"A many-stranded storyline, a cast of colorful personalities, and a pervasive sense of place: These qualities make *Fortune Island* a good, strong read. Here is a fit companion for the beach umbrella, the front-porch rocking chair, and the mellow bedside lamp. E.M. Schorb creates a world in which much happens—and all of it to the point."

—Fred Chappell
Recipient of the *Thomas Wolfe Prize*, Former North Carolina Poet Laureate

"*Fortune Island* is an exquisite reading adventure. We are hooked from the start by the poignant situation of William Makespeace Thackery McQueen, and are compelled forward both by the remarkable story and by the very human characters whom we love and identify with, not, despite their flaws, but because of their flaws---Bill McQueen himself, the beautiful and mysterious Susannah, and the remarkable Jessie Judas, whose life story is the real centerpiece of this skillfully written book. The setting of the Outer Banks is vividly detailed and contains the best description of Hurricane Hazel I have ever read. And finally there is a wonderfully despicable snake-handling villain, The Rev. Jason Petitt Cogburn, who makes a magnificent foil to the other characters. This is a must read."

—Anthony S. Abbott
Author of the Novello Award Winner, *Leaving Maggie Hope*

"I loved *Fortune Island*! I was driven by the suspense, and by the phrases that freeze you in place, mesmerizing you by what has been laid bare. E. M. Schorb isn't a prize-winning poet for nothing."

—Joy Calderwood
Reviewers' Choice Reviews

"A masterpiece in scope, characterization and drama, *Fortune Island* captures the imagination and excites the mind. A masterful achievement!"

—Pat Mullan
Author of *Childhood Hills*

ALSO BY E.M. SCHORB:

NOVELS
    PARADISE SQUARE
    SCENARIO FOR SCORSESE
    A PORTABLE CHAOS

POETRY
    MURDERER'S DAY
    TIME AND FEVERS
    THE POOR BOY AND OTHER POEMS
    A FABLE & OTHER PROSE POEMS

Fortune Island

E.M. Schorb

Cherokee McGhee

Williamsburg, Virginia

ISBN 978-0-9799694-2-3
0-9799694-2-5

First Printing 2009

Cover illustration by Braxton McGhee

Published by:
Cherokee McGhee, L.L.C.
Williamsburg, Virginia

Find us on the World Wide Web at:
WWW.CHEROKEEMCGHEE.COM

Printed in the United States of America

For

Patricia, my wife;

Selah and Leslie, my daughters;

and Laura, Ellen, and Hannah, my granddaughters

and

with thanks to

Lisa Williams Kline and Greg Lilly

Acknowledgement is gratefully made to the following authors and original publishers:

EPIGRAPHS

"The Darkling Thrush: A Centennial Appreciation"
by A.E. Stallings
"The Alsop Review"
Used with Permission

The Outer Banks Of North Carolina, 1584-1958
by David Stick
© 1958 by David Stick; renewed 1986,
University of North Carolina Press
Used with Permission

SONGS

"Don't Sit Under The Apple Tree (With Anyone Else But Me)"
by Charlie Tobias, Lew Brown and Sam H. Stept
© 1942 Alfred Publishing Co., Inc.
Used with Permission

"You Belong to Me,"
by Pee Wee King, Chilton Price and Redd Stewart
Hal Leonard Corporation
Used with Permission

POEMS

"The Diamond Merchant," Voices Israel, Tel Aviv
"The Souls," Stand, London, England
"An Appalachian Tale," The Coe Review, USA
"Leadbelly," Frank, Paris, France
"The Sex of Water," The North American Review, USA

Thomas Hardy's famous poem, "The Darkling Thrush," first appeared in print a couple of days prior to the last day of the 19th century. Hardy was watching the sun set on one century, and dawn on another.

> *The land's sharp features seemed to be*
> *The Century's corpse outleant,*
> *His crypt the cloudy canopy,*
> *The wind his death-lament.*

As Hardy did, we enter a new century (and millennium) with trepidation. May we find we have better grounds for hope now than Europe, on the brink of two devastating world wars, did a hundred years ago.

The Darkling Thrush: A Centennial Appreciation
A.E. Stallings, "The Alsop Review"

He that hath wife and children hath given hostages to fortune . . .
Francis Bacon

Stretching along the North Carolina coast for more than 175 miles, from the Virginia line to below Cape Lookout, is a string of low, narrow, sandy islands known as the Outer Banks. They are separated from the mainland by broad, shallow sounds, sometimes as much as thirty miles in breadth, and are breached periodically by narrow inlets which are forever opening and closing.

The Outer Banks of North Carolina
David Stick

Chapter
One

January 2000

The Lufthansa flight attendant, a tall blue-eyed blonde, strode down the aisle in her dark blue suit with its white, yellow, and black signature scarf a half hour after takeoff from Berlin and surveyed her passengers, mostly French and German, going and coming on business or pleasure. But she took special notice of a rangy man with dark hair and pale skin sitting toward the middle of the plane, by a window, an empty aisle seat beside him. He stood out from the crowd—for the second time, the first time being when he boarded, wearing a long taupe cashmere overcoat, and a Versace silk scarf—she had an eye for these things—tucked under his chin. When he boarded, she had noticed first how handsome he was, then how well-mannered, his Borsalino fedora crushed in his free hand. He had no bag, only a stack of papers and a magazine gripped outside his laptop. It looked as if he had been working up until the last minute before boarding. Now he sat tall in his seat, looking out at the tops of the sunset sand-colored clouds.

Another thing that drew her attention to him was that he was wearing evening dress, black tie, whereas almost uniformly the other passengers were travelling in blue jeans, leather jackets, and, in general, motley. His dark, even features and aquiline nose could have been Levantine, but his blue eyes sparkled with unmistakable Irish mischief. Adding things up, she decided that he must be an American.

His name was David Perle—she had checked. He had a loose, confident way with his long body, like a cowboy; otherwise he was thoroughly urbane in manner, a man who must have travelled widely in his youthful forty-odd years, a man who had been around.

As she approached him, the plane took a speed-bump and dropped, and the whiskey sour another attendant must have brought him flew from his hand. She almost caught the glass, got turned, and landed in the seat beside him. The plane steadied. She found his glass wedged between them, got back into the aisle and, with a slight risibility, asked him if she could replace his drink. "You can keep the next drink," she said. "There's little chance of two mishaps between Berlin and Paris. Of course, we have a stopover in Frankfurt. And you can get in trouble there. I should know, it's my hometown." She laughed.

"Oh, really?" He brushed his lapels.

"Yes," she said, then retrieved a fresh drink and a towel. As she patted his lapels, she said, "It's unusual to see anyone flying in evening dress."

"I'm on a tight schedule. I'm with the American Embassy in Berlin. I had to take time out because something very important is happening in Paris tonight." He showed her the cover of the new January issue of *Time* magazine. "That's my sister," he said, a forefinger tapping the cover. The attendant looked at the picture of a pale-eyed, red-haired woman of about sixty. Except for the fact that the woman in the picture looked much more Irish than the handsome man by the window, she could see the resemblance. The caption read:

PERSON OF THE YEAR—JESSIE JUDAS, WHO IS SHE?

"Your sister is Jessie Judas?"

"You've heard of her?"

"I've read her book. I read it in the German edition—*Andenken des Meeres. Souvenirs of the Sea* is one of the greatest books on the environment since *Silent Spring*. Of course I have read her book. Everyone has read it. It won the Pulitzer Prize, didn't it?"

"Yes, and tonight she is being awarded the Prix de Science. The ceremony is at eight and I haven't got time even to stop at a hotel or the American Embassy in Paris, which is why I'm flying in this monkey suit."

"You look very handsome. And you must be very proud."

"Yes, I am—very!"

"Have no fear, your jacket will look perfect. I'm honored to have spoken with you. I'll tell my friends." As she spoke she was looking at his fine, large, well-manicured hands. No wedding ring but in its place a large gold ring with ℒℒ on its face. "Your ring," she said. "Those are not your initials, are they?"

"It's a family heirloom. Love and Luck."

"Not a wedding ring?"

"No, no, I'm not married."

"Love and Luck. I like that. Let me give you something." She handed him a card, which he read:

Hildegarde Schnepp

Kant Strasse 34
D-10199 Berlin

(030) 706-3542   **hischnepp@aol.de**

"Perhaps you would like to contact me when you're back in Berlin."
"I'd like that very much."
"Then do. I look forward to seeing you again. Now I have others to attend to. Auf wiedersehen."

The momentary trappings of a vicarious celebrity, plus Fraulein Schnepp's directness, had left David a bit pleasantly flustered. He liked everything about Fraulein Schnepp—that she was beautiful, that she had read his sister's book, that her voice was soft and appealing, velvety English with a slight German accent, and that she was direct. During the stopover at Frankfurt, he stayed aboard, watching her when he could, as she worked. Near the end of the flight, she caught him looking at her, smiled, and he smiled back, then turned to the window in time to see the City of Light sprawled out below him like a great pinwheel galaxy of stars.

⌘ ⌘ ⌘

The building housing the Institut des Science was soot-gray, gothic, and gargoyled, and seemed to be pressing away the two modern glass buildings to each side of it—out with the new, long live the old—but they clung to it like two young guards desperately trying to do their duty by a difficult elder statesman. They were, in fact, a Bauhausian attempt to give wings to the heavy body of white stone and marble façade they flanked. And out of this contradiction in terms, between two fluted columns, rose the statue of a gray lady, gray of rain hat and hair, gray of face, gray of raincoat, stockings, and flat shoes, a gray umbrella tucked under her arm. But David looked for sharp, living, dark eyes, and found them in the statue's face, and found sudden animation as his mother opened her umbrella and swept down the wide marble steps toward him.

He paid the taxi driver and scurried through the rain and the crowd that climbed toward his mother, holding back her progress toward him, and was finally able to take her in his arms.

"So good to see you, Ruth. But where's Jessie?"

"We've got her tucked away backstage. Oh, David, she's been so ill! The chemo is taking a lot out of her. You'll be shocked. She's lost her beautiful red hair. But it's coming back. She's wearing a wig tonight. She still hasn't gotten over the nine-hour flight from the States. She's been vomiting the whole time, but she refuses to let anyone else accept the award for her. Do I look awful?" She took out a handkerchief and wiped her eyes. David took it from her and wiped the mascara streaks from her cheeks. They huddled under her umbrella, indifferent to the wake they were causing in the crowd around them. They were locked in the small invisible cage of their own concern.

"We don't have much time," Ruth Perle told her son. "I'm not going to sit with you. I'm going to stay in the wings, so I can be close to Jessie if anything happens. If she needs me."

Ruth and David made their way into the lobby, where they parted. David watched his mother as she went to the door leading to the backstage area and the wings. A standing sign read:

Ce soir
Jessie Judas
Gagnante du Prix Pulitzer
pour ses
Souvenirs d'une biologiste marine
recevra le Grand Prix en science

David patted the sign for luck, but he was worried: no unmixed blessings in life. He entered the auditorium in time to hear Jessie being introduced, "...Jessie Judas, auteuret specialiste en biologie marine. Mlle Judas a recu le Prix Pulitzer pour son livre, *Souvenirs of the Sea...*" David found a seat and added to the welcoming applause for his sister. "Ce soir on lui decerne le Grand Prix en science..."

Nobody had told him how sick Jessie was. Away in Berlin, he hadn't seen his family for six months. E-mails had hinted that she had been suffering health problems, but nothing so serious as his mother had just told him about. He felt the return of the benign paranoia of his childhood, the sense that his mother and sister were always trying to keep him from some secret they seemed to share. They had kept the seriousness of Jessie's illness from him as they kept everything from him and to themselves.

But now, as Jessie approached the lectern, he could see for himself how ill she was. She had always been an athlete, a great swimmer. But it was a red-haired wraith, in a sequin-glittering aquamarine gown, that unsteadily crossed the stage and stood looking out at the audience. Who here really knew his famous sister? He no more than the audience of strangers. Only Ruth, he supposed.

Jessie was accepting a plaque to more applause, when she leaned into the Master of Ceremonies and seemed to slide down his body to the floor. Ruth ran from the wings. Then David's view was blocked by a rising curtain of photographers stationed just in front of the stage. People in the auditorium, too, got to their feet and tried to see over the paparazzi, who were climbing up on the stage now. David, seized with dismay, was trapped in his place, with hundreds of heads between him, Jessie, and Ruth.

✂ ✂ ✂

At the "Gunpowder" Hospital—Pitié-Salpêtrière—where Princess Diana had died in August of '97, a nurse led him to Ruth. She was drinking coffee and chain-smoking in a room she had taken for herself, away from the paparazzi. Jessie was in the next room.

"What happened?" he asked his mother. "What is it?"

"Just a fainting spell," she answered. He saw that Ruth had been crying, but now her emotions were gathered—Ruth was never thrown for long, always right back on the horse—and she was focused. "I didn't think we should make this trip, but Jessie was determined. The literary prize for the book was wonderful, but this is a scientific award, you know. And this is her true life's work, she says. She made me bring her. She said it was the triumph of her life and she wasn't going to miss it for anything."

"Can we see her?"

"Yes. She's fine—for now," Ruth said.

Jessie was sitting up in bed, wearing a hospital gown, and not wearing her red wig. Her fading red hair was as short as a Marine recruit's. She smiled. "What a stupid stunt, eh?" she said, in her odd amalgam of North Carolina country and proper Bostonian. "Everyone knows an old hen can't do a swan dive." David kissed her. "I need a smoke and a Co-Cola," she said, fidgeting. "Well, I got my international scientific recognition, didn't I, even if I made a fool of myself just as I was being proclaimed a genius?" She snorted. "Now get me the hell out of here, Ruth. I don't want to be buried at Père-Lachaise next to a crazy American rock star, no matter how much a piece of attractive he is."

Ruth and David couldn't help smiling. Ruth winked at David, but shook her head as if to say, "What can you do with her?"

"David," Jessie said, "I guess Ruth has told you everything by now, so get your little ol' spankable diplomatic butt back to Berlin and do your job. I may need a doctor but I don't need a diplomat. And, Ruth, you get me the hell back to the States. If I should die, which I have no intention of doing, ever, I want to be cremated and have my ashes scattered where I was born—on Fortune Island."

Chapter
Two

Autumn 1941

Radio room German swing kids in a U-boat off the coast of North Carolina were picking up Jefferson-Pilot Radio from Charlotte, listening avidly to Woody Herman and one of their favorite crooners, Der Bingle— Bing Crosby—not crooning now, but belting out "Deep in the Heart of Texas." Clap-clap! Clap-clap! clapped the sailors, laughing, keeping time.

Kapitänleutnant Schnepp stepped into the radio room and said, "Do you Scheissköpfe know that Der Bingle wears a degenerate zoot suit?" To which one of the young swingsters replied in English, "Ja! With a reet pleat, and the drape shape, and the stuffed cuff."

"Schluss mit Englisch," ordered Kapitänleutnant Schnepp, "yetzt auf Deutsch! You understand that Der Bingle is our enemy, do you not? We are in battle stations. Turn that damn music off and get busy! We've got a target! There's a Liberty ship not more than three miles off, a tanker, probably carrying airplane fuel to feed the British Spitfires, a big fat target."

⌘ ⌘ ⌘

With every rumbling concussive explosion at sea a red flash penetrated the torn black air raid shades at the second-floor bedroom windows of the McQueen house on Fortune Island. Rainbow lights zoomed in at the edges and swooped through the room in a play of ominous shadows that gave the laboring Susannah the feeling of being on a terrifying carnival ride. As the dark stripes of shadows danced along the walls, floors, and ceiling of the bedroom, both the midwife Garcie and the birthing mother recoiled at their substanceless but tangible impact, and, for Susannah, painfully dilated, her baby's head emerging after thirty-six hours of labor, it seemed that the room itself was rolling in space, had toppled from the house like a roller coaster car.

"Even a momma's screams drowned down by them evil war drums," cried Garcie, "while another baby being born into this troubled world. God bless you, poor lil' darlin, you done done it, at last! Little red-top head, baldy but red, I swear it be!" A whack from Garcie's broad black hand brought the faint siren of Jessie's first breath.

"There now, how's that? They can hear that little gal way out on that burning ship, I'd swear, lungs like bellows."

"Don't talk about the ships! Bill might be on one of them. He could be dying out there."

"And you almost died in here. That was one bad hard birth, little Susie—one bad hard birth, and I seen many of 'em in my time. Sooner I take care of this baby, I take care of you—stitch you up tight. You wasn't made for birthing. I don't know what you was made for, you little narrow-hipped thing. And don't you go worrying about William Makepeace Thackeray McQueen. I birthed him, too—know him better than you do. Mister William's a survivor. It's you I worry about, you and this new helpless chile, this little girl born into trouble, born into the roar of war. Why you gonna call her Jessie?"

"It's a good mountain name. My mother was Jessie and her father was Jesse, after Jesse James, was said. But I came down the mountains to the sea. The sailors used to call me Mountain Girl. Why are you so good to me, Garcie? I'm just a half-blind whore he picked up in Wilmington."

"And married you and made you the lady of this house, because you have the heart of an honest woman. That's what my William could see. Garcie taught him to look beneath the skin. Southern boy that he is, he never used a bad word when he spoke of my people."

⌘ ⌘ ⌘

William Makepeace Thackeray McQueen bought a nice little linen postcard at the hospital souvenir stand and took it into the common room where there were pens, ink, and green blotters available for the use of the four hundred or so wounded seamen of all kinds—fishermen, crewmen of tankers and container ships, Coast Guardsmen, foreign sailors, and a large number of merchant marines like himself, who had had their Liberty ships shot or torpedoed out from under them—who filled the hospital to overflowing and who had the ability and the inclination to write something to family or friends.

The front of the card depicted a large, four-storied white stone building, pinked by afternoon sun, with a forward thrusting wing on each side, cement walkways, a few smallish unidentifiable trees, and a park-sized expanse of emerald lawn. Cottony pink-tinged clouds rolled in the azure sky at the top third of the card. Altogether, it was a tranquil and dignified looking place. Susannah would like the look of it and never guess at the amount of suffering within. The back of the card bore the legend, U.S. Marine Hospital, Norfolk, Virginia, so she would know where he was. He sat at a writing table, took a pen, dipped it in ink, and wrote:

> *Dear Little Susie,*
>   *I am okay. Has our baby come yet? I hope you and maybe baby are fine. I just wanted you to know where I was. After many examinations, I have to go now for a final medical evaluation. More later.*
>   *Love, Bill*

He addressed the card:

> *The McQueen House*
> *Fortune Island*
> *North Carolina*

Bill blotted the card, dropped it in the outgoing box, and went in search of his doctor and his immediate fate.

"At six-two," the doctor told him, "I'd like to send you home at a hundred-eighty, or at least a hundred-seventy-five. You're fifteen to twenty-five pounds below normal."

"Sometimes I can't hold food down," said Bill, stepping down from the scale.

"A touch of shellshock. Trauma to the nervous system. As to the concussion, headaches may recur, but, unless there's real dizziness, just take a couple of aspirins. If there's serious dizziness or fainting, see a doctor."

"There's no doctor on the island where I live." He sat down on the indicated straight chair across from the doctor.

"You should consider staying on the mainland for a while—until the symptoms clear up, which, we are certain, they will. As to the metal bits, we couldn't get them all out, so there'll be periodic bleeding as the metal pushes its way to the surface—"

"How long?"

"Weeks, months, years perhaps. If one of them gets particularly difficult, come back here and we'll pull it out for you. You know what stigmata are?"

"Hands and feet bleeding from the nails on the cross."

"Well, nothing wrong with your hands and feet, but it'll be a little like that on your chest, shoulders, stomach, and back. You'll just pop open every so often. As time passes, there won't be as much of it. Nothing to worry about. A bit painful, maybe."

"What about my hair?"

"Well, now, that's a bit different. No pain there, eh?" The doctor laughed. "It's quite striking, really. But you can always get some hair dye—any color you want, think of that!"

"When I was finally conscious—when I saw myself—"

"Yes, pure white at—"

"Twenty-two."

"Yes. Shock. Yours is the first case I've seen myself."

"But will it come back?"

"No one can say for certain, but I doubt it. But look, it's not so bad. I've heard the nurses talking about you. They think you're quite the thing, and they love your white locks. Your hair is thick and white and your face is young, makes a remarkable picture. Then, as I said, you can always dye it. Now let's get back to the important things. Your ribs have healed nicely, as have your leg and your arm. It's the concussion that concerns me. I want you to take life easy for at least six months, and I don't think you should sail again for a year. What did you do before you were a merchant marine?"

"In high school I played in a band. Guitar. We played road houses and juke joints and such, and did pretty well. I'm also a good carpenter and a pretty good mechanic."

"Well, for your health's sake, I suggest that you don't do anything for at least three months, maybe six would be better, and then only something light. Carpenter, mechanic, I don't like. Where did you play?"

"Honkytonks, juke joints—"

"Air! You should get lots of fresh air. I wouldn't suggest going back to that kind of place."

"Well, where am I supposed to work?"

"It'd be best if you didn't."

"Look, Doc, I have a wife, and maybe a baby at home. How am I supposed to take care of them?"

"My advice is strictly medical. I'm sure you can find something. How about clerking in a store—but stay off the ladder. What about your wife? Can't she work? A lot of women are out there working now. Rosy the Riveter put your ship together."

"She's not that kind—not very strong."

"Well, you'll have to do what you must, but my best advice to you is to take it easy. Concussions are tricky. You could have a cerebral hemorrhage and be laid up for months or years or even die. Then what would your wife do? I know it's hard. We're trying to get compensation for merchant marines, but there's a war on and there are more pressing needs. I'm sure you understand. I'm afraid you're on your own for now, son. I'm going to have to recommend release. We need the beds. We'll keep an eye on you for another week or two, then you'll have to go and take your chances. I'm sorry."

"Maybe that torpedo should have killed me."

"Now, now, son—buck up, you don't want a stay in the psych ward, do you?"

⁂

Same reason the rain can't stay in the clouds, same reason it pours down through the pines in streams and rolls across the foothills and flatlands to find its salt source, was the reason why Susannah, the mountain girl, came down to the land's edge. Some might call it gravity flow. Some might say she couldn't stay up there in the smoke of the mountains at the cliff's edge, because she hadn't the full strength of the eagle, and fell from the nest like a fledgling. Some might say she was prematurely driven from the nest by a mountain man determined that she marry another mountain man as mean and ugly as himself, but half his age. Some had it that that was the cause of the young girl's departure. Some thought her disobedience was innate and blameworthy, the mark of a rebellious spirit, her red hair the flag of that spirit; others thought of it as her escape from an oppressive mountain man rule and thought of her as courageous. Neither camp had it right. It was not blameworthy rebellion nor admirable courage, but fear that drove her down the mountainside and on to the Piedmont, along the Catawba and across the Old North State to the sea, a consumptive girl breathing in every kind of mill dust there was, and, at one point, accidentally wiping dye into her pretty young eyes, losing most of the sight of one, and with it many opportunities for honest work. She had a small stack of four years on her own to her credit before she found her way to the water's corrugated edge, before she found Wilmington, where there was lots of work for a war effort that she could not understand. But she couldn't take that hard work anymore at eighteen, sick and half-blind, and got talked into prostitution by a supposedly kind-hearted hooker. One eye so pale you couldn't tell the blue from the white, red hair so long that Bill held his hands nearly two feet apart to describe it, and not much else to her but what weak freckled flesh could cling to her long, delicate bones. Bill told his shipmate Smiley that he would have to see her for himself to understand what he meant when he said that she was beautiful, something meant to be loved and protected.

"I know the one you mean," said Smiley. "You're jawing about that mountain girl, what's her name? The one hangs out at the Anchor. She's a used-up hooker, Bill. What do you want with her? Why don't you get yourself a nice clean piece like my Ivy, works in a office and looks like a lady, not hiding all that tubercular exhaustion under a pound of paint? Not looking out at you with a white eye!"

Bill wasn't easy to anger but he felt a touch of the flame of it. He looked at Smiley's well-intentioned face and let the flame go out, let the rush of redness recede from his face. They had lost count of the number of times they had sailed together, had got drunk together on warm beer in Liverpool and on hot vodka in Murmansk, had been sunk and saved together. Bill wouldn't let Smiley's bit of lip annoy him for long, but his flare of anger made him realize how much the girl had touched him, how serious he was, which he didn't realize himself until then. "Love is a force as real and as invisible as the wind," he blurted.

"Look who's blushing," cried Smiley. "Let's go and get a second look at this fallen angel."

Bill believed that there was a point at which a young woman following the hooker's trade hardened and truly became what she worked in, but it seemed clear to him that Susannah had not reached that point; on the contrary, she behaved as if she were waiting to be saved by some stalwart like Bill, someone sensitive enough to see her for herself, more lost than bad, more sweet with love than sour with life; and, when Bill set her up in her own little place, she felt liberated from the life of the tight-skirted nightcrawler. Bill made several voyages and each time returned to find her, cozy in her little place and waiting like an suitorless Penelope, faithful in her stitching and unstitching. And Susannah's fidelity was confirmed by Ivy, who had befriended her. After one double date, Smiley told Bill that he had had her all wrong. "She's really a sweet kid," Smiley pronounced. "Good as gold." And Bill told his pal that he was going to ask Susannah to marry him.

"Now, hold on," said Smiley. "That's taking it a bit far, don't you think?"

"No, I don't think."

"You should. I'm no doctor, but even I can see that the girl is sick. You know what those flushes mean, don't you? She belongs in the St. James Infirmary."

"They mean she needs somebody to take care of her."

"You're too good for your own good, pal," said Smiley, downing a beer. But he dropped the issue there.

And so, Susannah was brought to Fortune Island, and became the chatelaine of a seven room house, a modest house but one beyond anything she had ever dreamed to possess. She had reached the very edge of the Atlantic and could step into it every morning if she desired, spread her toes and watch the foamy water fill the inlets and flow back out.

Bill heard Smiley throw his leg over the side of his hospital bed. He heard him light a cigarette, the scratch of a match. He heard Smiley exhale. The smell of tobacco smoke hovered in the air above him. He opened his eyes to see that he had slept into the evening, perhaps the night. Down the way, someone was softly snoring. Bill had taken to his bed that afternoon with a dizzying headache. He felt better now, but still sleepy. He realized that Smiley was talking to him. It seemed that Smiley was on deck and saw the torpedo coming like a white shark skimming the top of the water and leaving a long wake behind it.

"But wasn't it dark?" Bill asked, who could not remember where he was when the torpedo hit.

"You were down below that night, sleeping, just like now. There was plenty of moonlight and other explosions to see by. Another ship was burning orange, like the sunrise. I tell you, I saw that bullet coming and I said, shee-it! I thought right away of you, down below, trapped. And I thought that I would never see my soft-hearted old buddy again—the kid, who, in Liverpool, chose the ugliest whore for fear that nobody else would take her—and all the education in life I was giving you was going to be wasted, and of how you would never learn the rest of it and miss out on the benefit of my vast knowledge of the low and the lofty. For instance, pal, how you were never going to learn how to dance with anyone the way Ivy and I dance."

"You thought of all that, did you? In what—ten seconds?"

"Then the torpedo hit and I felt my leg being ripped off and I went sailing into the sky, and I remember tumbling over and over like I was doing some really terrific gymnastic stunt. I was way up in the air somewhere, like in a dream, and then I woke up into darkness. I must have been under water, deep, and when I came up again the water was on fire. I remember slapping at it, pushing the fire away. I must have blacked out again." Bill felt Smiley slap his hand. "Then I wake up with a stump that still feels like a leg and there you are, in the next bed, hair gone all white like an old man's. Who needs the leg, I said to myself, I've still got my buddy, my shipmate, my pal. But then the nurse told me that you were in a coma. 'What's new?' I asked her. But she said that I shouldn't be making light of it, that you were in serious condition, that you'd been like that for two weeks already. I asked her were you ever going to wake up and she said that she hoped so."

Bill's eyes were closed. Smiley seized his arm.

"Are you awake?"

"Umhum."

"I never told you this but when I was a kid, back home in Indiana, I was playing with a gun, quick draw, twirling it on my finger, tossing it from hand to hand, and the damn thing went off and killed my little sister. I was sixteen. It was my father's gun. The judge ruled it an accidental death, but he said that I needed to do some growing up and he ordered me to join the merchant marines. This was way before the war, even before they started recruiting. You know us merchant marines get no veterans' benefits. That's because they think we're all criminals, because of guys like me who were ordered to join by some judge, or draft dodgers, or Reds, and because we work for private companies, and have a union, and the armed forces don't like us because we get paid more than they do, and Congress don't like us because the services don't like us. But we got one thing. We got war insurance policies, but you got to be dead or permanently disabled, like me, and I'll get mine when we get out of here. I'll get my five thousand dollars compensation one of these days." Bill could hear him take a long drag on his cigarette and snuff it out. "And I've got some great ideas for when we get out of here. Ivy and me and you and Susannah are gonna be rich." He was gripping Bill's arm, then he saw that Bill had gone off again. But it was just a quiet sleep and no coma and he wore a little smile, Bill did, and so did Smiley, who thought maybe they were dreaming the same dream.

⌘ ⌘ ⌘

Dear Bill ain't nothing make me happier than getting that card but I am in a fix what with the new baby name of Jessie a little girl baby sweet as hony with reed hare Bill like me hope you know and Garcie is helping me some but this is me here writing this but like I said things is bad ain't had no money from you for months and I'm down to pennies but Christmas was better more like Wilmington when we first met. General store Walkups saw we had a bird and fixins me and baby and Garcie but I never imagin you can starve in a seven room house cuz its bad alone on this I'lan Mister and Miss Sherriff Walkup give me some to do in the store and a few dollar and some food and Garcie share with me what she got and take some good care of me and little Jessie but you gotta come home to help us please come home soon I am trapp with nothing I am so happy you must be alive and well just come home please your mountane girl Susannah. Love and Kiss I almost forgot.

Bill came into the common room waving his letter.

"Smiley, I got great news!" He had to yell over the booming jukebox.

"Which is?"

"I'm a daddy."

"Shee-it, boy, give me a cigar!"

"I can't afford cigars. Have a Lucky." Bill tossed a pack of Lucky Strikes on the table.

"I like that song," said Smiley. "Good dance number." He held one hand out for Bill to be quiet and cupped his ear in the direction of the juke box, listening and tapping the one foot he still had. He was waiting to be fitted with an artificial leg. Now he grabbed a crutch to tap the time.

Don't sit under the apple tree
With anyone else but me,
Anyone else but me,
Anyone else but me.
No, no, no, don't sit under the apple tree

With anyone else but me,
Till I come marching home!

The jukebox went dead. Now he looked inquiringly up at Bill.

"Boy or girl?" he asked, lighting up.

"A little girl, named Jessie."

"Hey, what could be better than a daughter to love her daddy?"

"It's just the finest thing in the world, good buddy." Bill turned a chair around and straddled it. He leaned forward against its back, smiling at Smiley, and Smiley wondered what was hidden behind the smile.

"What is it? Something wrong with the kid?"

Bill passed Susannah's letter to Smiley, who read it. He looked up at Bill and shook his head. "I didn't know she couldn't write. She never was much of a talker, but, when she said something, she sounded normal except for that hillbilly accent."

"She never had any schooling, poor kid. I don't know how she managed to learn to write at all. I give her a lot of credit."

"You sure do—maybe more than she deserves. Her letter is only semi-literate, and your mother was a school teacher. But, hell's bells, she sounds like she needs some help, eh?" Smiley brightened. "Is that it? Is that what's worrying you, son?"

"My money went down with the ship. Or somebody stole my money belt when I was out. You know I'm living on handouts."

"And you're leaving in a few days. Have no fear, Smiley's here! Ivy brought me a chunk of my savings." Smiley reached into his pocket and produced a fat wallet. He began peeling off bills.

"Ivy was here?" asked Bill

"A couple of weeks ago. The day you had your evaluation."

"Why didn't you tell me? Didn't she want to say hello to me?"

"Well, it went a little rough. I wrote her, but I didn't tell her about my leg; I figured she'd see it when she saw it. But she was really pissed about the leg, or maybe about me not telling her. The long and the short of it"—he pointed to each of his legs—"is she didn't like any of it."

"She took it hard, eh?"

"Yeah, a little. You know how she loved for us to dance. I told her I'd be back jitterbugging before she knew it. Here's a couple hundred bucks." He pushed the money across the table. "Ivy's got a couple of thousand of mine somewhere, stashed away, waiting for me."

"Where'd you get all that?"

"Go on, put it away, before somebody robs 'ya. Oh, son, I'm almost old enough to be your daddy. I've been sailing nigh on ten years now. Now take the money home with you to Susannah and your baby—Jessie, right? Take it home and feed them. But then, after you visit, I want you to meet me in Wilmington—Maffitt Village: it's a new development for shipyard workers. I'll write out all the details. I want you to meet me there and I'll tell you how we are going to get rich quick."

"Thanks, Smiley! This money is a godsend."

"You mean a Smileysend. You didn't think I'd let you down, did you?"

"I didn't know you had it."

"Smiley's always got it! You should know me by now. And there's plenty more where that came from. I'm going to show you how to make some real money. Look, I know you're up against it. I know you can't work, not with that banged-up brain of yours about to blow anytime you put it under a strain. What'd the doc say—about six months? You and Susie and the baby'll starve. Meet me in Wilmington in a couple of weeks and I'll show you the way out of this. Agreed?"

"Agreed."

Somebody kicked the jukebox.

Don't sit under the apple tree
With anyone else but me,
Anyone else but me,
Anyone else but me.
No, no, no, don't sit under the apple tree
With anyone else but me,
Till I come marching home!

⚜ ⚜ ⚜

" 'Home is the sailor, home from the sea, and the hunter home from the hill,' " said William Makepeace Thackeray McQueen, quoting Robert Lewis Stevenson. Misshapen moons of light swashed about in the wind-stirred waters of Pamlico Sound. It was sundown of an unseasonable February day of near shirtsleeve weather. After a supper of fried fish, black-eyed peas, collard greens, and cornbread, left them by Garcie before she went home, shaking her head—"My first black haired baby already white as snow and my latest little baldy baby already with long red hair prove how life whiz by"—Bill and Susannah brought kitchen chairs out onto their little porch facing the Sound and sat momentarily hypnotized by the restless water and the darkening sky slowly filling with stars. Bill held Baby Jessie in his arms and rocked back on the hind legs of his chair. Then Susannah stirred from her reverie. She looked at Bill.

"Will you get it back?" she asked.

"What?"

"The color in your hair."

"Not likely," he said.

"But it looks so strange," she said. "All that white hair around a young face."

Bill shrugged. "What difference does it make? We've got bigger problems than that." Bill felt a buzz in his head, the little electrical waves that he'd been feeling now and then. It reminded him of the doctor's warning that he must not stress himself. He had to care for himself in order to care for Susannah and the baby. He touched the baby's lips with his finger and she tried to suck it. "No, no," he whispered. "You've got the wrong thing there, little Jessie."

"Ain't she just beautiful?" Susannah said. "Garcie says she's a miracle baby—a miracle that she got born."

"A beautiful miracle. But I think our beautiful miracle is hungry. You better take and feed her."

"I'm dried up. I'll go inside and get some of Garcie's formula. She just made it."

Bill put the baby on his lap, so that she was looking up at him and he down at her. He said, "This is just between us, my little love, but right here and now I swear to you that I'm going to do everything in my power to give you a happy life." Bill was certain that he detected a smile on little Jessie's lips.

Susannah came back with a bottle in hand, took the baby from Bill, sat down, and began to feed Jessie.

"Bill," she said, tentatively, "I know you don't like to talk about it, but what was it like out there?"

"We got blown sky high, Susie-Q. Most of us died, either in the explosion or in the fire in the water. Smiley got his leg ripped off below the knee but was thrown clear of the fire. Nobody knows how I got out. I guess I got carried out somehow through a hole in the hull. I don't remember a thing. I was told I was picked up floating around, but how I got away from the ship and the fire—well, I guess that was a miracle. I was unconscious for weeks. Then I woke up, and there was Smiley. He must have sat with me a lot to be there just when I came out of it. He's a good friend. That's all there was to it."

"And your hair was all white like that."

"White as snow, like Garcie said."

She reached over and ran her fingers through his hair. "It's strange but it's beautiful." She sat in a kind of meditative silence for a while, feeding the baby. Then she said, "Jessie looks like both of us, don't you think? I mean, she's got my red hair and she's going to be tall like you, anybody can see that."

Yes, Bill saw that, too, and took pride in it—tall, like himself.

"Tell me about this old house that I own, just like a lady."

"I must have told you before."

"Only in bits. Tell me again."

"Why do you want to hear that?"

"Because it's romantic. And sad. It's like a love story."

"Well, I guess it was a love story. But it's getting too cold out here. Maybe we should go inside."

"No, let's sit on here. I want to listen and see the sky fill up with stars."

"Okay," Bill said. "We lived on the mainland then, outside Morehead City. Dad was a contractor and my mother taught in the school system there. My grandparents had a fishing shack right here on this spot, and my parents were over here visiting them, trying to avoid the coughing crowds of Spanish flu victims in Morehead City, when I decided to come out early. My grandma didn't know what to do and the men were useless so somebody went and got Garcie. She cooked and kept house for my folks, and they'd brought her along to keep her from getting the flu. She was part of the family—you know how it was in those days—her mother had been a midwife, so she knew what to do, and she brought me into the world." He lit a Lucky Strike and leaned back in the chair. "September 5, 1919."

"Your birthday."

"Garcie had been sleeping in a lean-to out back. She was only about nineteen or twenty then herself. After I was born my father built her her own shack, and I've been told that she never wanted to leave it. When the flu epidemic receded, my parents went back to Morehead City for a time. Garcie stayed on here to help my grandparents, who were getting pretty old.

"When the old folks died here—my grandmother was half Cherokee, you know—my father began building this house. 'Away from the madding crowd,' my mother said. That was about the time your friends the Walkups came to the island. Retired Sheriff Walkup and his teen-aged wife. There was a touch of a scandal there, at the time. But folks got used to them. That's when they bought the General Store, about then."

"They've been so good to me and Garcie and the baby. I told you about the turkey at Christmas—"

"They're good folks. They were a big help during the Depression when there wasn't much work for contractors. Especially in this part of the country. The Walkups were never hard about money. Always willing to wait. Anyhow, my dad would come over with a few old boys that worked with him in construction—they'd come over on week-ends—and, while I was still in high school, they finished it up. The biggest house on Fortune Island. The only real house. He even had a piano shipped over here for my mother to play. I sold it later. I even wrote a song about it called 'The Sold Piano Blues.' They were get-away-from-it-all people. Then everything reversed itself, and he'd go over to the mainland and work a job for a week or a month and always be glad to come back here to the isolation, to what we've got here now."

"It's so romantic, them wanting to be alone and all. It's sort of like us, don't you think?"

"So you think we're romantic, do you?" He smiled at her in the fading light. He guessed she was right. He truly wanted nothing more than to be alone with his Susannah and little Jessie.

"Oh, yes, don't you? I mean, living on an island and all. To a mountain girl like me it's romantic."

"Well, anyway, they probably should have stayed on the island, but instead they took a vacation on the mainland, and somewhere outside of Morehead City there was a car wreck, and they both died in it. That was in the '30s and I was on my own, out of high school, working at carpentry sometimes, sometimes playing the honkytonks with a few old boys from my high school band. We'd got a group together, playing anything from white country to black blues. My folks left me the house and Garcie that little annuity she's got. It was all they had left to give us, after the Depression years. But with them gone, I had to do better than I was doing, so I locked up the house and went in to Wilmington and joined the merchant marine. That was where I met Smiley, who lent me the money I gave you."

"I remember Smiley and Ivy, and how they loved to dance. But I never thought Smiley liked me much. Ivy was nicer, more friendly."

"Smiley liked you all right."

"I thought it was worrisome that he didn't, because he was your friend and I wanted him to like me. He always sort of brushed me off. It's like the story about your parents. That's what I meant—romantic and sad. Romantic because they wanted to be alone on an island and sad because— well, because they died like that, and they were young, not so much older than we are, I guess. I bet you felt bad, only being a kid and all."

"I guess I did, then; but life has toughened me up a lot. I just saw hundreds of my shipmates go down. Smiley got his leg torn off, and I've got something wrong inside my head. There's no damn time for feeling sad, only time for doing the next thing." He paused. "Now, I told you, I can't work too hard for a while; but Smiley's got something for me to do. I don't know what it is yet, so I've got to go over to Wilmington and see about it."

"You're not leaving me because of the way I acted in bed, are you?"

"Of course not, Susie. You just had a baby and that didn't surprise me all that much. New mother and all." He pulled his chair closer to hers and slipped an arm around her shoulder.

"It weren't that," Susannah said. "I'd have been all right for that."

"Well, what was it, then?"

"It's some feeling I've been having. I ain't a whore, now, but a true life honest wife, with a house and a baby—"

"And a husband," he said, pulling her closer, "who's going to take good care of you."

"I've been thinking about it. I know I've got wifely duties, too. I know that. It's just—I'm ashamed of the past, and it gets in the way now, somehow. Bill, do you understand?" She looked him in the face with her one blue eye and one white eye magnified by a pair of tape-repaired glasses.

"I understand. You're adjusting, and that's good. My mother used to say, 'This too will pass.' Everything will come out all right. You just wait and see." He studied her drawn face, her long red hair, and added, tenderly, "Got to get you a new pair of glasses, my love."

Chapter
Three

Ivy was proud to be part of the war effort and knew that "loose lips sink ships;" but, during their decade or more affair, Smiley had observed her to have something of a Jekyll and Hyde personality. As secretary to the assistant paymaster at the North Carolina Shipbuilding Company, she had proved herself to be a conscientious worker—by day, but by night Ivy was a party girl who, after a few drinks, couldn't keep her dress or her mouth buttoned up; and so it was that Ivy, by dribs and drabs, had told Smiley about the enormous sums that were passing through the paymaster's office of the North Carolina Shipbuilding Company; which, by then was employing about 20,000 people and was turning out something like fifty Liberty ships a year.

What William Makepeace Thackeray McQueen did not know about his friend Smiley was that he sometimes practiced the art of armed robbery between voyages as a merchant marine. Thus far, the self-proclaimed "improvident" Charles "Chuck" Smiley had not been caught. But his small-time successes had built a confidence in Smiley that amounted to hubris. With inside information inadvertently supplied by Ivy, Smiley planned to rob the payroll of the North Carolina Shipbuilding Company. He needed four men for the job. He enlisted two of them from the ranks of his former shipmates and the fourth would be Bill McQueen, whom he knew to be desperate for money and incapable for the foreseeable future of any sustained work. He thought of Bill McQueen as a "straight arrow," but he knew that desperation and a good sales talk can induce people to do things they would not otherwise do. All he had to do, Smiley thought, was to get Bill to show up at Maffitt Village in Wilmington, North Carolina.

In his hubris, it never occurred to Smiley that he could not depend on Ivy, his girl in the port of Wilmington. They had danced and loved their way through years of nights of abandon. He had come to trust her. So much so, that he had allowed her to hold his savings for him, now in the low thousands, as he reckoned, the sum of his labor as both merchant marine and bandit. But he did not bring his relationship with Ivy to any conclusion, such as a proposal of marriage or at least an engagement, and for her that time had passed. He had been away too much, though to Smiley being away was not being with himself, and so it had not occurred to him that she might think that he had neglected her. In time Ivy had begun to see other men, to go dancing, which was her passion, with others, and perhaps it was the shock of seeing that Smiley, her erstwhile dancing partner, had lost his leg, which was the final insult to Ivy's sensibilities. In his communications to her, Smiley had not mentioned so grave a fact as his loss of a leg. Discovering this fact by visiting him at the hospital had been a shock, and, though she had behaved stoically, by her lights, the immediately incalculable result of finding him legless had begun to manifest upon her return to Wilmington. After a time, she felt dread at his return. What was she to do? Did he expect her to support him? Not Ivy, not this good-time girl. She began to look in other directions.

The respectable and well-paid assistant paymaster for whom she worked had taken a shine to her, and they were soon dating on a regular basis. Smiley faded into a cloud, then a dark cloud hovering on the horizon of her life. She had to get rid of him. She told the assistant paymaster about Smiley's plan to rob the payroll. The paymaster told the police. The police told the FBI. The FBI saw no reason for federal intervention and turned it back to the police, with the warning that they did not want the police to allow the robbery to take place, did not want any interruption of the war machine, that Smiley and his three cohorts should be arrested before they attempted the robbery and charged with conspiracy, which would put them all away for ten or more years.

A trap was laid. Ivy accepted the presence of Smiley and his two friends while awaiting the third friend to show up. Bill McQueen knocked on Ivy's door, and Ivy let him in. Smiley and the other two were in the kitchen. A map of the North Carolina Shipbuilding Company lay on the table, its four corners held down by four pistols. Smiley leaped from his chair and clumsily drove himself toward Bill on his new artificial leg, his arms extended to give Bill a hug of greeting, but halfway to Bill he lost interest. He was looking over Bill's shoulder at a squad of policemen.

A month later, they were before a judge who apparently hated them. Though they had not been charged with any federal crime, it was clear that the judge thought of them not only as robbers, but as traitors to the war effort, to their country, and even in league with the Axis Powers, or perhaps with the Soviet Communists who were preparing for world domination after the Axis Powers were defeated.

Section One of the 1929 statute read, *Any person or persons who, having in possession or with the use or threatened use of any firearms or other dangerous weapon, implement or means, whereby the life of a person is endangered or threatened, unlawfully takes or attempts to take personal property from another or from any place of business, residence or banking institution or any other place where there is a person or persons in attendance, at any time, either day or night, or who aids or abets any such person or persons in the commission of such crime, shall be guilty of a felony and upon conviction thereof shall be punished by imprisonment for not less than five nor more than thirty years,* "and is still in effect," said the judge, "as of our present year, 1942." He would have given them more time, he declaimed in a stentorian voice, but for the fact that all four of them had been wounded in the service of their country; though they were not official members of the U.S. military, not sailors, not soldiers, not marines, but mere merchant marines. "However," the judge puffed, "you still deserve, at a minimum, what the law requires, and the statute requires five to thirty years. Twelve years each for all!" The judge banged his gavel. To Bill, it sounded like the blow of a sledgehammer.

After turning him in and testifying against him, as well as Bill and the others, Ivy had the nerve to write Smiley a dear-John letter in which she told him that she was going to marry the assistant payroll officer of the North Carolina Shipbuilding Company, and so had to do what she did. Furthermore, she said, she was not willing to betray her country for any man, least of all a dancing clown who could not dance anymore. No hard feelings, she hoped. As to the money Smiley claimed to have given her for safe-keeping, she had never heard of it and he had his nerve.

"My old man was right," Smiley told Bill. "Improvidence has pursued me through life."

After much procrastination, Bill wrote home:

My dearest Susie and baby,
I wish you had a telephone so I could hear your voice, but I wouldn't want you hearing mine, which must be full of shame and frustration at being such a fool as to get caught up in something so stupid. They said they would run a phone line out to the island

years ago, but they never did, and now I'm glad. I was a fool to think Smiley could help me in any way. I should have known better. He gets himself and everyone around him into trouble. You must be wondering why you haven't heard from me. I couldn't find the words with which to write to you before now. But things are settled. I am writing to you from the Central Prison in Raleigh. I'll be here for the next dozen years for something I didn't do. You must believe me. I am innocent. I'm only guilty of being a fool, which has made me your betrayer—a Judas—for I know how you depended on me and I've failed you and the baby, Jessie. I'm in prison for conspiracy to commit armed robbery. I had no weapon and I knew nothing about any robbery. I simply walked into Smiley's house and was arrested. He's here with me now. Of course he's very sorry about what happened, but that doesn't help much. He knows I'm innocent and told the police and the court and the judge the truth but it didn't help any. What all this amounts to is, that I have no idea of how to help you and the baby. My throat is so thick, I couldn't say these words to you if you did have a phone. I always remember something my mother used to say. She said the words came from Francis Bacon, a great writer. He who has wife and child has given hostages to fortune. I would change that to Fortune Island. At least, you have the house. Please don't sell it. It's wealth—not much, but something. You'll never be homeless, I have that comfort. But I don't know how you can make money to live. I know that Garcie will help you as she has always helped us McQueens. This is all I can say now, but that I love you and the baby.

Your Judas

Bill showed the letter to Smiley as they sat watching an early spring baseball game in the prison yard. He wanted Smiley to know how he felt. He wanted Smiley to feel the spot he had put him in. Helplessness had driven him into an insinuating vindictiveness when it came to his friend. But Smiley was too generous to let Bill turn into a crank. He read the letter placidly and handed it back to Bill.

"We've just got to do something about the situation," he said. "I'll write to Ivy and see if I can talk her into sending Susannah a few bucks." And he did. He told Ivy about Susannah's plight on Fortune Island, and reminded her of her quondam friendship with Susannah.

...we both know that you got me for a big chunk of money, and that's okay, no hard feelings, but you can spare a little bit of it, especially now that you're going to be rich with that boyfriend of yours marrying you, for Susannah and her baby stuck on that God-forsaken little island half way out into the Atlantic. Now be a good girl for old time's sake and send her a few bucks.

He enclosed Susannah's mailing address and posted the letter. He told Bill they would just have to wait and hope for the best. Smiley wasn't surprised but Bill was when Ivy wrote back promising to help Susannah. "It isn't her fault you two are a couple of jerks," Ivy signed off.

✷ ✷ ✷

Like a belle with a full dance card, the mail boat hovered at a distance and forced Sheriff Walkup to row out to it. Occasionally a visitor would come with the mail boat, or, if it were on its return voyage, a visitor or an islander might go. Sometimes the Sheriff's skiff wouldn't be adequate for what was coming to the island or leaving it, an article of furniture, say, or a body for the mainland mortuary, and he would commandeer a fishing boat for the emergency. But ordinarily there was only a small sack of mail, sometimes just a letter. The fact that the mail boat had stopped at all indicated that there was something of importance aboard, something for at least one of the twenty-odd islanders; and, if there were something on the island to be taken away, Sheriff Walkup would raise a red flag.

It was late in March when Susannah burst in on Garcie, waving the letter Bill had written from Central Prison in Raleigh. Garcie held little Jessie and listened as Susannah haltingly read her Bill's frightening words.

"Oh, my God in heaven, what will become of us? What will become of this little baby girl?"

"Twelve years, Garcie!"

"I know he innocent," said Garcie, with absolute certainty. "He never in a million years do such a thing."

"But he needed the money for us."

"Don't you doubt him like that. He never done it, I tells you. I brought that boy into the world and I know him like I know what's on them shelves."

"But what'll we do? I only have a few dollars of what he left with me.

What happens when that runs out?"

"When that runs out, God will provide. Wait and see. You know God wants this child to survive and she will survive because we will survive, hear? Now I got my little check come once a month, and you can work for the Walkups and—"

"They don't really need me. It's just charity."

"Then you takes charity. You takes what you can get. It's for this baby, not for you or me. I hear tales that things is booming on the mainland, factories agoing day and night in Wilmington, women working like they never done before, and we here like on the backside of the moon. But you must believe that the Lord will provide, even here. Now let me see you stick that little chin up in the air to catch those big tears. I'm going to make us some tea to talk by. We'll make out."

Two weeks later a check came from Ivy. It was for fifty dollars, and that was a goldmine on Fortune Island. Riches—for the moment. And Ivy had promised to repeat the gift every month.

"You see, there's so much money on the mainland, make your mouth water," said Garcie.

"Maybe I should go over there and get a job—"

"Baby, you can't do what they want there. Factory workers. Waitresses. You ain't got that kind of strength. You can't see too good, neither. You ain't never had no milk for the baby, even. Got to get that evaporated stuff. You lucky you didn't die when Jessie came. You lucky Jessie didn't die. You just stay on here with Garcie, and we get rid of that cough and them flushes before you think of anything like going to that wild place. It was even wild in the old days when I was growing up there. Did you know I was born right in the middle of the big riot of 'ninety-eight, just like Jessie was born right in the middle of this big war?"

"How far is Raleigh? Shouldn't I go and see Bill? They would let me see him, wouldn't they?"

"We ain't got no money for such a trip. We can just about afford all that evaporated milk. You stay put. Things'll work out. They always do."

But with each passing month the checks Ivy was sending grew smaller—fifty dollars, then twenty-five, then fifteen, ten, and, finally, nothing. No check came with the mail boat in August. No letter of explanation. Ivy had tired of her charitable noblesse. "They're on their own," she told her husband. "I gave her a chance to get on her feet. What more can I do? Does she think the world owes her a living?"

And so it was that Susannah found herself once again walking the streets of Wilmington, but this time seeking honest employment; not, however, at the North Carolina Shipbuilding Company, though new people were employed there every day, because she feared running into Ivy and in her desperation asking for help and being rebuffed. She couldn't bear that embarrassment, that hurt.

She had tucked her long red hair in a snood and, at first, had enjoyed the heat of the sun on the back of her neck, but by late afternoon her neck burned as salt sweat drizzled over it. She had begun to realize that her task was a hopeless one. The crowds on the pavement made her dizzy, so that she couldn't make sense when applying for a job. Her pocketbook, an old brown leather one that she hadn't used in years, was scuffed to rawhide in places. Her pink dress was faded, and thin as tissue paper, and limp with perspiration; and poor Garcie, who was losing her sight from diabetes, had painted the stockings on her thin legs unevenly, so that they looked mottled, as with some disorder of the skin. The flush of her cheeks and her cough, which had grown worse all day, warned of consumption, so that many people backed away from her as she spoke. She had been offered medical assessments. She had been told to see a doctor. She had been turned away everywhere. But at the end of the long, hot day she was welcomed in the coolness of the Anchor, the beer joint down on the waterfront that she had operated out of only a few years ago, where she had met Bill. And there was a gentleman in a black suit and black Stetson who seemed friendly and introduced himself as the Reverend Cogburn, a sad traveller. The patina of self-esteem she had acquired through her relationship with Bill had melted away. But being out of the sun and in a dark place and sipping a cool beer lifted her spirits, as did the fluttering interest of the man in the black suit. But it also brought back bad memories. And she wondered if she hadn't made a mistake in coming here. This situation was all too familiar. Why had she deliberately reminded herself of something that she was trying to forget? Was it desperation to be a success at something that brought her here, for this was the last place where she had been able to take care of herself? But she had escaped it and didn't want it back. She had an impulse to leave, to run out of the place, if her legs would carry her, but to where, to what? She was thinking so hard that at first she was only half aware that the man in black was speaking to her, only half aware of the familiar routine of the pickup. He ordered her a second glass of beer, the arrival of which forced her to focus on him.

"Did you say you were a what? A travelling man?"

"A sad traveller, my dear. I am an itinerate minister, a preacher of the word."

"A preacher? You gonna give a sermon in here?"

"Even such as myself need to cool off on a hot August day. Isn't that what such a young lady as yourself is doing? If you don't mind my saying, you look tired and woeful, alas, but I can see the beauty of your features. God's beauty. I believe you need help, am I wrong?"

Susannah hummed "Show Me the Way to Go Home" with the Artie Shaw rendition on the juke box.

"So you want to go home, then?"

"I'm tired from looking for work and I do want to go home."

She began to move away from reality—the day, the heat, the beer. Now there was a new beer and a new song on the juke box. She began to hum with "Don't Sit Under the Apple Tree." The man in black said:

"There's plenty of work. What's the problem?"

"What?"

"Why can't you get something? There's plenty of work."

"I don't know how to do anything or I haven't the strength to do it. I'm too dumb for office work and too weak to be a waitress. I'm nearly blind in one eye. I'm a mess!"

"Why, that's hard to believe—a beautiful girl like you. I could get you a job right now at a mission I know of. Would you like that?"

"Work? Yes!"

"I'll drive you over there right now, if you would like. Come on, take my arm. My car's right outside."

"Work? Yes!" Trancelike, Susannah got up, took the arm of the man in black, and left with him, as she had done in a time that she had tried to forget. She had done the same thing with Bill once, with others before Bill, but Bill had been different, and maybe this man was different, maybe this man wanted to help her, instead of use her. He was a preacher, a man of God, strong with the strength of God. It was so good to have someone to lean on. In the street he led her to his car, a dented, dusty '36 Ford that looked like it had spent its life on the backroads of the boondocks.

"Where are we going?" she asked.

"First we're going to Third and Market."

"What's there?"

"A statue of secretary of state George Davis of the Confederacy, his finger pointing to the Cape Fear River. But it's a funny thing about him. They went and built an ABC store right in between him and the river, so now he's pointing out to all the soldiers, sailors, and marines where they can get some hard liquor." He shut the car door on Susannah, went around to the driver's side, and got in. "You need a long cool drink, maybe a mint julep. How does that sound?"

It sounded wonderful. "But where can we make a mint julep? In the mission?"

"Why sure. There's all kinds of missions, you know. Some'll give you soup and some'll give you a mint julep." But Susannah closed her eyes to the breeze from the open window and later it took the Reverend Cogburn some effort to awaken her. "Come on, little lady, wake up. You been asleep for nigh on to an hour. Come on, wake up." He shook her arm and pulled her out of the car.

"Where are we?"

"Why, we're at the mission. Come on with me." He gripped her arm and led her inside a big, dilapidated, dirty looking place. She was in the elevator before she realized that she was in a hotel.

"Wait! Where're we going?"

"Just in here, to a nice big fan." He led her to his room and closed the door. "Sit down. There, in front of the fan. Feels good, huh? I like to sit there when I'm preparing my sermons. But you get the place of honor today." Something told her to get away, but she felt sick, dizzy. She sat down in a damp heap on the chair, a big leather thing with bumpy springs and stuffing poking from holes worn by fingers. But the fan picked up the air from the open window behind it and blew it on her in a cool shower, and in what seemed an instant the man in black was handing her a cold glass of ice and liquid. He kept on talking and she kept on trying to respond and he kept on bringing her cold drinks and the fan kept on whirring.

The situation turned into a dream, then a strange nightmare, then a waking dream. She was naked, and the man in black was naked now, and hovering above her. Bill kept looking at her and vanishing. Where did he go? Why did he leave her? Was any of this real?

Then she slept, deep, dark, dead to the world. And she woke with a crack of thunder in her head, a lightning bolt and a crack of thunder. She lay in his arms. He was snoring. She screamed and sat up in bed. The clock on the end table told her that she had been asleep all night and half the day. The sun at the window told her the same. But she was not back where she had started, or the man would be gone. She tried to comfort herself with that thought. She lay back down in his arms and went back to sleep. The next time she woke, he was up and about. He had made coffee on a hot plate and gave her a cup. He puffed on a cigar and watched her drink. Then he said:

"You told me last night that your husband's in prison. You didn't say what he'd done."

"It's called conspiracy to commit armed robbery."

"You told me he was up for twelve years."

"Yes. Twelve years." She sipped her coffee. "Did you put something in one of those drinks?"

"You're not saying you're sorry, are you?"

"No, I didn't mean that. It's just that—"

"Why, hell, you were exhausted, that's all."

"You don't seem like much of a preacher to me."

"I go where I'm called, from the Dismal Swamp to Cape Fear. I'll tell you all about the kind of preacher I am someday. Right now, let's talk about you. You also told me you owned a house on an island somewhere."

"Fortune Island. It's near Ocracoke, on the Outer Banks. It's almost a deserted island."

"Deserted? How many people on it?"

"About twenty. Fishermen, shrimpers. We've got a general store. Not much in it. Tackle and worms. Can goods. We've got a little church. Just clapboard. My house is the only real house on the island—seven rooms. The rest are shacks, more or less."

"I sure would like to see that house. How you gonna get back there without any money?" He puffed his cigar. "I'd like to see that island. What do you say I take you back. You told me last night there wasn't a chance of you getting any work here, anyway. You told me last night you had a baby to feed. I've been looking for a place where I could be quiet. That place of yours sounds perfect. I could rent a room from you. Then you'd have some income, and I'd be away most of the time anyhow. Just come back for a little rest and relaxation. Seems like it would solve both of our problems. What do you say?"

"But I don't even know you."

"You know me biblically already, little lady. A little socializing would take care of the rest of it. And we could stop this sex thing any time you want. You'll see, I ain't pushy. And I am a real preacher. You believe that, don't you? I can take and show you places I preach in and introduce you to other ministers who hire me to do them a slam-bang job."

He got up from the bed and began to sling on his black suit jacket, but his shirt sleeve got caught and he struggled with it.

"Is that a gun?"

"Oh that ain't nothing," he said, pulling his jacket on. He held his
jacket open. "Pretty neat, ain't it? Left inside pocket holds a Bible and
right inside pocket holds the gun. It's a holster sewed in. Now before
you go getting any silly ideas, I'll tell you why I carry this piece. I'm up
in the back country a lot and it's dangerous up there. Nothing scares me
like a snake, an evil serpent. I got to protect myself. From some of them
mountain folk, too. The moonshiners up there can be very dangerous.
Once I stumbled on to a pair of 'em and they beat me raw and kept me in a
cage till they decamped. I got saved by a revenuer come along. After that,
I always took this piece out on the road with me. Shoot, you got nothing
to worry about me. I'm as good as gold and as safe as God."

*Jason Petitt Cogburn, eight years old, born with the twentieth century,
stood between his mother Temple and his father Cletus in the Locust
Valley, Tennessee, Church of God with Signs Following, and shivered in
fear to watch and hear the great new prophet George W. Hensley hold a
dozen or so writhing snakes—copperheads, cottonmouths, rattlesnakes—
in his arms and speak in tongues, warning the poisonous serpents in a
strange, rhythmic, otherworldly language of deep-throated grunts and
groans, squeals and unintelligible shouts, not to sink their venom-laden
fangs into the flesh of anyone there who was touched by the Holy Spirit. It
was the voice of God, and the serpents would obey it; but, if a congregant
were not touched by the Holy Ghost, the snakes would know, and he or she
would be at the mercy of the evil in the snakes, for to the good, they would
bring good, but to the evil, evil. "Go on, now, boy," Cletus Cogburn told
his son. "Go on and take up the serpent. Your ma and me both done our
turn. I know yer scaret, but you got to be set free of the Devil. You got to
prove it to God, that you have faith in Him and not the Evil One." And
so Jason Petitt Cogburn overmastered his fear, stepped up to the great
entranced man and reached out to the belly-crawlers he held squirming
in his godly arms.
    Temple Cogburn screamed, realizing that her child had been bitten,
and the whole congregation seemed to roar at the boy, as if he had
committed a sin, and he must have done for the pain he felt now and the
sensation that his brain was being sucked out of his head. The last thing
he remembered was that there was open evidence of the evil in him and
that he was a shamed outcast, then the fire in his mind was clouded by
black smoke and the breathtaking smell of sulphur.*

He woke a week later in a small hospital in Cleveland, Tennessee, saved but never to be saved, and he would not speak to his parents when they came to see him. He turned away from them and all good. His hatred of snakes never abated, matched only by his hatred of people. He had small-boy dreams of killing the prophet, Hensley, and even of killing his parents, who had inflicted such days and nights of agony on him, who had caused his arm to be scalloped of necroflesh, leaving an ugly dent where there had been smooth flesh and pale tender skin. The small guilt his mother felt he interpreted as disgust, Cletus's consoling words were words of disappointment, and any member of the congregation of the Church of God with Signs Following who brought him loving hands and hearts he pushed away. He would bite their candy like a snake and spit it in their faces, and now they began to think of him as possessed. And that was fine with him, for he was. Within a year, he had burnt down his father's house. Whether his parents had survived or not he had no idea, nor did he care. He was on the road and through the woods at ten. At fifteen he was doing the only work he was suited for, being a child prophet and preacher who cold-bloodedly prophesied pain like a salesman and hypocritically preached the void in his heart with the words of the Book. He sat in the camps of the moonshiners and drank from their stills. He ravaged any female of whatever age caught away from the flock. He thought of himself as an outlaw of the God who had showed so little faith in him and in whom he had even less faith. He thought of himself as the snake that bit him, and of his being as snake-bit. When he raped the young sister of a moonshiner he was put in a cage and left to starve. When the moonshiner returned to find that Cogburn had escaped, word was put out to watch for him and he had to leave the Black Mountains and come down to the cities along the coast. Now he sought the anonymity of isolation on an island.

"But just till I recharge my battery," he told Susannah. "I'll pay you seven dollars a week, for that front bedroom."

"I was only going to ask for five."

"I'll stay put up there for a month, then I'll keep the room but I'll be going on the road again."

"How long? I mean, how long at a time?"

"Depends on how many churches I get called to preach at. Could be a week, a couple of weeks, a month. Can't rightly say till I go, but when I come back, you'll know. And I'll pay you at the same rate, either before or after. It'll be a steady income. That's what you want to know, isn't it?"

As soon as Susannah arrived home she told Garcie about her new tenant in a thrilled voice. "Twenty-eight dollars a month is enough to keep us going, Garcie, and I don't have to work, which I can't do anyway. I'm so grateful."

"Sounds like you struck gold, little Susie."

"He's good as gold and safe as God, Garcie."

"Well, then, we got to thank God for this preacher man, I think."

Chapter
Four

May 2000

W aking, David Perle watched through sleepy, slitted eyes as Hildegarde
Schnepp packed their bags for the next part of their journey. She
glanced out the window at the vast green vista of Central Park,
where they had taken a romantic carriage ride the evening before. They were
in a suite at the Hotel Plaza in New York City—a stopover rendezvous—and
were headed south, to North Carolina, to Chapel Hill to visit Jessie. He smelled
coffee.

Hildegarde was letting him sleep late—she had given him reason for
needing the extra time this bright Manhattan morning—but she caught
him watching her, came over, and threw herself down against him. "Ich
liebe dich," she cooed, snuggling up to him. "Come on, my big baby, we
have a plane to catch. I'm very anxious to meet your sister, the famous
Jessie Judas. She's my hero, you know."

"I thought I was your hero."

"Last night you were my hero," she said, laughing. "This morning I'm
back to Jessie."

In January, when David returned to Berlin, Jessie was the subject of
their first long conversation in a café Unter den Linden in view of the
Brandenburg Gate. David had told Hildegarde of his short visit to Paris
and of his sister's illness. Hildegarde knew of the fainting episode from
the newspaper and television reports. "So your mother has taken her back
to the States?"

"With those two, it's hard to say who's in charge."

"They are so close?"

"They've always been very close. More like sisters than mother and
daughter. They're less than fifteen years apart. Of course, Jessie is Ruth's

stepdaughter. They're like very close friends. Sometimes, when I'm with them, I feel positively de trop."

"Oh, pauvre petit Da-veed! For such a big man you are like a little boy pressing his nose against the window of women, ever shut out. Toujours de trop! We are not so different, you know. Women, I mean. I mean, from men. Just different enough so that we can fit together. My roommates are off on flights. We can go to my place if you like." And forty-plus David, bachelor and diplomat, succumbed to twenty-five year old Hildegarde Schnepp that night and every day since.

Finally, he was in love. He realized he had been since he first saw her on the flight to Paris, and this, for him, strange fact had been reconfirmed and intensified for three months now. When the chance came to go to the States for a couple of weeks, he asked her to meet him there, at the Plaza, promised to introduce her to Jessie, whom he knew to be a magnet for Hildegarde, and now here they were, heading for Jessie's house.

Driving a rented car from Raleigh, David said, "Have you noticed that there are days that are all one and days that have parts that are almost like separate days. This morning, when you woke me, seems now like several days ago, even though it was only"—he checked his watch— "about three hours ago."

"I'm a flight attendant. I'm used to broken time. Oh, look, David! What do you call those blossoms?"

"Which? I see dogwood, crepe myrtle, tulip trees—"

"Tulip trees?"

"They look like magnolias—probably are—but they call them tulip trees."

"The ones with the big purple blossoms?" she asked.

"The little ones that look like they have big tulips sitting on their boughs."

"Roll your window down," she said. "After New York, the breeze smells like a thousand cosmic perfumes. Chapel Hill is like a Bavarian village."

"A village of fifty thousand people is not a village anymore. That's a good-sized city. Sometimes it's called 'Blue Heaven,' for the sky-blue color of the Tar Heels."

"They are?"

"Athletes. Football and basketball players. They wear sky blue. Sometimes it's called 'the southern part of heaven.' Mountains, rolling foothills, forests, and a big blue sky."

He turned on to Franklin Street. "Here's the spot for sightseeing. This is the main drag. I can only go twenty miles an hour along here, so you can take a good look."

"And those old brick buildings—they are the University of North Carolina?"

"UNC at Chapel Hill. Thousands of students. Those scruffy people who seem to be searching for an angry fix."

"It is like any university. You wouldn't have recognized me if you had seen me when I was student. I even smoked then. I love all these little shops. Is it true that the woman who wrote *A Tree Grows in Brooklyn* lived here?"

"Betty Smith—yes." David turned off Franklin Street. "Many writers have lived here—writers and artists, great scientists. All sorts of well-known people."

"And Jessie Judas."

"Yes. She was teaching at the Institute of Marine Sciences—and doing research. She was in and out of here for years, so finally she bought a house—and there it is."

"And Tar Heels, what does it mean?"

"According to Ruth, who is the expert on these things, North Carolina was a big producer of pitch, turpentine, and tar since Colonial days. It seems that during one of the conflicts of the Civil War, North Carolina troops felt they had been let down by a regiment from Virginia, and carried chips on their shoulders when they were pulled back from the front after the battle. The Virginia soldiers taunted the North Carolina boys by asking if the North Carolina boys had run out of tar, meaning they hadn't stuck in the battle. The North Carolina boys retorted that there wasn't any more tar because Jefferson Davis had bought it all up, and the Virginia boys asked why that was. The North Carolina boys told the Virginia boys that old Jeff Davis was going to put it on the Virginians' heels to make them stick better in the next fight. General Lee, the story goes, heard about this exchange and blessed what he called the Tar Heel boys for sticking to the fight, and the nickname stuck as well—Tar Heels."

"So it means that they stick to their guns—right?"

"Jessie's a Tar Heel, so you can see for yourself."

David pulled in at a large, green-shuttered white frame house, beribboned like a gift with strands of ivy and climbing roses.

"Be prepared," he said. "She doesn't look like her picture on *Time* anymore."

An Hispanic woman of about forty answered the bell. "Buenos tardes," she said. "Señorita Jessie has been expecting—"

"Miss Jessie has finally arrived," called Jessie, "skipping along on her pogo stick. Juanita, you can bring the trays into the living room now." Jessie leaned on a metal cane with four rubber-tipped feet, and the usually poised Hildegarde towered uncomfortably above her like an oversized puppy looking for a lap to curl up in, wanting to worship upward at the ten-foot tall idol her mind still insisted on seeing. David, who seemed almost afraid to touch Jessie, so frail had she become, kissed her lightly on a clownishly rouged cheek. Hildy bent in a kind of curtsy and kissed the other cheek.

"It is so wonderful to actually be with you," Hildy said. "I feel that I know you. You will please pardon me, if I am too familiar, but you see you are my hero. The leaders of the world make wars, but people like you are saving the planet. You inspired me to join the Green Party in Germany. You are the second coming of Rachel Carson. Please forgive me if I gush. I've been containing my excitement ever since I first read your book. What a great and thrilling life you have led. I think it is women who will lead the world to better things." Hildegarde's eyes were glassy and her cheeks were flushed.

"Don't be embarrassed, my dear, but do catch your breath." Jessie patted Hildegarde on the back. "I quite understand. Rachel Carson was my own hero and inspiration. And I still remember how it feels to be young and idealistic; but, really, I'm just a quite ordinary old woman."

"But you are not very old," Hildy objected.

"A lifetime of physical and mental illness has made me older than my years. It's events that make you old, you know, not time."

"But you had to be so athletic—a great swimmer..."

"In my prime and for the purpose of my work. But as you can see... Now, come through to the living room. We have wine and cheese, Beluga and crackers, and I don't know what else Juanita may have put out. I'm not domestic, nor do I have any gift for entertaining." Jessie had made no effort to dress for company. Her head was covered by a red and black bandana—Hildy presumed she wore it to hide the thinness of her hair—and she wore an ice-blue, long-sleeved shapeless shift, spotted down the front by what was most probably red wine. Below the shift, green pajama bottoms reached down to a very beaten-up pair of pink slippers. She emanated a musty odor, mild enough not to be offensive, but suggesting that she had neither changed her clothes nor bathed in several days.

The living room was crowded and unkempt. Juanita had to push things aside on the large coffee table that filled the space between a smoke-colored couch and an overstuffed chair that Jessie collapsed into, her cane swinging about, dangerous as a ski-pole. "Platz namen!" she invited, as she landed and worked her bony backside into the chair, picking up a huge long-haired black cat. "This is Cinderella, my oven mitt." The cat's hair was everywhere and was picked up by their clothes. Juanita looked helplessly at Jessie's company. "It is not my fault," she said, "this disorder. She won't let me touch a thing."

"It's a cubist work of art," Jessie said. "If you like cubism—which is, my goodness—nearly a hundred years old—Picasso, Braque, you know—you'll just have to like my living room.

> 'A wild disorder in the dress
> Kindles there a wantonness...' "

"Robert Herrick," said Hildegarde.
"Very good," said Jessie. "You know your English literature."
"I took courses in English lit," said Hildegarde.
David had been here before and seen it all, but Hildy was intensely interested. The room was filled to the point of clutter with the relics and artifacts of a busy life. She identified honorary degrees from a number of universities representing a number of countries. They tilted this way and that on the walls, their frames arm-wrestling, as it were, with pictures of Jessie posing with celebrities from a number of fields. Copies of Jessie's book, *Souvenirs of the Sea*, were precariously stacked on the floor by the couch. There were several swimming trophies, some with dead flowers in them, scattered about the room. One whole wall was taken up by an aquarium filled with tropical fish, their colors and structures as exotic as the moon, a calm aquarium of dreams softly bubbling an otherworldly music. "I know where everything is," Jessie said, "and I don't want anything moved, or I have to go and find it again. Pour yourselves some wine—Juanita, pour them some wine." She held out her own stemmed glass to Juanita. "Come, fill my cup!"

David could see that Hildegarde was grateful to be at eye-level with Jessie. He remembered how tall and straight Jessie had been as a young woman, almost as tall as Hildegarde. And strong. She had lifted weights. Even last winter, in Paris, she had seemed tall and straight behind the lectern—before the fainting spell.

"Have you had another of those fainting spells?" he asked. His drink sat before him, untouched. Hildy was sipping white wine.

"That was just an aberration," Jessie said. "It was the pain. I hadn't been taking my pain medicine." Then, cheerfully: "It was embarrassing, though, all those paparazzi staring down and flashing their cameras at me." She reached out and tapped Hildegarde's arm. "I hope I had my legs closed."

"I saw a picture in *Der Spiegel*. You looked as dignified as a queen in her Schlafzimmer. Those nasty paparazzi wouldn't have dared to embarrass you. Millions of women like me would have come down upon them and thrown their cameras in the Seine."

Jessie told Hildegarde that she had heard much about her. Ruth had told her that Hildegarde and David were going to marry later in the year. Ruth had been down here trying to talk her into living with her in Brookline—"That's just outside Boston"—at the family mansion. Jessie had said No, that she wanted to live, or die, near her roots. All right, Ruth had said, I'll go back to Mass and get what I need and come down here to live with you. "So she'll be here in a week or so. And I suppose now that I am weak, she will take over my life as she did when I was a child. But I'm only joking. I'll be glad for it, to have her with me. I have Ruth and David—and now I will have a lovely sister-in-law named Hildegarde. How delightful is life! Full of new wonders to the bitter end."

"David told me that they are taking good care of you at Duke University Hospital."

"They can do wonders but perhaps not the one I require. Please forgive my appearance, I simply can't dress up anymore—except perhaps for a visit from Tom Hanks. Is he still popular? I don't watch television or see many movies. Have a glass of Beaujolais, you two. It's my favorite, but do have whatever you want. I see Juanita has put out a nice variety." She lit a cigarette and inhaled deeply. David noticed that the ashtray on the coffee table was overflowing with cigarette butts.

"You shouldn't smoke," he said. "It's debilitating."

"Ruth smoked, and she was my hero, so I smoked. You notice that I use a DeNicotia holder nowadays. Of course my doctor doesn't want me to smoke, so I have made this little compromise with him. Debilitating? My God, David, I'm dying. Can't you see that? What possible difference can it make? I'm only sixty and I look eighty. I look older than Ruth, my mother. More than my mother—my sister, my friend, my savior, all of those and still more. She won't mind if I smoke, or drink. She still smokes herself. We were always good company for each other."

"I didn't mean to annoy you," said David.

"Of course not, dear. I know that. It's just, all of this medical folderol has made me cranky. I should smoke some marijuana. I smoke pot now for the pain. I used to have such beautiful long red hair and now it's nothing but white wisps because of the poison they've pumped into me. I was never beautiful, but the hair helped. Now there's nothing. Oh, hell! Prosit!"

David and Hildegarde raised their glasses to Jessie. "Prosit!" they said in unison.

Hildegarde said, "Please forgive me, but you remarked on mental problems. I've heard nothing of this before. Such things are, of course, none of my business; but I am so surprised to hear you say it."

"Spells of depression, that's all. They started when I was quite young. There's a phrase we use down here in the south when someone has bad luck. We say that someone is snakebit. I feel that way sometimes."

"But you are a world famous woman," Hildegarde said. "I read *Andenken des Meeres* in German. You have done so many wonderful things. You have had for your friends some of the most famous, some of the greatest—"

"Look behind you there." Jessie pointed. "That's a picture of me with Jacques Cousteau aboard the Calypso. We were diving off the Great Barrier Reef in Australia. You would love to see the strange world down there, beautiful and terrifying.

> 'Full fathom five thy father lies;
> Of his bones are coral made:
> Those are pearls that were his eyes:
> Nothing of him that doth fade,
> But doth suffer a sea-change
> Into something rich and strange.'"

"Shakespeare!" said Hildy. "I love your description of the island where you grew up."

"The isolation and loneliness of those early days left their mark on me, but they are also probably why I have had my small triumph in life. You might say that I developed a one-track mind. That's why my book, that you seem to admire, is only about my work. There's nothing about my personal life in it because I haven't had any. Would you like me to read you a little of the book—in English?"

"Oh, I should love that—to hear you read it as it was really written. To hear your voice in it."

"Perhaps we shouldn't tax you," said David.

"Nonsense! Reading my own words gives me hope. It's like starting all over again." Her glasses were on a chain around her neck. "I wore that ring of yours on a chain for years—until I gave it to you. Do you remember? Love and Luck?"

"I remember," he said, holding his hand up, displaying the ring. "I wanted this ring from the time I was a little boy, and you always said you'd give it to me someday, and you did, when I graduated Harvard. I'm thinking of having it cut down—for a wedding ring, you know, for Hildy. Would you object to that?"

"Not at all. It's your ring now. We'll find out if it's gold when they cut it down. But I suppose they can tell by weight. It'll make a beautiful wedding ring. A member of our family gave it to me when I was a child," she told Hildegarde. "The double L has come to stand for Love and Luck, but the man who gave it to our relative in the first place thought that it stood for Lucky Lindy. But never mind that. It's a family heirloom, and Love and Luck is what it stands for."

She put her glasses on, and reached out for a little computer book on a table next to her chair. "Here we are. This is an eBook. Have you seen one? It lights up from the rear. Makes it easier for me to read. My publisher sent it to me."

"*Andenken des Meeres,*" said Hildegarde, "*Souvenirs of the Sea.* A Pulitzer prize winner!" This was what Hildegarde had been waiting for.

" 'Chapter One,' " read Jessie. " 'Fortune Island. To the best of my knowledge, Fortune Island was named for a plundered and derelict Spanish galleon, the Buena Fortuna, that, according to at least one history, scuttled on an island of the Banks in the sixteenth century. It's said that the gathering dunes eventually buried all but the prow of the ship, leaving only half of the name in plain sight, and so newcomers to the island looked upon the name of the ship as the name of the island and Fortune Island it became. But that's one, possibly the most likely, among many versions of how it got its name.

" 'By the eighteenth century Fortune Island was a considerable port-of-call, with a fluctuating population of around eight hundred people. These included fishers, shrimpers, crabbers, lobstermen, and tradesmen of all sorts involved with water traffic. And, of course, they brought their families to the island. But then the great disasters occurred, one upon another. A hurricane in the mid-nineteenth century shut the main inlet while opening another miles up the Banks. People left in droves for the new port. The 'fixed' population dropped to about a hundred, and continued to drop with the coming of Union troops during the Civil War. When the troops withdrew at war's end, Fortune Island was virtually depopulated, almost a deserted island.

"'As visitors to the island know, Fortune Island is a whale-shaped island, its head to the north and out to sea, its flukes pointing southwest to the mainland. Most of the northern end, or head, is covered with enormous dunes, as if the sea view had been walled away. The roots of the dunes are entangled with the roots of mummified trees which once stood tall in the sea wind but now are buried and grip the depths of the dunes like anchors. This area is referred to as Whalehead, the tail of the whale being the low narrow leeward end, which in my time was where most of the population, a few fishermen and shrimpers mainly, had little shacks along little streets of a tiny village. A small white church with a steeple that one could see from the heights of Whalehead remained from an earlier time. Out behind it were two cemeteries, one for black folk, one for white, each with a white picket fence not meant to keep people out but apparently to keep ancestral ghosts in.'" She dropped the eBook to her lap and looked up, saying, "I grew up on Fortune Island at a time when the outside world of authority didn't seek me out—there on my island far across Pamlico Sound—as other truants were sought, a time long before the authorities had computers with which to track truants down. I was, for all intents and purposes, unknown to the mainland." She paused, thinking. "It's still amazing to think that there were U-boats right off the coast during the Second World War, in the late thirties and early forties—I've been told I was born during an attack—sinking merchant ships, Liberty ships, they were called, not far out at sea. People could see the explosions from the shore, the great red fires from the airplane fuel that the tankers carried. The U-boats were like sharks out there. They sank many, many ships."

"The Nazis," said Hildegard, "I know. But that part about the U-boats was left out in *Andenken des Meeres*."

"No, no, my dear, that's not in the book. I was just thinking out loud. You're too young to know what it was like then, I should think."

"I am a history major. I know what they did, the Nazis—we did. I know all about the Holocaust, too. I grew up knowing about it. Back in the seventies there was an American television mini-series about the

Holocaust that shocked the German public. I've heard all about it, how
people my mother's age were embarrassed for their own parents, how
appalled all young Germans of conscience were."

Jessie said, "Sometimes I think that that has all escaped us, as
everything does, finally. Freud said something about infantile amnesia.
I must admit, I am too tired—maybe too drunk—to go on. Juanita! Do
you want coffee? No? No. Juanita doesn't have a green card, but what
the hell! Juanita, dame una copa de café, por favor. Just for me. I'm
sorry, I can't empty a bota bag as I once could at the bullfights in Spain. I
have actually seen El Cordobes, you know. The greatest bullfighter since
Manolete, I'm told." She found a handkerchief and wiped her eyes. "I'm
sorry. I'm sorry. Sometimes I suffer from logorrhea as well as amnesia—
my black hole. One theoretician believed that when I was young I suffered
from what is called pathological intoxication—one drink and I'd become
a zombie, an aggressive one with no memory of my aggression. But,
if so, I must have outgrown it. I can remember no other such incident.
Melancholia, perhaps. I must admit that every time I think about Fortune
Island I get upset. I really hate to think about it but it keeps coming back.
And in another way, strange though it may seem, I love the place. It was
the only time of my life that I could wander and dream. Maybe it's lost
love that brings the sadness on. But it's no good looking back. Ahead
is all we have—time's one-way arrow. I thought I could read you the
Fortune Island section, but I can't." She drained her wine and took a sip
of coffee. "Forgive me. You will stay here tonight, please? Your room
is ready. And we'll have a big Mexican breakfast together, outdoors on
the patio, if weather permits. It looks promising. Meantime, while I nap,
why don't you take a walk and see Chapel Hill? There are all sorts of chic
restaurants scattered about, but my favorite is the McDonald's on Franklin
Street. You see the most interesting characters in there, junkies and bums
with interesting faces."

While she and David window-shopped on Franklin Street, Hildy said,
"She's very different from the person I expected."

"What did you expect?"

"A sort of Katherine Hepburn, I guess. More positive. Was she always
so sad, or is it the illness?"

"Ruth said that when Jessie was a young girl she was full of *joie de
vivre*, lively and interested in everything; mind like a sponge, Ruth used
to say. But something happened—the depression Jessie spoke of. Bi-
polarism set in. From that point on she focused on her work. She became

fixated, one-tracked, almost fanatical. No men in her life, no interest. Ruth was always sad about that, but I've also heard her say that Jessie's singularity of purpose was probably what made her so good at what she did. You know, like an autistic-savant, having everything shut out of her life, she was able to focus entirely on her work."

"Before I met her," Hildy said, "I could almost envy her—a triumphant modern hero on the cover of *Time* magazine—but now she seems so sad to me, just a lonely old woman. Her life isn't a triumph, it's a tragedy of loneliness and depression. Even of alcoholism."

"I've heard you say that you thought Churchill was the greatest man of the twentieth century," said David.

"I have said that."

"Well? He was depressive and alcoholic."

"She is very brave," Hildy said. "I've never heard of anyone saying with such sang froid that they were dying."

David said, "Bloodied, but unbowed. I told you she was a true Tar Heel."

⌘ ⌘ ⌘

With Juanita's help, Jessie got to her bedroom, which was on the same floor as the living room. She did not want to climb stairs if she could avoid it, so her bed had been brought downstairs to her office. There were many things that she did not want to do anymore. She did not want to think of the past, but, of late, her thoughts had turned constantly back to the blankness surrounding her fourteenth birthday, a black hole in time some forty-five years before.

Jessie could see the irony in her fascination with biology; she, who had somehow undergone a profound change of life at fourteen, who felt no biological urges as she grew up, no desire to have a husband or children of her own, was fascinated by the reproductive cycles of animals. As she grew up, she thought of herself as a neutered savant and let the boys walk away from her in frustration.

When Jessie thought back over her career, it became clear that she had done her best work between the ages of twenty and forty. That work required her to be in top physical condition, like an astronaut. She had been a powerful swimmer since childhood. It was just before she was forty that she first fell ill. It was not the cancer she now suffered from. It was endometriosis, a condition in which bits of the tissue, the lining of the uterus, grow in other parts of the body. Like the uterine lining, this tissue builds up and sheds in response to monthly hormonal cycles. These uterine implants can be found even on the kidneys or in the lungs, menstruating every month. But there is no natural outlet for the blood discarded from these implants. It falls onto the organs, causing swelling and inflammation and is extremely painful.

Jessie, aware of studies in biofeedback, believed that her body, starving for the production of life, but suppressed by her mind, had turned on itself, that her untried womb had gone outside of itself in search of the expression of life. Her doctors did not share her opinion, but listened respectfully to it, because, after all, she was a biologist. Finally, how her condition came to be was of no consequence. Operation after operation—twenty-some— to remove the scattered bits of her womb ruined her once splendid health. These difficulties ended with the onset of menopause, but she was never the same, good for nothing now but writing about what had been, writing *Souvenirs of the Sea*, the book that had given her world fame and had in part at least brought Hildegarde to her door, wagging like a puppy.

Shamelessly neglecting her company, Jessie had napped until bedtime, leaving Juanita to take care of supper and the bedding down of her guests. When she woke, she was hung over and ordered a Bloody Mary. Juanita brought the drink to her room, with her night-time pills, her pain killers, her mild chemos, her sleep-inducers, everything she needed to drive out memory. The partial amnesia of disassociation had worn off weeks after her fourteenth birthday, but she had replaced it with a self-induced amnesia for forty-five years, her powerful will turning away from that which it did not want to know. But tonight, in a medicated half-sleep, her will unable to defend her, Jessie dreamed of an event that had caused her great shame.

Working with the National Oceanographic Survey, she was in a submersible a mile or more beneath the surface of the Atlantic, in the Atlantic Ridge, with mountains the size of the Rockies on both sides of her, and mephitic smoke rising through the water from fiery cracks in the tectonic plates, hell surfacing up through the murky density of the benthonic darkness. She turned off the white lights of the submersible and turned on red, for filming. Sea life could not see the red light; saw blackness, and swam before her in utter innocence. A hammerhead came up to sniff at the submersible, and suddenly she saw the Reverend Jason P. Cogburn, her freakish, frightening stepfather. She knew she was hallucinating but could do nothing to clear her mind of him and see the hammerhead again. Panic-hysteria overcame her, claustrophobia, and she screamed to be brought up. It was a costly misadventure, and embarrassing to all. It took her a long time to live it down. When someone on the boat had asked her what it was that she had thought she'd seen down there, she thought of hellfire and brimstone, but had replied, "My childhood." She sat up in bed, crying tears of shame. "What did I have... but the not knowing... to keep me going...?" She lit a lamp, and stared at the black window across from her until light gathered beyond it, till she heard an owl hoot and a squirrel chirp, and noticed that the smell of freshly brewed coffee was finding its way in under her door. "At last," she said, with a sigh.

Juanita knew that Jessie would be the first up. Coffee was ready on the patio and Señorita Jessie would want her morning cognac in it.

Jessie hobbled out to the patio on bare feet, stabbing her rubber-tipped four-pronged vade mecum at the flagstones, wearing only a slip, the last of her vanity hiding her once-beautiful, chemically betrayed red hair under a tight kerchief.

She was drinking coffee and cognac, smoking a king-sized cigarette, and admiring the roses climbing up the back of her house, and the centerpiece of the patio, a leafless, early-blossoming Eastern Redbud, when David and Hildegarde appeared, dressed, combed, and coiffed, an hour later. "Oh, I'd almost forgotten I had company," she said. "I hope you two slept well last night."

"We did," said David. "Did you sleep well, Jess? I hope you had a sweet dream of peace like Abou Ben Adhem."

"I'm afraid not. But look at this garden!

> 'Im wunderschönen Monat Mai,
> Als alle Knospen sprangen...' "

"Heine!" Hildegarde exclaimed. "Heinrich Heine.

> 'In the wonderfully beautiful month of May,
> When all the buds are springing,
> There is in my heart
> Love going into the world.' "

"Nice rendering, my dear," said Jessie.

"Yes, wunderschönen," said Hildy, bemused, pulling gently at a branch laden with the small purple blossoms of the Redbud. "What is this?"

"Cercis Canadensis," said Jessie. "It's called the Eastern Redbud.

But there's a private joke attached."

"A joke?"

"Yes. A bit of black humor. It's also known as the Judas Tree, or Flowering Judas. According to legend, Judas Iscariot hanged himself from a branch of the European species. It's my little identity joke."

"What was it that troubled your sleep," asked David, "pain, or a bad dream?"

"Neither, in fact. Memory. And then a further memory that the first invoked, one from childhood. I guess the closer you are to death the more you think of childhood. It's like Ruth's great poem, 'The Diamond Merchant.' Listen to how she puts it, this poem of the holocaust, or, better, its aftermath, and the imminence of death." Jessie closed her eyes against the morning brightness for a moment and began to speak the words:

" 'The buoys of memory have faint bells, noticed in the night.
I have left these chiming seamarks for the time of my return.
They ring out there, but faintly, so faintly I can hardly hear.
I think they want me to remember the severances of the soul,
if soul is more than mere electric tissue. If Death is king
and I do not reclaim what I have jettisoned, it goes to him.
I do not want the king to have my life. Therefore, each night at sea,
I must set out to find the ringing buoys and haul aboard
the lagan realities, for now my aging body, my emotional mal de mer,
lend renewed reality to the cold, damp camps. One numbered friend
should wear a wedding ring, another was engaged, and yet a third,
below and silent, had eyes like Tavernier blue diamonds set in Fabergé
eggshell by the master. I cannot put a name to the smiling face I see,
but she existed, who is now the faint dream of a denouement.

Shalom alekhem   *Shalom alekhem*

So now I sail all night to find them and their symbols, to
connect with them whatever seems appropriate, their rings,
their eyes, their ways: but not alone to find the persons
but to find the meanings of the persons to myself, the electric
mind, before the king should claim them from my life.'

"Enough of that," she said, and made a tipsy effort to brighten up. "I had a girlfriend once," she said, changing the subject, "a charming girl, beautiful and delightful—everything I wasn't. Did I ever tell you about Marie, David? Ave Marie! I have a whole stack of letters from her somewhere. We wrote for years. I told her of my adventures and she told me of hers and they couldn't have been more different. She found a rich man somewhere and they got married and she ended up living in New York on Park Avenue, wearing chinchilla coats and festooned with diamonds. She was the only girl, of nearly my own age—she was a couple of years older—with whom I've ever had an intimate correspondence. You know, telling each other our secrets and giggling on paper." She laughed a little. The laughing seemed to cause her pain. But she laughed.

Hildegarde and David busied themselves at a Mexican breakfast buffet brought out by Juanita. David wolfed down a platter of huevos rancheros, then two or three jalapeño corn cakes with his coffee.

"Whatever became of her, Jess, your girlfriend?" asked Hildegarde.

"We drew apart as I travelled the world in search of meaning and she sought more and more wealth through a series of marriages. Last I heard of her she was living on a Greek island with a Greek shipping tycoon. But that's of no importance. Not to me, nowadays. But once I thoroughly enjoyed reading about her adventures. Poor Ruth spent a fortune on tutors, prepping me so that I could get into Smith, but Marie taught me all the things about life that Ruth would have preferred I didn't learn, if you know what I mean. Strictly vicariously, you understand. What I am is—I'm over-medicated and a little drunk already."

"Your arm," said Hildegarde, "your shoulder. That round scar. I bet you were bitten by a barracuda or some kind of fish or something, weren't you?"

Jessie took a sip of her cognac-laden coffee, and looked down at her shoulder. "I was bitten by a snake."

"That doesn't look like a snake bite."

"Take my word for it, sweetheart, I was bitten by a snake."

"But snakes have fangs."

"Not all snakes, my dear. Who's the biologist around here? Juanita, bring me a wrap!" In a moment, Juanita floated a silk scarf around Jessie's shoulders. "Spring can be goddamned cold," Jessie said, lifting her coffee cup. "If I were you, Hildy, I think that I should prefer to read Marie's autobiography, had she written one, rather than mine. Marie could have written about men the way I write about sea life. Although sometimes I'm not sure there's a big difference—though, as many people believe, I'm one of the great experts on biology. Marie, quite a girl!"

"And you never had a romance?" asked Hildy, quietly.

"No, I had a career. I missed out on romance. I had to focus. That's how you do things in this world, my dear, you exclude and focus. Samuel Goldwyn said, Include me out. That's how I got this way, whatever way it is." She took a hefty drink and looked off over their heads. "I was a butterfly that closed myself up in my own wings and hardened into a chrysalis and emerged as an ugly caterpillar." She laughed again and held herself against the pain.

Chapter
Five

Spring 1943

The Reverend Jason Petitt Cogburn rarely told a joke, but he tried one of his own devising on Susannah McQueen as he drove her and little Jessie to the Central Prison in Raleigh. "What's the difference between a prisoner and a zebra?" he asked her.

She sat next to him, holding Jessie in her lap, and tried to think of a response, though she was not in any mood for jokes, riddles, or distractions of any kind, which was probably why he had tried his unpracticed hand at humor in the first place, to distract her from her fear of confrontation with William Makepeace Thackeray McQueen.

Receiving no answer, he said, "A zebra is white with black stripes, and a prisoner is black with white stripes." He snorted. "Black-hearted," he elaborated. "Like a nigger!" He turned from his driving to look at her— she turned her blind eye to him—and he turned back to the road with a scowl on his face. Little Jessie began to cry. "Can't you hush that child?" he said. When he looked at Susannah he saw nothing but weakness. He needed her to be strong. He had coached her on what to tell her husband and he needed her to follow his instructions. He had been soft with her up till now, not out of kindness, but because he had seen how a harsh word could make her retreat, and today, above all days, he needed her to be bold. The pot on the table was his possession of her and her house, ownership of a pliant slave and a home, his castle. Even today—if he hadn't driven her, she wouldn't have been able to get to Raleigh. She could come down the mountains to the sea like driftwood in a gravity flow, but she could no more climb than driftwood could.

He had found out that prisoners of the Central Prison in Raleigh could have visitors on the first and third Sunday of each month. This was the third Sunday, and he was taking her to the Central Prison to tell her husband that she was going to divorce him, that she was going to marry the Reverend Jason P. Cogburn, and that nothing he said could stop her. "You've got to show grit," he said, as they entered Raleigh's city limits. "You know what to say," he added. "We've been over it dozens of times. I want this to go right. This is costing me a fortune in gas. I've told you, we only get three gallons a week on rationing. I had to fill this tank on black market, and I ain't going to waste my money if nothing comes of it."

Susannah had not once visited William Makepeace Thackeray McQueen since he had been a prisoner behind the Wall. He did not blame her. He blamed himself for what he saw as his failure to live up to his responsibilities, for what amounted to his betrayal of her. "When you fail in your duty," he told Chaplain Baker, himself a decorated war vet—got it in the gut in North Africa with Patton, purple heart, and unable to return to active duty—"it isn't anyone else's fault, it's yours."

"Don't you think calling yourself Judas is overdoing it a bit?"

"How did you know about that?"

"Chuck Smiley brought it to my attention."

"None of his damn business."

"He's worried about you. I am too. How's your head—the concussion?

"The buzzing's faded out. But I still get headaches. Especially after I box."

"You shouldn't box. It's dangerous for a man with a head injury. Why do you do it?

"Cheap plastic surgery. Anyway, it has nothing to do with changing my name to Tom Judas, although it's a good boxer's name, and it's a lot shorter than William Makepeace Thackeray McQueen on a marquee if I ever get back to a musical career. It has a ring to it, don't you think?"

"Look, you come to me every week, but you have no interest in religion. You don't want to attach yourself to any denomination, you scorn every kind of ceremony, but you just keep coming. The question is, what do you want from me? Sometimes I think you have a messianic complex. Why don't you go to the psychiatrist? I don't know what I can do for somebody like you. Everybody in here claims to be not guilty, if not innocent, but, if Smiley is to be believed, you are innocent, and yet you behave as if you're guilty. What are you guilty of? You yourself tell me that you are innocent of the crime you're in here for; but don't you see that if you are innocent you have nothing to reprove yourself for? Why then call yourself Judas, the betrayer?"

"Because I was stupid, I left a wife and child to fend for themselves. I don't know how I can make it up to them."

"How were you stupid?"

"By trusting Smiley. He's not a bad old boy, but he himself says he's improvident. I should have known better."

"Smiley says you knew nothing, that he tricked you, knowing you wouldn't be part of his scheme if you'd known what you were getting into."

"Even so, I can't make it up to my wife and child."

"Maybe you can someday. You're still a very young man, despite that white hair. How old are you, twenty-two, twenty-three? You'll still be a relatively young man when you get out. Ease up on yourself."

"I can't help it. It's the way I'm made. My mother and father taught me responsibility. They bred it in to me. They were strong people."

"You've got years to do. More than a decade. You'll come out of here an old man if you keep this up."

Chaplain Baker liked these meetings with William Makepeace Thackeray McQueen, the white haired young man with the literary name. He tended to believe that McQueen was innocent. That he was also a sensitive and intelligent young man was clear. McQueen should have been seeing the psychiatrist, but Chaplin Baker didn't object to seeing McQueen on a weekly basis because he found him and his story to be interesting. The common run of convicts bored him. McQueen would have made a good soldier, duty-bound as he was. He suspected that McQueen preferred to visit with him because they had both seen action in the war. He looked forward to next week.

In the yard, Bill told Smiley that he had just come from the chaplain. "He doesn't get it," Bill said. "He thinks I should see the head-shrinker."

"I don't get it either," said Smiley. "I'm the only person in the world that knows for sure that you're innocent. Well, maybe he does now. I've been trying to convince him. I thought maybe he could do something to get you out of here. But they hear that all the time. I guess it goes in one ear and out the other. But I don't get it, why you suffer like you do. I hate to see it. I feel bad, too, because I got you into this. But look at me, I don't piss and moan all the time. And me guilty as hell and with one leg to hop around on."

"I don't piss and moan. And you don't feel the way I do because you don't take anything seriously, not even twelve years in prison. It's all just a lark to you."

"Hey, I have feelings, too."

"Yeah, skin deep. The worse loss to you is that you can't dance the way you could."

Bill had a small sheath of letters from Susannah. There was a new man in her life, a preacher, and he was taking care of her and their daughter. That was about all he could glean from her semi-literate ramblings on paper. There was no mention of love, either for him or for the preacher. He would have been better pleased had she written him that she had found someone to love, or some fulfillment of some kind; but what she wrote about was mere survival. But in the latest of these missives she had written that she was coming to see him, that they must settle up accounts. That's what it amounted to, and it was ominous.

Susannah shuddered at the sight of the Central Prison in Raleigh. This gargantuan, castle-like structure, that was five times, twenty, or maybe even a hundred times the size of the biggest mill she had ever seen, with sooty walls that seemed to reach the sky, was right in Raleigh, a nightmare placed in the heart of a teeming city. She had no words for its gothic façade, its gables and turrets, the ominous gloom of it all. In the parking lot, she looked about in wonder. Apparently even the baby felt oppressed and began to whimper.

The Reverend Cogburn lit a cigar. "Go on," he said. "You know what to do." He felt that there was nothing more that he could do or say. She was on her own. He leaned against the hot car and felt his shirt-sleeved back sting with the heat, the backside of his thin blue slacks grow wet, and moved away puffing, almost angrily, at his cigar. He wore a straw Stetson fedora soaked at the band, lifted it from his head, fanned himself and watched as she walked off in search of some entrance, some mouth of this monster who made black and white shadows in a sunny Sunday afternoon.

Now Susannah sat across from Bill wearing her rumpled Sunday best—a faded seersucker suit, a straw hat with artificial cherries on one side, and her beautiful red tresses bunched like a bird's nest in a ruddy snood—his horizontally striped prison uniform adding to her discomfort, holding little Jessie in her arms, and told him that she was going to marry the Reverend.

"I know it seems hard, Bill, but I got to be free now so's me and baby Jessie can have somebody to take care of us."

She had that flushed, consumptive look she acquired under stress. A serious little U had formed above her nose. Now he noticed that her red hair seemed to have faded to a salmon color and several sweaty strands hung down, escaping the snood. She coughed. Bill worried about the drooling, crying child, who seemed as agitated as Susannah.

"You must cover your mouth when you cough," he said. "You don't want Jessie to get sick, do you?"

Susannah shook her head, agreeing.

"Turn her around so I can see her face," Bill said. "Let me look at her."

Susannah stood Jessie up in her lap and turned her to face Bill. She was wearing a violet dress with white poppies, and her red hair reached to her shoulders. Then the most surprising thing happened: the child stopped crying, looked at him with the biggest blue eyes he had ever seen, and smiled. He smiled back and said, "Jessie," and the baby said something, a giggle or a gurgle that sounded like—he was certain of what it was, absolutely certain—"Da" or—was it?—"Da Da." Yes, she had definitely called him Da Da—hadn't she? He couldn't get over it—she knew who her daddy was, yes she did! He shook his head in wonderment.

Even in her distracted state, Susannah saw what had happened. Her eyes filled with tears, her lips grew tight, and several little tiny dimples formed on her chin. She caught herself up before she sobbed. Then, in a moment, she said:

"What can I do, Bill?"

"I'll divorce you," he said. Bill struggled to drive all emotion from his face and sighed. "I mean, you can go ahead and get the divorce and I won't interfere."

He wished he could hold the baby, his daughter, his Jessie, who kicked and squirmed in her mother's arms, but it was as if the huge wall that surrounded them was also between them, and there was the ever-present eagle-eyed, frowning, shot-gunned guard posted at every gate. Susannah put Jessie on the floor next to her, held her hand, and coughed violently.

"Hold your head away when you cough," Bill said.

"It's just worry making me cough. Mister Cogburn will take care of the expenses for the divorce," she went on. "You needn't worry about Jessie. He'll be a good father to her. He's promised me that."

"I hope the hell he better be. Do you love him?"

"What's love?"

Spring 1945

From the tower of his 245 foot U-boat, Kapitänleutnant Helmut Schnepp disdainfully eyed the dozens of reporters and photographers aboard the US Navy tug that had pulled alongside his great shark-like ship off the Isle of Shoals in a large patch of green water, dyed with chemicals to indicate the spot marked for their rendezvous, and said nothing, though he spoke perfect Oxonian English, his much-photographed face fixed in surliness. Im wunderschönen Monat Mai, Germany had surrendered. Kapitänleutnant Schnepp's U-boat was not the first to surrender nor the last. In the space of five days four U-boats had made the journey of surrender to Portsmouth Naval Shipyard on Seavey Island between New Hampshire and Maine, where the crews were briefly housed at the "Castle," a giant naval prison, before being transferred to the Charles Street Jail in Boston.

Kapitänleutnant Schnepp was described by a local radio personality as being "a typical Hollywood Nazi, wearing a long leather greatcoat and high leather boots, an Iron Cross tucked under his lantern jaw, who refuses to eat with his crew, few of whom show the same Nazi tendencies." In his cell at the Charles Street Jail in Boston, Kapitänleutnant Schnepp wrote a letter to his son, Ulrich, a member of the Hitler Youth, in which he proclaimed that there was no difference between a good German and a good Nazi, broke his spectacles, and used a jagged piece of lens to slash his wrists. When the guards found him, he was still alive, but nearly bloodless. He died soon after in a Boston hospital.

Summer 1950

The Reverend Jason P. Cogburn sat at his table in the kitchen of his house on Fortune Island and read a report in the "Wilmington Star-News" on the Korean War. He didn't know much about politics, but he knew that the North had invaded the South again, and that he must always, by heaven, side with the South. He couldn't grasp many of the finer points of the report because his mind was blurred by bourbon, as it inevitably was upon his visits home to what had come to be called the Cogburn House.

Susannah stood by in the uniform of the day for 1950's housewives, a cotton pastel print house dress with flowers as thin and faded into indefinability as herself. Nine-year-old Jessie sat across from the Reverend, balanced on a chair with her sandpaper soled bare feet under her and balanced as well between her desire to say something unpleasant to Cogburn and her desire to keep the peace for Susannah's sake.

Cogburn pushed the newspaper off the table for Susannah to collect and drew a deck of cards from his pocket. He dealt himself a hand of solitaire and began playing. He liked to play solitaire while he drank. He cheated but enjoyed the game anyway. Studying his cards, he said:

"Well, don't just stand there like a scarecrow, Magdalena. Pick up the newspaper and pour me a drink. And you," he directed to Jessie, "put your dirty feet on the floor. What do you people do when I'm not here? Don't tell me, I know. You live like pigs. Why do I have to come back from the work of the Lord to face two slovens in my own house? The Lord has put terrible burdens on this Sad Traveller. I do his work but there are times when I just plain don't like the son-of-a-bitch." He looked at Jessie. "It's all right not to like him. What counts is to believe in him. Now that's what a father is, what you might not like but got to believe in."

"Like you, Daddy? Are you what you done called the Lord? That son—"

Susannah snapped a look at Jessie that stopped her from what she was going to say, but could not stop her from snickering.

Cogburn looked at her blankly, drunken-eyed. "What?"

Jessie got her long legs out from under her and stood up. Her hair had the coppery fire and gleam in it that her mother's once had. But they were different. Susannah was petite, Jessie raw-boned and angular, a child who seemed destined to grow a foot taller than her mother.

Susannah put an arm over Jessie's shoulder. She could feel the strength in Jessie that she lacked, but she was afraid for her. Susannah could not see that Cogburn respected Jessie's spirit, even if he didn't like it.

"Child, what are you thinking?" he asked. "What's on that wicked mind of yours?"

Susannah squeezed Jessie. Please don't backsass, she thought.

"Sir, I was just memorizing as how we went to see those ships sometime back."

"She's talking about the old Liberty ships again," he said. "They sure put a dent in her. I took her to Wilmington once right after the war, remember? They had a couple hundred of them Liberty ships mothballed along the docks. I'm surprised you remember that, Jessie. You were just a tad. Been jawing on that ever since. I wonder what it was about them old ships. Could it be, was it because your ma knew someone once who sailed on one of them a long time ago?"

"There was a lady there who said"—Jessie deepened her voice—"*Please God, we have defeated the foe.* The *foe*—it was such a funny word."

"You're too slow, Magdalena." Cogburn poured himself another drink. "She must have meant that we'd won the war."

"Reverend, why do you call Momma Magdalena? She's Susannah."

"It's just a nickname Mister Cogburn has for me, honey."

"That person your momma knew who sailed on a Liberty ship was a very bad man. Even now he's in a place where they put bad people. Ain't that true, Magdalena?"

"You are never wrong, Mister Cogburn. I must admit to that. But I would like to remind you that we are abiding in his house, in the house that was his mother's and father's, and isn't it true that we should show respect for people when we live in their house?"

"It's your house now and that makes it mine. That makes me the master of it. He left you and yours as hostages to fortune, and I am your good fortune. Didn't I teach you both to read, so that you could study in the good Book how to gather up snakes in your arms and speak in tongues, just like my own beloved mother and father that let me get snakebit and betrayed me for lack of faith? To learn of the hell on earth? Don't I put food on the table by my good works and snake-tongued talk, my sermons on every mount in the woods, my Job's job? Damn to hell, I'm away most of the time, and all I ask when I come home is that you give me peace and quiet in which to meditate. Pour me another drink, Magdalena mine. Pour your lord and master another drink." He dealt a hand of solitaire.

Within an hour, his head lay like a turnip in a card-patch on the table, suffering with nightmares of hellfire. Inside there, he roamed from table to table, picking up glasses of whiskey that immediately ignited, as if someone had put a match to them; outside, he snored from nose and mouth and heard screams in his ears. The screams were a few whispers exchanged by Susannah and Jessie, as they sat at the table and looked at him. Susannah poured herself a large tumbler of bourbon containing at least four shots. "Peace at last," she said with a sigh.

"Don't drink, Momma. Come outside with me and look at the stars."

"You're clinging to a rope with your arms and legs," said Susannah, "and that rope is pitched betwixt the two sides of a big canyon, like what they got out west, and you pull yourself along to the other side, but when you get there, ain't nothing there but a black wall, and then you cling to that rope as long as you can, until your strength gives out, and then you fall and keep on falling forever, and you know where you fall to, child, why, right into them stars you want me to look at."

"Momma, you can't fall down into the stars. They's up."

"Oh, yes you can, baby. They's up *and* down."

Susannah studied the top of Cogburn's unruly, thinning hair, like that of an old, smelly sheep, and said, as if talking to it, "For folks like us there don't seem to be much we can get out of this life." She drank down half the tumbler of bourbon. The coughing did not come from the choking sting of the bourbon but from the crackling phlegm in her lungs.

It was a painful, concerning sound to Jessie, who gently patted her back. "Momma, try to get hold of it," she said. "Spit it out."

"Baby," Susannah said, and swallowed the other half of the bourbon, "you got to get all you can out of this life. I wish sometimes that even the devil himself had gone to the trouble to help me learn when I was a little girl in the hills. I been thinking, it ain't right you should get no schooling out here. I'm going to show you something that'll help you get some learning."

"What, Momma?"

"You ever hear this saying—a treasure trove?" Susannah whispered. "Do you know what a treasure trove is, honey?"

"No ma'am."

"It's like a beautiful container filled with wonderful, secret things. Was somebody once upon a time showed me this treasure trove and let me know some of the beautiful things in it. Come up to the attic with me," Susannah said suddenly, decisively, and Jessie's pulse grew fast to hear so much new, unprecedented—forbidden attic, and decision itself—in such a few short words. Susannah stood up, swayed, and Jessie hurried to support her. "Was your daddy, girl."

"The Reverend?"

"No, no, baby, he ain't nobody's daddy. You come on along with me."

"I'm here, Momma. I'm hearing you."

"Shoot," said Susannah. "Your real daddy was a sailor boy, pretty as could be, once upon a time. A good sweet man, too. You can't have supposed you could have come from that there, whatever you call it. No, you had a handsome sailor daddy with snow white hair like an angel."

"Snow white hair?"

"Well, not at first, but after he got torpedoed in one of them Liberty ships you so interested in, got torpedoed and come home with snow white hair, like them foe people had done scared the color right out of it."

Jessie had heard reference to this several times before but couldn't quite get a hold on it. This time it came clearer. Once, when he was drunk, she remembered Cogburn saying that she was none of his, so she wasn't amazed or surprised or anything like it. She'd known it all along somehow. It was in the air. And she was glad to know it more clearly now. Now she knew there was white-haired hope for love out there somewhere. Just white-haired hope was better than Cogburn in the flesh.

Susannah's face was pale but flushed high on the cheeks. Jessie didn't have the thought for it but she saw the delicacy of her mother's face, the bones, the nose so thin she could break it with her fingers. But for that one strange eye that had got the dye in it, her mother looked like a child, but a child full of dry lines and starved hunger. She wondered could there be an old child. If that could be, then her mother was it. Excitement at what next gripped her, what more to come. But she said:

"You shouldn't drink, Momma. Garcie says it's not good for you. Garcie says he makes you drink with him and that you're not strong like him and could die from it. Garcie says—"

"Hush up about Garcie and give me an arm to help me up to the attic. Bring that oil lamp. Now never you say a word to Mister Cogburn about this, you hear? Thank the Lord he never goes up there or he'd skin me alive."

"Why, Momma?"

"Because I disobeyed him. When it was that I made the mistake to marry him, he done ordered I get rid of all the McQueen furnishings in the house. He don't like the McQueens none and their things just reminded him of how this wasn't really his house—plus you know how he likes everything bare and plain. No decorations, no pictures, nothing to make a house a home, nothing to warm it up some—he loves his emptiness, does the Reverend, like he's feared both of heaven and hell." At the foot of the stairs she cast a look back at Cogburn. Yes, it was safe. "Well, when the Reverend was away and I was getting rid of the McQueen stuff by some old boys needed work, I had them take a few things up to the attic. I had them put a padlock on that door, and I hid the key in a crevice in the floorboards on the steps. He don't have no curiosity about it, and we got to be thankful for that. Just so's everywhere he looks is empty, that satisfies him."

Jessie, holding the lamp, was partly pushed up the narrow stairs by her mother and partly pulled her mother up behind her. The door was at the top. Susannah said, "Hold the lamp down here," and found the key. She unlocked the door and Jessie followed her in, Susannah's long and broken-looking shadow projected by the lamp behind her. There was a flapping and fluttering of unseen birds. The roof beam of the A-framed roof felt low and the walls closed claustrophobically upward on each side. Jessie felt fine silken strands of spider webs draw and snap. Draped sheets or tarps showed gray, here and there in the room, as the lamp swung about, like ghosts of strange creatures, some tall, some flat, some angular, ghosts of imaginary animals. "What are they, Momma?"

"Just a few pieces of furniture I managed to save."

"Why you showing me this here, now, Momma?"

"You ever hear a body say *I'm at the end of my rope?* Means they can't take it no more. Means they reached their limit. Well, baby, I done reached my limit. And when people reaches their limit they got to plan to pass something on to somebody they love, so now I'm passing this on to you, this secret place and what's in it, the treasure trove I was telling you about. It's all I got to give you."

Jessie knew Susannah was drunk, and, though she hadn't heard her speak of ends of ropes or limits before she had heard her say that one of these days she was going to walk into the sea and be gone forever. Jessie told Garcie, and Garcie told her that she had heard Susannah say that, too, "but none come of it," so Jessie wasn't too worried about what Susannah said about ends of ropes or limits but most of her mind fixed on what Susannah said about "that there treasure trove."

"Where is it, Momma? That there treasure trove. I don't see nothing but them ghosty things. I hear the wind going through, fine, but you can't see none of that, 'cept when it moves the ghosts and makes them behave."

"Bring that lamp down here, baby. See here? Look here!" Susannah pulled a dusty sheet away and showed Jessie a trunk. She opened it. It was full of books. "You learned to read by Mister Cogburn and now all them worlds in these here books can belong to you."

"Who do they belong to now?"

"They belonged to your daddy who owned this house and to his momma and daddy before him. Some are real old. Here, blow the dust off this. This here's the key to the whole thing. This is called a dictionary.

Any word you don't know, your daddy told me, that word is in this book and all you have to do is find it, and it will tell you what it means and even how to say it. I was set on learning myself once. Then Mister Cogburn come along, and stopped me. He don't like you to read nothing but the Bible, even though he reads other things himself."

"Why is he so mean to you, Momma?"

"Cause once upon a time I didn't know no better than to do wrong things and he says he's is learning me how to be a better person." She began to cry.

"Don't cry, Momma."

"I told Garcie, I could walk into the sea and fill it with my tears, if it weren't for you. Jessie, baby, don't start out making mistakes. Learn from this treasure trove. It'll give you guidance. That is what your daddy told me, but I didn't have the sense to listen or the braveness against the Reverend to keep up. I had low sense because I had low strength in my body, but you're strong."

She shuffled through the books. "Now I found one. Look at this one, Jess. This one here, your daddy told me, was how he got named. William Makepeace Thackeray. He wrote this *Vanity Fair: A Novel Without a Hero*, and your daddy's mother loved this book and named him his full name of William Makepeace Thackeray McQueen. Ain't that something? What a name for a sailor boy. First time I heard him say it I liked to fall over. William Makepeace Thackeray McQueen! Ain't that a mouthful, Jess? Well, that's the real name of your real honest-to-goodness daddy."

"Will he ever come back, Momma—will William Makepeace Thackeray McQueen ever come back?"

"I don't suppose, Jess. But now you know who he was. You got him now. But don't you say a word to Cogburn. You keep all this a secret."

"What happened to him?"

"He's not a bad man, Jess, like what Cogburn said, but he done a bad thing and he got put in to a place for people who do bad things. Lord knows what'll ever become of him."

"But he'll get out?"

"He'll get out."

"And he'll come back for us."

"Maybe for you, baby."

They heard Cogburn call from below—"Magdalena, where are you? Magdalena, help me!"

"He's awake. I've got to go down. Mind what I've told you, now.

But keep it to yourself, hear? Lock up and hide the key in the crack. Quick!"

Jessie followed Susannah down the stairs. Cogburn was looking for something.

"What are you looking for, Mister Cogburn?"

"This bottle's empty. Where's the other one? If you drank both of them up—"

"Right here in the cabinet." Susannah found the bottle and brought it to the table. "Do you want me to have a drink with you, or not?"

"Pour two drinks and tell me what you've been up to."

Jessie knew that she no longer belonged to their evening, what could turn into their night, what with this new full bottle of Wild Turkey, so she got a few things together and slipped out the door. She would spend the night at Garcie's, as she often did when the Reverend Cogburn and her mother sat down to drink together—before the march of the parade of abuse.

Chapter
Six

At the end of June and for several Junes in the past few years, the sounds of construction, of hammering and sawing and planks being tossed about, could be heard coming from behind the great Wall of the Central Prison at Raleigh. Street urchins convinced one another that prisoners were being hanged, but over the years the gallows had given way to an electric chair, nicknamed "old Sparkey," and ultimately to a gas chamber. The sounds the children heard were the sounds of the construction of an outdoor stage, complete with a standing microphone and loudspeakers, at which certain of the floodlights would be directed for the evening performance of Capt'n Jack Midgett's Jamboree and Amateur Hour.

Capt'n Jack Midgett was a white-haired, red-faced, walrus-mustached, rotund man of over six feet, well-known to the politicians of Raleigh, the capitol city, as a performer, reformer, union organizer, and fellow traveller. Some called him a pinko commie, but usually not to his face, for, from wherever it emanated, Capt'n Jack had juice. It was rumored by the opposition that Capt'n Jack was a friend of the governor, or sometimes it was bruited about in the legislature that Capt'n Jack had something on somebody important. In any case, he got what he wanted, and he wanted to perform with and for the prisoners. His striped-suited minions were already at work in the yard, hammering and banging to beat the band, as it were, getting things ready for the big show that was to take place within a week.

Capt'n Jack needed a pirate for his sea shanties and Smiley was perfect for the part. He could jig and spin on a pirate's peg leg while waving a wooden cutlass above his head. He wanted Bill McQueen to join in— "Good for you," he told Bill. "Gets your mind off your troubles." But

Bill, who had been a performer, seemed to prefer his troubles, and, for several years, had been reluctant to join in the fun. Smiley told Capt'n Jack about Bill. "He's a real professional—writes songs, sings, plays the guitar. It'd be worth it to you if you could talk him into it." Capt'n Jack told Smiley to get his friend to compete in the Amateur Hour portion of the show, told Smiley that his friend sounded like a real winner. "He's a real artist," Smiley went on, "a very sensitive guy. He's got a guilt complex about getting into trouble. He don't mind boxing because he don't like it much, even though he's real good at it, but he loves to play and sing. He really enjoys it, and that makes him feel guilty. That's my take on it. You gotta help me get him up on the stage. You won't regret it."

"You say he was a merchant marine?"

"My shipmate, torpedoed out of the water when I lost my leg."

Capt'n Jack had been a merchant marine himself and would do whatever he could for such comrades. "They're all down on us, you know," he said, "that whole Red-baiting, right-wing press, the Westbrook Peglers, the Walter Winchells, that whole gang, they're all out to hang us, and we've got to stick together."

Capt'n Jack asked the warden about Bill McQueen and was told that he was an odd case. The warden advised Capt'n Jack to talk to Chaplain Baker. Chaplain Baker told Capt'n Jack that he thought that Bill McQueen was probably one of the few innocent men behind the Wall. "He's like clockwork. The same story once a week, every month, every year. He's one of the best boxers on the team. For some peculiar reason, when he boxes, he calls himself Tom Judas. He wins, but he doesn't protect himself. Every week, black eyes. I think he's had his nose broken three times. It looks to me like a form of self-punishment. He's a perfect prisoner. Never gets in trouble. But maybe that's because the other convicts don't bother him. He's pretty much of a loner. They respect that, and that he can fight. The only one he's close to is his pal, Chuck Smiley."

"Yes, I know Smiley. From what Smiley told me, he's a very talented musician."

"I'm no expert, but I'd say he was. I've heard him play." And so Capt'n Jack Midgett got permission to visit this Garbo of the guitar. He wanted Smiley to be present, to introduce him to this reluctant musician, and to help him convince him to perform. "Play for Capt'n Jack," coached Smiley. Bill McQueen was not anti-social, so he played willingly enough in the cell he shared with Smiley, and Capt'n Jack was delighted by his performance. So delighted, in fact, that he turned over his own guitar to him. It immediately occurred to Capt'n Jack that he may have discovered a big talent. He used all his persuasive powers, and they were formidable, to talk Bill McQueen into entering the amateur hour, and, when Bill finally agreed to enter this year, Capt'n Jack was delighted.

"This could be the beginning of a great career," he told Smiley, as they left Bill to contemplate the meeting. Smiley hobbled along beside the big, Burl Ives-sized Capt'n Jack Midgett.

"He's as good as I thought, then?" asked Smiley.

"Yes, I think we've got something here."

Later Smiley told Bill, "If I could play like you do, I'd be in that amateur hour every year. I look forward to doing my little pirate jig. Breaks the monotony."

"I know all about it," said Bill. "I was playing in tap-houses before I went into the Merchant Marine. Having any fun at all makes me feel guilty, though. Look at what I've done. Left my wife and daughter in the hands of a stranger—"

"Look at me," ordered Smiley, "everything's gone but the future. Here, Capt'n Jack brought me some hair dye. The warden okay'd it."

"What's it for?"

"What do you think? It's for you. I won't kid ya that you look like you did when you came in here. But you'll look a lot better with this in your hair. Why don't you grow a mustache? Your beard comes out black, anyway. You're still a pretty good-looking guy, despite letting everyone pound your face." He feinted a punch at Tom's head. "Keep that guard up. Me and Capt'n Jack are going to make a new man out of you. You want to call yourself Tom Judas? Okay, let's look like him. Let's look like this here Tom Judas you've got in your mind."

The big show every interested party was preparing for was divided into two parts. Part one featured Capt'n Jack and some of his singer-musician group doing a variety show consisting of everything from bawdy sea shanties to slap-stick routines. Part two brought in the inmates. The more daring of the stripe-suited clan went on stage to see how well they could entertain their fellows. There were usually only about ten men in the whole prison who would try their hand and most of them were very bad indeed. Most would be hooted off the stage to return to the evening shadows of the yard, to sit or stand with the others who had hooted them off. A fiddler had done well, as had a drummer. Tom had rotated with the others—three chances; in Tom's case, three self-accompanied songs. He had started out with a lively, minstrel-like rendition of "O Susannah," using a banjo borrowed from a member of Capt'n Jack's band. The cons had liked the nonsense humor of Stephen Foster's lyrics and Tom the boxer's high-stepping dance. It was lively, hand-clapping fun, and had won the convicts over. Only the hardest faces remained stoic, and even these didn't lose respect for him because they knew he could fight. On his second turn, Tom had used the new guitar Capt'n Jack had given him and sung one of his own songs, "Sold Piano Blues:"

> "Sold the piano,
> I sold the piano,
>   sold it to the husband of a blind soprano,
> because I needed money
> so I could pay the rent—
> I needed money
> so I could pay the rent—
>   they had to make their living,
>   I had to pay my rent.
> (kept my guitar)
> Sold that piano,
> I sold that piano,
>   the gap-toothed one that wobbled on three legs,
> my poor piano,
>   that made that sad soft sound
> like when you're breaking eggs,
> one dead pedal,
>   many missing keys,
>   its ivories all yellow and its broken knees.
> Sold my piano,
> oh I sold my piano
>   and now I have to do a cappella blues.
> (No, I don't—kept my gitfiddle)
>
> Got no piano,
> I sold it
>   because I needed money so I could pay the rent.
> Sold my piano
>   and now I wonder where all that dirty money went
> because I didn't pay the rent.
>   I bought a month's supply of booze

and now I sit and sing a cappella blues,
a cappella blues.
Ah... I sing the sold piano blues.
(good thing I kept my geetar)
I sing the sold piano blues,
sold piano blues... "

First he rumbled the song out like a riff, then went back over it in his slow, medium baritone, a touch country, a touch bluesy. What the prisoners, and Capt'n Jack too, liked about the number was that Tom made it seem funny the first run-through and almost sad on the second, a joke and then a tale of loss. For his third number Tom sang a heartbreaking rendition of "Amazing Grace," only occasionally touching a string of his hanging guitar. Tom dominated the stage without effort, as many present had seen him dominate the ring. He won by acclamation and the imprimatur of Capt'n Jack's raised thumb.

In half an hour men in stripes began to remove the big banner that read CAPT'N JACK MIDGETT'S JAMBOREE AND AMATEUR HOUR. Groups of prisoners were being herded away from the bandstand and back to their cells. A cluster of men stood to one side—Capt'n Jack, the warden, Chaplain Baker, prison guards with shotguns, and Tom. Smiley hobbled by on his peg leg, a black patch over his eye. He gave Tom the thumbs up and a big grin.

"Yes sir, warden," said Capt'n Jack, "we got us a winner here! When he gets out, I'd like to see if we can't get him a recording contract."

"He's a good man," said the warden. "I never knew he was such an entertainer."

"I had a hunch," said Chaplain Baker. He put his hand briefly on Tom's shoulder.

"I know some important people," said Capt'n Jack. "Senators. Congressmen. Library of Congress types. I'm serious. Maybe we can get him a couple of years knocked off his sentence."

"I'd put in a good word for you, McQueen," said the warden.

"I call myself Tom Judas, now."

"That's okay, too," said the warden. "A man can call himself what he wants as long as it's not for criminal purposes."

"It's a stage name," said Capt'n Jack. "Right, son? Well, then—*Tom*—I want you to look me up when you get out, so it's either I'll see you next year here on this stage or I'll see you sooner at my homestead in

Manteo, my dacha. If you've ever been to the Soviet Union you'll know what that is."

"I have, in fact. When I was just a kid, during the war. We made several runs to Murmansk, to keep the Ruskies supplied. Smiley was with me. But I still don't know what a dacha is."

"It's a vegetable-growing country house. You come to my place and you'll see. Now don't go shooting that hundred dollar prize on a crap game. Save your money, boy. You'll need it when you get out, which'll maybe be sooner than later."

"His money will go into the safe," said the warden.

"It'll be waiting for him," said Chaplain Baker, patting Tom on the back. "I meant to tell you, I like your dye-job. Black hair suits you." In his sincerest voice he said, "We're proud of you, son."

"You're going to be a big star," said Capt'n Jack.

⚵ ⚵ ⚵

The Reverend Jason P. Cogburn ranted on in an alcoholic haze. He had been up all night, atop the Tower of Babel, and into the fine June morning, perfect for rhapsodic preachment. "The elders sinned against Susannah, but Magdalena sinned on her own. Susannah was innocent, but Magdalena was a whore. You must be re-baptized. Born again." He was inspired, the bourbon burning a red spot on his forehead, his tufts of a beard pointing in every direction, his snake eyes bright and focused for a strike. But he was disappointed to realize that Susannah was asleep in her chair. It was the morning of which night? He had Susannah all to himself and there were still a few drinks left in the bottle. He reached over and shook Susannah's shoulder.

"Come on, woman, let's go out on the water. I'm going to baptize you. You're going to be born again—purified, clean, and innocent. No more a whore, but fit to be a holy man's wife."

Susannah, exhausted, in a state of surrender if not total defeat, followed him like a Roman slave across the dunes, down the embankment, and to the beach, where he kept a rowboat with an outboard motor. "Out in the water you shall be baptized, cleansed of the filth of your sins. You shall become a new woman, one with whom I can bear to live." Susannah had heard it all before, a hundred times. Hope had deluded her. She hated hope.

Out in deep water she sat and waited for him to instruct her. Passivity was her only friend. Water caught the bouncing sunlight and was bleached to a blinding glare, with ripples slithering through it like black eels. Gulls shrieked above the swash of the sea. Only the salt smell kept her awake, a mollusk smell, like clam broth, like salt zephyrs in her flared nostrils. Rabbits think they hide by being motionless.

The Reverend Jason P. Cogburn drank from his bottle of Wild Turkey, the oars resting on his lap. "Go ahead!"

"What?"

"Cleanse yourself."

"You want me to go over the side? You know I can't swim."

"I'm here. What have you got to fear, Magdalena? When you return, you shall be born again."

"I don't want to be myself again—ever."

"Then be what you will."

"You want me to die?"

"You disappoint me."

"You asked me to be honest with you. I've been honest with you. I told you what I've been. You knew it all before you married me."

"But you have no desire for me."

"I have no desire for any man."

"Then you're not even Magdalena. You are no woman at all. Just a bundle of disease and sin. Jump, I tell you, and cleanse yourself!"

Susannah agreed with the Reverend Jason P. Cogburn. She rose to her feet in the boat.

"But who will take care of Jessie?"

"Garcie will take care of Jessie. I will take care of Jessie. We will take care of Jessie better than you can. You can't even take care of yourself, let alone us."

"Why don't you kill me? Why don't you push me overboard?"

"You must redeem your self."

"I understand." Susannah wasn't sure if she'd tripped or jumped, but now she was helplessly beating at the swaying water, like a bird with a broken wing trying to fly.

Startled, now, Cogburn looked on from the boat. With the suddenness of inspiration, he pushed an oar out for her to reach it. She seized it, briefly, then closed her eyes and let go of the oar and sank below the surface. Now Cogburn wanted to save her, but she was gone. He rowed around the spot where she had disappeared beneath the churning water, looking for some sign of her. Then he settled the oars in his lap once again. He was no less drunk than he had been, but now he wondered if he had gone too far. He wondered because of a sudden sense of loneliness—the sky so vast and blue, and the round watery horizon. He already missed her. Useful, she had been, when he came home.

The brisk salt breeze was clearing his head. He realized that the situation might look suspicious, that his situation might be precarious, dangerous. Someone might think that he had murdered the woman. Someone might misinterpret what had happened. What had happened? Why, she had just slipped off, just slipped away. But he put the oars in the boat, and began tugging at the outboard's pull until the motor sputtered and started. He would go to Ocracoke, just across the inlet, then, in a day or two, take the mail boat back. He would be shocked, then, to hear that she had walked into the sea, as she had often said she would, that she had vanished from Fortune Island.

✂ ✂ ✂

Beneath the turmoil at the top, where the black water chopped itself to pieces and foamed, slate sliding about, Susannah, indifferent in death, rode the undercurrents that bent or straightened her arms and legs to make her seem a swimmer luxuriating in the alien atmosphere. How deep she went and how long she stayed no one would be able to say for at least three days, when her body washed up on the shore of Fortune Island, eyeless, bloated, and waxen, not hard glossy wax, but soft melting wax, how many sea forms approached her curiously or hungrily could only be guessed at later in Wilmington where she would be sent in preparation for burial. What touched her down there, what kissed her down there, what painlessly bit at her ankles, who could tell? Her death was the mermaid's life. When she was missed, Garcie on shore believed she heard the echo of Susannah's silenced voice in the waves that rushed to her brown feet in white foam. Then, on that third day, they found the bloated grey ghost of the mountain girl gripping the land's edge, ignorant of land and water and itself.

It appeared that the Reverend Cogburn had gone to the mainland to carry on his hypocrite's crusade before anyone had noticed that Susannah was gone. Even Jessie had not noticed for over twenty-four hours of heavenly escape, for she had gone to stay with Garcie the night that Cogburn had drunk himself into a stupor and her mother had tried to join him in it, the night of William Makepeace Thackeray McQueen. That night she told Garcie what the situation was at home, both guardians of her well-being drunk, and how Susannah had told her of her father; and

Garcie, finally able to speak freely, told her of how she had been the midwife at the birth of her father, told her of the fine young man he was who did not deserve his fate.

※ ※ ※

The huge stench of Susannah's decomposing body emanated from the old Ford station wagon. At first, pinching her nose against the smell of rotting flesh, Jessie sat down on the running board, plagued by flies. Ordinarily, in June, it was swarms of mosquitoes that attacked, but these buzzing bluetails seemed to bite, too, and she slapped them away, angrily, with both hands, a dead red bird in one fist. At three o'clock in the morning, Garcie's snoring had awakened her and she had come to the pier to be near her mother. From the dunes she had picked up the dead bird, pretty and crested and still. She patted its little head with her finger. Her momma was just inches away, but the doors of the station wagon were locked. Momma was doing what the dead fish did. They rotted. If it was all just that, then what was she, herself? Was everything just that?

Sheriff Walkup drove up to the dock in a pickup that beamed lights on her, and began to unpack equipment. Jessie walked up to him. "What's the matter with you?" she said. "Let my momma out of there."

"Got to send her over to the mainland, honey. Got to get her ready to be buried. Can't help it if the mail boat don't come every day and the danged radio don't work. Got to spray out the station wagon or there'll be a God-awful stink. Now you keep away from there. You get back or I'll spray you down with this here disinfectant. Fact is, you look like you need it. And what in hell are you doing out here in the middle of the night?"

"What are *you* doing out here in the middle of the night?"

"I got to be alone when I do this. Don't want nobody watching me. Now you get on home."

"No, no, no! Don't you do that to my momma. There she is! I see her. I see her hair. Leave her alone. Let me in. I'll wake her up. I'll wake her up." But Jessie did not believe that she would be able to do that. It was the only way she could say good-bye.

Sheriff Walkup looked down at her. "What's that in your hand? What's that—a bird? Throw that dirty thing down and get on home. And wash your hands when you get there. I can't have you out here in the middle of the night watching me. Now skedaddle!"

On diabetic legs and nearly blind, holding a stick for guidance and support, Garcie approached them.

Sheriff Walkup turned to her for help. "What's everybody doing out here? Woman, can you get this child away from here?"

"Why you done sneaked out of the house when old Garcie is sleeping? Now you come with Garcie, baby. Come home with Garcie. I checked at y'alls' house. I was looking for you. The Reverend ain't come back. He probably don't even know your momma's done walked into the sea like she said she would. Did you ever hear her say that, Sheriff?"

The Sheriff shook his head. "I never heard it, but I'm not surprised."

"He's not my daddy, that man. My daddy's somewhere and he's coming back. I know he is. I want him to so bad, he has to come back."

"That's right, baby. Coming back with his banjo on his knee. You come and wait for him with Garcie. He's my boy, too, just like you're my little girl, my little red-head. Come on, now, Garcie'll fix you some hush puppies and chicory coffee." With a strong grip on Jessie's arm, poking her stick before her, Garcie half-walked, half-dragged Jessie toward home, across the dunes; but somewhere in the starlight Jessie broke free from Garcie and ran into the night.

As was her wont, Jessie dug a little hole in the sand and sat down in it, and this is what she said, thought, felt: *Momma, wherever you are, can you see the lighthouse blinking on and off on Ocracoke? I can see it from here. And there's a glory of stars. Can you see them? Momma, Garcie snored so loud I couldn't sleep, so I came out to be with you, and I found this here dead red bird. I don't know its name. It's got red feathers like you and me. Momma, I want to know where you've gone, so I'm going to take this jack knife and open this bird and look in its breast until I found out where its song has gone.* She laid the bird on the sand and, holding it with one hand, stabbed it in the breast with the other and twisted the knife to break open its small rib cage. *I'm not afraid because it's either in there or it must be somewhere else in a place where I can't understand any of it. Don't you think that's true? Momma, I don't want to know about places where I can't understand any of it. I only want to know about a place like this, a place I can figure out if I work hard at it. I'm waiting for you to tell me what I should do. I only have Garcie now, and she's sick with the sugar and will probably be with you soon. Momma, you said that you would walk into the sea and fill it with your tears but for me. But you didn't keep your word. You did it anyway and left me alone. Why did you do that to me? Couldn't you wait? Well, I guess you couldn't, even though you loved me. Can't you send me somebody? Momma, please, either come back or send me someone. And look, Momma, look, there's nothing inside this here dead red bird but guts and that big red ball has begun to peep up over the ocean. Isn't there something, somewhere?* Jessie got up out of the hole she had dug and pushed the bird into it with her foot. She pushed more sand on top of it and patted it down. She made a cross out of some twigs and stuck it on top of the little mound. *Bird, I don't know if you were a Christian or even if I am, but I thought you might like a marker. If you aren't a Christian, don't be bothered by it. Either the tide or the wind or the rain will take it away.*

✄　✄　✄

On the morning of Susannah's funeral the Reverend Jason P. Cogburn climbed down from the mail boat into the skiff that bobbed beside it and appeared shocked to be told by Sheriff Walkup that Susannah had drowned.

"Seems like she walked into the sea and washed up about three days later, fish-gnawed and bloated to twice her size."

"God in heaven why didn't somebody tell me about this?"

"When you leave here no one knows where you go."

"Oh, of course. You say she walked into the sea?"

"That's what people say."

"Are you trying to tell me she committed suicide?"

"That's what it looks like. I'm told she couldn't swim."

"I've gotta have a drink of bourbon. Will you take one with me, sir?"

"I'll take a small slug. The body arrived early this morning, all ready for burial."

"Oh, my tragic bride! What did you do it for?"

Cogburn's eyes were watering. The Sheriff wondered if they watered out of emotion, breeze, or bourbon. He had never been able to make this man out. Perhaps twenty years of retirement had dulled his detection skills. Albeit, he had never liked Cogburn, as he often remarked to his wife, "not even one little bit." It made him feel guilty. The man deserved some sympathy at a time like this. He handed the bottle back to Cogburn and pulled at the oars in frustration. He wanted to get to shore. He wanted to get out of the skiff and away from Cogburn, who now sat looking at him enigmatically and sucking drink after drink from the neck of the bottle. Sheriff Walkup's mind shrugged its shoulders while his shoulders pulled at the oars. He wondered why he could not feel the sympathy for Cogburn that he ought to feel. "Funeral parlor sent your wife's body over this morning on a boat of their own, along with an undertaker's assistant and a Baptist minister to do the service. We had to proceed."

"Who ordered all this?"

"I did in the name of your daughter and Miss Garcie and yourself. Like I said, it had to be done. You weren't here or anywhere to be found. Your daughter's holding up. Strong little girl."

"Oh, true, true! How is the little dear?"

"She's holding up."

"Yes, you just said that," Cogburn said, irritably.

"You didn't ask. I thought you might want to know."

"Of course. Of course. Can't you see I'm in a state of shock?"

"The bourbon helps though, doesn't it?"

"Takes the edge off my great pain."

"I guess you're in great pain, aren't you?"

"Do you doubt it?"

"No, no. I don't doubt it," said Sheriff Walkup. "I know I would be in great pain to hear such news."

"Indeed! But if you ordered all this—who's to pay? I'm just a poor itinerant preacher—and no rich Baptist. I'm a Pentecostal."

"I expected that when you returned you'd be glad to pay. The funeral home knows me. So they went ahead with it. I told them you'd pay."

"Well, how much is it going to cost—all this?"

"As much as a few cases of Wild Turkey, I suppose."

"That much!"

The Sheriff wondered, as they pulled in to land, what was the primary cause of the Reverend Cogburn's mourning.

Like a crow with broken legs, black-suited Cogburn lurched off across the dunes.

"Noon," Sheriff Walkup called out after the retreating shadow in the bright, morning light. "The burial's at noon."

Back to Walkup, the lurching Cogburn shot an arm into the air. His voice came on the breeze. "Noon!"

Cogburn knew Susannah was dead and gone, but when he reached the front door of the house he expected her to be there. He even called out, "Susannah," but he knew she was dead. Where was Jessie? Where were those who were expected to attend him? Oh, Jessie would be with Garcie. His bottle was empty. He went to a cupboard, found a new bottle, and opened it. The sweet fever of sour mash entered his nostrils and became a delirium. He chug-a-lugged from the bottle. His Magdalena had deserted him. How could she desert him in his great work? And why should he pay for the deserter's death? Questions puzzled his mind. He gave no thought to the fact that he looked like a wild man. "From walking up and down in the world, and back and forth in it," his mind, not his mouth, quoted Job. He would go as he was.

But as he was was not fitting.

"You are not fit, sir," said the Baptist minister sent over by the funeral parlor. "You have been drinking."

"And you, sir, are a money-grubbing Baptist. How dare you charge me—how much? Fifteen cases of Wild Turkey in order to plant this skinny creature? Fifteen cases, sir! This woman, pitiful thing that she was, was my wife." Cogburn was causing a small scandal in the graveyard. Fishermen, shrimpers, and their pious wives stood by uneasily.

Garcie and Jessie were horrified. It was as if a sanctuary had been broken into by a man with firecrackers. Jessie said, tears springing from her eyes, "They wouldn't let me look at her. They promised they would."

Sheriff Walkup, standing with his embarrassingly young wife, Betty Lou, or, as he called her, Buttercup, whispered to Garcie, "They couldn't let her see her mother. Her eyes had been eaten out by fish. They put in glass things just to keep the shape of the lids."

"Why should a Pentecostal pay for a Baptist funeral?" yelled the Reverend Cogburn, seizing the Baptist minister by the collar.

Garcie squeezed Jessie's hand. "Be brave, now," she said. "Don't even listen to that man. He's making a drunken fool of himself."

The Baptist minister pushed Cogburn away. Sheriff Walkup took Cogburn's arm. "Steady, man. I know this has been a shock to you, but you're going too far."

"I say," cried Cogburn, "it is a sad fate to begin in sin and end in suicide, but this woman deserted her duties long before she deserted this life."

"Sheriff, can't you do something about him?" begged the assistant funeral director. "He's making a spectacle of himself and a mockery of this ceremony."

"I haven't been a sheriff for twenty years and I have no police authority, but I'll do what I can." He took Cogburn's arm. "Come away, Reverend Cogburn."

"But I want to tell everyone what led her to this," Cogburn whined.

"She is an object lesson. She deserted me in my hour of need."

"You're drunk as a skunk, Cogburn," said Sheriff Walkup. "I'm going to take you to the general store for a sit down and a sober-up."

Garcie felt Jessie shaking as if she were about to burst into a wild dance.

"Praise be!" cried the pastor. "Come on, folks. Let's sing the little lady out. Let's lower her in and sing her out."

Sheriff Walkup was trying to lead the Reverend Cogburn away from the gravesite. Buttercup was trying to help. Cogburn burst into "Amazing Grace." Walkup clapped a hand over Cogburn's mouth and he and Buttercup dragged him off.

SPRING 1954

For the last six months, Tom Judas had tried to keep his mind off the day of his release, keep to the prison schedule and ignore the calendar, the devolving days. But he couldn't help wondering what kind of world awaited him. A U-boat had torpedoed his Liberty ship in 1941, and in January he had read of the launching of the first atomic submarine, the "Nautilus."

In the clanging hall where the prisoners ate he looked about and saw both strange and familiar faces, most of whom he would probably never see again. Down the long table Chuck Smiley was stuffing a duffy, a prison biscuit, into his mouth and preparing to wash it down with coffee. If it hadn't been for Smiley, he would have been out of here already. Improvident Smiley had tried to make a one-legged run for it while out on a work party and Tom had run after him in an attempt to stop him. Even if Smiley had got away, how long would it have taken to spot a one-legged man, limping along on an artificial leg? The incident had earned Smiley an indeterminate extra year or more, depending on his behavior, behind the Wall. It had also made it impossible for Capt'n Jack to get Tom out early, as he had tried to do. Chaplain Baker believed Tom when he told him that he was just trying to stop Smiley. His recommendation had saved him from time in the dark cells. Still, it had cost him any hope of the early release. But Smiley didn't ask Tom to run after him. He ran after him because he had had a flashback of himself and Smiley in Liverpool when they were young merchant marines, Smiley dancing, holding up a mug of stout, cigarette between his teeth. The Liverpudlian barmaid had said, "Yank, your mate's a crazy bastard, but a real charmer." He had run after

Smiley and tackled him before he could take another improvident leap-before-you-look step, but the horse-backed guard refused to see it that way. Once more, thanks to Smiley, he was stuck for his full twelve years. After saving Smiley from himself, he felt like knocking the stuffings out of him, but settled for the silent treatment, maintained for about a month, by which time Smiley's persistence and charm, evincing gratitude, weakened Tom's resistance and finally won him back.

Now, two years later, in the mess hall, it occurred to Tom that he might not ever see Smiley again. Surprisingly, it was a hard thought. Smiley had polished off the duffy and was pouring coffee down his throat, holding the tin cup at least an inch away from his mouth. The gesture was typical, familiar. Smiley had burned himself a number of times doing it. Smiley had burned himself and others a number of times by just being Smiley, but there was no real harm in him, only his admitted improvidence, his unthinking impulsiveness. What would become of him? Time, the huge mouth with stars on its roof and life on its tongue, was lifting him in, closing behind him, locking its jaws. For a moment, all Tom could hear was jaws grinding in the enormous room filled with devouring men. Tomorrow he would go somewhere outside the Wall and eat a meal in solitary peace.

Tom recalled the day when he had been summoned by Chaplain Baker and told of Susannah's suicide. His first thought had been, What will happen to Jessie? "But she has her stepfather," said Chaplain Baker. As to why Susannah committed suicide, Tom need not wonder. Once the fact of it was there, so was the inevitability. He remembered being surprised that he felt no surprise, only remorse. Chaplain Baker had said that it was not his fault, but he could not agree. She came down from the mountain and washed into the sea like a twig with one red leaf on it. Tom felt the fate in it. She had been lost when he found her and he did not save her.

Now he was here to bid Chaplain Baker farewell. "Well, Tom, twelve long times have come and gone. I'm going to miss our conversations. I think they've done me more good than they've done you. When we first talked, the war had left me bitter and the bitterness had become indifference in here, behind the Wall. I was *pro forma*. Spoke the usual words. Scarcely listened at all. But I listened to you and you taught me to listen to the others again, to hear their stories and to empathize with them as they told me their troubles. As Eugene O'Neill put it, you have a touch of the poet, Tom."

"It's certain that every poet is a fool, but every fool is not a poet. I read that somewhere."

"You've read a library of books in here, haven't you?"

"They only allow two books a week."

"Twelve years of books at two books a week is quite a lot. Are you going to go into the music business?"

"Not right away, although I know Capt'n Jack wants me to."

"He told me that he'd sent out some demo tapes and had received some positive responses."

"Sam Phillips at Sun Records in Memphis has shown some interest, but he wants me to come in person. Capt'n Jack tells me that there are no style limitations at Sun. Phillips named it Sun as a sign of a new day and a new beginning. Nothing's fixed there. They mix up gospel, blues, hillbilly, country, boogie, and western swing, mix it all up and come up with something new. They like what I do, on tape, but they've got to have a look at me."

"Naturally, I suppose they'd want to see you in action. Speaking of which, look at this." He shoved Tom's files across the desk, turning them around for Tom to see. "Who is that?"

"That's William Makepeace Thackeray McQueen, someone who doesn't exist anymore."

"A face like a baby and an old man's white hair. You couldn't look much more different."

"It was the boxing."

"And the hair dye. The mustache. And twelve years hard time, eh? But—what are you now? Thirty-five?"

"Thirty-four. I think I might be a little old to start off in the music business, no matter what Capt'n Jack says, don't you? Besides, I've got other things on my mind."

"Tom, you still look like what you are, a young man. Don't start off with a negative attitude. I'll miss you, Tom." Chaplain Baker stood up and reached across the desk for Tom's hand. "Write to me. Maybe we can continue to do each other some good."

Next morning, in the warden's office, things went much the same. But the warden had a surprise for Tom. He had summoned Smiley to see Tom off. The warden gave Tom a handshake and his best wishes and told Smiley to behave himself, "I know you two men have been through a lot together, so I'm going to step outside and let you say good-bye, but don't you pull any hijinks, Smiley. You keep an eye on him, Tom. Don't let him steal anything."

"You've been real decent to do this, warden," said Smiley. "I wouldn't let you down."

"You've got five minutes." The warden left them alone.

"I asked the warden if he'd let me see you before you left. I had a feeling you might just skip out without saying good-bye."

"Since when did you become so sentimental?"

"I just wanted to tell you not to get another buddy like me, one who gets you into all kinds of trouble. Keep your nose clean. I'm gonna come see you on that island someday." He stepped up to Tom and threw his arms around him.

"You're a bear," said Tom. "Let me breathe."

"And you're one weird son-of-a-bitch," said Smiley, "but I love you just the same."

This was the last of the gothic grayness of the Wall—to put on the clothes he'd come in with, to collect the four hundred dollars he'd won beating all comers at the amateur hour, to put the money in his beaten up old wallet, to find there the photograph of Susannah holding Jessie in her arms, to sling the case of his triumphant guitar over his shoulder, and to step through a door in the Wall and out into the spring of 1954 and the bustling streets of Raleigh, where he looked like a refugee from the forties. Rebirth. The primal scream. No, it was the sound of a horn. Then he saw Capt'n Jack, the midwife of his fate, or what he saw was a big bus with the sign on the side: CAPT'N JACK'S MUSICAL JAMBOREE.

Chapter Seven

July 2000

High over the Atlantic, heading for Boston, Mr. and Mrs. David Perle talked away their nine-hour flight from Germany.

David explained to Hildegarde that the Smileys were like family. "I guess you'd say that Buttercup was my nanny, and Chuck was a stand-in father—and an uxorious husband to Buttercup, his one true love. You'll see his limp. He lost his leg as a merchant marine."

"What happened?"

"He and my father were torpedoed by a U-boat off the coast of North Carolina. Dad had a fractured skull and a serious concussion. Ruth thinks it contributed to his death in the accident, years later. Smiley lost his leg. Ruth has had him refitted with better and better prosthetic legs over the years, but they couldn't get rid of the limp. He's a very old man now. I guess after nearly sixty years, the limp is a habit with him."

"You love him, don't you?"

"Yes! Oh, God, yes. And Buttercup, too. She's a lot younger—at least twenty years—than Smiley, who is now... Maybe in his mid-eighties, and, sad to say, suffering from Alzheimer's. But he was quite a character back in the day. Got me into all sorts of trouble when I was a kid. He'll be doing Fourth of July fireworks later tonight. He does fireworks every Fourth, out in the garden. When I was a kid, I was always afraid he was going to blow us all up. Damn near did, as I remember, one year. But don't worry, Buttercup watches over him. She watches over all of us. She won't let him near fireworks unless she's there. I don't know what we'd do without her. It was one of the smartest things my mother ever did—bringing the Smileys up from Fortune Island to run the place."

"I can't wait to meet them," said Hildegarde.

They landed at Logan, rented a car, stopped for fried oysters at the Union Oyster House, and were now headed for the family mansion in Brookline. Hildegarde knew downtown Boston's brick streets, had mentally aimed the guns of "Old Ironsides" at the disruptive, enormously expensive Big Dig, but limited stopover time had always kept her from visiting Brookline's stately avenues. David would show her the mansion, maybe spend the night, then take her out on Cape Cod to Provincetown, to see Ruth, who was doing a fellowship at the Fine Arts Work Center there.

David turned in through a gate only a little smaller than the Arc d'Triumph, or so it seemed to Hildegarde, as she passed through it, and the car growled and sped up a long gravel driveway to a distant house—on closer view a massive mansion—with several connecting buildings and several more free standing structures in the same style of calm and stately Georgian symmetry. This five-and-dime castle was the prize and product of Grandfather Perle's war against Grant's, Woolworth's, and Kresge's, a monument to himself and his empire, founded on nickels and dimes.

David was such an unassuming person, it had never occurred to Hildegarde that he could be so rich, nor that his famous sister could have spent her teen years in such a setting, a setting gone unmentioned in Jessie's book. *Souvenirs of the Sea* had stuck pretty much to Jessie's scientific adventures above and beneath the ocean—to public, not private, life.

David braked the car in front of the house, got out and led Hildy up to an elderly waiting couple. "Meet the Smileys," he said, "the keepers of the keys here at Castle Perle." The old woman was plump, gray, and grandmotherly. She was still pretty, with wide-set, happy blue eyes. She kissed David on the cheek, took Hildegarde by the hands, and looked her over. "Oh, David, she's beautiful!"

The old man took a little dance-step forward, and half-bowed. David said, "This is Charles—Chuck—and Buttercup. Smileys, meet Hildegarde—my bride."

"Have we met before?" Smiley asked David. He seemed confused.

"It's David and his new wife," urged Buttercup. "You know David. You used to take him to baseball games."

The old man looked hard at David. He squinted, then his mouth dropped open, he tilted his fuzzy, freckled bald head, and said, "David, it's you!" He looked at Buttercup and said, "It's my little Davy Jones, my little shipmate. How did you get so big? You remind me of somebody,

somebody I sailed with once. Now what was his name, Buttercup?"

"Tom—Tom was his name. David is his son, remember?"

"Bill was his name—*Bill*—William Makepeace Thackeray McQueen was his name. Wasn't it? And this is my little Davy Jones back from the sea. David, David, David, I must remember. I'm sorry, I get all mixed up anymore."

"Never you mind," Buttercup said, patting his back. "It'll all straighten itself out." She gave the newlyweds a wink. "Let's go inside. I didn't know if you would eat or if you'd eaten elsewhere. I have something ready, if you're hungry."

"We stopped at the Union Oyster House," Hildegarde said. "I'd really like for David to show me around."

"When you're ready, I'll show you your room. Your bags will be up there. Go ahead, take the grand tour. I'll get things ready. You'll be staying the night, won't you?"

"Of course, we'll stay the night," David said. "Then we're off to Cape Cod to see Ruth. But I've got to spend a little time with you and Chuck. It's been a long time."

"Too long," said Buttercup.

"They've dressed up for you," Hildegarde said, as Buttercup bustled off. "She acts like a mother whose movie star son has come home for a visit."

"Well, they dressed for you, too—to meet the movie star bride of the movie star son."

"How long has Mister Smiley been like that? I mean—"

"It was only recently diagnosed. Ruth and Buttercup take it in their stride, but it's heartbreaking for me, I must say. He almost didn't recognize me. He's the closest thing to a father I've ever known. We played like kids together. He taught me to sail out on the Charles River when I was a little boy. He took me to all the games at Fenway Park."

"Baseball?"

"The Red Sox. He told me about Babe Ruth's curse on them, and we said prayers together to overcome it. Now he doesn't remember any of that, I guess. "

"He remembered you. I could see it."

"Yes, finally. After I got out of the Marine Corps, he took me out on the town in Boston and bought me my first legal drink. He ordered me a whiskey sour because he liked them. We had great fun that night. It's like losing a father, watching him fade. Every time I come home there's less of him here."

Hildegarde was to discover that the house had seven bathrooms, an indoor swimming pool, a gourmet kitchen, a billiards and media room, a gym, a library, an entertainment center with a dance floor, and a formal dining room, as well as a butler's pantry, a family room, an office and, of all things, a secret spiral staircase from the office to the master suite. "The Smileys," said David, as he showed her about, "live here year-round. As I said, they manage the place. Well, Buttercup has always really managed the place. She hires and fires. You know, workmen, grounds people. My mother brought them up from the south, before I was born, where they ran a general store. Ruth spent years in Appalachia and along the Outer Banks collecting folklore for her books. Over twenty books now. And she's been working for years on a collection of narrative poems taken from her collection of folk tales. She's in her seventies and still a roaring girl."

"I know," said Hildegarde. "Your mother is as remarkable in her way as Jessie is in hers."

"Jessie got it from my mother. I'm just naturally more laid back."

"They're extraordinary women. I admire them beyond words."

"We all lived here when I was growing up, before I went off to prep school, before Jessie went off to Smith, before she got her Doctorate, and Ruth went back into the field. We lived in one of the cottages, sometimes. Ruth never liked the ostentatiousness of the house. She's an old-time fellow traveller, you know, very left-wing, at least in those days.

"It was great to have Chuck when I was growing up. Two forceful women—three, counting Buttercup—and you can imagine, living in a place like this, I didn't have many little boy friends, so it was good to have a rough and ready guy around who was always willing to get me into some Tom Sawyer trouble, talk me into whitewashing the fence, as it were. He kept me normal enough so that when I joined the Marines I wasn't shocked by what I found. He also taught me how to deal with these dynamic women, say the right things to them at the right time. He taught me never to argue with women, just agree and do what you want to do. I credit him with my becoming a diplomat. You can imagine what growing up in a place like this can do to a kid."

"But this place—it's amazing—it must be worth millions. The upkeep alone must be a small fortune. Why doesn't your mother sell it, if she doesn't really live here or care about it?"

They turned down a dark corridor and walked toward a large window at its end. They stood, looking out over the grounds. "The current market value is about twenty million," David said. "But you see, we can't sell the place. It was handed down by my grandfather with restrictions and must be kept in the family. It's his monument. There's a trust fund to take care of everything and a whole law firm in charge of that. But don't worry, our lawyers and brokers and bankers have pushed our net worth up to somewhere between fifty and a hundred million since Grandpa died."

"Gott im Himmel, I had no idea! How can I ever convince you I didn't marry you for your money, a poor German flight attendant?"

"Don't be silly. I know you didn't know. I was almost afraid to tell you. It seems to overwhelm people. Even to frighten them."

"It frightens me a little."

"You'll get used to it. Even the Smileys are used to it. It's their mansion, more or less. We come and go, but we don't live here. None of us is really interested in living with Messrs. Hepplewhite, Sheridan, and Chippendale, anyway. Ruth's life is with writers, artists, Jessie has been submerged off the Great Barrier Reef in Australia until recently—I'm joking—and the diplomatic service supplies me with homes of sorts. I'm afraid our child will be stuck with this white elephant, though, and his or her children as well. Eventually, the lawyers will probably turn it into a museum. You're the first guest we've had here in years, as far as I know." He took her hand and led her back down the corridor to the stairs.

"I'm honored."

David took her out on the grounds. Summer buzzed around them. Hildegarde couldn't keep count of the aromatic gardens, the lawns, and little lakes that separated them. Twelve acres, a good-sized park, a park one could get lost in: the perfumes of perennials in clustered blooms, aromas of all-summer-long roses, the sticky pulchritude of lilies, filled their nostrils. Scattered fountains lifted cool water into balmy air. Occasional menhirs, pushed down by the ice age, dominated where they landed, like fat Buddhas. They walked, hand in hand, in a little Eden.

David said, "My grandparents had three children, of whom my mother, Ruth, was the youngest. Both of my uncles died bravely, I like to think, in World War Two. Ruth eventually inherited everything. That's about all I know about that. Ruth and Jessie have always been a bit sketchy about the past. You read Jessie's book. It makes for exciting reading, God knows—adventures, celebrities—but if it's made of bits and pieces, she's also left bits and pieces out. Big chunks, in fact. She doesn't even mention our father, though she uses his stage name. Ruth told me he was a folk singer in the fifties and died in an auto accident. She said he could have been as good as Hank Williams or Elvis. I'm told I look like him. So does Jessie—her body, when she had one—except that he had black hair like me—he was part Cherokee, you know—and hers is red, or used to be."

"But why are you named David Perle and she is Jessie Judas?"

"Ruth wanted us both to use the name Perle, but Jessie has always insisted on using the name Judas. That started when I was a baby, I guess, so Perle I was and Perle I remain. All I know is what I've gleaned from Ruth and Jessie over the years. None of it really meant much to me. My father died before I was born. Except to say that he was my father's best friend, Chuck never said much, either—*Any questions, Davy Jones, I'm under strict orders to refer you to Ruth.* By the time I reached the age of reason, it was all ancient history."

Hildy said, "We never know for certain what went on back there when our parents were young. Or our grandparents. Before he died, my father told me that his father had been a U-boat commander. I couldn't help thinking of what Jessie said about the U-boats off the coast of North Carolina. I don't know where my grandfather was stationed. Nobody would talk about it. But it was strange to think that he might have been in command of one of those boats. I asked my father, who, as a child, had been in the Hitler Youth, if my grandfather had been a Nazi. Not a real Nazi, he said, whatever that meant. When I asked my mother about it, she said there had never been a Nazi in our family, but I could see she was lying. She's a transparent liar, but a bold one. To her, the past is one thing one day and another on another day, but, somehow, always a glory, at least before the German defeat. The Allied bombings, her father told her, were a martyrdom, completely uncalled for. She told me once that her father was a Duke. German aristocrats didn't like the Nazis, but they were just as bad in their own way. Mother is extremely difficult."

"Uh huh. Not attending our wedding was mean enough, but calling your wedding ring, which is actually gold, a cigar band was to my mind even meaner. It's a prized family heirloom. Doesn't she realize that I have money and could have bought you a diamond as big as the Ritz?"

"She didn't know that because I didn't. But I wanted this, the ring you were wearing when I first laid eyes on you." She looked at the ring. "Love and Luck, what could be better?"

"Nothing, my dear, absolutely nothing could be better. And we have both. But let's not talk about your mother. Let's try to forget about her and enjoy being together."

"But you see," said Hildy, "there's a skeleton in everyone's closet... And some of them have flesh and blood and walk around fully clothed."

Years before, Ruth had had a large, well-appointed apartment made for the Smileys, right in the mansion. Hildegarde was surprised to see that they lived in the style of the Park Avenue rich, at least as well as her own mother in a Frankfurt high-rise. Buttercup had had the cook prepare southern fried chicken, a typical Sunday dinner. They sat in a dining room as lovely as the main dining room downstairs. Hildegarde thought of Chinese boxes, this inside of that. Over supper, Buttercup chattered, asked questions, listened, and chattered some more. David tried to talk to Chuck, who smiled, sometimes, showing a germ of interest, but often went blank. Despite Buttercup's ebullience, a sadness shrouded the room. But Buttercup, determined to keep things cheerful, said that she was going to do the fireworks, and that they must follow her outside, where she had things prepared. "I think that Charles has forgotten that it's the Fourth," she said. "It's just as well. I have to do it every year now, anyway." Out on the terrace, which was the size of a small aircraft carrier, overlooking the grounds at a height of at least thirty feet—"the deck," as Chuck called it—there was a champagne wagon and a wagon loaded with Megabanger fireworks—sparklers, fountains, cones, Roman candles, rockets, and aerial repeaters. Buttercup had summoned someone from the grounds crew to help, a young man who seemed to know what he was doing. As the small group toasted the Fourth with champagne, the young man began lighting the fireworks. "Don't I get to do any?" asked Chuck.

"Not this year, sweetheart," said Buttercup, firmly. "You just stand here with us and enjoy it."

Fireworks from other sources were making Van Gogh stars and swirls in the night. They could feel as well as hear the thunder and thuds, and see the bright distant rainbow pinwheels. "Happy days!" cried Buttercup, lifting her champagne in a toast.

"God bless America," cried Hildegarde.

"God bless America," parroted Chuck, as Buttercup removed the glass from his hand.

"I promised you a sip of champagne," she said, "but it's not good for you."

"Davy Jones, make her give me back my bubbly," Chuck implored. Then, with a bang and a buzz, one flaming thing went wild. In a dream-like instant, Chuck seized it from the air, flame in his hand. It was an impulsive but, nevertheless, an heroic act. He dropped the relentlessly flaming demon and kicked it and ran after it and stepped on it, a young man for the span of a minute, a minute-man. Then he was old and holding his burned right hand under his left armpit, obviously in pain. But, possibly, he had saved one of the others from serious injury. He looked about, dazed. "Once... out at Fenway... DiMaggio had the bases loaded," he said, staggering toward them, "and knocked a long high one out to the fence... but the kid out there—I forget his name—jumped higher... higher than the outfield wall... and caught it. DiMaggio... he never got flustered, you understand, but this time... this time he lost his temper and kicked the dirt. Very unusual... for DiMaggio... you got to understand—" He sat down, lay back, and passed out. In ten minutes the EMS was taking him off to the hospital, third degree burns on his hand. Buttercup, David, and Hildegarde stayed at the hospital well into the night, only surrendering to exhaustion and going home when assured by the doctors that Smiley was going to be all right.

Early Wednesday morning David kept his long weight off Hildegarde's swollen stomach. "*Jessie* or *Jesse*?" he asked her, as he ran a hand over her belly, and she told him sleepily that it would be one or the other and that she would rather wait and see than find out from a machine. Even the remaining Fourth of July thunderboomers, from greater Boston and Boston harbor beyond, could not keep her awake.

Wednesday afternoon they went to Boston General to see how Chuck fared. He had a bandage the size of a football on his hand. "Now I'm down to one hand and one foot," he complained. "I don't care. I want to go home. Buttercup, please take me home," he whined like a child. But the doctors insisted, because he was a very old and a very sick man, that he should remain in the hospital for another night. They returned on Thursday and picked him up.

In the car, Hildegarde said, "You did a very brave thing, Mister Smiley."

"Did I?" He didn't seem to remember the incident. "Oh, well, all in a lifetime," he said.

On Friday, David and Hildy drove out to Cape Cod. They passed Barnstable, Wellfleet and Falmouth, location of the Woods Hole Oceanographic Institution.

"Oh," cried Hildy, "Jessie writes about that place in her book."

"Yes, she spent a couple of years there. Also, when we were kids, we spent a lot of time out here on the Cape. Jessie was a great swimmer, even then."

"What's it like beyond the trees?"

"Mostly flat, but with sand dunes, low hills, small lakes. The Cape is the nation's largest producer of cranberries, you might be interested to know, but its biggest business is tourism."

"How far is Provincetown?"

"Not far now, but if you mean from the mainland, it's about sixty-five miles."

Hildegarde did not want to see Plymouth Rock. "I have read that there is another rock that I would be more interested in seeing."

"And what rock is that?"

"The rock that marks the spot where a pier went out into the water at the end of which was a fish shack that was converted into a theatre by the Provincetown Players. Eugene O'Neill put his first plays on out there. I studied the Provincetown Players at school. Part of my English courses. That's the rock I want to see."

"I'll take you there. We're coming onto Commercial Street now. Your rock is just up ahead there to the left. I'll pull in."

They got out of the car and crossed the road, the slow-moving exodus of vehicles honking at them, more out of holiday fun than impatience.

"But it's just a boulder," she said, reading the plaque.

"The pier must have taken off from about here and gone out to about there," said David, pointing. He pointed to the spot where he thought the shack must have been. Two young men joined them at the rock. They were bare-chested, heavily tanned with rings in their red nipples, and holding hands. They stood about ten feet away and kissed. Their kiss seemed to bring a challenge to Hildegarde. She turned and kissed David with a passion equal to that of the young men. She withdrew, saying, "While I was kissing you, I saw Eugene O'Neill and Edna St. Vincent Millay walking out on the pier."

"I have a strange effect on you, it seems."

"Maybe because you're so much older. You bring back a more romantic era."

"I'm not that old. It's just that you're rather young. You're not saying I'm too old for you, are you?"

"Of course not. It's just that all Jews are ancient. They go back to the beginning. There's a—what do you call it—? An aura!"

"Ancient days in the Levant. I hate to disabuse you of such cherished notions, my dearest Teuton, but I was born in Boston, and Smiley told me once that my father was Irish, making me half-Irish."

"Ich lieber dich," she said, laughing.

"I love you, too," he said, smiling down at her.

Back in the car, she said, "What is this fellowship that your mother has got herself?"

David was looking for the turn-off. "Call her Ruth. We all do. There's a foundation that supports a Master Fellowship Program at the Work Center. They select writers and artists who are at least fifty years old to come and live and work there for a time. She gets a few weeks of peace and quiet and an honorarium—a couple of thousand dollars, I think."

"But she's rich. She won't take their money, will she?"

"She'll probably end up writing them a check. There it is." David pulled in. "And there's her red Hummer. Unmistakable. Like a fire engine."

Hildegarde looked up in time to see the sign: FINE ARTS WORK CENTER.

"It's a charming place," Ruth said. "Rustic and impervious to the outside world. Let's have some cold white wine. There's no air conditioning and it's hot as hell, isn't it?" The bronzed septuagenarian wore white strands of fluency—a long white skirt with a tunic top—stirred by a large electric fan. The stubby toes of her brown feet were tipped by shell pink nails. A pair of sandals lay aside, where she had been sitting. Her salt and pepper hair fell damply about her shoulders. She was firm, with muscular arms and legs, like someone who had done a thousand lakeside laundries. She looked like anything but an heiress, more like a peasant prepared to stamp grapes; and yet, for all, she was beautiful, with a straight, determined nose, and gleaming, excited brown eyes set in eggshell seas of white. "And how are the Smileys?" she called, as she pulled out a bottle of chardonnay from an old, throbbing refrigerator in the kitchen corner of a cavernous room of the remodeled, apartmentalized barn.

"Old Chuck had an accident."

"Surprise, surprise," she said. "What did he do now?" She was extracting the cork from the bottle with a troublesome corkscrew.

"He burned himself on some fireworks—burned his hand—had to be taken to the emergency ward."

"Poor Buttercup! She has to watch over him as though he were a child. She's a very competent person. I've taken care of things in case she has to put him somewhere, in a home or a hospice. How is she?"

"Full of vim and vigor."

"Yes. Well, she's much younger than he is. Her first husband brought her to Fortune Island when she was just a girl and he was an aging man. Old Sheriff Walkup."

She returned to David and Hildegarde with the uncorked wine bottle and three stemmed glasses, lit a king-sized Marlboro while still standing, held the cigarette away and looked at it, took a long drag on it, exhaled a jet stream that made Hildegarde cough, and sat down, oblivious. "Pour us all a drink, won't you? What do you think of this gig, David? I was sitting down at Chapel Hill, going crazy worrying about your sister, when the invite came." She looked at Hildegarde. "What can we do? Jessie's operation really didn't do any good. She's been in the hospital twice over the last five weeks with congestive heart failure. I don't know if I passed this along earlier, but she had surgery for lung cancer, and she still has dozens of little characinoid tumors in both lungs. She's home now and doing much better. Nurses still around the clock, though. That's why I couldn't come to Frankfurt for your wedding, but I still needed a break from the stress of it, so when they called up and said I had a Senior Fellowship up here, I figured, well, two weeks—it was just the respite I needed. I'm supposed to do a reading of my poems tonight. It's my last night and I'm going to give them the works. You'll be there, of course."

"Of course."

"Then I'm going to get into my Hummer and drive down to Chapel Hill and stay with Jessie."

"Isn't it dangerous for you to drive alone?" asked Hildegarde.

"I've got a .357 Magnum in the glove compartment."

"Ruth," said David, "you don't mind about it, do you, that we decided to get married on the spur of the moment?"

"Of course I don't mind. I didn't tell you about Jessie's operation, which came up suddenly, because I didn't want to spoil your wedding. And I'm sorry. My apologies to both of you. But mind? On the contrary, I'm delighted." She reached out and took Hildegarde's hand. "You are a most beautiful and—from what Jessie has told me—highly intelligent young woman. I warmly welcome you into our family, such as it is. David, isn't that your Love and Luck ring, the one Jessie gave you?" But she didn't wait for an answer. "How clever of you to have it cut down for her. It makes a perfect wedding ring, a gold band. How lovely!"

While she was lighting another cigarette, David took the opportunity to say, "We're expecting a baby. Hildy wants to name it after Jessie. Boy or girl."

"I noticed, and I am delighted. And Jessie will be delighted, too. A new world begins. A new Jessie. What could be more wonderful? I was afraid I was never going to be a grandmother, you know," she told Hildegarde. "Due to an early injury—a trauma, you might call it—Jessie has been unable to have a normal...well, it's more psychological than physical...unable to enjoy the full life of a woman... In any case, I had the early disappointment of realizing that she would probably never marry and have children." She seemed to brush the thought away with her hand. "So, naturally, I placed all my hope in David. Then one day I woke up with the recognition that I had a bachelor on my hands as well as a spinster, and not a grandchild in sight. So you see, my dear—my dears—I am joyous at this late surprise, absolutely joyous! In fact, a toast to the baby! In fact, to the old Jessie and the new Jessie! Prosit!

"And I have more news," said David, lowering his glass. "We're going to move to Washington. I have finally battled my way into Foggy Bottom."

"Oh, splendid!"

"Now I can be near the two of you," he said. "I want to be close—because...to be frank, I know she's going soon."

Ruth looked at him quizzically. "Neither Jessie nor I are afraid of the truth. And for God's sake, my boy, don't surrender to death so easily. Sometimes it takes a long time for the gentleman in the dustcoat to woo the maiden. We're all tougher than we think we are. Don't you agree, Hildy?"

"I hope it is true."

"And Hildy has quit Lufthansa," David said. "She's going after her master's degree at Georgetown. International politics."

"I want to qualify myself for the world of diplomacy," Hildegarde said.

"Then learn to shoot," said Ruth. "Diplomacy comes out of the barrel of a gun, or so Mao said."

At the reading, the great poet Chanley Jarrett introduced Ruth as Doctor Ruth Perle, the folklorist and poet. "She will read from her collection-in-progress, *Folkways*." First Ruth read a poem called "An Appalachian Tale." The literary crowd filling the hall had leaned cautiously into the rough folk humor of the piece, but about half-way through appeared to catch the spirit of the thing, and, by the time Ruth had finished, seemed pleased with it, laughing and applauding. Next Ruth read a piece set in the Mississippi Delta. It was about an angel who discovers and likes the fleshy ways of the world so much that he forgets his mission on earth.

This piece, too, was humorous, and brought scattered applause. Ruth sipped from a bottle of water, cleared her throat, and introduced her third and final piece:

"The nonagenarian of the next poem," she said, "is a woman with a mind of myth, of untutored, almost Jungian archetypes, of casual comments made by others more than eighty years before the time of the poem's events, comments become memories and memories grown more vivid and meaningful over time. She would occasionally find me working about my daughter's property in Chapel Hill, this woman, who is a compound of several, and in a cracked, but still strong, voice would regale me with her anecdotes, stories, tall tales. 'The Souls' tells of her response to a flock of blackbirds that landed on my daughter's lawn. I hope to pass her folk wisdom on to a new generation. That generation may pass it on to others. I think that she would be pleased with such an outcome. I wish I could read the poem to her, but she has joined

'THE SOULS

Outside on a green lawn a giant water-oak conducts a sunset.
    Some unsteady hum has summoned us out of our houses.
My ancient lady friend, who lives nearby, is jawing now, and wears
    an awed-holy expression as she says they are souls, yes sir.
And they are everywhere, they wade the dusky clouds, they are
    giant black-winged fruits hanging, falling, bouncing. The green
is black with them. And neighbors stare; they worry for their

cars and pickups. If they get into the red berries, it's hell on
    paint. Shoot them. No, they are beautiful. They are a menace.
Look out below! They rise and wheel, kaleidoscopic, inside rings
    of themselves. They set themselves against the sky, black on blue.
They caw. They are telling themselves, or us, something.
    They caw and caw, and what is it they are saying, so
earpiercingly, holes through your eardrums, through your brain,

as if lasered? Then they settle again, like a black blizzard
    of huge coal flakes. The souls come back to visit us, to tell
us that they know everything now. Now their sharp yellow beaks
    pierce the lawn. They are busier than worms, in a feast
of famishment, an ecstasy of appetite. Now, she says,

the nonagenarian, I'll soon be with them, and then
it's always now for me like them. The souls have found their

bodies. I don't know which is which, but somewhere, there,
   is everyone who died, all the loved ones, and even the others,
the ones that nobody loved, they are all there now, she says.
   I stare as deep as I can see. They are every blessed
place—on roofs, looking down, in trees, on bushes, under,
   over, and around. Some seem to be waiting, some tug
at the turning-emerald lawn in the lowering light: and now

how do they know to rise suddenly, and become one wide
   black wing? How do they know to circle and circle in unison,
one boomerang black wing composed of so many blood-beating,
   sky-rowing black wings? How do they know when it's time
to fly along a horizon, rimmed with rising red? The souls,
   they know, they know! I think it must be out of some distant
folklore that the old lady speaks, eyes fixed, waving them goodbye.' "

Chapter Eight

Summer 1954

The few remaining souls on Fortune Island feared that Sheriff Walkup would close the general store for lack of trade, which would greatly inconvenience them. They bought bait and tackle from him, canned goods, and the general store was also the post office, where news of the outer world came and, sometimes, was responded to. Though pleased that he kept it open, why he did was a matter for conjecture among the fishermen, shrimpers, and crabbers who frequented it, people who preferred isolation, the last stubborn remnant of the League of Solitary Souls. But they did not discuss the question. They simply wondered and went their own way.

The only person on the island who might have welcomed a bit of gossip was the sheriff's young wife, Betty Lou, herself a matter for silent conjecture—as was the hermit of Whalehead, the book writer, Ruth Perle—among the few, stony, stoic fisherfolk of Fortune Island. Wagging tongues had it that she had been a girl in trouble and was saved by the old sheriff from a sad fate—there was the sense of, was it the unmentionable, an abortion? She was young enough to be his daughter, perhaps his granddaughter. Curvy, bouncy, and dimply, Buttercup, as the sheriff had dubbed her, intrigued her few customers. The sheriff must have won her at a shooting gallery, like a Kewpie doll. And it was a fact that he had saved her from trouble; and she, having no better prospect in view, had amazed him by accepting his marriage proposal. As old as he was, he was more of a man than most, and in time she had come to care for him.

Upon his retirement, and expecting better days to come to Fortune Island, he had taken his savings, bought the general store, and brought the curiosity of his May-December marriage to the island. In short order, he found his young bride to be a very competent business partner, and gradually, as he grew older, handed over most of the business responsibilities to her. Quick with numbers, efficient with stock, liking her customers—all but the Reverend Jason P. Cogburn, who gave her the creeps—she was the great asset and gift of the sheriff's old age.

But even now Buttercup could feel the Reverend Cogburn's eyes on her as she reached for a tin of tobacco. She could feel the very place he was looking—her hair, her hips, her legs—he made a chill wherever he looked, a chill on a hot June day.

Cogburn eyed Buttercup's backside from the other side of the counter. He wore a worn and sweat-soaked, spindrift-soggy black suit, his usual dented Stetson. His short, spiky, gray beard itched and he scratched it with long fingernails. At his feet, between his scuffed and cracked Wellingtons, stood a bag containing four bottles of Wild Turkey. He had saved several hundred souls as far north as the Dismal Swamp and as far south as Cape Fear, and he looked forward to a few quiet days of drink, introversion, and tobacco, which pleasures he usually denied himself while on his circuit.

It was on the trip across Pamlico Sound that he realized that he had forgotten to buy smokes—meant to get them in Morehead City, where he had hitched a ride to Fortune Island on a fishing boat that was pursued, much to his annoyance, by wild-winged, shrieking gulls. He was just about to run out of patience with the birds, when he saw Fortune Island emerge from the water like a humpbacked whale. He had lost many of his teeth and much of his hair, and now he was losing his sight. Time was, he had been able to see the island from half-way out on Pamlico Sound. When he had taken off his glasses to wipe them, the island had disappeared like a whale in a dive; when he had replaced his glasses the island was there again, rolling in the Atlantic.

But these breaks were no longer what they had been, no one to talk to but the kid, Jessie, no Susannah, waiting at home. Damned if he didn't miss her! Snakebit loneliness was the only companion of the Sad Traveller in this life.

He disliked having to go to Sheriff Walkup's general store—the ex-sheriff of Carteret County always eyed him suspiciously—but he had to have tobacco. Thank God the sheriff wasn't there.

Buttercup pushed a bag across the counter and took his money. She was glad to see the humped back of him as he left.

As he traversed the mud flats toward the dunes of Whalehead, as he eyed Garcie's shack with disdain, as he climbed the slope up toward the dunes, he watched his shadow mocking him, distorting him, running around his serpentine path, a shape-changing spook. And as he came to the front of his house, his shadow loomed before him on its façade. He opened the door and stepped to the other side of his dark self. He did not expect anyone to be inside, but was not surprised to find Jessie there, at the kitchen table, reading.

"What's that you got there?"

"*That* is *Vanity Fair* by Mister William Makepeace Thackeray," Jessie said, breathlessly but boldly. He had caught her out. She was shaken up. She looked down, back up, dagger-eyed.

"You know what I think of those kinds of books. Where did you get a thing like that? I want that out of my house!" He walked over to her, seized the book from her hands, went back to the door and threw it out, flapping. It landed pages down like a square brown dead bird on the dunes. "What are you doing here, anyway? Why ain't you with Garcie?"

"I got a right to be here—more'n you!"

"All right. All right. I'm getting too old to contend with your backsass. I ought to just smack you up side the head."

"Don't you try it, old man. You try it, I'll kill you in your sleep."

"Do you hear that, Lord? This child's threatening to kill me! Get me a glass instead. Try behaving like a good daughter. Like a loving daughter. You know you and me are alone in the world, 'cept for that nigger woman, but we are stuck together alone in this world, so why can't you try to behave? You got none of the sweetness of your mother."

"Here." Jessie put a glass on the table. "Drink yourself blind."

Cogburn rolled up his shirt sleeves and sat down at the table. He poured himself a drink and lit a cigar. "I miss your momma to be here welcoming me. I miss her more than I thought I ever would." He fanned out a deck of cards on the table, then set them up for solitaire. "Let me see..."

"You drove her to suicide—everybody says."

"She took herself off to her drowning, one way or another. What I did, I saved as much of her as I could. I mean, her soul. That's my job. That's what I do. And I'm going to save yours, too, little girl. Damned if I won't! Now you go look in that bag over yonder and you'll find what I saved her from."

"What do you mean?"

"Just look."

Jessie went to the bag and found a magazine in it, *True Detective Magazine*.

Cogburn let a glassful of bourbon run down his throat, his head back like a baby bird taking in a worm. "Phew! I needed that. Thirsty as an A-rab! Bring that over here." Jessie brought him the magazine. He thumbed through it, opened it to a story, turned it around and pushed it across the table. The last rays of the evening sun Venetian-blinded the page. "Sit down there and look at that story. There's pictures."

Jessie, curious now, did as she was told.

"You see that there white-haired boy?" He tapped the picture with a dirty-nailed finger. "That there is your daddy, a criminal bank robber and probably a stone killer, as bad a man as your poor momma could have found herself in the ways of her sinful life."

Jessie moved the magazine around, trying to get the picture clear in the flashing sun and the darkening room. It was a faded picture that had been printed on pulp paper. A gaunt boy with a shock of white hair stared vaguely back at Jessie from the magazine. He seemed submerged in time, an image staring up through sun-streaked water with a row of illegible numbers across his chest. The caption read, *William Makepeace Thackeray McQueen*. He looked scared. Three other pictures in a row across the page meant nothing to her. One was a picture of Smiley. The story was entitled *THE MERCHANT MARINE GANG OF THE FORTIES: HOW THEY ALMOST STOLE VICTORY FROM THE ALLIES*.

"The pictures are on the cover, too, along with the title. I saw it on a stand in Morehead City and plucked it off just for you to see the evil that sired you, so's you could get it straight in your cement head about what is good and what is bad."

"This is my real daddy?"

"That is the blood that runs through you. Now you must see why I must take a strong hand to you. But that don't mean I don't care about you, little Magdalena." He grabbed her wrist and pulled her around the table to him. "Now give your good daddy a kiss." She pulled away from him. "You stink of liquor," she said. "You just plain stink. Let me go!" He sat smiling into space, took another long drink of Wild Turkey, put his glass down, and lunged for her from his chair. But she was more limber than he was and he landed on the floor. He wasn't angry. He had just enough bourbon aboard to find the situation humorous. He laughed and got himself back up and into his chair. Jessie told him she was going to Garcie's. "You won't come after me there," she said. "Garcie'll take a skittle to you."

"I believe she would," he said. "Sure do miss your mother," he added, pouring another drink with one hand and picking his cigar from the ashtray with the other. The room had become dark and smoky. Jessie could see the embers of his cigar go red and dark and red again as he puffed on it. She was gathering what she needed—the magazine, a blanket, a few other things—and she left him there, stepping out into the starlit and moonlit night.

When night came to Fortune Island it was like a big hand reaching out from the mainland, its fingers making dark shadows among the dunes, but before that happened, there was often an horizonless silver of sound-water and sky until it darkened; then to the northeast the soft steady recurring blink of a lighthouse appeared like a star. That softly winking star was Jessie's special friend.

Jessie searched the dunes for the book, the book from which her father's name had been taken and given, William Makepeace Thackeray. She found it a couple of yards from the house, pages bent and torn, dog-eared by indifference, by destructiveness, picked it up and wandered out into the dunes that seemed to glow golden in the dark.

About fifty yards from the house she dug a foxhole, laid the blanket in it, and laid herself in the blanket. She had another foxhole back up against the house where she had often gone in winter to escape Cogburn, the heat from the house warming her, but she preferred distance tonight and the dunes were still warm from the all-day June sun. The mosquitoes and sand fleas seemed to target her. And she feared the fire-ants. But she pulled the blanket around her, shaping a sort of tent, and lit a flashlight, playing it on the picture of her father in the magazine, his dark young face and all that white hair stark in the beam. "Got to admit," she said, "I never did, in all my born days, ever see a young man with hair like yours." This man put his milt on roe and here she was—Jessie McQueen, who swims like a fish. She switched off the flashlight.

She could still see that strange, time-distant face as she snuggled down in the blanket, the magazine falling away. She looked right up at the stars and at first they seemed to come at her but after a bit it was as if she were going to them, drawn deeper and deeper into them, and, heavy-lidded, she fell asleep.

❊ ❊ ❊

At three o'clock in the morning, the Hermit of Whalehead woke at her typewriter.

Ruth Perle lit a Lucky Strike, held the cigarette out, and looked at it.

She took a long drag, and, with a heave of her chest, let the smoke roll from her mouth. Her crowded shack sat in the night and she sat in the fluttering oil lamp light within it, sipping yesterday's cold black coffee from a sticky white mug.   In a picture on the wall, she saw the dark face of her young flyer husband, killed in Korea, and the pale face of her dead child—hers, her husband's, dead daughter, born even before their marriage in 1944, dead of meningitis even before her husband was shot down. Her guilt was that they had not been important enough to her. She had not even taken her husband's name. It was not that she hadn't loved them—oh, she had!—but had always been so much otherwise involved. Then it had been her doctorate that had consumed her. As far back as she could remember, she had been consumed by projects, achievements, the perpetual escape from the giant shadow of her father and his famous name and his enormous wealth. Sometimes she wondered if she hadn't married her husband, a goy, a non-Jew, just to hurt her father. Her daughter had died at the age of two, the void in her life, her husband at the age of twenty-five in 1950. She had been a widow for four years, a bereaved mother for ten, a lost daughter for nearly thirty, from birth, it seemed, all her days. If her mother had died first, she would not have inherited, but her mother outlived her father, and so she was rich. Or the wealth would have gone to her brothers, most likely, but both had died in the Second World War, heroes, as her mother told her. They had been older. She hardly knew them. What she had always wanted was a life with ordinary, shit-kicking people, some paradigm of the ordinary that she had fixed in her mind as the opposite of whatever she had come from. *Volk*, the people, the five-and-dimers—folks, just folks. She had developed a tough surface to hide and protect the romantic within, the lover of poems and tales of the people, the folklorist.

But did what she had in mind conform to reality? Or had she from childhood created a dream world? Her weakness—perhaps her only discernable weakness to an outsider, meaning anyone not herself—was that she couldn't let go of her wealth, had kept the stack of it in the shape that her father had left behind. Was it not the chink in her armor? The lie of herself?

She snuffed out her cigarette and went to the door to look at the night sky. She looked out on the glowing, deep-shadowed dunes and thought of Robinson Crusoe. Her refuge was a nearly deserted island, nearly a desert island. Wellaway! A writer must have isolation. Many a writer would give his or her soul for a shack on a deserted island.

Why not walk out on the dunes? There was no one—or very few, asleep at this hour—to see her there. She need not take her pistol. What large animal would she encounter? What human monster? There was no one and nothing to try to do her harm. She almost wished for danger. Ah, she was just plain lonely.

Bare feet in the sand, a salt sea breeze running its fingers through her hair, the smell of the sea, of fish and foam, the sound of the sway of the sea, a half a snowglobe of stars overhead, they entranced her, set her to wakeful dreaming. Barefoot, she took a few quick steps in the sand and whirled in a little secret dance, digging her toes in, extending her arms to the sky—Nature Girl.

Mystery had claimed her, when something rose up out of the sand at her feet to breathtakingly stop her—her feet—her heart? At first a darksome, enormous figure, then, shrinking down and taking shape, a girl-child, who had whirled up out of the sand.

"Oh, my God!" she cried—then, seeing—"You scared the bejesus out of me."

"Don't be scared. I'm just a little girl."

"Not so little, Stretch."

"I'm tall for my age."

"Which is?"

"I'm twelve, almost thirteen."

"What are you doing out here on the dunes so late?"

"Sleeping. I guess a crab got into my blanket. Anyway, something was crawling around inside and I woke up and I jumped up and there you were. What are you doing out here so late?"

"I'm afraid I couldn't sleep. Why were you sleeping out here in the sand? Don't you have a bed at home? It's after three in the morning."

"I don't want to be in the house with my father. I mean, my stepfather... I mean—"

"Did he chase you out? Scare you away?"

"He's drunk and mean as a snake."

"What about your mother?"

"She's dead. Swam out to sea and drownded herself."

"Oh, yes, the young lady at the general store told me about that. So that was your mother. I'm so sorry. You see, I come and go."

"I've seen you before," Jessie told her. "You're the one the fishermen and their wives call the Hermit of Whalehead."

"They call me that? Well, I'm not a hermit at all. I'm out and about all the time. Don't you have somewhere you can go? A friend's house?"

"I can go to Garcie's, but I don't want to bring her any trouble."

"Garcie is your friend? An older woman?"

"She looks after me. She bore me into the world."

"Oh, Garcie, yes, the midwife. I've met her. I see. Well, my name is Ruth Perle. What's yours?"

"I'm Jessie McQueen. I never heard anyone talk like you. You ain't from around here, are you?"

"I'm from Boston. Up north. I'm doing some work down here."

"What work is there to do down here? If you're not a fisherman—"

"Never mind about that now. I'll explain later. Why don't you come on home with me and spend the night? My shack is right across the dunes. You probably know it. Are you hungry? I can fix you something."

"That'd be mighty nice of you. I didn't eat no dinner or supper." Jessie began to gather up her things—flashlight, magazine, and book— and put them in the blanket. She made a sack of it and threw it over her shoulder.

"What's that book you're reading?"

"That's *Vanity Fair* by—"

"William Makepeace Thackeray."

"How did you know?"

"It's a classic. I mean, a famous book. Isn't it a bit difficult for you? Can you tell me what it's about?"

"No'm. It's about a poor beautiful lady name of Becky Sharp who is trying to get a good house and something to eat, and maybe some jewelry, if she can. I can't pick up on some of it, but I'd say that was the main heap. The main reason I like it though is because that's my daddy's name, my real daddy."

"Becky? Becky Sharp? It can't be."

"Oh, no ma'am." They were trudging across the dunes now and Jessie leaned into Ruth's shoulder, laughing. When she caught her breath, she said, "My daddy's name was William Makepeace Thackeray McQueen. His momma was a school teacher and she named him after the man who wrote the book."

"That was a big name for your poor father to carry around on his shoulders."

"That's the truth! Sometimes I think he must be all bent over with it." Jessie started laughing again, then grew serious. "I ain't laughing at him, you understand."

"I understand," Ruth said.

"No, ma'am, I wouldn't do that!"

As they approached Ruth's cottage, Jessie said, "You live here? This cottage used to belong to an old man and his wife. They kept to themselves, so I didn't get to know them. They was hermits!"

"What happened to them?"

"The wife died, and the husband was taken off to a nursing home in Beaufort."

"What did you say your name was again?"

"Jessie McQueen. The wife died and the husband is in a nursing home because he is so old—that's biology. Did you know that an octopus has his sex thing in one of his arms, and that arm breaks off and swims away to find a female to make pregnant and then it dies but it never leaves her. She's got the dang thing stuck to her forever. Think of that!"

"Goodness! Is that a fact?"

"Oh, yes, ma'am, that's biology. All animals die. I can tell the old ones. They get grayed up like people. And I'm always finding dead ones on the beach. Sometimes I bury them. If it's a bird, I sing a song. Sorry for jawing on like this. Just things come into my head sometimes and I out and say them. I talk to myself, too. Nobody around much to talk to. Heavens to Betsy!" Jessie exclaimed, as she stepped into Ruth's cottage. "Just look at this place! What's that?"

"That's a tape recording machine. I use that in my work. It takes down what people say and I can play it back."

"I ain't never seen nothing like that before. Big, ain't it? Can I hear my own voice? I ain't never heard my own voice before."

"Later. I'll record your voice later."

"I ain't never seen a room like this one!" The room was loaded, wall to wall, with books. There were uneven stacks of books that looked as if they were about to fall over. There were books on the floor, on the tables, books everywhere. Where there was wall space, there were posters, prints of modern paintings—Braque, Picasso, and others. A pump-action shotgun and a hunting rifle rested on pegs. A wind-up record player stood in a corner. Jessie was drawn to a typewriter, which she petted as if it were a cat. "Lord a Mercy! What's this?" she said.

"Just an old Remington."

"What's a Remington do?"

"It's a typewriter. I write on it."

"And it prints out, like a book?"

"Like this." Ruth picked up a stack of manuscript sheets beside the machine and held them out for Jessie to inspect.

"That Remington sure is a beautiful thing." She looked intently at the pages in Ruth's hand. "Does that mean that you're a writer? What do you write? Do you write stories?"

"In a way. I'm a folklorist. I write about legends and... Well, here, let me show you." She turned to the bookcase, pulled out a volume, and handed it to Jessie.

"You wrote a whole book?"

"Five books, in fact."

"*Legends of Ap-Ap-*"

"Appalachia."

"Appalachia," Jessie said, trying out the new word. "I read a book by Miss Rachel Carson. It's called *Under the Sea Wind*. It's the only book I've ever seen that was written by a woman. Do many women write books? I never heard of any beside Miss Rachel Carson. I love that book because it's about everything I really know—the sea, the tides, the beach, the little animals and such."

"Have you never heard of Margaret Mitchell?"

"No, ma'am. Don't think so."

"Who wrote *Gone With the Wind*?"

"No, ma'am."

"She's about the most famous woman writer in America."

"I ain't never been off this island. Well, once, when I saw the Liberty ships near Wilmington. 'Please God, we have defeated the foe!' I always remember them, but I was a little girl then."

"It seems I found myself a Kaspar Hauser."

"What's a Kaspar Hauser?"

"A little boy who was kept away from the world."

"That's me, I guess; but I'm Jessie McQueen. At least, that's what they tell me, and they been calling me that forever—well, as far back as I go." Jessie rocked back in her chair, surveying the room. "What's that," she said, pointing at one of the posters.

"That's a painting by Picasso. He's a famous artist."

"Why is it like that—all those blocks?"

"It's called a cubist painting."

"Cubes. Well, if you ask me, all inside here is like a cubist painting. See—all the books and everything."

"I suppose it is, a little. That's a sharp thought. Aren't you hungry?"

"Oh, my God! What's that?"

"That's a .38 Smith and Wesson revolver. I keep it for protection. I go into some pretty dangerous places in my work. And it's very isolated here, too."

"Can you shoot—are you a good shot?"

"I think so." Ruth went over to the desk, picked up the pistol and showed it to Jessie. "You see, there's really nothing to it. This is the safety. Just press it back with your thumb. Then you point it at whatever you want to hit and pull the trigger. Here, try it. It's empty." Jessie stood beside Ruth, hefted the pistol, clicked the safety, aimed at the doorway, and pulled the trigger several times.

"It's easy," she said.

"But it's not to be played with, you know."

"The handle is pearl, like the inside of an oyster shell. And it's so shiny. It sure is a beautiful thing."

"And very dangerous, like a cobra. I don't want you fooling with it, hear?"

"Yes, ma'am. I'm sorry if I'm being impolite, nosing around. I just never seen anything like this before. I mean the whole place—all these things. It just does so warm me. Our house is bare as a bone." Her eyes lighted on a small framed photo on the wall. "Oh, who's this soldier and the little girl?"

"That's my husband and my daughter."

"That's Mister Perle?"

"His name was Robert Latham. I'd already written a couple of books when I met him, so I kept my name—Perle. He was killed in the Korean War. He was a pilot. And just so you don't have to ask, the little girl was my daughter. She died of spinal meningitis, a very terrible disease. She would have been just a few years younger than you, now. So you see—I'm all alone, sort of like you."

"My momma killed herself. Yes, she went and throwed—threw—herself in the sea, like I told you. People tell me that it was an accident, but I heard them say what she done—did. And that man—he made her do it, I think. He called her names and they hurt her. I always thought he wasn't my daddy because in biology, things that come from things look like them, don't they?"

"Most of the time," said Ruth, "not always."

"Your little girl looks like you. Looks like her daddy, too. Here, this is my daddy." Jessie went over to her blanket sack, which she'd dropped by the door, and dug around until she found the *True Detective Magazine*. She thumbed through its pages until she found the page with the photo of her father. She took it to the table and held it beside the kerosene lamp. "See this one here? That's my Daddy. He's a criminal. That's probably why he has that white hair."

Ruth sat down at the table and lit a cigarette. She held the magazine and looked closely. "It's very small and blurry. Hard to see. He's very young."

"I know. I can't even tell if I look like him from that. I used to dream about him coming home to get me—well, not him exactly. But somebody who cared about me."

"You mean like a Prince Charming who comes to save you? We all have dreams like that."

"Even you?"

"Even me. But I should know better."

"It's just that—that—that man who was sorta my father, at least he's real. But he ain't my father, really, and, this here fellow, he ain't exactly real, if you see what I mean. So what have I got now? I got no mother, and two fathers that ain't my father. Ain't it the craziest thing you ever heard of?" She expelled a long sigh and looked at Ruth as if she expected a solution to the enigma of her life.

"I didn't think there were any children on Fortune Island," Ruth said.

"I'm it," Jessie said. "I've always been it. When a baby gets born they take it away. But no babies have been born for years, that I can remember. I guess you know there's under twenty people out here now. I try to keep count. You're twenty-one, maybe."

"It's true, but that's why I like it here. You'd be surprised how hard it is for a writer to be alone. But I've seen you before, I think. You're so tall, I guess I thought you were somebody's wife. It was only earlier when I saw your face out there on the dunes that I realized how young you were. Yes, I've seen you wandering around out here. Do you go to school in the winter?"

"No'm. Never been to school."

"Never? Didn't anybody from the school system come out here looking for you? Didn't anybody here report you?"

"Nobody ever came looking and nobody ever told. People mind their own business. There ain't no Nosy Parkers on Fortune Island. You ain't gonna tell, are you? It would mean a heap of trouble for me with the Reverend Cogburn. He sure wouldn't like to have to worry about getting me back and forth or set up on the mainland."

"I'm not going to get you in any trouble," Ruth said. "So, you've never been to school at all, and you can read Rachel Carson. How does that work?"

"Well, the Reverend taught me my letters when I was nothing more than a tad, and then he taught me to read from the Bible."

"That's the way the pioneers did it," Ruth said.

"And then my momma showed me the treasure trove."

"The treasure trove?"

"My daddy's books up in the attic. Momma told me to use the dictionary that was with them books to cipher out any word I couldn't understand. Well, there were lots of words I couldn't get the meaning of anyway, but I got the idea of what they meant from inside the books—"

"You mean, from the context?"

"From what the other words meant. What they said. I could sort of sniff it out. Hell and damn, there wasn't much else to do. Only had Garcie to talk to, sometimes the Reverend, when he weren't—I mean, wasn't—drunk. I know from the books that I don't talk right every time, but that's because I don't know anybody who does—except you. You talk like a book. Is that the way a book is supposed to sound—like it's from Boston?"

Ruth laughed. "You're quite a girl, Jessie McQueen. Do you know that there's a book about children your age in supposedly good schools who can't—well, who can't read—and here you are out here all by yourself reading books by Thackeray and Rachel Carson with no help or guidance. It's amazing. You're an amazing girl, do you know that?"

"I know I'm the dang loneliest girl in the world—until now."

"What other books have you read?"

"One I can think of right away is *Treasure Island*. That reminded me of here. And I read some of *Pilgrim's Progress*, but I didn't like it much. Something about it reminded me of the Reverend Cogburn, and I don't like much that reminds me of him. I hate the Bible. What I especial like is books about nature. I like nature, the way things get born and the way they die, and what they do in between, and how many ways they change in the in-between time."

"What would you like to be some day?"

"Just me, but I would like to see some place beside this old island. I am so tired of this island. I swear, I have been over every inch of this island, and much more'n twice. That's what I like about books. They

take you to places you ain't never been and you get to meet people that
are different from the people you meet most of the time. Like Miss Becky
Sharp. I love this old island, but—"

"What if you needed a doctor?"

"I never get sick 'cause I never take a bath. I swim. Garcie says I
should swim in the ocean. It's full of salt and that's good for you. She
says a bath can be a blight to your health. She never gets sick either,
except she had to go to the mainland on account of her diabetes, which is
making her blind. But Garcie says I should thank my stars I'm out here,
because on the mainland there is every kind of sickness you can think of.
I never had the scarlet fever, but they have a lot of that on the mainland,
Garcie says. And they got this real bad polio disease, and Garcie says
all the children get it on the mainland. That's another thing that scares
me about leaving the island. I suppose those little bugs are all part of
biology, though, like that crab that bit me. *Pinched* me. But I did get to
go one time to the mainland. The Reverend took me. I was four or five
years old, I think—don't rightly remember. Momma was coughing up
blood and Garcie had to tend to her. Momma asked the Reverend to take
me with him to a place called Wilmington. He was a preaching there, and
there was a whole flock of people, and he yells down at me like he hated
me, I remember, *Do You Believe?* I didn't know what he meant. And he
shouts again, like this: *Do You Believe?* He looked like a big black snake
I saw once jump into the air on its tail. *No*, I shouted back. I'm just a tiny
little girl then, you understand, and he scared the stuffings out of me. All
I could think was whatever it was I didn't want any of it, I remember that.
Then he ups and twists my earlobe until I cried. So I got the idea, and I
shouted back, YES, that I did believe because that was the way he wanted
it, I could see then. But after that, I did not—no ma'am—and I could not
never believe whatever it was he wanted me to believe—whatever it was,
coming from him. I looked around for some of the big people to help me,
but it seemed like they thought he was right to hurt me, and they just kept
on jumping around with him and his snakes."

"What?"

"Yes, ma'am, snakes! Any old how, I remember I couldn't stop crying,
and, later, I found out that we had been at a church on the banks of the
Cape Fear River, and when we all went outside, I could see across to that
big city of Wilmington. I was still crying. My momma never did anything
like that. Neither Garcie, but she said she slapped me to get my first
breath. Anyway, I'm standing there crying and looking across the river

at what a church lady told me were Liberty ships, hundreds of them. The lady said they were a mothballed fleet, that's what she said, a mothballed fleet, a long line of gray masts against lines of gray cypress trees, beautiful trees, tall and pointy, and that is how I remember it, 'No need to cry,' the lady said, and she wiped my eyes with her lacy pink handkerchief. 'We have defeated the foe.' I could never get that out of my head. 'We have defeated the foe.' "

"That must have been right after World War Two. She must have meant that we had won the war. Thank God that we had won the war."

"Well, that ain't what she said. Lordy, I must be keeping you up with all my chatter."

The room was filling with morning light. Ruth reached over and turned down the oil lamp.

"What we both need is something to eat and some shuteye. I'll make us some breakfast. I have to go way up the Banks, nearly to Virginia, day after tomorrow. Would you like to come with me?"

"Oh, yes, ma'am! I sure would!"

"Would anybody mind if I took you? We should get permission from somebody. Your—the preacher? Garcie?"

"I'll get permission. I wouldn't let anything stop me from going."

"What I meant before, Jessie, was what would you like to do with your life? Like a job?"

"Oh, that. Well, I know I could never do what I want."

"Which is?"

"I would like to be like Miss Rachel Carson and tell people about the tides and such."

"You want to be a scientist—a biologist? That's it, isn't it?"

"I guess that's it. I would dearly like to be like Miss Rachel Carson, that's all I know."

Chapter
Nine

"Sunnyside up," that was how Ruth described the eggs they had for breakfast. Garcie never made them that way. Hers were half scrambled, half fried, so that the yolks rolled through the whites, like wavy stripes. And there was no chicory in Ruth's coffee. Jessie felt guilty thinking it, but she liked Ruth's cooking better than Garcie's. She guessed it was because Ruth could see and Garcie couldn't, not so good. The coffee didn't keep her awake because she wanted to sleep and dream of the upcoming adventure that, maybe, if...and she was almost asleep before Ruth had finished zipping her into a sleeping bag.

"It's like a big cocoon," she told Ruth, but Ruth just patted her head and disappeared. Then she was on a ship that was going as fast as a car over land and water and, sometimes, off the top of a big mountain and into space, and then Ruth unzipped her and told her that it was time to get up.

Ruth had put a record on her wind-up record player—"You Belong to Me."

> See the pyramids along the Nile,
> See the sunrise on a tropic isle,
> But just remember, darling, all the while,
> You belong to me.

"There's a bowl of water," Ruth said. "Wash your face and come and have some coffee." The coffee smelled good. Jessie splashed her face with cold water and sat down to have coffee. It was hot in the room and she could see through the window that it was short-shadow time, the sun blazing straight down.

"It's almost one o'clock," Ruth said, smoke escaping her mouth. "I want you to go home and get permission to go on our trip in the morning.

I want it in writing. Just a signed okay will do."

Jessie gulped down a cup of coffee. "I was a travelling all morning in my dreams. But maybe it was that song in my head. Now I'm awake, I got shudders in me. You know how it is when you get excited and your heart beats fast and your stomach goes to shaking—that's how I feel. But I got something to fear about, Miss Perle."

"Call me Ruth, honey. Now what would you have to fear about?"

"Plenty, Miss... Ruth. All I got to wear is this old raggedy dress. Shouldn't I be dressed up or something, if I'm going out into the big world?"

"Don't worry about that. I'll fix you up with some clothes. I've been thinking about that, putting together something for you to wear in my mind. Now what else have you got to fear about?"

"If the Reverend'll let me go, that's what!"

"I could go over with you and talk to him."

"Oh, no, ma'am, please don't do that. He's going to be mad at me already because I left him alone on his time off. I run out a lot on him when he gets drunk, which he does just about every time he comes back from his circuit. But if you came over after me spending the night out, he'd just plum blow up. If he's feeling good, after a time, I might be able to bring him over here and you could talk to him and maybe make him see that I should get a little trip to go off somewhere sometime. Maybe. I got to hope."

"I'll hope with you. I'll get things ready anyway and if it turns out that you can go, then I'll be ready to take you. You go along now and see what you can do."

"It looks hotter'n Baptist hell out there. That's what Garcie always says on hot days. Some people can't walk barefoot on a day like this, but the bottoms of my feet are really tough. Hot sand only makes me go faster."

Her full and proper name was Gullah Garcie Garson. There it was on her birth certificate. She could not see clearly the contents of her tin memory box, but she knew what was in it, the few prizes of her life. There was her grammar school diploma, torn in its folds, a photograph of herself with the first McQueens, Jessie's Grandma and Grandpa (taken when they first came to Fortune Island), other oddments, and, most especially, her ring. She tried to put it on her ring finger but her finger had grown too fat. She held it up to the light, close to her eyes, and turned it about. Gold glitters, and it was real gold. Nothing fake about that ring or the man who gave it to her. No sir!

"Nothing fake about this ring," she said aloud, and just then Jessie rumbled in the door like a surge of the surf. The door flew open and Jessie was sitting at the table across from Garcie so fast she was still talking to herself.

"What's that?" Jessie said. Garcie could not see her too well but she could tell that Jessie was full of beans, piss, and vinegar. "That's a pretty ring." The bright little music of Jessie's words was high and happy. "That's a real pretty ring, Garcie," she sang.

"Can you see what's written on it?" Garcie asked. "Can you see the letters on it?"

Jessie took the ring from Garcie's hand and looked it over. "Says L and L, two Ls. That ain't you, Garcie." She handed the ring back to Garcie.

"No, baby, that stand for Love and Luck."

"Where'd you get it?"

"Got it when I was a young girl from a bass player who was playing in Morehead City. His name was Jimmy 'Twango' James. Oh, he was so handsome, with his neat little mustache, slicked down hair—we used to call it a conk—and skin like cocoa-butter. I swear he had the girls crazy. He played in a jazz band, and he could make the wildest sounds you ever did hear. Thump, thump! Twango, twango! He was about thirty when he came to town, and he already a hero in the big world, and I wasn't much older than you are, and he had the sweet-eye for me. I could tell, because, when he played, he'd be banging and plucking on them strings, but he'd be looking at me and smiling bright with them big white teeth of his. Even asked me to go off with him. Yes he did! I swear to it! He wanted to take me away with him. But I was too young and too scared to do it, and, besides, I had to take care of your maw-maw and paw-paw. They couldn't get along without me. Mister McQueen once said that I was indispensable, *indispensable*. So when Twango was going to leave town, he up and took off this ring and put it on my finger and kissed me good-bye. Just a kiss on the cheek, mind you, but I knew he wanted a lip-smack. He was the sweetest man, was that Twango. Nothing rude or crude about him. Love and Luck, yes siree! And ever since then I have had a weight in my heart that I didn't go off with him. I curse myself for being scared. Listen, baby girl, never be too scared to try a new life. Them's the best words old Garcie can give you. This ring is the only thing I ever got from a black man, besides heartache. It is the golden treasure of my lost love."

"How 'bout the Love and Luck part, Garcie?"

"But the mojo come true. The love I got from your folks, and who can say that you ain't a piece of pure luck? So it all come true. Just that one little thing—Mister Twango gone, but I got him right here in this ring, got him for keeps."

"I got news about that, Garcie, 'bout that very thing, 'bout what you said, not being afraid to try new things?"

"What news, baby?"

"First, the Reverend Cogburn has gone off again. He left this note." She waved a piece of paper before Garcie who could see the whiteness of it with the light on it. "It says that he'll be gone for about a week. He left money with it for us to eat on." She put an envelope on the table. "Oh, and this don't matter, but he also said that he thanked me a lot for keeping him company, meaning, I figure, that he don't thank me at all and was good and sourpussed when he left. But that don't matter. This is the exciting part—there's a lady in the cottage on the dunes says she's gonna take me up the islands on a trip, and you just said that I should make sure not to miss a chance to go someplace, ain't that right? Well, she would like you to sign this paper that says it's okay to take me."

"You talkin' about that Miss Perle up there?"

"Do you know her? Oh, sure you do. She told me she knew you."

"She come by once in a while, sit and talk. I told her the story about the church so full of sinners the tide came and carried it out to sea, and every so often, once't in a while, some fisherman see the mast sticking up like a white water spout out on the ocean, all them sinners drowned. She liked it, that story, said she was gonna put it in a book. She a real nice young lady. Tell you what, I'll sign for you. Gimme that paper and show me where to put my John Hancock."

And at five o'clock, Jessie ran up to Ruth's door waving Garcie's okay like a document of armistice.

"I guess this'll do," Ruth said. "She's *in loco parentis.*"

"Oh, no, ma'am. She ain't crazy. She dang well knew what she was doing when she signed this here paper. And I didn't have to fox her none, neither."

"I'm sure she did and I'm sure you didn't."

Ruth was wearing a terry cloth bathrobe and nothing else that Jessie could see. Her dark hair was hanging down wet and she was rubbing it with a towel. "I just took a bath and I want you to strip down and pop into that tub of water. It's still hot. It took me over an hour to get it all in here in hot bucketsful."

"I didn't expect no bath," said Jessie, eyeing the galvanized, shoe-shaped tub with suspicion.

"We're going on a trip tomorrow morning. We're going to meet people. I don't want you smelling like—"

"I only smell like the sand and the sea."

"And a few other things that come from them. Now come on, get ready. Don't you want to smell nice and sweet for the big world?"

"Does the big world smell nice and sweet? Ain't we all on a big ball of mud and droppings? I'm used to the way I smell."

"That's why you don't notice it."

Ruth wrapped the towel around her hair, took off her robe, and began to dress. Her breasts were large, her body athletic, Venus-like. Jessie gaped at her, awe-struck.

"Wow! I ain't never seen a grown woman naked before."

"Just strip and get in there, young lady. If you knew the trouble I had to go through to get enough hot water for this bath, you'd jump right in. I had to heat all this water outside in the kitchen shack and drag it in here, and I had to drag the tub in first. Now get in there while it's still hot."

"Yes, ma'am."

Ruth looked over the naked Jessie clinically. "God, you're not a tabula rasa, you're a bas relief of bites, abrasions, and bruises. Let me look in your mouth." At first Jessie clamped her mouth shut, but, with a pliers-like combination of finger and thumb, Ruth forced it open, and forced a forefinger inside with an intermittent hum, as if she were looking for pearls and finding sand; but no, she pulled her finger from Jessie's mouth. "It's amazing. Your teeth are in good condition. I don't suppose you get much candy, do you?"

"Don't eat much of anything most of the time."

"Long Tall Sally, thin as a rail. We've got to pack some weight on you. Stay there for a minute. I'm going to take a picture of you so we can check on your progress. One of my jobs is to document everything. I can't exclude you. Right now, you're my most important project." Ruth went to the table and picked up a pack of Lucky Strikes, lit one and let it hang from her lips, then she aimed a Polaroid with a flash bulb at Jessie. "Stand up straight. Good. There. Got it."

"That was like the sun hit me in the eyes. I never seen—saw a camera like that. What kind of camera is that?"

"It's just about the latest thing. It's called a Polaroid Land Camera.

Watch this. This is the best part." She drew a print from the camera, fanned it about for a minute, handed it to Jessie.

"It's a picture of me! I thought you had to send pictures away to make them work."

"Now get in that tub and hurry up and scrub. I've got a pair of blue jeans that should fit you. We'll have to roll the cuffs down, but otherwise... And then we'll take another picture of you, tomorrow morning, dressed and all prettied up."

"I didn't know an adventure was going to be this much work."

"All beginnings are difficult, sunshine. Everything takes effort."

"But I bet everything don't take a bath."

"I'll make us some supper, we can talk and listen to some music and hit the hay early. I'll zip you into that sleeping bag again. We have to be up and at 'em early, dressed and ready to catch the mail boat. Okay, sunshine?"

"This hot water's breaking up my skin. I can feel things falling off me."

"Barnacles, no doubt."

✴ ✴ ✴

Later that night, as Ruth zipped Jessie into the sleeping bag, Tom Judas checked into the hotel across the street from the bus station in Wilmington. He felt satisfied that he had given Capt'n Jack some of what he owed him; the full measure of his indebtedness to Capt'n Jack could never be paid, he knew; but he had spent valuable time that his emotional makeup, the one way arrow his soul had aimed at Fortune Island for over a decade, could ill afford in order to satisfy some of the debt.

Sun Records had decided that there was nothing special about him, nothing unique, which may or may not have been true. Capt'n Jack had thought they had been dead wrong. Tom didn't really care. Success in Memphis might have led him away from his true goal, Fortune Island and the sight of his daughter. If it hadn't been for Capt'n Jack's hectoring insistence, he'd of gone straight to Jessie, not *to* her, but to the sight of her, for he was determined not to interfere with her life, so long as it was a reasonably good one. He had missed so much of her growing up, he owed her so much ungiven attention, that he was determined to watch her and to guide her if he could, but from a distance. He had no fear of being recognized. The dark, rough-hewn man he saw in the mirror was not the white-haired boy who had left the island over a decade ago. He wondered if the idea of disguise had been lurking in him when he took up boxing in prison, or had it come without volition, an accident of time. How long the germ of his present motive had been building in him, he didn't know. It had just come to be. With each passing year of the dozen he had spent in prison, a plan that had almost eluded even himself had been formulated, stage by stage, to a kind of clarity: approach but avoid. Do not bring to your daughter what you brought to your wife. He faced the ceiling of a darkened room and anticipated his first sight of Jessie. She was twelve years old now, nearly thirteen. What would she look like? His heart yearned out of his chest and into the darkness above him. Plus, there was the painful recognition that he must avoid Garcie. Surely she would know him, surely she could see through the dozen years of beatings and black hair dye right into his soul, even with her half-blind eyes, and know him. But if he were to keep watch over his daughter he must avoid the woman who was like a second mother to him. He was used to the fact that for everything given something was always taken. He was used to a lot of sad facts, but he would not inflict them on others. Sometimes he felt himself to be what Garcie might have called a bad mojo man, unlucky, and a bringer of bad luck to others. Deep in the night he scorned himself. Ambitious, optimistic Capt'n Jack had been taught the lesson of disappointment his bad luck brought. But when he boarded the mail boat in the morning for his long-anticipated passage to Fortune Island, where a job he had acquired through an advertisement and an interview-by-mail awaited him, he was determined to be wearing more than his best suit and hat and carrying more than his guitar and suitcase. He would wear and bear the weight of a smile.

✄ ✄ ✄

Jessie's eyes popped open to pearly light. By red morning Ruth had her prepared for the trip. Under an early blue sky Ruth took a photograph of her protégé. In that treasured time-blurred shot, which Jessie would keep and study for over forty-five years, her ringleted hair had been combed and brushed by Ruth to near tameness. She wore a tee-shirt with SMITH COLLEGE written across the front, a pair of unrolled jeans, still an inch or two short for her, and a pair of Ruth's sandals, also a bit short, for her toes curled over the soles. Her first pocketbook, another gift from Ruth, a small leather one, hung on a long thin strap from her shoulder and rested on her hip, a little to the front, her hand holding it there. It was the first time it had occurred to Jessie that she might be, well, if not pretty, at least presentable in the way a young woman ought to be.

"I look like a real girl," she said.

"A very pretty one," Ruth said. "All you needed was a scrub down and a comb out. Now here's our itinerary—"

Jessie looked blank.

"This is what we're going to do." And she told Jessie, as they trudged across the sand dunes with Ruth's logistical haversacks on their backs and cameras dangling from their shoulders, that they were going to stop at the general store, and the sheriff would row them out to the mail boat in his skiff, or motor them if his outboard was working, which it rarely was, and then they were going to take the mail boat to Ocracoke, where a vehicle awaited, and from there they would drive up the Outer Banks to a place called Manteo and interview a musician named Capt'n Jack Midgett.

The mail boat was a pretty little white steamer about fifty feet long with gray trim and a red, white, and black smokestack emitting dark, immediately dissipating little puffs against the now deep-blue sky and the silken white clouds that hovered in it. Down its starboard side hung a black metal platform with stairs leading to the deck, where a passenger stood waiting to disembark. Gay and glad, the mail boat bobbed out there, ready to take Jessie away to her first great adventure, itself a glimpse of a heretofore unknowable world.

The Sheriff pulled at the oars for a time, puffed and pulled, then stopped about thirty feet from the mail boat to wipe his wet forehead with a damp handkerchief. "I'm getting too old for this," he said; then, brightening, "Lookee yonder, ladies! You see that there feller waiting to get off? That's my new strong back standing there. Don't look like it, does he, in that there seersucker suit and straw Stetson, but I'm gonna have him in dirty work clothes before this skiff has to go out again," and he began pulling painfully at the oars once more, drawing the skiff closer to the mail boat, so that Jessie and Ruth could get a better look at the newcomer, the mysterious stranger who looked intently down at them.

"Look," Jessie said. "He's got a guitar case."

"Quite the dude, ain't he?" said Sheriff Walkup. "But he looks strong enough for what I need."

"He looks good enough to eat," Ruth said.

"He's beautiful," Jessie whispered.

"Watch out, ladies," said Walkup. "He's mine."

They climbed aboard as the stranger tipped his hat in greeting and gave them a big smile, aimed, it seemed, especially at Jessie, who noticed that his hand was shaking with surprising violence. The hand holding the hat had a hard time finding the head to put it on, like a silent screen comedian with a cane up his back. Ruth noticed that, but in the excitement of boarding a found curiosity was lost.

This was his daughter, Tom thought, with a ninety-nine and nine-tenths percent certainty, this was Jessie, the object of his hopes and fears for a decade, the invisible visitor to his cell, to his consciousness, his conscience, and his dreams, and he felt the shock of recognition as he had felt many a punch in the gut when he had boxed. That was his own gangly body in young female form, that was Susannah's hair, the flame of Susannah's youth, before the fading began. Prison had hardened him. He thought the armor he had acquired there could not be dented, let alone fall away, as he felt that it was doing now, with a secret crash on deck. Behind the Wall he had learned the trick of letting his tears run down the backs of his eyes, unseen, and he gripped himself with a will to pull off this trick again, now, to hide the tears of joy he felt but could not show, would not show, that they should betray him, his purpose and plan. He helped Jessie—he thought he felt an electric shock when he took her arm—and her friend up with their paraphernalia, handed down the mail bag, his guitar case, and a battered old suitcase. Up close, his creased and leathery face looked just as good to them, but surprisingly pale, as if he had spent too much time in juke joints, playing that old guitar, or perhaps hadn't slept for several days. They were sorry to see him go, climb down into the skiff.

Walkup put him right to work. Set him to rowing back to the island. Before he got very far from the mail boat, he stopped, turned around, and waved his Stetson like a cowboy. It struck Ruth as an impulsive gesture. "He's a romantic," she said.

"What's a romantic?"

"Somebody who would do that."

Tom put his hat back on and pulled at the oars. "What's the matter with the outboard?" he asked.

"I was hoping you'd tell me," said Walkup. "Sometimes it works, sometimes it don't."

"Spark plug?"

"I tried that."

"I'll take a look at it. Where are those two going? I hope they're not moving away, just when I get here."

"Just up to Manteo for a day or two, I think."

"Who's the lady?"

"She's a writer. Down from Boston. She's been down before. Interviews the locals. I suspect she's a wealthy woman, but what I like about her, she don't act it. Nice as pie."

"And the girl?" Tom said, feeling certain that he knew, that no one could tell him that that wasn't Jessie, that that red hair could belong to anyone else but Susannah's child.

"That's Jessie McQueen, the only kid on the island. I don't know if you realize how isolated you're going to be, Mister. I tried to make that clear in the ad and in my letters, but people always think, Well, it can't be that bad. Let me tell you about Fortune Island, son. There ain't many people here and most of them are planning to leave. Me and Buttercup—that's my wife—we'd leave too, but I can't sell the store. Beside the general store there's only one real house on the island—the McQueen—I mean, the Cogburn house. Used to be the McQueen house, but the McQueens are all gone, except for Jessie. Cogburn is her stepfather. He's what they call a Sad Traveller, a preacher, off on the mainland most of the time. Their house is up on Whalehead, high ground, mostly dunes, at the northern end. Only one other dwelling up there, but way on the other side, and that's a shack owned by Miss Perle, the woman with young Jessie. Just in front of the dunes there's another shack. That's where old Garcie lives. Black woman. Good old soul. Then there's a whole stretch of nothing, sand flats, mud flats, ankle deep in water a lot of the time, sun-cracked the rest. South of that, where we're going, is Fortune Island Village—our general store, back of which is the shack where you'll live, the church, the black graveyard and the white graveyard, and about twenty-five fishing shacks, only a little more than half occupied. There's no phones on the island. So you won't be calling your girlfriend, if you have one. There's no electric power. We islanders cook in what we call summer kitchens, little shacks, or lean-tos, outside the big shacks. It's too hot to cook inside in the summer. They cook with kerosene. Even Miss Perle cooks with kerosene in her summer kitchen. See what I meant? She's regular. She's good folks. Down-to-earth. The only real kitchen, aside from ours in the general store, is in the Cogburn house. Everybody heats with kerosene in winter. The general store has got a generator, so we can play a radio and listen for the next storm, and the storms hit us hard here, each and every one, like they just aim for us. So far, it's only the skirts that have whacked us. I'm afraid a big one will wipe the island clean some day. And now there's a lot of talk about the National Park Service taking over the island. I bought a pig in a poke, son, a big mistake but too late to take back. Frankly, I got to wonder about anybody who'd come out here. Did I tell you that I was Sheriff of Carteret County once? You're not running away from something, are you?"

"Only myself, Sheriff. Love gone wrong. Everything you describe as bad sounds good to me. I just want to do my job and be left alone."

"A time for healing, eh?"

"Do I row this skiff to that dock or up on the sand?"

"We'll tie up at the dock. I believe my Buttercup will have something to eat waiting for us. You know, son, I can't afford you, but I've got to have you. You don't want to buy the store, do you?"

"Don't have the money."

"I'll sell cheap."

"Don't have cheap."

"I figured."

Chapter
Ten

J essie thrilled at everything she could touch, smell, or see—the rust on the iron rails of the mail boat, rails that she gripped, white-knuckled, the wake coming from the bow and scudding out in milky foam, spraying her face, the spindrift that dampened her hair, the sudden distance between herself and Fortune Island, the clouds racing across the sky, competing with her fearful enthusiasm for the future. The lighthouse she often saw from Fortune Island, the one that seemed a low, twinkling star in the night, was soon looming before her, tall, conical, and stark white.

She turned to Ruth. "I feel all mixed up with wanting what's up ahead and scared of it and glad to leave that old island and scared of leaving it, too."

"When you've been as many places as I have," said Ruth, "coming and going doesn't mean that much. You'll get used to it."

On Ocracoke, Ruth unveiled a miracle. Behind a building housing a restaurant in the center of town, Ruth pulled a tarpaulin from a huge, squarish vehicle, with a "Voila!"

"Well! I have never in all my born days seen anything like that! That's the biggest, toughest looking, flat-faced dog of a thing I ever did see. What is it?"

"It's called a Land Rover, one very expensive dog. When I get it barking, it'll take us over mountains and dunes and—" Ruth folded the tarpaulin as she spoke. "—well, just about anywhere. That's what it's made for. Come on! Climb in!"

The Rover bulled out of the alley between the restaurant and the building next door and on up the street. In minutes it was roaring along a road of pounded sand, then flying along a beach near the surf. Thrilled and scared, Jessie looked admiringly at Ruth, who drove this monster nonchalantly with a cigarette clenched in her teeth.

Jessie yelled, "I just plumb don't think you're scared of anything, Miss Ruth."

"What? I can't hear you."

They bounced, jumped, and leaped on for fifteen miles, sometimes on the beach, sometimes on the road, sometimes, it seemed to Jessie, they stayed in the air for miles on end. Her first lovely hairdo was in wild disarray by the time they reached the Frazier Peele ferry landing at Hatteras Inlet. Ruth drove the Rover up planks and on to the ferry. They got out of the Rover to stretch their legs. As they made the crossing to Hatteras, Ruth, unfazed, spent some time reshaping Jessie's hair. "I don't want you looking feral," she said. She saw the blank look in Jessie's eyes. "Like a wild girl."

"Do I look like a wild girl?"

"Not now," Ruth said, smoothing back her hair, pushing here and there. "Now you look like you're ready for Atlantic City."

"Where's Atlantic City?"

"Up north. That's where the Miss America contests are held. We're going to get you ready to be a Miss America, in more ways than one."

"Miss America. That's real good, isn't it? Do you think I could do that?"

"You never know what you can do until you try, honey."

"Where are we?"

"Just a hop, skip, and a jump from Cape Hatteras. If you like lighthouses, they've got a big one there."

And then they were bouncing along again and Ruth didn't even slow down when they came to the big lighthouse, bigger than the one they had passed in Ocracoke. "That's the Cape Hatteras lighthouse," Ruth called, dangerously taking her right hand from the jumping steering wheel of the Rover to point at what Jessie thought was one of the greatest wonders she had ever seen—or almost seen, so fast did it recede from view, that lonely giant peppermint stick. Her eyes glued to it, she had to pull them loose, and turn her head almost all the way around to face front. Everything was like that with Ruth—whizzbang! "We're heading up Hatteras to Oregon Inlet," Ruth called. Jessie nodded her agreement. She had noticed by now that disagreeing with Ruth was useless. But then she yelled, "When are we going to eat?"

"When we get there," Ruth yelled back over the growls of the Rover and the roar of the surf. "Eat one of those peanut butter sandwiches I fixed. We don't have time to stop now. I want to get to Manteo in plenty of time to do my work and take you to a play tonight. We're going to see 'The Lost Colony,' by Paul Green—"

"Get where?" Jessie yelled, aiming a bouncing sandwich at her mouth. "See what? Who's Paul Green?"

"Manteo," Ruth yelled back. "I have friends there. I told you about Capt'n Jack Midgett, didn't I? The play's about Virginia Dare, the first English child born in America."

"But if you have friends, Ruth, why do you live so far away from them? Why do you live on Fortune Island, where there isn't hardly anybody but me and Garcie and Buttercup and a few others?"

"What? Why do I live on Fortune Island?" She looked over at Jessie, who nodded affirmatively. "Because it's the perfect place to write, my honeylamb. I do my collecting up and down the Banks—like this—then I bring it back to Fortune Island, where there isn't anybody to bother me, and I can concentrate and write."

Jessie thought about that for a moment, then said, "Ruth, am I going to bother you?"

Ruth gave her a quick, disturbed look. "Not you, honey, never you. Don't you ever worry about that."

But, once thought of, it did worry Jessie. She sat on in silence until they crossed the Oregon Inlet. The ferry here was much bigger than the one they had taken earlier, full of cars below and people on the promenade deck.

"Why the frown, honey?"

"I been thinking. All this is maybe too good to be true."

"It's as true as your red head, honey."

"But you'll go away and then it'll be over."

"It won't ever be over, I promise you."

"I want to be just like you, Ruth."

"That's sweet, honey, but I don't want you to be like me. Nobody should be like anybody else. I want you to be like you. I want you to become more you than you are, more than you know you are." She gave Jessie a hug at the shoulders. "Carpe diem, quam minimum credula postero. Seize the day, sweetheart, don't worry about tomorrow. It'll take care of itself."

"I feel blubbery."

"Let it go, then. No one will see. Just keep your face to the water and the water birds. Watch their great wild rising. They'll lift your spirits with them. After all, sweetheart, you're just excited. You really have nothing to fear and everything to look forward to."

The young woman and the young girl held each other and looked out at the perpetually undecided sea with its appearing and disappearing fractals that was Oregon Inlet until the ferry landing loomed before them, breaking the spell of intimacy in infinity, of constancy in eternity, of bonding. Water shuffled and gulls fluttered off into space, seeking organization out of the tropism that is loneliness—formation, order, perhaps the victorious V of migration. Time had paused in what had already become the past, but it was on the move again.

Whizbang! In fewer than twenty miles of paved road, they came to a populated area, took a hard left and crossed the bridge to Roanoke Island, where they stopped for gas at a very dirty filling station with a redundancy of drunken, rednecked attendants. Just beyond that, they turned off onto a dirt road and drove under a wooden ranch-style sign inviting them to enter CAPT'N JACK'S DACHA. There was a sandy, quarter-mile, roller-coaster ride downhill, to a trestled wooden bridge about fifty feet long and ten or fifteen feet above the deepest declivity of a small flood plain, a kind of canyon, rip-rapped in places, an ice-cream scoop out of the earth, that must have been well below sea level. The Land Rover rumbled across the bridge and began to climb a crushed-shell and gravelled road up to the house, giving the illusion that the house sat on a hill, although it could not have sat any more than five feet above sea level. Off to both sides of the road were scrub pine, clumps of tall wild grass, and waves of rock-strewn sand, as far as Jessie could see, but at the top of the prominence, not to say, hill, she saw a huge oak, a big green leafy hand that seemed to hold the house in place. On the grade, a few feet below the house, Jessie saw a small flagstone patio, a kind of lookout, with stone steps unevenly leading up to house level. Then the Rover veered to the left, toward the big oak tree, and stopped beneath it. Jessie's telescopic young eyes spied garden plots to the left and right of the house, and thick trees beyond. But she focused on the ramshackle, frame house, sprawling with jerry-built additions, separated second floors, like huge gables, at each end of the sprawl.

"What a crazy-looking place!" Jessie cried. "But I like it! I love it! It's like fifty fishermen's shacks all stacked up on each other."

"Every time Maggie has a baby," Ruth said, "Capt'n Jack builds another room." Ruth lit a Lucky Strike, took a good look at it, then savored a drag. "Every time I come out here," she said, exhaling, "the house has either climbed out to the sides or up into the oak tree."

"How many children does he have?"

Ruth sat relaxing behind the wheel for a moment, enjoying her Lucky. She was tired from driving. "Countless, it seems. Come on, shybaby, let's go face the music." It was hard to get the doors open for the crowd that had gathered around the Rover. Maggie Midgett appeared on the porch, waving, a big, round matron in full command. "You kids get your little asses back to work and let those people breathe," she called, and what seemed dozens of big eyes vanished from the Rover's windows. Maggie approached, like a fast tank on rolling treads, as Ruth and Jessie hit the ground.

"Hi, Maggie," Ruth called.

"Hi, yourself! Been cooking up a storm." She gave Ruth a kiss on the cheek. "Now who's that hiding behind you?"

Ruth pulled Jessie to the fore. "This is Jessie McQueen, my very good friend. Jessie, this is Maggie Midgett—call her Miss Maggie—my very old and dear friend. We just ran into a bunch of rowdies down at the filling station, Maggie, and I think they scared Jessie a little bit." Ruth caught Jessie by the shoulders and planted her firmly in front of Miss Maggie. "She's not used to people in bunches."

"Didn't scare me none," Jessie asserted, feeling a little ashamed of herself. She stared at her feet, at her long toes curling over Ruth's short sandals. When she looked up, a huge man stood behind Miss Maggie. He was wearing nothing but bib overalls and was puffing on a pipe.

"Don't let that old hootenanny of redneck greasemonkeys and pumpjockeys down at the filling station scare you any," he said. He had a barrel chest from which a voice not so much deep as powerful seemed to come in controlled explosions, like the hum of the Land Rover. He adjusted his pipe and reached a huge paw out to Jessie. "Call me Capt'n Jack," he said. Capt'n Jack saw before him the fabled child of Tom Judas, the, to him, famous orphan of Fortune Island. A tall, slim, slip of a thing, her body belonged to Tom's, and the mass of her unruly red hair at the top of it proclaimed her to be the daughter of Susannah, the redhead of whom Capt'n Jack had heard so much. Capt'n Jack clenched the stem of his pipe with his big strong white teeth and puffed a honeyed smoke signal up before his eyes in reminder of the fact that he had vowed to keep Tom's secret. And he would honey his words for this girl's sake, and they would be the words of an amnesiac when it came to his knowledge of Jessie's origins. Tom's secret was safe with him, though he doubted that Tom had chosen the right course of action.

Jessie knew that she was being awkward, but somehow couldn't control herself. She was having a mild fit of what looked like St. Vitus's dance, stepping back and forth over her own feet. "Calm down, baby," Ruth said, holding her shoulders. The gas station attendants had unnerved her, it was true, but she hated the fact that people could tell. And now there was all this: children looking at her, some laughing—why?—children everywhere beyond Capt'n Jack and Miss Maggie, children of all sizes and ages, it seemed, running in and out of the house with trays of food, too busy, as yet, to greet her—or not allowed to come forward—for which fact she was grateful. So many pairs of eyes to look at her, to see the loneliness in her, to see that she had never had a friend her own age, scarcely a friend at all. It was daunting. She was desperate to think how to act, what to say, and do.

Now, as if her ears had popped open, Jessie heard Miss Maggie say, "You must be hungry after that long drive—well, you just scoot over to that table and dig in." She pointed to the huge picnic table. "There's cold chicken and potato salad and iced tea or, if you want, Co-Cola. I won't bother introducing you to all these brats, you just meet 'em as you may." But she called out to one of the kids, "Marie, come over here and drag this girl to the table."

A pretty blonde girl, a bit older than Jessie, came over and took Jessie's hand. "Come on," she said, pulling her. She led Jessie over to the picnic table, overhung by oak tree boughs. The table was covered by a white sheet pretending to be a table cloth and laden with food.

"She's got stage fright," Ruth told Maggie. "I'll tell you about her later."

"Well," said Maggie, "she better learn quick the boarding house reach or she won't get anything to eat, with this wild bunch. Nobody around here can afford to be shy. I better see to her." Maggie winked and went to the picnic table. "You come, too," she called back.

Ruth said: "Good to see you again, Jack."

"Must be six months, darlin'. I've got a new collection of songs to sing into your machine. After lunch, I'll get out my banjo. Oh, and I got me a beautiful new balalaika. I'll play some Russian folk songs for you later. How's your book doing?"

"My agent quit and ran off to Hollywood with her actor boyfriend. I'm looking for somebody now."

"The one that handled *Legends of Appalachia*?"

"Same," Ruth said, exhaling smoke from nose and mouth. "She threw away a successful career for the guy. Wants to be the wife of a movie star. Wants a picket fence in Beverly Hills—shop at the Farmer's Market in Hollywood—buy her house dresses and aprons on Rodeo Drive. How many writers she left sitting on their books, God only knows!"

"I may have somebody for you. My anthology of folk songs is about complete. It's sort of an alternative to Sandburg's *American Song Bag*. Of course, Carl's got a bigger name than I have—"

"You're more famous than you know."

"Whatever! But this agent... She's the first black graduate of one of the Ivy League law schools up north. Her name's Victoria Underhill. She's the daughter of the Reverend Edgar Underhill, the civil rights activist. I'm sure you know of him."

"Of course."

"I'm sorry to say he won't be able to be here for our party, but Victoria's expected. She's just a kid, but brilliant—graduated law school at twenty-two, but had no interest in practicing. Instead, she joined some big literary agency, stayed long enough to learn the business and develop some clients and slam-bang opened her own agency. She's hungry for new talent. I'll introduce you. Say, you heard about Brown versus the Board, didn't you? I mean, who knows what you heard, off on that desert island of yours—"

"Yes, it's wonderful!"

"If jingle-balls Ike would come out of his coma once in a while, kids all over this land could get an equal education. Now that we got Brown versus the Board out of the Supreme Court, separate just plain ain't equal. That's the law of the land now and what it should have been from the beginning. So why doesn't Ike do something about it? There's black kids all over this country, in second-rate schools, waiting for something to happen."

Stepping up to them, Maggie said, "Let's lay off the politics, Jack. Let's have some fun this afternoon."

"That's what you get for marrying a Red, Maggie, my darling."

Maggie said, "Come on, Ruth, and get something to eat. You can't live on cigarettes."

"Did Jessie eat?"

"Like a bird. Marie is giving her the grand tour. Who is she, anyway? Where did you get her?"

"I found her in the middle of the night wrapped in a blanket, sleeping on the sand dunes, being eaten alive by sand fleas, mosquitoes, and crabs." Ruth went on to tell Maggie what she knew about Jessie.

At the picnic table, Capt'n Jack slugged down half a water glass of vodka, showed interest in Ruth's variations on Jessie, but said nothing, only occasionally grunting and puffing on his pipe.

Marie and Jessie went to Capt'n Jack's workroom. As Marie always did, she ignored the KEEP OUT sign. They sat on the floor, surrounded by Capt'n Jack's albums. *"Capt'n Jack Sings Songs of the Great Depression* was Pa's first album," Marie said, handing it to Jessie. There was a picture of Capt'n Jack on the cover, an apple in one hand and a tin cup in the other. The tin cup bore the legend, "Brother, Can You Spare a Dime." Marie said, "Next came *Capt'n Jack Sings Sea Shanties*, and so on—sings this, sings that."

"Was your daddy a captain in the army?"

"Lord no! He's against the military. He's a pacifist. Some of his friends just started calling him Capt'n. I guess 'cause he looks like some kind of captain, don't you think?"

"What's more important than a captain?"

"A major, a colonel, a general, an admiral."

"I think he looks like an admiral. He sure is big enough to be an admiral."

"He says Captain is good enough for him. He don't like big-wigs and he don't like high-faluting people, no siree, not one little bit, that's the way he says it. He always says you should be able to talk with kings but never lose the common touch. He likes to say that but he doesn't like the man who wrote it. Kipling—that's the man—was an imperialist, he says. Do you know what that is?"

"No."

"Neither do I—exactly—but it's something bad if Pa don't like it. My daddy knows more about everything than almost anybody I ever heard of. He sure knows heaps more than my teachers at school, and you should see the people that come to see him. We had a senator here one day. Spent the whole day listening to Pa play and sing. And they stoked away a whole case of beer between them, too. Say, what's the matter with you?"

"I don't know," said Jessie. "Since I ate that chicken I've been having cramps something awful."

"Well, it wasn't the chicken. Those chickens were fresh killed. We got a chicken coop out back with enough chickens and eggs for the whole county. We grow most of our own food. That's what a dacha is in Russia, a little private family farm. I done wopped off one of their heads myself. Ain't it the wildest thing, how chickens run around with no heads? Pa says they're Republicans."

Jessie scanned the walls. "Who're all those people in the pictures?"

"That one there," said Marie, pointing, "is Pa with Carl Sandberg, the poet, and that's Pa and Burl Ives, the singer—they look like brothers, don't they?—that there is an old picture of Pa when he was younger with the governor of Louisiana, Mister Huey Long. Governor Long wrote the song 'Every Man a King,' and he and Pa were singing it together, Pa playing the guitar. That black man over there, that's Mister Jimmy 'Twango' James, the bass player. That's a bass fiddle he's holding. He's a great jazzman. He'll be here tomorrow, but he don't look like that picture anymore. He's real old."

"Now that name sounds really familiar to me, like I heard it somewhere—that 'Twango.'"

"Oh, he's famous! And that one over there, that's Mister Tom Judas. Ain't he pretty, all dressed up in that cowboy outfit?"

"Him, too! I could swear I've seen him someplace."

"You ever go to the movies?"

"Never been."

"Never been to a picture show? Wow! Well, if you ever had been to a picture show you would see his likeness to Henry Fonda, who is a big movie star. I could just fall in love with him."

"You could? Why?"

"Cause he's pretty! Can't you see that? When Mister Judas was here, he looked so much like Henry Fonda, I almost fell in love with him, I swear I did. Pa says Tom Judas could be a big star but that he don't care enough about his career. Ain't that a shame? Oh, and that one over there—that's Woody Guthrie, a famous singer and songwriter, and that's Pete Seeger with him. He's a singer, too. Hey, what's the matter with you? You look green. I got to show you to momma. Come on."

In the living room, Ruth and Capt'n Jack sat across from each other, Ruth's large tape recording machine between them. Capt'n Jack pounded on a banjo and sang—

> "What shall we do with a drunken sailor?
> What shall we do with a drunken sailor?
> What shall we do with a drunken sailor?
>   Early in the morning?
>
> Way-hay, up she rises

> Way-hay, up she rises
> Way-hay, up she rises
>   Early in the morning.

> Put him in the long boat 'til he's sober
> Put him in the long boat 'til he's sober
> Put him in the long boat 'til he's sober
>   Early in the morning.

"Of course, there are other responses," said Capt'n Jack. "You see, you've got shanties for every kind of activity. That's what you call a heaving shanty. There's short-haul shanties, halyard and long-drag shanties, capstan, windlass, and pumping shanties, a shanty for anything you might be doing. It's the rhythm of the shanty makes the work easier, keeps the morale up."

"I didn't realize that," said Ruth.

"Sure, it's like workers in a cotton field, you know how the rhythm helps them to pick." For emphasis, Capt'n Jack picked a few bars of "Swing Low, Sweet Chariot" on the banjo. "Like that," he said. He put down his banjo and picked up his pipe just as Maggie came in.

"Better come with me, Ruth," she said. "Your little friend is having a problem."

"Hold that thought, Jack," Ruth said. "I'll be right back." She snapped off the tape machine.

"I'll just get the next number ready," said Jack, lifting a tall glass of vodka to his lips. "You're going to like this one, especially. I heard an old fisherman humming it and I put the words to it myself."

In the hall, Maggie said, "Marie brought her to me, green at the gills. When I said she looked sick, she ran into the bathroom and locked herself in. Now she won't answer the door."

"Maybe it's all the excitement. I told you how isolated she's been. Maybe the excitement has upset her stomach."

"I know it can do it to me, around here. Poor baby. I thought putting on the feed-bag would do her some good, but maybe it was too much for her."

The bathroom door was closed and locked. In front of it, Marie was waiting for help. Ruth knocked on the door. "Jessie, it's Ruth. What's the matter?"

"Ruth," Jessie called, in a weak voice, "please, help me! There's something wrong with me. It's terrible!"

Ruth turned to Maggie and Marie. "You two go ahead, I'll take care of this."

Maggie said, "I hope she's all right, poor kid. Call me if you need me."

Ruth said, "You've got to let me in, Jessie, or I can't help."

The door opened a crack. "Have they gone?"

"Nobody's here but me."

Jessie opened the door and let Ruth in. She closed and locked it behind Ruth. "Oh, Ruth, I'm so scared! Something terrible has happened to me." Ruth studied her for a moment, and whirled her around. Just as she thought. "Oh, baby, you've had an accident, that's all."

"What do you mean? I'm bleeding! I'm bleeding from my secret place."

"Is this the first time?"

"Yes, ma'am. It never happened before."

"It never occurred to me, but I don't suppose anybody's ever told you a thing, have they?"

"About what?"

"You see, honey, most girls are told by somebody before this happens."

"This happens to other girls?"

"To all normal girls. You're having a period. You've become a woman. You can have a baby now. And if you aren't made pregnant—"

"How do you get made pregnant?"

"Sort of like that octopus story you told me, but by a man. I'll tell you all about it when we get home. But right now, there isn't anything wrong with you."

"But I've got cramps."

"A lot of the discomfort will leave you now that you know it's perfectly normal, which it is. I'll get you a couple of aspirins." She went to the medicine cabinet, found the aspirins, and something else. "And here, you can take a couple of spoonfuls of Lydia Pinkham's Vegetable Compound. At twenty percent alcohol, you ought to be feeling no pain in no time."

Inspired, Jessie said, "I never put what animals do together with what people do. But we're nature, too, aren't we?"

"Of course. What else would we be?"

"But the Bible says—but the Reverend Cogburn says—"

"The Bible is a poetic way of telling about life, but not a scientific way. And as for the Reverend Cogburn—"

"He can eat spit!" cried Jessie.

"Well—"

Jessie laughed, and Ruth saw a little color coming into her cheeks. She realized that Jessie had been scared to death. Then Jessie frowned. "You too?"

Ruth thought for a moment, then saw what Jessie meant. "All women. All healthy women. Now you stay here and I'll go and get you a clean pair of jeans and underclothes. I'll be right back with a Kotex pad. You take off your pants and wash yourself up a little. There's nothing to worry about. I'll be right back. Throw some cold water on your face. Brighten up. There's nothing wrong with you."

Ruth started to go, but Jessie seized her arm. "Biology?"

Ruth nodded. "Biology, baby."

Maggie asked Ruth if she thought it was a good idea to take Jessie to see "The Lost Colony" that evening. "Oh, she'll be all right now," Ruth said. "It was mostly overexcitement and fear. We can get through the play. If we didn't see it, after I promised her, I think she'd be pretty disappointed. But I've been thinking about driving home right after the play. I think the poor kid is worn out, and she can sleep all the way home."

"You can't do that," Capt'n Jack said. "I've got a load of people coming tomorrow—a lot of people you'd want to meet—jazzmen, R and B, folk singers—people from all around the country. It's a big chance for you to meet them. We're going to have a regular Capt'n Jack's Jamboree! You take the girl to the play and let her get a good night's sleep tonight and you'll see, she'll settle in. She'll be fine. There'll be music all day and she'll love it. Besides, the ferries won't be running till morning."

"I thought we might camp on the beach until morning."

"Nonsense!" exclaimed Capt'n Jack. "You'll be eaten alive. Besides, are you forgetting? Victoria Underhill will be here. We both have business with her."

Jessie and Marie came in. Jessie was wearing a clean pair of jeans and a pretty pink blouse, borrowed from Marie. Maggie said, "Now look how pretty our Jessie looks."

Marie said, "She wanted to wear a dress but I told her she shouldn't wear a dress out there to see that play out of doors in the evening, that the mosquitoes'll eat her alive."

Capt'n Jack slapped his knee. "What'd I just say?"

Marie said, "I gave her some citronella to rub on her arms. She's fine, Ruth. She wants to go, don't you, Jess?"

"Honest, Ruth, I feel heaps better. That Lydia Pinkham's stuff is really great. I could drink some more of that."

"You've had enough Lydia Pinkham, my girl," said Ruth. "I told you it was twenty percent alcohol, more than some wines."

"And I sure do want to see a real play," Jessie went on, "like 'The Lost Colony' by Mister Paul Green. Marie's been telling me about it. She's seen it, how many times, Marie?"

"I think it's six times. It's really good. It's all about the first English settlers and what happened to them and how the first English child born in North America—named Virginia Dare—got lost with the whole colony. Once I saw it, Andy Griffith played Sir Walter Raleigh. He was great! Very handsome with his mustache and goatee."

Jessie said, "Please, Ruth!"

"Okay," said Ruth, "if you think you're up to it. Lost Colony, here we come!"

Chapter
Eleven

The waterside amphitheatre on Roanoke Island was surrounded by a thick forest of trees. They parked the Rover in the crowded lot and walked with others down a footpath to the theatre. It was about dusk. The trees swooshed in the wind. As they came into the theatre, looking for seats, there was plenty of light, but soon darkness fell on the audience and the stage lit up. Sitting next to Ruth, stars overhead, hearing the strangely clear voices of the cast, the wind-ruffled costumes bedazzling her, Jessie whispered to Ruth, "It's like magic, it's like magic," over and over again during the course of the play. And when the settlers on the stage walked off into the dark woods, surrendering to the time that never came, when the ship would return with supplies, such a tortured cry came from Jessie's mouth that those sitting nearby turned to her, momentarily distracted from the play, afraid of what might be wrong with the sobbing girl, and, realizing she had been overtaken by her emotions, turned back to the stage in relief. Jessie seemed to take, not the memory, but the actuality of the play home with her. "How could England just leave those poor people there? It's the worse thing anybody can do to anybody else—desert them." And even as mooncrowned night fluttered black wings outside the window, even as sleepy Ruth and wakeful Jessie were tucked in bed, Jessie kept the play alive. "I almost cried when the sail moved away against the night sky. I mean, you know the ship is never going to come back and find them. And what will become of poor little Virginia Dare? What do you suppose ever happened to her, Ruth?"

"Maybe she grew up like you—on an island by herself."

"Do you think so?"

"Jessie, honey, I'm exhausted. You said you could only go to sleep if you slept with me, and here you are, wide awake in the middle of the night. Poor Marie was so hurt that you wouldn't sleep with her."

"I'm embarrassed. I don't have any nightclothes."

"I should have brought you something, but Marie would have lent you some jammies."

"But suppose I had another accident? I didn't want to spoil Marie's pretty things."

"Oh, flapdoodle! Everything's under control. But I'm glad to see that you liked the play so much."

"Oh, I'll never forget it! It'll be stuck in my memory like those Liberty ships in Wilmington. I'll never, ever forget 'The Lost Colony.' Thank you so much for taking me to see it. It must be wonderful to see Shakespeare—Romeo and Juliet, the kissing and all. And you know that man who played Sir Walter Raleigh? He looked like a picture from a book of Shakespeare's plays I've got in my treasure trove, with that pointy beard and that mustache curled up at the ends. Ruth, what are men like? I mean—"

"I know what you mean. I'll tell you what, I'll put it this way, men are like an adventure—difficult but worth it."

"Do men care about the same things as women?"

"Women have their problems and men have theirs. But basically, you might say, men and women care about the same things in different ways. Men want families, homes, just like women."

"And I'm a woman now, ain't I?"

"Aren't I. You know better than that. And yes, baby, I guess I'd say that you are sort of an apprentice woman, and before you ask me what apprentice means, apprentice, in this context, means a woman starting out, learning the ways of being a woman."

"Ruth, you know what I would like to be? I would like to be a great woman, like you and Miss Rachel Carson." Jessie pushed at Ruth's back. "Ruth, you're snoring!"

"Was I? Well, I was listening. So you want to be a great woman like Miss Rachel Carson, do you? Here's how to do that—act the way you want to be and soon you'll be the way you act."

Jessie thought about that. She thought about it until she heard Ruth begin to snore again and then she thought about it some more. "Act the way you want to be and soon you'll be the way you act. I'll do it," she vowed. She heard an owl hoot and shut her eyes to listen, shut her eyes to listen, shut her eye... But the best she could achieve was an intermittent, shallow sleep, like a swimmer just below the surface, and, when she flung herself on her back, light had invaded the room. She opened her eyes to see the light traverse the ceiling and then dim. Their guest room was ground level. She realized that a vehicle was parking outside. Now she could hear it, and voices too, and she got up to look. To the east, the big red yolk of the day had already broken somewhere out on the Atlantic, and she could see that a very large vehicle, a bus, had pulled into the front yard. She blinked to clear her vision. She could just make out what was written along the side of the bus: CAPT'N JACK'S MUSICAL... JAM... JAMBOREE. Ruth snorted in her sleep. Jessie turned to look and saw that the room was filled with feathery, opalescent light. Beside Ruth, on the night table, were a few of Ruth's things—a pair of dark glasses, a cigarette lighter, a pack of Lucky Strikes, some coins. Jessie jumped up from the floor by the window and went to the night table, shook out a cigarette from the package, put it to her mouth, and let it hang the way Ruth did. She had noticed that everyone did whatever they did in a special way. This was the way Ruth did it, put it between her lips and let it hang. Often she talked over it, or around it. Then, sometimes, Ruth would hold it out and look at it before she took a puff. Jessie thought Ruth was probably trying to see how much of it was left. She pretended the cigarette was lit. She held it out and looked at it, but of course it hadn't shrunk. Everyone walked differently too. Ruth took long steps. Jessie let the cigarette dangle from her lips, and took three long steps back to the window. She sat down and watched the men, who were no longer trying to be quiet about their work, as they set up a platform. The thud and hollow ring of lumber coming in contact with lumber broke slumber, woke Ruth, who sat up and said, "What's going on?" Jessie jerked the cigarette from her mouth and threw it in a dark corner. "There's a bunch of men working out there," she told Ruth, in a shaky voice. Ruth's thick black hair was in wild disarray. She shook a cigarette from the pack, lit it, and held it away to look at it, then put it between her lips and let it dangle. Jessie watched intently, stifling a giggle. "What is it?" Ruth said.

Jessie caught her breath and said, "Everyone is so..."

"What?"

"...themselves!" exclaimed Jessie, after a moment's thought.

Ruth said, "That must be Capt'n Jack's boys setting up for the party. We better get our clothes on."

Jessie strode across the room and got in bed next to Ruth. "It's exciting," she said. "What's going to happen?"

"I expect Maggie'll be in the kitchen, fixing everybody a big farm breakfast. A lot of people will be coming in all day, black and white folks from all over. Mostly musicians, I expect. There'll be a lot of playing. A lot of getting to know each other." She lit one cigarette from another. "I expect Maggie'll put out a big buffet so that people can help themselves. We'll have to chip in and help her get things together. In fact, I think I hear another car coming in now. Hey, sleepyhead, wake up." Ruth nudged Jessie. "I bet you didn't get a wink of sleep."

Jessie heard Ruth's voice, but Ruth seemed far away, in another world. She heard cars, voices, music, and, when she woke, Ruth was gone, and the room was bright and hot. Jazz poured into the cups of her ears but she didn't know what it was, only that it was warm and happy music. She jumped up and got dressed, pulling on Marie's jeans and her Smith College tee-shirt, slipping her feet into the undersized sandals Ruth had given her, and went to join the others in the exciting world outside the window.

"Heavens to Betsy!" There were more people around that house than had ever lived on Fortune Island, old, young, black, white, and there was even an Indian beating a tom-tom. He smiled at her as she passed him by. Clusters of people, here and there, scattered about the clearing, played to their own delight, looking at one another, frowning, smiling, winking, blinking, nodding. The confusion was dazzling, dizzying.

But there was Ruth with Capt'n Jack and Marie. As she approached them, Capt'n Jack said, "Well, here's the sleepytime gal." He was holding a big glass of vodka and really did look like an admiral today. No bib overalls. He was wearing a huge red jacket with epaulettes, blue pants with a stripe down the side, and on his head some kind of hat with a feathery thing sticking straight up—a shako, in fact. It was his bandmaster's costume. His face was red and his eyes were glassy. Ruth's eyes were glassy too, under a widebrimmed straw hat. She wore big hoop earrings, a white poet's blouse, and black toreadors. Her feet were bare. Marie looked sassy in cat-eye glasses, pink cotton, poodle-appliquéd skirt, and her hair up in a palomino pony tail. Jessie thought Marie looked perfect. She could not see that Marie had her tongue in her cheek, that she was mocking the teenage costume of the day. Marie lifted her glasses to better observe Jessie's sandman sleepy eyes. "You didn't dress for the party," she said. "I left a costume like this one on the chair in your room, Sissy. We could have looked like twin geeks."

Ruth said, "I thought you probably hadn't slept all night, so I let you sleep late."

Marie said, "But you sure slept most of the day, even with all this racket going on. Come on, Sissy, let's go over to the buffet and get you something to eat." Jessie felt a bit bereft. She saw that Ruth was holding a glass, too, and she and Capt'n Jack had gone back to an animated conversation. Marie said, "The grownups are all half drunk. All except him," pointing at an old white haired black man who sat, his chair leaning back against the house, watching the festivities.

"Who's he?"

"That's Twango James. He's too old to drink. He's too old to do just about anything. He just likes to watch and listen to the music. Pa says he can listen to all the different groups and all the different styles and hear each one as if it's playing alone. Compartmentalization, Pa calls it. That means each part of his brain is picking up something different all at once. But I'm not sure he can see."

"Twango... Twango... I know that name from somewhere."

"Oh, he's famous, I told you. He's probably one of the most famous bass players in the world, and I mean the world! Remember that picture of him I showed you?"

"Oh, yeah... I guess that's where I know him from, that picture."

"Come on," said Marie. "Let's go up in my room and talk about boys. I got a bunch of pictures showing you their things, up and down."

"Wait," said Jessie, tugging back at Marie's hand like a recalcitrant dog. "I know who he is," she almost shouted. "He's Garcie's Twango!"

"Who's Garcie?"

"My friend. Let's go over and talk to him."

"Oh, God, he must be a hundred years old!"

But Jessie pulled her over to Twango, where he sat, and stood looking at him, not knowing what to say. For what seemed a long time he appeared to be unaware of them, though they stood close by and he could certainly feel their eyes on him. Then he said, "Well, what do you young 'uns want from old Twango?"

"My name is Jessie McQueen," Jessie said boldly, "and this is my friend Marie, Capt'n Jack's daughter."

"You want I should sign an autograph?"

Now Jessie could see it, some of it, what Garcie had said, that he was handsome, very light-skinned, and he still had that small mustache that she mentioned, but it was white, as if someone had marked it out in chalk on his tan upper lip. But what was different from Garcie's description was the dime-sized pennies all over his cheeks and up on his forehead, copper-colored freckles. Garcie never mentioned them. His hair was neat and white and slicked down. When he turned his eyes to them, the browns had wisdom and the reds of the whites made him look very old. "Well, what do you want, young ladies?"

"Do you remember Miss Gullah Garcie Garson?"

"Can't say that I do. What is it, some old girlfriend after me? If she is, she must be mighty old."

"Somebody I know who says you were in love with her once."

"Whooo! Hold up there! Ain't been in love with anybody for fifty years. Don't know if I was in love with anybody before that. Married—or half-married anyway—four or five times, down south and up north. Out west, too. Tell me something more about this—what'd you say her name was?"

"Gullah Garcie Garson."

"Wow, some folks really name their children, don't they? Well, what about Miss Gullah Garcie Garson, or—did I get that right?"

"You gave her a ring, a gold ring, don't you remember? It had Love and Luck graven on it."

He looked down at his knees. The girls could see that he was trying to remember. They looked down at his knees, too. He was wearing shiny black trousers that Jessie could have fitted into. That's how slim he was. She saw that he was wearing patent-leather shoes, dusty and scratched. She looked up, waiting. He wore a white, ruffled dress shirt, a band shirt, collar open. "I bet you'd like to be playing," she said.

"Can't stand up. How'm I gonna hold a big bass upright and pull its sweet strings back? I remember what you're talking about, girlie. A little skinny black girl no bigger than you. It's that ring that brings it back. Every juke joint I played, that big-eyed girl showed up right out in front. It was her enthusiasm. I'd toss her a smile. Then the day came I had to go. Now this is where the explaining gets a little harder. Maybe neither one of you young ladies has heard of Lucky Lindy, the pilot Lindbergh who flew the Atlantic in nineteen twenty-something. First person to do it."

Marie said, "I've heard of him."

"Anyhow, I was in a poker game one night more'n two hundred years ago and caught me four aces and a king, so this fellow ups and hands me over that ring. He told me that ring had been owned by Lucky Lindy himself and was pure gold. So I took the ring, smiling all the way, like a good Pullman porter, which I was, like Huddie Leadbetter, and I got the hell out of there. I had got my law degree in Washington, but could make more money on the trains, you see, and that playing poker, too. I bet that surprises you. Yeah, I'm a lawyer. Well I wore that ring for a while. When somebody would ask me what the double L meant, sometimes I'd tell them what I was told, that it meant Lucky Lindy, sometimes I'd tell them something different. If it happened to be a woman who asked, I'd always tell 'em it meant Love and Luck. Well, that poor little girl with her big pop-eyes, she just touched me, kid like that, and I had plenty of money in those days, like I said, from the Pullman cars and the poker, so it was nothing to me to pop that ring off my finger, and hand it to her, and give her a kiss on the cheek, to boot, which I remember doing now that I've been thinking about it. Or maybe I misremember because it's been so long now, but I think I do remember that little girl with the big eyes. How is that poor little old thing doing, still alive and kicking up those skinny legs like she used to do, I hope?"

"She's still alive, but her legs ain't skinny."

Twango chuckled, a quiet chuckle of remembrance. "Gained some, has she?"

"She's twice as much as us three put together."

"That's what the quiet life will do for you."

"Thank you, Mister Twango."

"Are you gonna tell her about this, little girl?"

"You bet! I got to!"

"Then don't you tell her what I said, none of it. You tell her that those initials mean exactly what I told her they meant and that I gave it to her because it broke my heart to part with her. You tell her that's what old Twango said, you hear?"

"You want me to lie?" said Jessie.

"There's a lie and a lie," said Twango, "and what I told you to say—you listen to me, now—what I told you to say, is the truth. You get a little older, and you find out that there ain't one truth. There's lots of versions of the truth, and the older you get, the more you will realize that we need them all. I got my version of the truth and Gullah Garcie Garson's got hers. Ain't nobody around here a-lying. Do I look like a liar?"

"No, sir."

"No, missy, Jimmy Twango James don't deal in lies. Now scat out of here. Let me listen to that music, all the versions."

"I understand, Mr. Twango."

"See that you do, young lady."

Jessie couldn't find Ruth when she went to tell her about Twango.

She asked Maggie where Ruth had gone. She was told that Ruth was engaged in business with Capt'n Jack in the house, probably in Capt'n Jack's workroom. Marie pulled Jessie away. "Let's get out of the crowd," she said. But Jessie was bursting to tell Ruth about Twango.

"No," she said. "I've got to find Ruth."

"Can't it keep?" asked Marie.

"No," said Jessie, "it's so exciting. I've got to tell her about Garcie and Mister Twango."

"Oh, okay, if you have to," Marie assented. "Follow me."

Capt'n Jack sat in his workroom, listening to Ruth and Victoria Underhill, puffing his pipe, occasionally taking a drink. It was very pleasant, watching two beautiful women animatedly discussing business. They seemed to hit it off.

"You have a great track record," said Victoria Underhill. "Your books sell. There's a special category of the marketplace for folklore. We can count on that for a base. If we transcend it, if you come up with something special, we may even be able to get a best seller out of it."

"I'll send you what I've got as soon as I get back to Fortune Island. Do you want me to sign anything?"

"We'll just shake hands on it," said Victoria, and they did.

"Well, that's settled," said Capt'n Jack. "Now let's get back to the party. Damn, I wish your father had been able to come."

"Oh, he'd have had a real good time," said Victoria.

Marie had led Jessie to the workroom door, and, when the three inside stepped out into the hall, Jessie looked up at the beautiful black woman in awe. She was tall and slender and just wonderfully elegant-looking in a white dress and a large-brimmed white hat, and, when she looked down at the girls, her perfect teeth glimmered in a frame of smiling red lips. Small gold earrings glistened at her ears, and the delicate cheeks of her dark-skinned face formed dimples. There was a rose on her bodice that matched the color of her lips. In all her born days, Jessie had never seen a more beautiful black woman, better than a match for most of the white women she'd ever known, even the real pretty ones. The adults brushed past the girls in the hall and went on outside.

"Did you ever see a black woman who looked like that?" Jessie asked Marie. The sight of Victoria Underhill had knocked the thought of telling Ruth about Twango right out of her mind.

"Oh, sure! Where you been? There's all kinds of beautiful, up-to-date, black women around nowadays. Singers, actresses... Up in New

York they got this fashion model..."

"All I ever knew was Garcie."

"A domestic? I mean, your friend!"

"Well... maybe... I guess so."

"Oh, you're behind the times, Sissy. Modern women, black and white, are coming on strong these days."

"Well, where have I been?"

"Not in New York, that's for sure!"

There was a shower late in the afternoon but everyone stayed outside and let it rain on them. Then there was one last burst of sun before evening fell, and the uproarious music began again, and, to Jessie, her stomach comfortably filled with deviled eggs, it seemed a golden moment, but so fast did the sky streak with black and red, it made her gulp, realizing that one of the most amazing days of her life was coming to an end. But not quite yet. The sunlight might have been going, but Capt'n Jack's crew had already turned on artificial lights that flooded the area and the music rolled on. Jessie and Marie walked from group to group, holding hands, pausing to listen, walking on. "It's like a dream," Jessie said. "No, never in my born days did I dream such a dream, but I will from now on."

"Me," said Marie, "I get damned tired of it. Too many kids, too many grown ups, too many, too much of everything. It's like living in a carnival."

"I've never been to a carnival. If it's like this, it must be wonderful."

"Come on," said Marie, "let's go sit on Remembrance Rock."

"What rock?"

"I'll show you. Come on." Marie led Jessie down the uneven stone steps to the patio she had seen on the way in. "You can still hear the music but it's quieter here. I like to sit here and watch the cars go by on the road at night. Get away from the house, you know. Pa calls it Remembrance Rock after his buddy Carl Sandburg's novel." To Jessie, Marie seemed more grown up, like Ruth. It wasn't that she was so much older. Only a couple of years. But she had the same air of certainty that Ruth had, the way she took things for granted. "Will you write to me?" Jessie asked her, sitting down, wrapping her arms around her knees. "I don't have any friends. There's nobody on Fortune Island, nobody my age."

"Pen pals! Sissy, I'll come out here on this patio at least once a week and write to you. Okay?" She caught and squeezed Jessie's hand. Jessie thought she was wonderful, so beautiful, so worldly. She wanted to look at Marie and think about her, but something distracted her, the thought of the filling station, the thought of the rough men there, and the smell of the place, the smell of gasoline. She sniffed the air, like an animal sensing danger. It seemed that she could smell gasoline, wafting up to her on Remembrance Rock.

"Do you smell anything?" she asked Marie.

"Booze—from the party."

"Does it smell like gasoline?"

"Some of it smells exactly like gasoline. I hate the damn stuff. Only I like a cold beer once in a while."

"That must be it," Jessie said. Now, with a new burst of enthusiasm, Jessie said, "I love your father and mother. Your whole family. They all seem so happy."

"Are you kidding? At school they call us the midgets. They hate us around here. It's because Pa's a Red. You probably don't know what that means, so I won't try to explain it to you. It's too hard. Ruth's a Red, too, whether you know it or not. That whole bunch back up there, they're all Reds. They call us the Midget Reds. All of 'em but one, my boyfriend." She lifted her skirt, and got a pack of cigarettes that were tucked in the top of a stocking. "Want one?" She gave one to Jessie and lit one herself. Then she lit Jessie's. Jessie puffed and choked. "Oh, that's okay," said Marie, patting Jessie on the back. "You'll get the hang of it. Then you'll like it."

"Ruth likes it, I know that, but right now I don't understand why."

"Do you know what he does?"

"Who?"

"Pa! Pa, he walks around naked and lets us all look at his dangler bouncing."

"His what?"

"His dangler. His thing. Don't you know anything? He walks around naked all the time. He says it's natural, but my boyfriend—he's a football player—he says Pa's a pervert, that his pa never did such a thing. But then—"

"You tell your boyfriend about your pa?"

"Course. Got to have somebody to talk to. But my boyfriend shows me his thing, too. I guess he's a pervert, like Pa." She held her hands out in description. "It's about this big. How you doing with that cigarette?"

"It's not so bad when you get used to it." She held it away and looked at it. "Looks like I've smoked it about half way down."

"You don't know shit, do you, Sissy?"

"I guess not. I never heard tell of anything like this stuff."

"What stuff?"

"All of it—all what you've been saying."

"When I write to you, I'll tell you more about it. It'll be fun to have somebody to explain my life to, what I want and all. What I want, is for my boyfriend to hold my arms down and ram it into me."

"Gee, Marie, I don't know if I—" Marie had looked like a princess, but now she was frightening Jessie. She didn't know what to say. But it had gotten easier to breathe the smoke in and blow it out. She tried to feel the way she imagined Ruth felt. She held the cigarette away and looked at it again. There was only a long ash left. The music up behind them came to a crescendo, then stopped. The crowd whistled and applauded.

Capt'n Jack seized the microphone from a female singer who had just finished belting out a rousing rendition of "Blues in the Night." By now, most of the guests had gathered at the bandstand and were taking turns entertaining one another. Capt'n Jack said, "There's somebody here to honor somebody who is not here. Now, listen up, folks! We've got Doctor Ruth Perle here, and she's going to read a poem she has written about Huddie Ledbetter, that is—LEADBELLY!"

Ruth stepped up to the mike. "I'm sorry I can't sing it for you, but here goes—

> Leadbelly, grim with your Cajun accordion,
> with your harmonica blues, with your knife
>   flicking down the twelve strings of your guitar
> —the Rock Island Line was a mighty good road—
>   bowing, scraping, white-suited trainman . . .
> made your pride sick, but you sang,
>   fast, strong, quiet, like a driven
> demon, like you had to get it out
>   before a razor dumped your guts
> on a blood-mud taphouse floor,
>   or some drunk crazy rednecks
> nailed you up like Christ, in a dangerous world
>   for anybody but most America for a black
> poet of low-down places and sky-high loves.
>
> Leadbelly, thirty years hard time murder,
> six and a half, sang your way out, ten more, intent,

then Alan Lomax and his bro, John, folklorists—
makes you laugh inside at night—white boys,
    playing—but they get you out again and in
the Library of Congress, that grinding
    voice part now of something big, like
storm darkness, like that lifething,
    love, always beyond somewhere or
crying deep inside, in a dark place,
    yeah, big like music, big like that gal you
call Irene! How many Irenes, you think?

    Even the Lomax bros, even them white boys,
they know Irene—you driving them through
    New York traffic, them folkloring in back and you
being their folkloring black chauffeur.
    You drink sharp liquor in Harlem, play
with Woody Guthrie, Sonny Terry, Brownie
    McGhee, the Headline Singers—radio too,
Hollywood and *Three Songs by Leadbelly*,
    a French tour... You show 'em your razor
stretch marks, your shotpitted pot.
    Good night Irene I'll see you in my dreams . . .
all that good hot mean hard American life
    and Lou Gehrig's *amyotrophic lateral sclerosis*.
It's *The Midnight Special*! Fade me, Death!"

Capt'n Jack put one big arm over Ruth's shoulders and squeezed
her to him and with the other arm raised his glass on high, and began to
chant, "Leadbelly! Leadbelly! LEADBELLY!" And the crowd joined in:
"Leadbelly! Leadbelly! Leadbelly! Leadbelly!"
    Jessie and Marie could hear the chant of the crowd on Remembrance
Rock, where they sat, looking down now into an opacity of night punctuated
by white spots Jessie pointed out to Marie, cones of white that moved
about; then fire snaked its way up an invisible pole until, with a startling
suddenness, it shaped a towering cross against the night sky.
    Then they saw Capt'n Jack barrel down the drive, pumping shot into the
air. Headlights beamed, tail lights flared, a pickup sped off. Capt'n Jack
fired after it several times, his shotgun coughing red in the darkness.
    Then Ruth was there, with Victoria Underhill, with Marie and Jessie,

on Remembrance Rock, a pistol in her hand. "Come on, girls—move it, back to the house. Quick!" Victoria Underhill's long, bejeweled fingers and sharp red nails dug into Jessie's shoulder.

"Ouch," she cried.

"Move it," Victoria commanded.

That night on Remembrance Rock gave Jessie a new view of Ruth. She had warrior blood. People up by the house were singing, "We Shall Overcome." They were being brave, Jessie understood that. But Ruth would have shot down the danged bastards, and Jessie knew it. She even scared Jessie, waving that big pearl-handled pistol around.

Before the cross was reduced to embers and ashes, some of the guests began pulling out. Some wondered if the sheeted ones weren't waiting for them on the road. Capt'n Jack reassured them. "Those bastards are to hell and gone. Yellow sons-of-bitches! Once you're off on the road, you'll be safe. They're just a bunch of bums at the local filling station. They ain't gonna bother you. I know exactly who they are. But, if anybody's worried about leaving, he or she can spend the night and go out in the morning. We've got plenty of room. But if you choose to go, you poor black Americans, you second-class citizens, you won't be able to get a sandwich or even a soda-pop until you get up beyond the Mason-Dixie line, which is the disgrace of this country. If you wait till morning, we'll fix you some sandwiches and something to drink to take along with you."

"I'm bunking with Ruth," said Victoria, "she's got a gun!"

"Fine," said Ruth, "and Jessie can bunk with Marie."

"Oh, yes," Jessie and Marie chorused.

"We can talk all night, Sissy," Marie said.

"And you can tell me all about boys," Jessie whispered excitedly, "the dirty stuff."

Back inside the house, Ruth said, "We ought to call the State Police."

"Call Mars," said Capt'n Jack. "It don't cost a cent."

"What do you mean?"

"I mean, I don't pay the goddamn telephone bill. The FBI pays it for me, so they can listen in. I call Moscow whenever I feel like it, and they love it."

Maggie shook her head in agreement, said, "It's the truth. They were bugging our phone for years until we got wise to them, then we decided not to pay the bill anymore, and nobody ever turned the phone off. The

FBI is paying, just to see what we're doing."

Ruth said, "So you don't think it'll do any good to call the State Police? To report it?"

"No. I'll handle it myself," said Jack. "I'll go into town tomorrow morning and confront the bastards. They're probably hiding under their beds by now. You know, they have an affinity for bedding—sheets and pillow cases—you might even say it's a fetish with them."

"If you're going into town tomorrow, Pa," said Marie, "I want to take Sissy to see a movie. She's never been to the movies. 'Streetcar Named Desire' is playing at the Old Pioneer on Budleigh. If you're going to drive in tomorrow, will you take us along, Pa? Can she go, Ruth?"

Ruth looked at Capt'n Jack. "Do you think it's safe?"

"In broad daylight? Sure. Nobody'll bother them."

Jessie looked pleadingly at Ruth. "It's okay, Ruth?"

"Yes, if Jack thinks it'll be okay, I think it'll be okay."

Before noon the next day Capt'n Jack drove Jessie and Marie into town. He drove right into the filling station, got out of his pickup, looking like a man who could pick up any four of the skinny pump jockeys who sat about the station, and asked outright, "Did I put some birdshot into any one of you assholes last night?"

"We don't know what you're talking about, Jack."

"Of course you do, you stupid sons-of-bitches! I've got the phone number for the Grand Giant in Elizabeth City in my wallet, and I could go in on that pay phone and tell him exactly what you bums did last night. Did you boys know that there was a half dozen reporters up there with us? Grand Giant wouldn't like that one bit, now would he, him running for public office and all. At this point he'd denounce the lot of you. He's working his ass off at the State House trying to get himself legitimized, and you all boys are embarrassing him, putting him on the spot like that. Ten to one you called him to ask if you could do what you did and he said no. Am I wrong?"

"Then why don't he resign?"

"Because your Grand Giant is trying to hang on to your sucker votes. When he's a senator he won't even know you. Now fill 'er up, and be quick about it!"

From the cab of Capt'n Jack's pickup, the girls could see that the wolves of the night before had turned back into sheep. Like a real Grand Giant, Capt'n Jack stood amidst them and stuffed his pipe. They were cowed by his contempt for them. Marie squeezed Jessie's hand and gave her a grin, and Jessie wasn't afraid anymore.

After the movie, smoking, waiting for Ruth to pick them up in front of the Old Pioneer, Marie said:

"Ain't that Marlon Brando a piece of ass, or what!"

⌘ ⌘ ⌘

Jessie had a thousand questions for Ruth but the heat of the sun knocked her out and she slept in the Land Rover on the long trip down to Ocracoke, bouncing about, and even almost walked in her sleep as she boarded and disembarked the two ferries at the inlets between islands. At Ocracoke, Ruth parked in her usual place behind the restaurant, unloaded their gear, including the tapes she had made at Capt'n Jack's Dacha, and a suitcase full of textbooks that had once belonged to Capt'n Jack's children, and were meant for Ruth's use in teaching Jessie, and, with Jessie's zombie-like help now, covered the Land Rover with the heavy sailcloth tarpaulin and tied it down.   Ruth had timed the trip down from Capt'n Jack's so that they wouldn't have long to wait at the dock for the mail boat. Hauling their heavy load of bags and suitcases to the dock had brought Jessie back from the land of Winkin, Blinkin, and Nod, and, as they waited for the mail boat, the sleep-suppressed questions bubbled up to the top of Jessie's consciousness like effervescence in soda water. They stood amid a small group of people waiting for the mail boat. Nothing covered them, and the nearly noonday sun, a bronze gong, could almost be heard in the bird-peppered, vermillioned sky.

The boat was late. Word spread that there had been mechanical trouble up the line. Ruth, sweating profusely, said, "I'll light a cigarette and the damn thing will come along." She seemed tired. Jessie felt much better, refreshed by her nap. She asked Ruth what a piece of ass was. For an instant, Ruth seemed angry. She looked at Jessie sternly, exhaling smoke, then, gradually, a smile formed on her face. "It's a very crude expression, and I'd prefer if you didn't say it again. It's slang. It means that somebody is attractive. I guess you could say it means somebody is attractive to the opposite sex. But don't put it that way, don't say what you said."

"I didn't say it, Marie said it."

"I should have known."

"This actor that Marie said it about raped this nice lady, in the movie, you know, and that's what Marie said, and then she said that about him— that he was... Attractive, you know, the way you said."

"I'm going to have to have a long talk with you about some of these things."

"That's what I want. I want you to have a long talk with me about some of these things. I have a whole lot more."

"I just bet you have. Oh, thank God, there's the boat."

At Fortune Island, the skiff was waiting in the water to fetch them, but things had already changed. It was the new man only he didn't look like the same man who had disembarked when they had boarded two days before. Jessie was sorry to see that he was not all duded up as he had been that day, looking like something out of a picture book. Now he wore only bib overalls and a hat, the same big white wide-brimmed Stetson he'd come to the island wearing, but now he was slightly bearded and actually kind of dirty looking. But he did have the same big white-toothed smile on his face, that smile that made you think he was glad to see you, and that's what he said, as he helped them aboard the skiff. "Glad to see you! Have a nice trip?"

"I'm sorry," said Ruth, "I've forgotten your name."

"My name's Tom Judas, and you're Ruth Perle, and the young lady is Jessie . . ."

"Jessie McQueen," Jessie said.

"But aren't you the Reverend Cogburn's daughter?" he asked, tugging at the outboard's cord, the muscles of his naked shoulders, his arms, rippling.

"He's my stepdaddy. I don't know where my real daddy is now. He was in—"

"Her parents were divorced," Ruth said.

The motor sputtered and the prop went into motion. Tom steered the skiff away from the mail boat, toward shore. "And you're looking after her while the Reverend's away?"

"Miss Garcie Garson looks after her most of the time. The Reverend's away a lot. But Miss Garcie is getting old, and I plan on being a big help to her when it comes to Jessie. I saw your guitar case when you arrived. Are you a musician?"

"I guess you'd say I'm a sometimes kind of person. Sometimes I'm a musician, sometimes I'm a carpenter, sometimes I'm something else."

"You'll not get any work as a musician on Fortune Island. I guess you know that."

"Then I'll just have to play for myself."

"Are you a cowboy singer?" Jessie said. "Because I saw a picture of a cowboy singer kinda looked like you."

"Not exactly," Tom said.

"No, I guess not. This here feller was a real dude. You know, had on one of those cowboy shirts—all different colors, with fringes on it. Saw his picture and somebody told me he was called—well, I don't rightly remember, but it was a name like yours. Couldn't be, though, could it?"

"Wish it was," said Tom, frowning. But the sun wasn't in his eyes, Jessie observed. And, in a few moments, there was something else she noticed. The gregarious fellow of a few minutes before was gone; what was left was a mysterious, dark-jawed stranger, tight-lipped, now, but still polite, willing to help. When they landed, he seized up the suitcase of books and several bags. "I'll just take these up to the cottage for you."

"Thank you," Ruth called after him.

"Look at those muscles," Jessie said. "But he reminds me of somebody."

Trudging up the sand flats from the dock, Ruth wondered aloud about him. "He comes and goes so suddenly. I mean his personality. It's as if he wants to be friendly and then something stops him, like he's afraid of giving away too much."

"Like he's got a secret," Jessie said. "But he sure is some piece of attractive, ain't he, Ruth?"

"Some piece of attractive," Ruth said, almost to herself.

Chapter
Twelve

October 2000

D avid had known Victoria Underhill all his life. She had been his mother's literary agent and friend for over forty years, their friendship annealed by a nineteen-fifties cross-burning, or so the story went. Victoria had also been an editor, a publisher, a feminist, and a civil rights activist. Her father was the late, great Doctor Edgar Underhill, assassinated martyr of the Civil Rights Movement. David could still see her remnant beauty, the beauty that had amazed the young Jessie who often mentioned her first encounter with Victoria, but the decades had painted streaks of grey in Victoria's hair and pulled and etched her face. Light bounced from her glasses.

"Now just exactly what am I doing here?" he asked her. "What's expected of me?"

They sat at the bar of the Inter-Continental Hotel in Frankfurt, where Victoria had booked rooms for them both, and had told him to meet her. Beads of rain rolled down his trench coat. Victoria's white suit was crisp. He was having a whiskey sour. Victoria sipped a martini. He had never smoked, and fanned her smoke away with a damp hand. "You're here to accept a prize for Ruth, for *Folkways*, if she wins in the poetry category. I thought it would look good if a member of her family accepted for her— better than her agent—and you had only to come down from Berlin. You were married here in Frankfurt, weren't you?"

"Yes. My Ice-Queen mother-in-law lives not far from here. But I was only in Berlin on state department business. I live in Washington now."

"With your lovely wife... I know." She looked at him over her glasses. "For a man who grew up with writers, you don't know much about the book business, do you, little David?"

"Not really. I hear about it from Ruth, occasionally, but it goes in one ear and out the other. I guess I'm not a literary type."

"Well, this is the big time! The Frankfurt Book Fair is the world's oldest and largest. What really kicked it off was the Gutenberg Bible. Think of it, little David, moveable type!" Victoria was still an enthusiastic woman, wide-eyed faux innocence hiding a litigator's mind.

"Yes, wonderful," he said. He adored Victoria, and knew that she always had the family's best interest at heart, and so tried to be accommodating. He would even allow Victoria to take him on a tour of the fair. Reluctantly, he finished his whiskey sour, helped Victoria on with her London Fog, and let her lead him out into the rain again.

The Frankfurt Millennium Book Fair occupied a dozen or more floors of five huge halls, housing nearly 7,000 exhibitor booths from a hundred-plus countries, and Victoria dragged him, for Ruth's sake duty-bound to stick with her, through more than three hundred thousand people, among whom were Boris Yeltsin, the Russian Premier, whose memoirs were up for grabs, Posh Spice, ditto, and a fellow American named Brian Greene, who had been paid two million dollars for the rights to his book, *The Fabric of the Cosmos: Space, Time and The Texture of Reality*, so that, by late afternoon, David's usual upright posture had fallen into a round-shouldered slump. The little electric trolleys that moved the public from hall to hall had only afforded small relief to his burning feet. Vox populi had gratefully drowned out Victoria's running commentary, but he still had a headache. Yeltsin was one thing, but Posh Spice—that was quite another.

If Victoria hadn't asked him to do this, he would not be here now, not with the baby so close to coming. After his business in Berlin, he would have scooted right back to Washington. Of course, the baby wasn't due for another month—a November child, the doctors at Georgetown University Hospital had assured him. In any case, the women in the family had conspired to put him on the literary hot-seat. Had he wanted to make speeches, he'd have become a politician. But, to be honest with himself, David knew that he had assented to come to Frankfurt to do more than represent Ruth.

There was an opportunistic inspiration involved. Attending the book fair gave him the excuse he felt he needed in order to visit his mother-in-law, dear Mother Schnepp, that gnädige Frau, the next day. He had never told Ruth that Frau Schnepp wouldn't attend his and Hildegarde's wedding on the unstated, if clear enough, grounds that Hildy was marrying a Jew. She had claimed illness; the fact that she had made any excuse at all was grounds for hope; and, being David, and a diplomat, he hoped for reconciliation, hoped that she had thought better of the situation; had relented, but was too embarrassed to make the first move.

Frau Schnepp lived alone, but for servants, in a five-thousand-square-foot condominium, not far from the Inter-Continental. Her condo was within easy walking distance, for all the good that it did. He had called her, but she had no intention of visiting him. Neither had she asked him to see her, to come and visit, as he had done anyway, hat in hand.

A tall, elegantly coifed silver-blonde, with Tavernier blue eyes, Frau Schnepp wore a simple black dress with a collar of pearls hiding her skinny, wrinkled, long-necked throat. She drank cognac but offered him nothing but coffee and sat blowing streams of acrid Gauloises Blonde smoke in his face while he tried to drink it. When he told her about the baby, she warned nobody in particular about negative genes. But David had to listen.

"Think of it," she said, "the child will be Jewish, Irish, and, as I understand, American Indian."

"And German," David said.

"Hardly!" Frau Schnepp seemed shocked at the idea.

"You don't want to lose your daughter, do you?" he asked her gently.

"It is only incidental to a greater loss," she said. "Now, David, if you have satisfied yourself about my intentions, I suggest we end this interview."

She wasn't really one of the old guard, David knew, but a large, gilt-framed portrait of one of the old guard hung on her wall, an officer in a Wermacht uniform, epaulettes, Iron Cross, blue sash, and all. "My father-in-law, the Baron," she said, proudly, looking at the portrait of the man as if he were a god. "A Prussian officer of royal blood. He was not a Nazi, as some have claimed. He despised Hitler, a common corporal, held him in contempt. He was an aristocrat. They had their own code." But he wore a Swastika on his sleeve. David could easily imagine the Baron shooting a nuisance in the head. He looked the type. Frau Schnepp looked the type, too. The reconciliation he had hoped for, for Hildy's sake, and for the baby's, seemed out of the question.

David had lived, off and on, for years in Germany, and tried to comfort himself with the thought that he had only on rare occasions come up against a person of Frau Schnepp's ilk. She was one of the few unreconstructed things that he had crossed paths with in Germany. She wasn't even a product of the war. She had been a post-war baby, but somebody back there had gotten hold of her when she was young and turned her into this monument to the futility of superiority. Leaving her, he felt sick. At the corner, a block from her building, he had to pause, to place a hand on Gothic stone, and vomit thin, acrid stuff. Even her coffee was poisonous.

Early that rainy evening David reconnected with Victoria at the Inter-Continental bar. Now he was wearing a tux, and she wore a lime green Ralph Lauren gown. They were ready for the Prize Ceremonies at the Old Opera House. The bar was full of people in evening dress who were also attending, and limousines waited outside to take them. They had about an hour to kill.

"Whiskey sour for me and a martini for the lady," David ordered. He had drunk as much in the company of diplomats and had not felt it to the same degree. Perhaps it was exhaustion from the long tour of the fair, perhaps it was worry about the home front, about Jessie and her chemo, and Hildy and the coming baby, and perhaps it was about how Ruth, who, after all, wasn't really the roaring girl that she once was but now, it seemed to him, still pretended to be. Perhaps what was draining him was the thought of Ruth and how she was bearing up under the stress of Jessie's illness, terminal illness, after all—he had to face it—even while that cold blonde monster within walking distance sat and endlessly smoked her Gauloises and drank Remy Martin Cognac in a perpetual stupor of no-regret.

Yes, Frau Schnepp was the enigma he most puzzled over, the person who, the problem that, most exhausted his emotional resources. Anger and frustration rose in him as he thought of how her bigotry had made him sick, of how his fixation with her continued to nauseate him, of how he couldn't get his mind off her, the puzzle of her repulsive disease, the disease that she was. He took another, longer pull of his whiskey sour, prompting Victoria, who was, as the saying is, feeling no pain herself, to warn him that he might have to accept an award for his mother at the Old Opera House later that evening and that he might have to say a few words—that he mustn't allow himself to overindulge before the event. "A lot of famous publishers, agents, and writers will be there," she warned. "I don't want you making a fool of yourself. So take it easy on those drinks, little David."

"That's what you're here for, Aunt Vicki," David said. "You'd be better accepting for Ruth than I would. You know the book business. You know what to say. I'm just a humble civil servant, the Kissinger of Brookline."

"I think you're drunk already," Victoria proclaimed.

"Have you heard this one?" David said, his voice louder than he intended. "It's a great mother-in-law joke. A young cop, in training, is asked what he would do if he had to arrest his mother-in-law. The cop thinks for a minute, then says... *I'd call for backup!*"

The bartender apparently got the joke, because he slapped the bar with his bar rag and guffawed, delighting David, who bowed slightly to him. David ordered another whiskey sour despite Victoria's objections. "Plus ça change, plus c'est la même chose," he said.

By the eleventh hour, David was back at the Inter-Continental bar, almost certain that he was sitting on the same stool he had left so reluctantly earlier that evening, dragged out to a limousine by Victoria, who found him an amiable drinker. Getting him in and out of cars and finally seated at an eight-person round table had been the hardest part of dealing with him. He drank steadily and said very little during the long evening of speeches and awards.

Later, he remembered walking a red carpet and going up the stone steps of the Old Opera House—a huge canvas advertised "Porgy and Bess"—and being led through by a hostess who for some reason took him and others on out the back door. Confusion abounded. Ed McBain, the mystery writer, asked the hostess, as they stood outside the back door wondering why they were there, "Was it something we said?" David thought the writer was a great wit and laughed uproariously. Victoria elbowed him in the ribs. "Dignity," she had whispered. Then they were all led back into the Old Opera House and finally into the enormous ballroom where the ceremonies were being held. David realized that there were TV cameras everywhere and he tried to straighten up, to re-acquire his diplomatic dignity, but the whiskey sours were winning the evening. Italian, French, German, Austrian, and American cameras trained steadily on his unsteady person. He was embarrassed because he knew he was drunk, but not too embarrassed to order another whiskey sour. As if possessing some deeply held religious faith, he believed that this one would straighten him out, perhaps even up. The food served was that of a diplomatic dinner, but the drinks made the curly carrots and the twirly mashed potatoes appear gnomic, and he found it hard to look at them. And what was that meat under it all? Lamb? Lamb something, or something? He was surrounded by carafes of wine, but the waiter was good enough to bring him more whiskey sours. It must have been the way he twirled his finger. He became convinced that the waiter was the only person in the Opera House who understood him.

Even later, he remembered being attracted to the Mayor of Frankfurt, a beautiful middle-aged woman who was Mistress of Ceremonies. She had started speaking in German, which he understood perfectly, then, for some reason, had switched to English and continued in it. He remembered understanding her German better than her English, but maybe that had something to do with the fact that he had continued to order whiskey sours, consuming them during the whole program, thus determining Victoria to accept any award Ruth might have coming. "If Ruth is mentioned," she said, "you just sit tight—and I mean tight—and I'll go up and take care of it. Get it?"

"Got it!"

"Good!"

Later still, back in his seat at the bar at the Inter-Continental, David remembered some of that. Unfortunately, Ruth did not win. Victoria, who had stopped drinking when it became obvious to her that David would not, decided, in her disappointment at the unexpected outcome, to join David in his battle against sobriety. How it was they joined a group from the ceremonies at a table, David could not fathom, but there he was, somehow embroiled in a heated discussion led by a Frenchwoman, a stranger to them, who had lost in her category—non-fiction, a biography of Louis-Ferdinand Céline. "Céline was superior to any American writer of the twentieth century," she affirmed.

"A great writer," said Victoria, "but a Fascist anti-Semite of the worst sort."

This warmed David to the subject. "For three thousand years," David said, "Europe has been making scapegoats of the Jews. J'accuse! J'accuse!" He jabbed his finger, from a safe distance, at the Frenchwoman.

"Au contraire," the Frenchwoman said. "The Jews have bought up all the great art work of Europe. I bet your family even owns a Van Dyke. I know who you are. You're unspeakably rich. I don't know why you work."

"I work because my mother taught me the great American work ethic."

"Mais oui, I see you Americans marching down the Champs-Elysées in short pants like overgrown little boys with cameras slung around your necks and I know you immediately. We sit at café tables and point you out. It is a joke. Your noses and your knobby knees prove who you are."

"For God's sake," Victoria cried, "this is a party and David's a Jew."

"Secular," said David, "and half Irish."

"The French certainly earn their reputation for rudeness," said Victoria. Ruth's loss had put Victoria in a bad mood, and her warm brown eyes had gone as cold as brown can go as she stared voo-doo at the Frenchwoman. "What happened to liberté, égalité, et fraternité? In the new world—"

"You are in the old world," said the Frenchwoman. "What used to be called the new world is intellectually the old world now—old in the sense of behind the times—unsophisticated—even primitive. And we French often find that American manners leave something to be desired."

"We may be in the old world, but France is the old Europe," Victoria snapped back. "The New Europe—the Europe that matters—is what used to be the Warsaw Pact Nations. America finally wrestled Poland free and what help did we get from the Frogs?"

"That's enough for me," David said, getting to his feet. "Congratulations, everybody, well, anybody." He leaned over and took the Frenchwoman's hand. "Bonne nuit, Madame. Aufweidersehen." He waved. "Good-night all!"

"Where are you going?" asked Victoria.

"To get some fresh air, Aunt Vicki. Take a walk. Sober up."

"Get your coat. It's cold out there."

"Don't need it," he called back. "Ciao!"

He straightened himself up, tugging here and there at his tuxedo, flattening his unruly black hair with his hands, and walked unsteadily out through the lobby and on out the door, a tall, thin, wavering figure. He was offered one of the several limousines waiting outside, but waved them away, waved away the mostly Arab drivers, and walked toward the corner. The diplomat in him surrendered to the dipsomaniac. He had to see Frau Schnepp again, to confront her. He wanted to push her off her pedestal, to break her poise of condescension. That's what he wanted to do, dammit, but he turned the corner and walked down toward the moonlight sparkling Main, just a short distance behind the Inter-Continental, to cool off. It occurred to him that he could take a sight-seeing boat, along the Main, south to Munich, where folks were having fun, where it was Oktoberfest and beer bellies were bulging at the moon. Where he was, there was a railing along the embankment. He leaned over it—Don't fall in!—and vomited a stomachful of whiskey sours into the broody, moody, moonlight-spoony Main. "That's twice in one day," he told himself, wiping his face with his handkerchief. He bowed—apologized to the river. He was not a heavy drinker. That bitch made out of golden ice had prompted this drunkenness. She'd gotten under his Semitic skin in a big way. He tried to do some thinking, watching the silver spoons of the moon stir up little silver shark fins in the gentle flow of the dark river.

For no reason he could fathom, he decided to walk downtown, to the center of Frankfurt, a banking town, like Charlotte, with its New York-like imperative traffic. That was the reason! It was cold. A brisk walk in the cold would clear his head. He looked up at the sky, beseechingly, lost, for a moment, in space, and stepped off a curb. He heard brakes squeal in a slam, cars around him gearing, changing their courses, curses, excited exchanges in German and English, could make nothing of any of it, his mind blind, but for the night sky, yet finally penetrated by a version of reality. "I'm drunk as a skunk," he told himself. "I better go back to the Inter-Continental." He turned on the dime of his heel in traffic that seemed to be on all sides and, like a lucky blind man who has lost his cane, his dog, and his dark glasses, found his way back to the curb and safety, then back to the hotel. As he traversed the lobby on wobbly legs and eggshell-careful feet—"Dignity, dignity!"—he was thrown from his course by a call from the desk.

The concierge handed him a phone. "Call from Washington, Mr. Perle."

He took the phone in hand and leaned on the counter looking at the bar, where his drinking partners remained. It appeared that the boozy polemic, not to say near intellectual riot, was still in full force.

"Hello!" he said.

"Is that you, David?" It was Ruth.

"Mother?"

"I've got some important news, but first, let me tell you that I saw the whole awards ceremony on the computer. I bet poor Victoria is in a bad mood. Is she tight?"

"We're all a little drunk here."

"Well, it probably won't do much good, but tell Victoria that I'm not a bit upset about losing. Now, David, I've got some exciting news! Are you sitting down?"

"Leaning against a marble counter," he said. "What is it?"

"Everything's fine, David. Hildy had the baby—and it's a girl! I know you wanted to be here, but what can we do with Mother Nature? She sent little Jessie into the world a month early. She's fine! She's got all her parts. Everything works. Absolutely nothing to be concerned about. Little Jessie and Hildegarde are both doing fine. I left big Jessie with her nurses and flew up to Washington as soon as I got word. I'm with

Hildy now. She's exhausted. It was a complete surprise, not to say shock. Hello? Are you there?"

"I'm speechless. But tell me, what color is the baby's hair?"

"She's bald, David.   Think of it, you're a daddy!   I'm a grandmother!"

"I'm thinking! I'm thrilled. I'll be there tomorrow. As soon as possible. Tell Hildy I love her. Can I talk to her?"

"She's sleeping. I'm sure she'll call you when she wakes up. But I couldn't wait. I feel guilty—stealing her thunder—but it was all so sudden. Are you sure you're all right? You sound a little... odd."

"I've had a few drinks with some people here. Believe me, Ruth, this is one of the happiest moments of my life."

"All right! I'm off! I'm going back to look at my little granddaughter. I can't get enough of her. Love you, David. Later!"

"Night, Mother." He heard Ruth click off and handed the phone back to the concierge, to whom he said, "I'm a father!"

"Congratulations, sir!"

As he approached the group at the table near the bar, he called to the waiter for drinks all around. "I just got a call from Washington," he told them. "I'm a father!"

A winner said, "Well, that beats my prize!"

Even Victoria, though quite tight, understood. "But the baby's early, isn't it?"

"Couldn't wait to get here," David said. "I guess she wanted to beat the millennium."

He looked down at the group of slowly-comprehending faces, torn from their antagonistic polemic, and saw an almost magical transformation occur.   Hesitantly, smiles appeared, an armistice was declared, and fellowship was rung back into the world. It prevailed, triumphed! Finally, even the battle-flushed Frenchwoman lifted her glass, and cried:

"A toast to the new father!"

Birth being the ultimate argument for no argument at all, they raised their glasses to David and saluted the mother, the newborn, and, finally, the dazed and sobering father.

"It was quite an achievement," he said, swaying, "if I say so myself."

"What are you naming her?" asked Victoria.

Without thought, David exclaimed, "Jessie!" because he and Hildy had already agreed on that.

Chapter
Thirteen

Autumn 1954

Back in the thirties, the McQueens had built the only true house on Fortune Island, the house now known as the Cogburn house, where, on occasion, resided "the evil gnome of the island," as Buttercup called the Reverend Jason P. Cogburn. Even then, during the Depression, even before that, during the rich and roaring twenties, Fortune Island was on the ropes, an old boxer with a history of losses written on his face. It had lost to countless storms that had buried Whalehead's greenery in dunes, and altered its inlets so many times that trade had been lured away to other, more promising ports up the Banks. Buttercup, sweatered and wearing woolen slacks, a scarf around her neck, was taking her constitutional. She was in her thirties now and felt the need for exercise, felt that she was, if still pretty, a bit too plump. As she climbed the dunes toward the Cogburn house, she wondered how its weathered white could look so dark on a crisp, bright October morning. It came to her that it must be the fault of Cogburn that darkened its façade. At three stories, the house was the tallest structure on the island. Was it just the cast of the morning sun that gave it that crooked look, or was it aging on its footings, sinking on one side in the dunes that she rarely climbed to? The surprising cross currents of wind, bringing flashes of heat and cold, were enough to make you wonder if you were catching something... or losing something, losing the company of the birds that were migrating south across the horizonless October sky. The island had lost every pastor who had tried to make a living on it. They went like the escaping birds.

The ever-changing weather, its sudden darkenings and brightenings, made the island seem a moody place, at least to Buttercup. Men didn't seem to notice. Her husband, being old, lived in the past, and Tom Judas resided intensely, it seemed, inside himself, apparently not noticing externals like the weather, the year-round humidity.   She wiped her forehead on her sleeve.

Tom was a luxury she and the Sheriff could ill-afford, a hired hand to do the things that her aging husband could no longer do; indeed, things that no longer needed doing. It was a good thing that the Sheriff had his retirement checks, a good thing that he owned the store and the property outright, otherwise they would be destitute. He had no business sense at all. He should have consulted her about hiring a man. His assumption of superiority to her in the business of living she recognized as a carry-over from his days of authority, but authority in a completely different field, and also as a product of his age, of his nearly thirty years of extra experience, which actually counted for nothing in business. No longer a child bride, she knew herself to be the practical one, and she knew that somewhere inside of him he knew it too, but would never let on. She said a little thanksgiving prayer for Miss Perle, who was paying her to tutor Jessie in arithmetic.

Buttercup was, yes, outright amazed at herself, for never suspecting that the child wasn't being taught, but of course there was no school on Fortune Island. She supposed the nearest school to be the one-room school on Portsmouth Island she'd heard tell of. She guessed she had assumed that Cogburn had been tutoring the child. She was ashamed to say that she hadn't thought much about it. Of course, Miss Perle could have taught Jessie, but, as she told Buttercup, she had her writing to do. She was finishing a book. Buttercup had always been a very quick study, if she said so herself, but, as she told Miss Perle, Jessie was easy to teach. "You tell her something once and she's got it. The thing is, Miss Perle, arithmetic isn't a problem to her like it is for some girls, it's a game, and she just loves to play it." It was so easy teaching Jessie, and so much fun, she felt that she was hardly earning her money, but she was grateful for it. "It's hardscrabble these days, and we can use it." When Buttercup had started out that morning, the horizon looked like a big lipstick smile. Now there was a fiery ball above the globe. She looked at her watch. It was nearly eight. Jessie would be waiting at the store for her lessons. They worked at the counter every morning, now, Buttercup on one side and Jessie facing her on the other, spinning books and papers about, breaking pencils and sharpening them, and in general having a good time.

Occasionally, Tom Judas would stand by, a quiet, lanky presence, almost always nowadays needing a shave. More rarely, he would help out with a suggestion. Like Buttercup, he was good at math. He was a mystery, though. Buttercup wondered why a young, able-bodied man would hide himself away on a dying island, but the Sheriff said he was an all-right fellow, a man with something on his mind, probably unrequited love. The Sheriff said, "He'll leave us soon enough, when he gets over whatever it is he has to get over. He fixed the outboard, didn't he? Something I couldn't do for all my trying. And he's a good checker player."

"And we're keeping a man in bed and board," said Buttercup, "so you can have a checker partner?"

The checker partner was behind the counter this morning. He had coffee waiting. And there was Jessie, eager as beginnings, with her books and papers spread out on the counter. She said, "Do you know that letter I've been waiting for, Buttercup? Well, it ain't come again today."

Buttercup said, "Hasn't! Hasn't! Didn't! Has not! Did not!" Buttercup took a sip of coffee. It was hot. "I know perfectly well that you know perfectly well that that is not correct and will you please stop using that country talk! You also know that mail can't come until the mail boat comes, so why do you ask every day?"

"Haven't you ever heard of hope?" asked Jessie. "Hope can make things happen that might not without it."

"Hope is good, but patience is better," said Tom, surprising them.

"We'll get her whipped into shape," said Buttercup, "or know the reason why."

"Now, Buttercup," said Jessie, "Ruth is paying you to teach me arithmetic, not English. She gives me English in the afternoons, and she's even started me on French!"

"Mustn't backsass," said Tom.

"Oh," said Buttercup, "she just likes to give me a hard time. Fact is, she likes to give everybody a hard time, don't you, you little brat?" She gave Jessie a hug and joined Tom behind the counter.

"Butter, Butter, Buttercup," said Jessie, "I sure wish we had started this sooner. It's some of the most fun I've ever had."

"Might have done," said Buttercup, "if it hadn't been for you-know-who. I don't care if I do say it. His neglect is criminal." She was speaking to Tom, whose face darkened.

He looked at Jessie, and she thought for a moment that he was going to ask her a question, but then withdrew behind that hard, handsome, dark-jawed face. It was as if he had put on a mask. But, next morning, he was back, and smiling, when Jessie came in with her books. It startled her to see him smiling. "What is it?" she asked.

"That letter you've been looking for has finally come." He flopped the thick letter on the counter. "I hope it meets expectations," he said.

At sight of the envelope she dropped her books and grabbed up the letter, turning it this way and that. "It's my first letter! It's the first letter anybody's ever written to me. There it is! Look at it! It's from Marie. She's my friend, up in Manteo."

Tom saw that she had tears in her eyes, tears for one letter, one out of the thousands that he might have written her from prison. But he could not, would not, have written her from there, and, though he felt sure that he had done the right thing in staying out of her life, nonetheless, he felt a pang of regret. It was hard to be made aware of how little he knew of this young girl's heart.

He watched her run out the door with her prize in hand. He looked away, and looked away from whatever he had just looked at. He lit a cigarette with his back to the door, blew a puff of smoke that he stepped through as he had stepped through fog on board ship when he was a merchant marine, with his useless eyes shut, but his ears, like a bat's, listening to close small sounds and distant obtruding ones, whistles, horns and bells, a clanging chain—now Jessie's running feet, their faint echo on the porch outside.

Up on the dunes, where it was gusty and she noticed that the sky was overcast, Jessie found a spot she hoped was away from all prying eyes but those of the migrating birds overhead or the little stalking, stalk-eyed crabs in the sand. She cupped her hands, lit a Lucky Strike under Buttercup's fluttering wide-brimmed straw hat, and began to read Marie's letter, the pages going dark with the darkening sky, but bright and brassy with Marie's spirit.

Hey, Sissy,

Sorry I haven't written sooner, but I had to wait for some news and nothing ever happens here, except my bratty brothers and sisters falling down or something, which is a big zero. You know where I am? I'm out on Remembrance Rock! I know you remember because of all the excitement that night. I got to tell you one of those stupid guys from the filling station saw me downtown and flirted with me. Can you believe it? Maybe he heard about me and my boyfriend the football player I told you about, breaking up. These dumb local boys think I'd trade one of them for another one of them? They're all dirt poor and I got better things to do. And I did one. Some friends of Pa came down

here from New Jersey to visit him and brought their daughter who is
maybe a couple of years older than I am, and they took me back to
New Providence, New Jersey with them. But there was really nothing
to see. Here I am in Yankeeland and it looks just like any old wide
spot in the road in any old place. Big old house, kinda nice, kinda like
home, same old thing, like the old dacha down here. Anyway, the girl,
whose name is Teresa Delgado, well, Teresa says, like this, "Let's blow
this joint!" So we hop a bus and go in to Newark, which is a really
big place, just the sort of thing I wanted to see, and then we take some
kind of train in a tunnel and go all the way over to New York. Wow!
Now this even makes Newark seem small. So we go down to believe
it or not Greenwich Village, just the most exciting place in the world!
You wouldn't believe the people that live in Greenwich Village, they're
the most interesting people I have ever seen. This is for me, I said! We
sit at a fountain in a place called Washington Square, which I am sure
you must have heard of, which has all these students from New York
University and all kinds of other characters in it, and we get to talking
to some girls who live in the Village and they say come on home with
them, their parents are in Europe or some silly place and they have a
house all to themselves. They're about Teresa's age. So we go with
them and the house is just beautiful and we sit in the kitchen and they
give us beer out of the refrigerator which has hundreds of cans of it
and they pass out cigarettes, regular ones but I was hoping for one
of those fancy ones, you know, REEFER MADNESS, but they didn't
have any, and we had a blast playing real music, not that damn folk
singing stuff I hear night and day, not that old shit-kicking country
crap, but Frank Sinatra and the Platters. People like that and we
danced together the girls and us and naturally I get sick as a dog and
heave everything up and splash some cold water on my face and start
pouring down the beer again and it was just about the greatest time
I ever had! That's the way to spend a night—drinking "P. Ballentine
and Sons, Newark, New Jersey"—that's an ad you hear on the radio
all the time up here—in Greenwich Village, and listening to Frank
Sinatra. I tell you Sissy I want to live in New York just as soon as I
can. I'm gonna see if my folks won't send me to school up here. They
might like the idea of the New School for Social Research. It's right up
their alley. That's what Teresa says. Anyway, sometime late that night
Teresa gets all scared and worried, probably from being drunk—I'm
having too much fun to worry about anything—and she calls up her

folks and they come over from Jersey and get us. They are FURIOUS! They tell her that she should have better sense, taking me off like that and letting me drink because I'm underage and she's older and ought to know better. Good thing for me she doesn't. I like her fine, Sissy, but I wish it was you that I'd been with and maybe some day the two of us can go to New York. Wouldn't that be great? And of course my folks are mad at Teresa's folks, sortof. But they're old friends so they don't make so much of it, but Momma says Marie you have to learn to be careful who you go off with because New York is a dangerous place for young girls and I say back to her shoot, Momma who is this Alligator guy that they are talking about on the radio? Is he from New York? No he ain't. Have you heard about it, Sissy? Well, BOO! They think there's some crazy man going around killing young girls, and maybe other people too right here in North Carolina. Momma I said they don't have no Alligator Man in New York—he takes bites out of them—whole chunks. They say they find most of the bodies in swamps and near rivers. And he's right here in the Old North State.

Sissy, you be careful down there, though I doubt if you're in much danger on that old island of yours, but a girl about your age was found dead floating in the Cape Fear River just last week. Her throat was cut and she had been molested, which you know what that means, I hope. RAPED. And about a month ago another was found up near Elizabeth City. Same thing. Pa says there's a wolf on the loose, so be careful, I doubt if you have anything to worry about. You know who it probably is, it's probably one of those goons down at the filling station, just the type, like the one who flirted with me. So maybe you should worry about me. You know what they say, I'll take Manhattan! Anyway, a dacha is supposed to be a country house you visit on weekends, not an all-year prison!

> *Your loving Sis,*
> *Marie*

Jessie lit another Lucky Strike and read the letter over again. Then she sat and thought about it, thought about Marie's adventure in New York and wished that she could've gone with her. She tried to imagine Greenwich Village. It sounded like a small place in a big place. It sounded like a place where people had a lot of fun. She was going to ask Ruth about it, because she knew that Ruth would know all about Greenwich Village. Ruth knew all about the biggest cities in the world. Ruth knew about

London and Paris and Rome. Ruth had been everywhere. And now Marie
had been some place important too. She decided to read the letter again,
so she lit another Lucky Strike and began:

Hey, Sissy...

A drop of rain splashed on the page, bleeding Marie's ink, making a
pale blue blot. Jessie pressed it to her heart to dry it.

❇ ❇ ❇

There was a damp, rutted, serpentine road, made so dark by the over-
hanging branches of the surrounding forest, dominated by red maple, with
swamp tupelo, sweet gum, tulip trees, and cypress, that, though it was
only late afternoon, and rays of sun, like gleaming swords, struck through
the interstices of the autumnized, dripping trees, the Reverend Jason P.
Cogburn decided to turn on the headlights of his new, used Ford station
wagon, big enough to hold a coffin, as he drove north from Elizabeth City
up to the edge of the Dismal Swamp. He had maneuvered this narrow,
bumpy road many times before. Only when it rained did it present a
real problem, otherwise it was merely an uncomfortable drive which he
mitigated with a pillow under his behind and a cigar in his mouth.

He was heading for Mumbo, a hamlet of inbred denizens who made
their living by hunting, trapping, or catching a variety of mammalian
swamp creatures—everything from bears to bobcats to beavers—reptiles
and amphibians—turtles, snakes, lizards, salamanders, 'gators, frogs and
toads—and over two hundred species of birds. They sold these offerings
on the outskirts of Elizabeth City to people of exotic tastes, thus making
enough money to keep the Reverend Cogburn coming to their collapsing
one-room church in order to re-supply himself with what he considered
the necessities of life, booze and smokes. Swamp people are hard to scare,
but Cogburn knew how to do it, which is why the local pastor liked to have
him come. Without Cogburn's visits, the local pastor would have starved,
or possibly been eaten, but Cogburn's visits at three-month intervals
reaped benefits for the pastor that lasted even until Cogburn's next visit.
A banner, hung over the front door of the ramshackle little church, caught
the imaginations of the swamp people by announcing FRIDAY NIGHT:
THE SAD TRAVELLER, THE REVEREND JASON P. COGBURN,
BRINGS YOU HIS SPECIAL BRAND OF TRUTH. FEAR THE LORD!
He drove into the clearing, his headlights scanning the banner, and saw,
on the sinking front porch of the church, the wicker baskets that held the
snakes, awaiting his performance.

"The congregants are gathered and waiting," said the pastor.

"I want only those men who gathered the snakes to work with me."

"They're the only ones who will," said the pastor.

Cogburn banged open the church door and marched up the aisle to the "oohs" and "aahs" of the congregation, their pastor deferentially following him. It was clear who was in charge, the man with the crazy-quilt gray stubble going this way and that. He looked out at these Holy Ghost people with a contempt that they could see and it only made them feel more in awe of him. He was a God-driven magic man, shaman and spook, and parents tucked their children close to them. He was not here to make them happy, he was here to teach and terrify, and he had not failed them yet.

Two snake gatherers brought the snakes to Cogburn and opened the wicker baskets. Unhesitatingly, he pulled snakes from the baskets and unwound snakes from snakes as if sorting them and had the snake gatherers lay them across his arms like a big stack of squirming kindling. The snakes flicked their forked tongues, smelling first the fear in his sweat, then, immediately, the fear receding, being replaced by something that held them from striking, the, to them, horrid odor of camphorous, charismatic confidence. They were overpowered by the stink of his will.

The Sad Traveller had always been afraid, and just as surely had always conquered his fear. It was as if he held the Medusa's head in his arms, her long dark braids squirming and snapping, but helpless to bite, hallucinatory. This was how he made his living, the only job he had ever known, and he hated it; snake-bit, he hated those who made him do it, those who had set him on this course, this life among the low and ignorant, his mother and father. He was drunker now than if he had consumed a quart of bourbon, drunk with the power that overcomes fear, but he had not touched liquor. He never drank on the job. Rule one, this, God's darkness, was his business, his stock and trade. God's hatred of the human animal, that was his business.

He said, in a voice that started low, so that the little congregation had to lean forward to hear him, some of them even cupping their ears, "He will send floods and tornados, water to drown the race of evil and winds to sweep the earth clean of them."

Now he raised his voice. "The honest serpents proved me a sinner and I was snakebit and outcast to wander the world alone, a sad traveller, in a world so evil it can't be described in any language of man, but can only be understood by those who can feel it on their skins, like the snakes. It is their fear that makes them strike at ours and ours at them. Also at ourselves, doing the wicked Juba, like coiled serpents in combat or in the throes of wicked, voluptuous sex.

"Once upon a time, wicked brethren, wicked women of the wicked brethren, serpents roamed the earth, serpents bigger than houses, who could spit fire like men spit hot tobacco juice, some who could fly, and beat great ugly bat wings above the heads of our little likenesses, the mice, the shrews, those whose hearts pounded like trip hammers with the speed of humming birds in fear as mine does now, holding these little replicas of the great ones, these copperheads, these squirming water moccasins, these noisy rattlers—shut," he cried, throwing a rattler down and stepping on its neck to hold it, with an alligator boot—"and they ruled because God made them to rule, the evilest things possible to think of, I say, were made to rule; the poisonous, the venomous, the vermin; the big fish eat the little fish, the great, the small, and this is all the creation of our God whose disgust at himself, whose purgation sent forth what evil he could rid himself of, them, us, else, whatever, that could manifest his disgust at sin, the sin he knew and understood, and, with us, through us, this and that, great and small, could purge himself, and must make the death to go with it, this and that, and here, there, and everywhere, make the death to go with it, that is proper to such evil; he ripped all this from himself and put it here and we are it, not the worst, for that came earlier, but also not the worst yet, and—" he threw the snakes forward out of his arms, people screamed, jumped on chairs, and snakes slithered into shadows—"*I am free of them,*" he whispered, then shouted, "*I Am Free Of Them!* You gather them, if you will, if you can. If they sink their venom into you, if they cause you with their ugly, dirty fangs to writhe in pain, as I have done, in a delirious visit to hell with a million needles in my skin, if they prove you not to be the innocent children you would wish to be, that is hell and that is here and now, that is the serpent and that is you, this and that, and everything but God himself, and both are the things of God, his love for his own goodness and his hatred of all that don't share it, those whose only redemption is to be of the poison, so immune to it, like the hoopsnake that bites its own tail with venom-dripping fangs and keeps on rolling down the hill to the land of the dead but never gets there, for death is life to our good God, and life bad death in hell, where his fallen-away evil has collected in a huge stinking, venomous, snake pit heap called the world."

He threw his head back, his Adam's apple bobbing, and a strange voice in a strange language emanated from his throat. Some said he sounded like a rooster, some said he hissed like a snake, some said he gobbled like a turkey, some said that it was none of these things but something different entirely, a child's scream that went on and on and was suddenly gone, like the ever-silent, agonized voice of God that speaks in storms through teeth of locusts, and it was over, and the Sad Traveller had done it again, had confused but transfixed them, like the slithering frightened snakes that had found the corners of the walls and floors of the tiny church in the primeval forest to hide in. The snake gatherers began to gather the frightened, spitting snakes with long forked sticks, cut for the purpose, pinning them at the neck, lifting them by the tail, and putting them back in the wicker baskets, while other members of the congregation, breaking into gurgling mindless song, collected the Reverend Jason P. Cogburn's alms in dented cups and frayed hats. He had done it again, earned his keep. He called to the crowd, "Let a young girl who is not a woman yet bring me a snake, and I will recompense her." He waved a dollar bill in the air, and scanned the crowd to see what female child, perhaps the chosen one, would have the courage to seek out and bring him a serpent. He spotted a girl of about Jessie's age who had already begun to search for a snake. He thought how much a dollar would mean to the child, the same dollar her parents would give him but never her, for he knew her parents, as he knew his own.

When the church had finally emptied of all but the pastor and himself, Cogburn sat at a table, counting and sorting his money, a good haul.

"You better watch out for thieves on the road," said the pastor. "Some of the same people who put the money in the hat tonight might decide to take it out again tomorrow."

"If I can overcome my fear of those stinking serpents, I don't think I have much to be afraid of from these slope-headed swamp hicks. Besides," he opened his jacket to display his pistol, "I always carry this, and I've got a shotgun in the station wagon." He pushed some money over to the pastor. "Maybe you ought to be careful yourself."

"Where is the Sad Traveller going next?"

"Oh, I'll be out on the road for another week or so."

"There's a radio report—"

"About that Alligator Man? He ain't after money. He's after thrills."

"No, I don't mean that madman. There's a storm coming. A big one, I heard."

"I saw the sky on the way up here—gray and drippy as wet cement."

"They're calling it Hazel, hurricane Hazel."

"Just more of God's ugly darkness, my friend. I'm heading inland,

away from it, maybe as far as Tennessee. So I don't give a damn what
he does out on the coast. First trick is to bump and bang my way into
Elizabeth City, then find a highway and climb up the Piney Mountains,
and over top the Smokies, where there's a church no bigger than a hangnail
that's been waiting for the Sad Traveller for months now, and right down
the road there's a juke joint, with a still out back, with white lightning and
black, red, high-yeller, and paleface Magdalenas. They even got a Chinee
fortune cookie there with a message inside her hot as fire I can warm my
feet at."

"I don't believe it," said the pastor.

"Believe it, Good Samaritan, believe it! You should come with me
before God drowns you in this here coming storm or these slope-heads eat
you for breakfast."

"I've always meant to ask you," said the pastor, "where do you get your
ideas for your sermons? They're... unusual. Not typically Pentecostal."

"I earned them." The Sad Traveller got into his rattletrap Ford station
wagon, blasted some fire and smoke from its tail pipe, and drove off under
the mixed green and autumnized canopy of the tunnel-like, kudzu-covered,
winding boondock road, the beams of his headlights bouncing off its maze
of walls, Appalachia bound.

Chapter
Fourteen

Even now, in Garcie's shack on Fortune Island, Ruth was about to recite a poem to Garcie and Jessie. "It's called 'An Appalachian Tale,'" she said—clearing her voice, deepening it—

"Played the devil's fiddle, stomping to it, shaking it out,
   full of corned blood, his boot down down down!
Days before the corn, his old bitch Lucy lay by his piston heel.
   Said later she smelled it, stayed by it, waiting
for the meaty bone; said later never done him no harm at all;
   said later not even a ghost of evil but Lucy got it,
old bloodhound bitch like red clay, wrinkled old lady hanging
   from her own bones—could make her moon-howl,
pointing his wild bow—do that at dances. Devil in a Baptist,
   playing the fiddle. Gradual as the mountains,
he found out how the devil got in. Fiddle under his spiked,
   gray chin, corn jug thumb-hooked and cradled on top
his elbow—capful for Lucy—then stomp stomp stomp: music
   through Blue Ridge pines! Could choo choo it
so's you see smoke and steam, hear that wheezy accordion whistle;
   could conjure with it up a trainload of places
or turn you back home to the station of pines and blue smoke
   mountains, bring musical rain, or put the devil
in your heart, winking and drinking and stomping. Everybody loved
   him and his Lucy, including said devil, as the corn dropped
down into his right big toe. Said it hurt to stomp. But it don't
   stop the fiddler. Don't nothing stop the fiddler! He was
one thing else than music; he was a man. Take more'n corn going

through, dropping down in my right big toe, says at
the May dance, everybody seeing him stomp, ouch ouch ouch on
    his big red gray spiked old corned face. Devil
got in through the corn, slick as silk; got down in my boot,
    but I'll stomp him out; give old Satan a head-
ache—stomp stomp stomp! But that corn went to killing him.
    His bow was flying! Went on like this, folks say,
a tad's five year, him stomping the devil in the corn and the devil
    stomping back. Said now he couldn't play no more if
he don't get rid o' that old devil. Takes him a broad wood chisel
    out back on a stump, sets his right foot up, sets
that chisel to his toe, and strikes down with a good hefty hammer.
    When he pulls back his foot, that devil in the corned toe
stays on the stump, says looka me, I'm off! Has brought him
    some fireplace soot and some gingham. Sticks that foot
in that black soot, to staunch the blood, and wraps it in gingham
    rags. Said never done him no harm again, quiet as a bone,
and he goes back to stomping in peace, rid of the devil. But
    first, he throws that old corned toe to Lucy. Says:
I knowed you always wanted it. Now mind the nail, Lucy; don't let
    the devil get you, you drunk old droop-skinned hound
bitch, cuz I love you. And Lucy goes to lickin' that toe, pops
    it in, and goes to grinding up that devil in her old ground down
chops. And next time we see them, the fiddler and his drunk bitch,
    they both full of corn, and ready, now, for the dance!"

"Ain't that good, Garcie?" cried Jessie, clapping her freckled hands until they hurt.

"It's a signifying tale," Garcie pronounced, "but a poem should rhyme, bang-dang, moon-June! That's the way the old timey raps done when I was a girl. But, got to admit, some of 'em wasn't fit for a young girl's ears. You ever heard tell of 'The Signifying Monkey,' Miss Ruth?"

"I've heard versions of it," said Ruth, "and you're right.

'There hadn't been no shift for quite a bit
so the Monkey thought he'd start some of his signifying—' "

"Don't you say that, Miss Ruth," cried Garcie, "not in front of the baby!"

"Shit!" Jessie exclaimed. "It's got to be shit!"

"I wasn't going to say it," said Ruth, "and I wish you hadn't."

"Amen!" said Garcie. "If I could find you, I'd whop you one!"

"Ruth says modern poems don't need to rhyme."

"Well, I'm sorry, Miss Ruth, but poems must need to rhyme," Garcie persisted.

"Carl Sandburg don't rhyme," insisted Jessie.

"Doesn't," said Ruth. "Carl Sandburg doesn't rhyme."

"Now what I'm supposed to say about that?" Garcie asked. "Should I change my mind because this old Carl Somebodyberg can't rhyme up two words? When I was a girl, poems rhymed up, and I liked 'em that way. How you know them old raps, Miss Ruth?"

"I'm a folklorist. It's my job to know things like that. About 'An Appalachian Tale,' Garcie, if you want to think of it as a story, it's okay with me. It's really a story, anyway, a tall tale, like 'Signifying Monkey.' I heard it up in the Black Mountains when I was collecting old English ballads. A mountain man told me the story and I just shaped it up into a poem—or maybe not a poem."

"Like I say," said Garcie, "it's signifying."

Jessie was at the door. "It looks like night out there."

"And it's only four in the afternoon," said Ruth.

"Storm's coming," said Garcie. "The banshees are out."

"And it's cold," said Jessie, pulling on a heavy sweater.

"I want y'all to stay with me, hear?" said Garcie. "Since I got good and sugar-blinded, don't like being alone in a storm. Tell us another story, Miss Ruth. Don't mind if it rhymes or if it don't."

Ruth said, "Tell us one of yours."

"I'll tell you one of mine," said Jessie. "When I was up at Capt'n Jack's, I met somebody you know, Garcie."

"Now who can that be?"

"I met Jimmy Twango James!"

"Twango? You never met no Twango! Twango got to be dead these many years." She thought for a moment. "Oh, my God!" she cried. "I know what you met, you met a ghost. You met the ghost of Twango James. He come to you to send me a message. That must be it. Was he all gray like a ghost?"

"His hair was gray. But honest to God, Garcie, he wasn't any ghost, just an old man, and he remembered you."

"He never! That must have been fifty years ago. I was no more than your age then."

"He sure enough did! He remembered about giving you that ring—the one with the two Ls, Love and Luck? Only he had the story a little bit different."

"Different? How? You know what? I don't believe you met the real Twango James at all, you little fibber! I believe you're making this whole thing up just for the sake of a good story." She laughed heartily. "Or maybe it was a ghost you saw, like I said. Twango James! He dead and in his coffin long since. Must be! Must be!"

"Alive and kicking," Jessie insisted. "Well, not exactly kicking, but sure enough alive."

"He was there," Ruth said.

"You know him, Miss Ruth?"

"He's world famous, Garcie. Old and famous. Everybody who likes jazz knows who he is. He was the best sideman in the business."

"Is that true, Miss Ruth? Famous? My own Jimmy Twango James? Well, I'll be!"

"No ghost," said Jessie, shaking her head.

"Well," said Garcie, "it's just like hearing about one. Makes a chill go up my spine to think that he come back after all these years. You know, Miss Ruth, we were in love once."

"Oh, listen to that," said Ruth. "It sounds like a thousand nails being driven into the roof. Garcie, do you have some more lamps? We'd better light them."

"Sounds like a church full of sinners got taken away and sunk in the sea and come up just a screeching and wailing like banshees. You girls, close them shutters! Somebody put a chair against that door. Sounds like it's gonna push in. Now, what's that?"

"Someone's knocking," Jessie said.

"There's water coming in under the door," Ruth said. She called, "Is anybody there? *Hello?* There's somebody out there. I can hear them but I can't hear what they're saying." She lifted away the chair that she had placed before the door and opened it.

Sheriff Walkup stood outside in a yellow slicker, holding on to his yellow hat. "Have you folks heard?" he called over the wind. "We've got a hurricane coming our way."

"No," said Ruth. "Garcie doesn't have a radio, and the battery's out on mine. Jessie left it playing when we went away. Do you want to step in?"

"Naw, I just wanted to warn y'all. We're about ankle-deep in water down at the low end of the island. Y'all up here are on high enough ground, I think, and y'all probably be all right; but if you want to, I can get y'all down to a Coast Guard cutter that's evacuating anybody who wants to go. What do you think?"

It was hard to be heard over the wind and the rain. He looked questioningly at Ruth. "Did you get that?" he yelled. "Did you hear me?"

Garcie called, "Somebody please close that door! Rain's flying in. I can feel it on my face!"

Ruth signaled for the Sheriff to bend down, and she stood on tip-toes and spoke into his ear, saying, "I don't know how we could get Garcie down to the boat. She can hardly walk."

He said, "I can help you now. I might not be able to, later. Y'all folks got to make up your minds. Can't stand here long."

Garcie got the drift, and called, "Garcie ride it out like she done many another." Ruth asked the Sheriff if he had heard. He nodded. Garcie yelled, "Those cutters have come down before and nobody's gone off on 'em. They just like to keep busy. I stay put."

"Tell her I agree," called the Sheriff. "I've ridden out quite a few of these storms myself."

He waved and vanished in a wet, yellow blur. Ruth pushed the door shut and put the chair back under the handle. "I'm sure we'll be all right," she said. "Want me to open some canned meat and beans?"

"Do that, Miss Ruth," said Garcie.

"I'm hungry," said Jessie. "I'm always hungry now that I'm doing all this brain work."

During supper, with the help of the howling wind, Garcie told them about the mysterious stranger who had come to her door and given her a kiss on the cheek and left her a bottle of Southern Comfort. "He didn't say a word," she said. "Not a whisper."

"You must have been dreaming, Garcie," said Jessie. "Once, I dreamed I was inside a whale and it was like Greenwich Village in there with all these strange people drinking hundreds of cans of beer and smoking reefers. Wow!"

"Wasn't no dream and wasn't no village," said Garcie, "and I can prove it."

"How you going to do that?" asked Jessie.

"You just look in that cupboard where my hand come upon it and you'll find that bottle. But don't taste it like I done! You're too young for such bad warm sweet goodness. Maybe you'd like a drink of it, Miss

Ruth? Warms the insides on a cold day."

"Maybe later," Ruth said.

Jessie jumped up from the table and went to the cupboard. "Danged if there ain't a brand-new bottle of Comfort up there! But there's five empties up there, too—old, spider-webbed and dusty, sugar-caked around the mouth. My fingers are sticky. That how you got the sugar in your blood, Garcie? That what made you blind?"

"Can't afford to buy Comfort every day. I'm a poor old woman. All I got is my allotment from your Maw-Maw and Paw-Paw. Used to pour sugar in it to soften it up, like to sweeten it. Oh, I had to stop drinking it, but Mister Mysterious, he don't know that. It used to be my favorite drink," said Garcie, "and that mysterious stranger, he done knew it, else how come he brought that to me?"

"It was a dream, Garcie," Jessie insisted. "You just had that old bottle left over. You just done forgot about it."

"You think nobody would bring old Garcie a gift? You think nobody would kiss old Garcie on her black cheek?"

"It was prob'ly the ghost of Jimmy Twango James come back to find his love," said Jessie, "but that ain't no ghost of Southern Comfort in the cabinet. That's rock-hard, hot-as-the-devil liquor up there!"

"I told you so," said Garcie, droopy-eyed, her head rolling to one side.

They roused her and put her to bed. She told them that in that nodding instant she had dreamed of Twango. "...And it was before I got old and fat and blind... and he was dancing with me... looking down at me with those big eyes of his... and I reached up... and touched that little black mustache of his... and he just smiled at me so sweet... and I began to cry. It seemed so real. But, Jessie, I believe you saw a ghost... a ghost..."

She closed blind eyes in a dark room the better to see her dream and perhaps saw it all again, felt the soft kiss once more. But how could she sleep? The tin-roofed shack was like a drum being beaten by one of the great, flying-haired, sweat-spraying drummers, Bellson or Krupa, or the pounding, ecstatic little genius, Chick Webb, that Jimmy Twango James had often jammed with.

"That gives me a headache," Ruth said, looking at the ceiling.

"Ruth, what's *Reefer Madness*?"

"I was going to ask you where you heard that," Ruth said. She looked at her cigarette, brought it to her lips, and took a drag. "A reefer is a cigarette made with marijuana and not tobacco. Where did you hear it?"

"Marie mentioned it in her letter. She mentioned a few things that I didn't understand. What's Greenwich Village like?"

"It's a place in New York. I have friends who live there. I'll take you there someday. Where's that bottle of Southern Comfort you and Garcie were talking about? Is it real, or were you just teasing her?"

"Ruth, have you heard of the Alligator Man?"

"No. Who's he?"

"He eats people. I thought you could tell me more about him."

"Never heard of him." Ruth was looking through Garcie's cabinets. "Oh, thank God! There it is!" She poured herself half a glassful of Southern Comfort and sat down with Jessie at the table. She slugged some of the amber liquid down and focused on Jessie. "What else has Marie been writing to you about?"

"Oh, lots of stuff. She went to New York and got drunk in Greenwich Village."

"I'll have to have a talk with Capt'n Jack about Marie."

"Why? You drink."

"I drink, I don't get drunk. Oh, maybe once or twice when I was in college." She gave Jessie a serious look. "I want you to go to college. I'm going to get you ready to go to high school and to college and all the way."

"Why? Why, Ruth? Why do you do so much for me?"

"It's just something I want to happen. You want it, too, don't you?"

"I do—so much! I want to be like you. I want to be like you and Miss Rachel Carson."

There was an ominous intangible tension in the air, a distinct feeling they caught from the atmosphere that something bad was going to happen. Jessie thought of how, during a storm, Garcie always said that God was moving his furniture around, but this sounded like he was stamping his feet in fury, and that reminded her of the Reverend Cogburn's God. She told herself that she did not believe any of it, that it was just nature acting up.

But Ruth saw that Jessie was shrinking in her chair. "I'll teach you a song," she said. "Do you know 'All Through the Night'?"

"No," said Jessie.

"It goes like this—

    Sleep, my child, and peace attend thee,
    All through the night;
    Guardian angels God will send thee,

All through the night;
Soft the drowsy hours are creeping,
I my loving vigil keeping,
All through the night . . ."

By the time Jessie had the words right, she'd stopped singing. Ruth carried on with the lullaby until she saw Jessie's eyes close, and even after that, sporadically, until Jessie put her head down on the table and fell asleep.

She woke in what seemed an instant, but must have been hours, when the storm intensified toward daylight. A particularly sharp strike widened her eyes. She asked Ruth, "Are you scared?"

"Of the storm? No!" said Ruth, filled with Dutch courage from Southern Comfort. "But I'm not crazy about it."

"Then I'm not scared, either," Jessie announced, sitting up tall and throwing her shoulders back.

At that moment the door broke open and water poured into the room like foaming ink. Instantly, it seemed, they were up to their knees in it. They could hear themselves screaming in shock. Then the water began to recede, leaving a room full of flotsam. Trying to shut the door, they saw in the morning light that the lowlands were awash. Then they saw something huge and black rolling toward them, a tidal wave like nothing they had seen before. And it struck, instantly lifting the water level in the room to the height of Garcie's bed.

"What's that?" Garcie cried, feeling the water and what it had brought with it—a small tree limb—no, a wriggling snake!—and the warm round belly of a just-drowned possum. "Oh, my God! Oh, my God!"

Now Ruth and Jessie saw a shrimp boat coming toward them from the lowland. The great dark hulk had been beached, down by the village, for repairs, and had been lifted by the surge and driven toward Whalehead. It came right at them, until something, a twist of the wind or a gyrating roof beam, something out there in the murkiness, had caught it and spun it around like a top. Then, so close to the shack that they could almost reach out and touch it, its bow aimed off in another direction, its whole huge dark port side passing in front of them like a wall that they themselves were passing, but not quite passing, because its bulk slammed into a corner of Garcie's shack, and, with a tremendous shuddering, the shack flew apart, leaving them in whirling black water, whirling black sky above, torn boards from the shack spinning around them, careening into them like little battering rams; and they were up to their necks in a maelstrom, half swimming, half dancing on their toes, and Ruth was trying her best to keep Garcie from drowning.

She swam holding the big soft woman up somehow with one arm and knocking debris aside with the other, shouting to Jessie, "Are you all right? Are you all right?"

Jessie went under and came up with a mouthful of brackish water. She started to go under again, for the water was filled with powerful hands, undertows and riptides, devil fingers, pulling her down, this way and that; but an angel hand pulled her up by her hair, pulled her aboard a bouncing, bucking skiff, and plopped her in its bottom like a netted fish.

She could hear Tom Judas calling to Ruth, "Get her up! Push her up! Push her up so I can get hold of her."

Finally, seizing the gunnel of the skiff with one hand and clinging to Garcie with the other, Ruth was able to get Garcie within Tom's reach; and, with a tremendous display of desperate strength, he pulled her aboard. Then, like a pair of trapeze artists, Tom and Ruth caught hands and he swung her up, so that, for an instant, she seemed to fly, and then landed in the skiff.

"The water's full of backtows," he shouted. "If I can maneuver them... they'll take us to the general store."

"Is Jessie all right?" Ruth called.

"Just got a stomach full of salt water, I think."

But Jessie, choking and spitting, had slipped over in her own vomit so that she could see the others, dancing gray shadows, see who was safe, and, stalk-eyed, saw pass over her, just above Tom's bobbing and weaving head, what she thought were birds but on second look in the slow, two-timing, instantaneous movie of this nightmare chaos turned out to be fish, she'd swear later, *fish*, a small school of silver fish flying through the air, as if swimming.

"Where did you come from?" cried Ruth.

"Rode the surge up. Look at that! The whole village is ten feet deep."

Tom couldn't control the skiff. It whirled and whirled like some kind of crazy, gyrating carnival ride. Everything was spinning, topsy-turvy, and jittering black and white like a silent film. Ruth couldn't have said whether it was day or night, though it was about eleven o'clock in the morning, and should have been bright day, near noon. She looked out through the surreal light for some orientation in this pandemonium, some landmark, but there was only water, black water, white water, coming down in gales, rising up in geysers.

Then she saw the sign sitting at the foundation of the store. It had been knocked down. But no, it hadn't been knocked down. It was just below the second story windows where it had always been; it was just that the second story was all that could be seen. The water had risen to the sign. But still, it was reassuring to see it, the white board, the black lettering—WALKUP'S GENERAL STORE.

The starboard side of the skiff banged against it, bounced back, then banged into it again. Tom and Ruth tried to anchor the skiff to the sign, first with their hands, then with a line pulled under the seats in the skiff and hooked along the back of the sign—"If the sign doesn't tear off," shouted Tom. The port oar jumped from its oarlock and slid away, bouncing and spinning atop every crest, almost flying.

Jessie's head snapped back as she was lifted from the skiff. The second floor window, just above the sign, had been torn from its frame, making a tableau of several people in the building. Jessie saw Buttercup, along with others, reaching out of it to pull her in.

Inside, she was dropped to the floor, where she lay limp and vomiting. She heard a struggle at the window.

Outside, Tom and Ruth were trying to get Garcie upright in the bouncing skiff. Garcie was limp, weighed over two hundred loose pounds, and the skiff was an unpredictable platform. It seemed an impossible feat until the skiff jumped above window height and Ruth and Tom put their shoulders behind Garcie and pushed her in, with a wash of water, toward waiting arms, and she was seized, slippery-gripped somehow, by those inside, pulled, by both arms, and pushed from behind, by Tom and Ruth, all in an instant; and down sank the skiff, like an elevator dropping a floor, and back up it came, and Tom pushed Ruth into the room, climbed onto the sign, and was pulled into the room himself. Instantly, the skiff tore away and was lost to the receding surge.

Chapter
Fifteen

Ruth stood in the middle of the room and counted nine people, including herself, some she knew, some strangers. Bloodied and matted, or merely muddied, none of them appeared to have been seriously injured by floating or flying debris. Seven of them stood like soggy Raggedy Anns or Andys and looked questioningly at each other, lacking a child's words for speech, and two lay prostrate, one choking, one showing no signs of life. They dripped on a wet beige rug in a small bedroom with a neatly made bed with a red spread and a ripped-out window and their rags fluttered like tattered flags with small gusts of the big, hazardous wind outside. The instant was surreal.

Jessie sat up, choking, coughing, wanting to ask for Garcie but strangling with every attempt.

Tom went to her. He seized her shoulders and shook her. "Are you all right?" He saw that she couldn't answer for gagging and slapped her several times on the back. "Are you all right?" he repeated. He looked in her eyes for answer and saw that she was safe, nodding her head. He wiped the blood from a few minor abrasions on her face; then went over and kneeled down by Garcie, who lay, like some kind of beached sea creature that showed no signs of breathing, in a heap of twisted wet nightclothes. "Somebody get me a rolled-up towel to put under her neck," he called. He checked her pulse, her heart—nothing!

Buttercup brought him a towel and he put it under Garcie's neck. He opened Garcie's mouth and leaned down into it, forcing breath down her throat, once, twice; then pressed his large hands on her chest and threw his weight into them, one, two—fifteen—times. Two more measured breaths into her mouth, and he repeated the process that he had learned as a young lifeguard.

Finally, water leaped from Garcie's throat, pinkish, foamy. He turned her on her side and let it run. Then he stuck his finger down her throat and explored her air passages. They were clear. He laid her back as she had been and gave her more breath, more powerful pumping pressure on her chest with his hands, then turned her on her side again and more fluid poured from her mouth. At last, she heaved and began to breathe. "She's all right, I think."

"Good job!" cried a ruddy-faced, Moses-bearded man wearing a captain's cap. "You brought her back to life! Couldn't have done better myself."

He recognized the fishing boat captain, Captain Baft, then the Captain's son, the Captain's wife, and his daughter-in-law, from their occasional visits to the store.

Jessie was finally able to speak. "You did do it! You saved my Garcie's life!"

Buttercup said, "Let me get you a cup of coffee. It's not hot anymore, but I'm sure it'll help."

"I'd rather have a shot of whiskey."

"I'll second that," said Captain Baft, "and one for my boy, here, too."

"We could all use a drink," said Ruth.

"Then you'll have it!" Buttercup went away and came back with a bottle of whiskey and poured some into Tom's coffee, then poured them all a drink. "Where do you suppose my husband is?" she asked. "Has anybody seen him?"

"He's probably up on the high ground," said Tom, "up on the dunes of Whalehead somewhere. It's not flooded up there. He could have gone to the Cogburn house. It was still standing the last time I looked. Or he could have gone to Ruth's cottage."

"I'm sure he found some shelter somewhere," said Ruth.

Tom said, "A Coast Guard cutter will come back as soon as it can. They'll send a life boat out to us. Buttercup, why don't you get everyone some blankets. We have a storeroom full. We might as well try to get some rest."

"What if the water rises up here?" asked the Captain's daughter-in-law, obviously terrified.

"It's already receding," Tom said.

"How do you know?"

"Because the same skiff that took me up to Garcie's on the surge brought us back down here without any help from me."

"I'd say it crested long since," said Captain Baft. "We just have to wait for help. The Coast Guard'll be along."

"This is a general store, after all," said Buttercup, returning with blankets. "There's plenty of canned goods. We could eat something. I was going to suggest that we go into the storeroom, but all the windows in there are broken. We're probably better off staying here. It's not so bad."

"Bad enough," said Captain Baft's son.

"How about a game of cards to kill time?" said Captain Baft.

"I'm sure somebody can think of something to do," said Ruth. "We've got oil lamps. Let's get some light in here."

"There's a box of dry matches in the dresser," said Buttercup.

"There, see," said Tom. "Everything's okay."

Buttercup said, "Tom, I know you know the Bafts."

"I know them, too," said Jessie.

"Ruth, this is Captain Baft and his son, Robert, and their wives. I'm sorry, I don't know your first names."

"Louise," said the older woman.

"Cathy," said the younger woman.

It occurred to Buttercup that this was the friendliest they had ever been, although they had visited the store many times.

"Garcie's shaking," said Jessie.

"She could get pneumonia from having all that water in her lungs," said Ruth. "We should put her to bed. Do you mind, Buttercup, if we put her in your bed?"

"I'll help you," said Buttercup, and Tom and Ruth and Buttercup struggled to get Garcie across the room and into bed. Garcie could help now, a little, and, once she was in bed, and Ruth had gone off to help Buttercup get supplies, Jessie tagging along, Garcie spoke, saying something in a broken, muffled voice about a mysterious stranger—at least that's what it sounded like. "Mysterious stranger? Is that what you said?" Tom put his ear close to her mouth. "Talk to me, Garcie. Please, talk to me . . ."

Garcie whispered, "Don't tell me it ain't... Billy McQueen... come back." She grew excited. "I know you, Billy... I know the touch of you."

"Oh, my dear Garcie!" Tom whispered. "*I love you . . .*" He squeezed her hand and felt pressure back, then release as she slipped into sleep. He stood back and looked at Garcie, then Jessie came up and stood beside him.

"Will she be all right, now?" Jessie asked.

"I believe so," he said, realizing that Garcie's recognition of him would change everything.

"I'm going to snuggle up to her," Jessie said. She crawled in beside Garcie, who seemed to know and opened an arm for her. Seeing them like that, Tom was reminded of when he was a child and slept in Garcie's arms, just as Jessie was trying to do.

He went over to the window and looked out on the flood, hearing the rumbles and roars of lions of wind, and seeing gray, sparless, torn sails of rain. Black water just below him lifted and dove in a desperate search for floodgates. Now that Garcie knew about him, his plans must change. He could no longer be the guardian angel of Jessie's life, watching over her from a distance without interfering, without bringing his own troubles to her, making them part of the difficulties of her life, except in the most extreme circumstances. Trouble, not always of his own making, was all that he had ever brought to others. He did not want to be guilty of bringing more.

He felt Ruth come and stand beside him. He remembered hugging her, pushing her body through the open window. He had not felt the closeness of a woman for many years. He looked at her. She looked at him. They had learned a lot about each other out there on the water, more than some learn about each other in a lifetime.

"You saved our lives," Ruth said. "It was very brave of you to even try it." She put a hand on his shoulder and pulled him down to her, kissed him on the cheek. "Thank you," she said.

"You saved Garcie," he said, "in the water back there. You're strong in every way. Strong and brave, too. I've got a lot of respect for you."

"And I for you."

✄ ✄ ✄

Garcie slept, Jessie drowsed. The crackling ballet of lightning-footed thunder could not rouse them.

Jessie's head had found a place on Garcie's chest, her right ear buried in Garcie's left breast, beneath which Garcie's heart beat with a comforting, steady thud, the iambic squeeze and thud of a pump, and Jessie had drifted off into a dream of soft drums, until the heart sound sharpened and hollowed into a rapid tom-tom beat, and, with one final burst, stopped. Startled awake by the silence beneath her ear, Jessie called, "Garcie,"

shaking the old woman by the shoulders—"Garcie, wake up! *Please,
Garcie. Wake up!*"

Tom came over.

"It's Garcie," Jessie cried. "She won't wake up." She shook Garcie
uselessly. "What's wrong, Garcie?"

Tom felt for Garcie's pulse, wrist and neck. "*Oh,*" he sighed. Suddenly
everything was the same as before. Garcie no longer knew him. She
would never know him again. Billy McQueen was dead, absolutely dead.
He had belonged to Garcie, and she was gone and he had gone with her.
He didn't want to tell Jessie, but the words just fell from him. "She's
gone," he said.

"Oh, no!" screamed Jessie. "*No, no, no, no, no!*"

Tom stood looking at Garcie, watching Jessie tugging at the old
woman's body, his mind gearing to no effect.

Ruth came over and tried to pull Jessie from Garcie's arms. Jessie
wouldn't let go. "Stop it! Stop it!" she cried. Ruth pulled her fingers free
of Garcie and pulled her from the bed. "Come over here with me, baby."

Jessie was wild, desperate, hysterical.

Ruth made her drink some whiskey.

She choked it down, red eyes shooting hot tears.

Everyone was awake now and gathered by the bed.

Buttercup pulled the covers up over Garcie's face.

"She was holding me," Jessie cried, sobbing. "I could hear her heart
beat. Why did it have to stop? Why did it have to stop?"

"She's gone on her way," Tom said, finding his thoughts at last. "It
was time for her to go and find the people that she lost in this life. She'll
be with them, and she'll always look down and watch over you. I know
she will. You believe that, don't you?"

"No! And I have no one now. Who do I belong to?"

"Don't be afraid," said Ruth, hugging her. "You belong to me."

"And to me," said Tom.

"Who are you?" Jessie cried. "I don't know who you are. I don't
belong to anyone! My mother and Garcie belonged to me. My father
must have belonged to me. My real father, not Cogburn. I'm talking
about Bill McQueen, the criminal who deserted me." In a fury, she tried
to pull free of Ruth. "He deserted me and my mother and left us with that
evil old devil Cogburn. If he ain't been hanged, he should be. I'm talking
about Bill McQueen. He's the real evil one—to leave us for the Devil to
take. He's what belongs to me—nothing! The most evil, selfish man in

the world. He's the reason my momma's dead. I hate him. I hate him like he was a copperhead snake. If I ever got hold of him, I'd cut off his head like a snake oughta be done! Leave me alone." She sobbed with a broken heart.

Tom was nonplused at her outburst. She only echoed what he thought of himself, what he had thought of himself during the whole long twelve years of his imprisonment, the guilt over his failure that had grown larger and larger in his conscience until it dominated his being. It had turned on him the way the body turns on itself until it had consigned every good in himself to shadows and cast unbearable lights on his failures, even inadvertent, as a man. Now—how could he ever tell her the truth?

The building quaked. "Hear that? We're in trouble here," said Captain Baft. "That's at least a hundred knot wind out there." For an instant they all stood still, fell silent, listening, like platformed window washers hearing a line snap. Even Jessie stopped her keening. She looked from face to face. Then Louise Baft cried:

"Trying to ride this one out was a big mistake!"

"Your idea, Pa," said Robert. "I was for getting out of here."

"Me, too," said Cathy Baft.

"I thought we should stay with the boat," said the skipper.

"Look," cried Cathy, "I can see the street!"

Tom went to the window to look out. "Be careful, fellow—both of you!" exclaimed the skipper. "You could get sucked right out and find yourselves up a tree in Ocracoke before you know it, or get your heads bashed in by a flying beam."

"The wind's shifted," Tom said. "My God, most of the water's gone already."

They had grown used to the flapping on the roof, probably some loose shingles, almost unconscious of it, but now it grew in intensity, like great beating wings. But now there was something else. They tilted their heads up to the ceiling to the sound of a big zipper being pulled and getting stuck and being pulled again. Then a whole section of the roof was gone. Rain travelled horizontally above their heads in silver streaks like bullets aimed to the north. Beyond the glittering rain was a black sky. They found themselves standing in a whirling shower containing bits of wood and plaster. That portion of the roof that was gone had taken the stove pipe with it, and smoke rose in the room, wet black dust, but dispersed almost immediately in the tides of air.

"We've got to get downstairs," Tom said, "before this whole level is blown off. The water's gone. It's the wind now."

"I agree with Mister Tom," Captain Baft said. "This is no time to be at the top of the mast. But what about the dead woman?"

"She don't feel nor know a thing about it," his wife said. "I could almost envy her. Let's let her be and get down before the roof goes."

"No!" Jessie screamed. She ran to the bed and threw herself on the body, arms and legs reaching for the four corners of the mattress in an attempt to shield Garcie from the pouring-in rain. Tom went to the bed and began to push it across the floor to a drier corner. Ruth seized the foot of the bed and pulled. The Baft family joined Tom in pushing. Together they got it out from under the downpour. "Not that it'll do much good," Captain Baft said. "There's a freight train made of water and wind right overhead and it's heading north."

"It's for the girl's sake," Tom said to him. He reached down and took Jessie by the waist and pulled her away from Garcie. He carried her out to the hall, toward the stairs. "Somebody bring a light," he called.

Jessie thrashed and screamed, but he could hold her in one arm and raise the lamp Ruth had given him with the other. Ruth and the Bafts followed, then Buttercup. Ruth called down, "Be careful! You and Jessie and the lamp will all go down together in a heap."

"At least there's no reason to worry about fire," Tom called back, "everything's drenched."

The stairs were littered with debris, some of it soggy, some of it dangerously hard and sharp—clothing, canned goods, soggy boxes of cereal—and the way down was narrow, Jessie making the way down even narrower with her thrashing. He slipped, almost falling, righting himself against the slimy wall of the stairwell, and decided to put Jessie on her feet and drag her if he had to. He could hear her now sobbing, panting, and coughing behind him as he pulled her by the wrist, and then his lamp opened the room before him on a display of ruin.

Buttercup, the last down, put a hand to her mouth, then a hand to her breast to steady her heart. It looked like a complete loss. All the goods that she and Tom had so neatly stacked on the shelves were on the floor—a mine field of ankle-breaking canned goods, fishing gear and tackle, hooks and broken glass, seaweed, even a few dead animals. There was still an inch of muddy water on the floor, which would have to be swept out, once the floor was cleared of its heavier, harder, and more dangerous debris. All the windows were broken. The doors stood open, or were torn from their hinges, she couldn't tell. "We're ruined," she cried.

"Pardon," said Captain Baft, "but this is no time to be worrying about the store. If we're to worry about anything, we got to worry about the rest of this building just standing."

"Everybody find a place," said Tom, "and try to make yourselves as comfortable as you can." He spotted a small, wriggling water moccasin, seized it by the tail, and whipped it out the door. He watched as the snake seemed to fly across the flats on the unrelenting wind. "Look around before you sit down," he said. "Don't get a cut or a bite. We don't have much in the way of medical supplies. Be careful."

Ruth asked, "How long do you think before the wind settles down?"

Captain Baft said, "If it's moving along at about thirty knots—"

"You said a hundred knots," his daughter-in-law, Cathy, said.

"The big circle is going at about a hundred knots, is what I meant, but the whole damned system is moving north at about thirty. Now if it's moving along at about thirty knots, three-hundred miles in diameter, say, the big wind should be north of us by dark, maybe sooner. Safety by five, is what I think."

Jessie sat on a soggy burlap bag of cornmeal and thought of how many times she'd come to get Garcie a bag full of the ground yellow grain, how no one had minded as she used the tin scooper to fill a brown paper bag of the stuff for Garcie, who never had enough, it seemed. Jessie was ashamed to discover that she was hungry for Garcie's hush puppies and chicory coffee. Hungry! With poor Garcie above her there, dead in that soaked bed, how could she think of food? She would never eat again! Never!

Ruth put an arm around her. "You're shaking like a leaf," she said. "If only we had something warm for you to drink."

Tom joined them. He had an unopened pack of cigarettes, a lighter, and a bottle of whiskey. He said, "Give her a drink of whiskey," handing the bottle to Ruth, and tore the cellophane from the cigarettes.

"Want one?" he asked Ruth.

"They dry?"

"Sure they're dry. Packed in cellophane. If I can only get this lighter to work." He thumbed the wheel of the lighter several times and caught a spark, then a flame. "It's amazing, isn't it? Some things still work." He pushed a cigarette toward Ruth and held out the lighter to her.

"It's a godsend," she said, drawing on the cigarette as if the smoke were made from the clouds of heaven.

Jessie's brain seemed to drift sideways in her head, like a pellucid jellyfish, but it wasn't a bad feeling. "Can I have another sip of that whiskey?" she asked. "I don't think—" Ruth began to object, but Tom said, "Give her another drink. It'll do her good—anesthesia." Ruth let Jessie take another sip from the bottle. "It burns, but it burns good," Jessie said. "Is this why you grownups like it so much?" Her brain, that jellyfish, seemed to swim out of her ear, leaving a dark void, and a few hours later she woke, crumpled like a scared black snake that's turned itself into a stick, a fallen tree limb, and immediately felt that something had changed, something was missing. The roar of the wind was missing. And so were Ruth and Tom.

She found them out on the porch of the general store, where the winds hounded their clothing but did not blow them away. Even Jessie could stand in it now, her hundred, swaying pounds rooted by Earth's weak gravity. Ruth turned to her. "It's over, baby. It's heading up north."

"Let the Yankees have her," said Captain Baft, standing, now, behind Jessie. "She's none of ourn now."

Jessie looked out on the rain-curtained devastation, turned on her heel and scrambled back inside and up the slippery stairs to Garcie. Much of the roof was gone. She pulled the cover down and looked at Garcie's face. "Are you smiling at me, Garcie, or are you smiling because the storm has gone up north to visit the Yankees?" She leaned over and kissed the dead woman's lips. "Oh, Garcie, I loved you so much! Good-bye!"

Downstairs, the Bafts had decided to go and find their boat. "It's just a squall now," said Captain Baft. "I calculate the eye of the storm came up to hit the mainland southwest of us. We got the south to north surge of it. Thank the Lord the eye didn't pass over us or we'd gotten it coming and going. I reckon things are quieting down now. We'll just go and find our boat."

Robert said, "Forget it, Pa. That boat's done sunk or gone to fishing by herself."

"That boat rode out the storm, don't you worry none," said Captain Baft. "I had her anchored good so she could run like a dog on a chain. But as far as I'm concerned, folks, that's it for Fortune Island. I been thinking for some time that it got put in the wrong place. Well, this time I'm going to find me a better place. I'm through with Fortune Island. It's damned to hell."

"You're a leader among the fishermen. If you leave, they'll all follow you," said Buttercup, "and the Sheriff and I will be out of business."

"You should leave, too, Mrs. Walkup," said Louise. "This here island is snakebit, and that's for sure! I been telling the Captain that for years."

"But—"

Tom and Ruth stood by, helpless to help, almost hopeless themselves.

With no more to be said, the two Baft men had already trudged off through the rain. Now the two women followed them, sullen and silent, and vanished behind the torn gray sail of the late afternoon.

"If you need anything," Buttercup called after them, "the storeroom is full of goods. Some of it's probably all right. Whatever you might need!" she called. "You know your credit's always good here!" She wondered if they could hear her. "Well," she said, turning to Ruth and Tom, "it's just us chickens now." She hardly knew what she was saying; but she knew that she was afraid of being left alone; and she didn't understand why the Sheriff had not appeared; why, as soon as the weather had improved, he hadn't, he didn't come to help her. Was he lying dead somewhere? Had he been swept away? She felt like a woman on a widow's walk. No!

Just then Jessie put an arm around her waist. She said, "Don't be afraid, Buttercup. Garcie's not afraid. You should see her up there in bed, eyes shut and a smile on her face like she's dreaming something good."

Buttercup gave Jessie a hug and said, "Lord, y'all are still soaking wet! We've got some dry boxes of jeans and shirts upstairs. Ruth, why don't you take Jessie up and find something to put on? Then Tom can find him a dry outfit. On the house."

"I'll hear nothing of that," said Ruth. "You've still got a business to run, you know. I'll pay for everything." Ruth saw desperation in Buttercup's eyes. "And don't worry, Buttercup," she said, putting an arm over Buttercup's shoulder, "we'll help you set things straight."

"It's the Sheriff," Buttercup said.

"He's probably asleep up at the Cogburn house," Tom said.

"Let's go," Ruth said, taking Jessie by the hand. Inside, she picked up an oil lamp, and they made their way up the dark stairs.

Buttercup turned fear-stricken eyes to Tom. "Really, Tom, where can the Sheriff be?"

"He probably doesn't want to wade down here in the dark any more than I want to wade up there in the dark. He's a sensible, patient man. And I hope I am, too. We'll wait till morning to check out the houses on Whalehead. A lot of snakes will be washed down in the mud flat and the water will be up to our knees in places. For now, we can go inside and clear some things away and set up camp. We've got Sterno. We can heat up some canned goods and eat something."

When they were all in dry clothes again, Tom said, "How about some kind of word game? Something to do. Do you know any word games, Ruth?"

"Have you heard of Botticelli? Not the artist—the game? It'll keep us busy till we fall down somewhere."

"I know how to play," said Buttercup, "but it might be too hard for Jessie."

"We'll keep it simple," Ruth said. "But I don't think anything's too hard for Jessie to pick up."

"What?" said Jessie. "Do I look dumb? How do you play?"

They began clearing a space inside as they talked.

"The main way is that one player thinks of a famous person, gives the others the first initial of that person, and then answers yes or no questions to allow other players to guess the identity of the person they're looking for," Ruth explained. "The game gets its name from the question, 'Did you paint a picture of Venus Rising?' And the answer to that would be *are you Botticelli?*"

"I've got a T," said Jessie. "You know who it is? William Makepeace Thackeray who wrote *Vanity Fair*."

"That's not how you play," said Ruth.

"I don't care," said Jessie. "I don't give two heaps from a horse's rear end."

They heated up some food on Sterno burners and ate and played Botticelli until nearly midnight, by which time Jessie had learned the rules, and was playing fairly well. She would never forget the strangeness of that night, them playing, and even sometimes laughing, below, and Garcie dead above them. Life seemed cold and cruel, but what were they supposed to do, what choice did they have? She was a scientist, she told herself, and must look things in the eye. She guessed that was what the others were doing. Losers weepers. She put Garcie out of her mind for the time being and tried to guess who was next. Ruth was the chooser and was asking for a 'G.'

"Are you God?" Jessie asked.

"We don't use God in this game," Ruth said.

"We do use water," said Tom, distracted. "A lot of the cisterns down here will be polluted, but the ones up on Whalehead should be potable. We can bring water down here in buckets, if we have to."

"Ruth's got a cistern and Cogburn's got a pump," said Jessie, something she had not thought much about before the storm. There was a mechanical pump in the kitchen. Jessie could see Susannah working it with her bony, freckled arms. But the water was brackish, salty, whereas the water from Ruth's cistern was sweet clean rainwater. "The water at Ruth's is better," Jessie said.

"We'll take a couple of buckets with us," said Tom, "and bring you down some fresh water, Buttercup."

"I don't care about water. If I want a drink, I've got Co-Cola. I want you to get up there and find the Sheriff, that's what I want."

"Do you want to come?"

"I better stay here in case he shows up."

None of them slept that night. Jessie hadn't slept for two nights in a row, only that nap in the afternoon. And the game went on, the game of talk, and the talking game, it all went on and on, endlessly. The wind howled like the banshees Garcie used to tell her about, slamming, now, at the front of the building instead of the back. The wind came right into the room and made their clothes flap and made them wet all over again, no matter what plaster shield or onyx tabletop they set up to block it. Tom poured himself glass after glass of whiskey but showed no sign at all that it was having any effect. He'd cupped his own and Ruth's cigarettes to light them with his large hands. They were steady. Finally he said, "It's lightening out."

"Lightning?" asked Buttercup. "It's been lightning all night."

"No, lightening, getting light! We'll need some slickers and some rubber boots. Let's gather things up. It's time to go."

Outside, in the dim morning light, the little expeditionary group paused, before going on to Whalehead, to peer down at the Flukes, where there was a warren of ramshackle fishermen's shacks, which must have been submerged by the tsunami-like surge. The huge area of the Flukes was dark with distance and there was something of a fog between themselves and it. Closer up, they could see the church, a blocky steepleless whiteness; closer still, the steeple itself lay pointing north. There was no sign of life down there. A rain like hovering spindrift dampened their faces. Without a word, but with one will, they turned north, toward the mud-flats, where light seemed to pool and vanish and pool again just ahead of them, like the water of an oasis in the desert. Their boots sank in mud and came up tangled in soggy seaweed and clumps of marsh grass. The flats were littered with small dead mammals, food for snakes that slithered in what looked like disorientation. Tiny crabs ran across their boots, shrimp paddled in new, impermanent ponds, where clumps of fire ants floated on rafts of their own dead, and superior, stilt-legged heron hunted and feasted.

All was unreality, or an unrecognizable reality, all that Jessie felt and saw. Suddenly she was wading knee-deep in refuse-strewn muddy water—and where was the light coming from? There was no sign of the sun, but from behind a blotched sky a weak light emanated. They could see without flashlights now. And gradually the ground cleared of the pools of water, as they climbed up to the dunes, which were twenty or more feet above sea level, and gained the consistency of wet beach sand, making for better footing. Ahead was the ridge of the dunes, in places an escarpment—in one such place Garcie's shack had stood—in other places a climbable rampart, or slope.

Garcie's shack was gone. Nothing remained but strewn rubble, sheets of corrugated tin from the roof, torn and twisted. It had been built into a cave-mouthed escarpment and the cave remained, inside of which, on its side, lay Garcie's stove, which had stood in the main room. It was all gone, the place where Jessie had been so happy with Garcie on numberless days and nights, all gone.

She tried to go into the nothingness of it and stumbled over something—Garcie's little metal memory box. She seized it up in her arms as if it were a drowning baby. "Look what I found, Ruth!" she called. She opened the box and pushed things about with a long slender finger that slipped into Garcie's golden ring, hooked it, and lifted it from the box. Even without benefit of much light, it glittered.

"It's Garcie's Love and Luck ring," Ruth said, as Jessie held it up for her to see.

"Is it mine now?" Jessie asked.

"I think she'd want you to have it," Ruth said.

"It's too big."

"I'll get you a gold chain and you can wear it around your neck. It'll be a memento, a keepsake, something to keep Garcie with you over the years."

"I'll wear it forever and forever! I'll never take it off!"

Tom knew the ring better than Jessie did. He remembered the buzz about the house when his parents discussed Garcie's infatuation with the jazzman Twango James. He remembered their concern for her, that she not be hurt by a sophisticated older man, and their relief to find out that Twango James had treated Garcie with gentlemanly respect and kindness.

As he grew up, he had heard her embellish this story until it had become a great romance, the ring her proof. "Let's go to the house," he said, with surprising abruptness, and began seeking a new path—the old one had shifted away—up onto the dunes. It was then, around a bend, that they saw it: the shrimp boat. The prow of the boat was wedged in the dunes like a spear in a tree. "That's what hit us," Ruth said. "That's what shattered Garcie's shack."

"It's going to take a crane to pull that out," Tom said.

"Do you suppose that's Captain Baft's boat?" asked Ruth.

"Don't know," said Tom.

"Hope not," said Jessie.

"Come on," said Tom. "Let's go."

They climbed up onto the dunes, and there, not fifty yards ahead of them, stood the great old house, noble of height for the island, if ramshackle, firmly footed in affirmation of Tom's father's building skills.

"It looks all right," said Ruth. "You'd think that big full sail of a house would have ripped down the middle in a wind like that."

"When I was young," Tom said, "I spent a lot of time at sea. I learned that it isn't just one wind, it's a million going at different speeds and not all in the same direction. Some snap this way, some that, like the lashes of a cat-o'-nine tails. They'll skirt around one thing and catch another. They call it multiple vortices."

"*Vortices?*" shot Jessie. "It didn't hit it because the old bastard wasn't home."

"Jessie!"

"You mean Cogburn?" asked Tom.

"Well, I don't mean the Sheriff. Now he might be there, and he's a good man, and maybe that's why it didn't get hit."

"Let's go have a look," said Tom.

Tom was first to reach the porch, the porch where he and Susannah had last sat together as man and wife. He could see himself and Susannah sitting there, over a dozen years ago. He was holding baby Jessie. He touched the façade of the house behind the invisible chairs where they had sat. But the past was intangible. Jessie skirted by him, pulled open the front door, and walked in. He and Ruth followed.

"A few broken windows," Tom said.

"Nobody was here," Jessie said. "There's no bottles on the table. Everything's slick clean."

"We better check out all the rooms," said Ruth.

Tom took the first floor, Ruth the second, Jessie the attic. In a few minutes they gathered again in the kitchen.

"I don't see any structural damage," Tom said.

"There's nobody in the bedrooms upstairs," said Ruth.

"The roof is making a flapping sound," said Jessie.

"Any leaks?" asked Tom. "Water on the floor up there?"

"Dry as a bone," said Jessie.

"I think it got away pretty clean," said Tom.

"No sign of the Sheriff," said Ruth. "I was hoping, for Buttercup's sake, that he'd be here."

"Where can he be?" asked Jessie. "I hope he didn't go off into the sea like my momma done."

"Well," said Tom, "let's take a look at your place, Ruth."

But the Sheriff wasn't at Ruth's cottage, either. "He may have found his way back down to the General Store," Tom said.

"Let's face it," Ruth said, "he may be dead. He could have been washed away."

"Not if he was on Whalehead," said Tom. "The surge didn't get up here. The only damage up here is wind damage. There's a big hole in the side of your cottage. Something must have hit it. But it looks like you got spared, too."

"I'm scared for the Sheriff," said Jessie. "I'm scared for Buttercup."

"Don't look at the dark side," Tom said. "The Sheriff could have found a cave out on the dunes somewhere. Under all this sand there's soil and under the soil there's rock with a lot of caves in it. Haven't you ever gone exploring, Jessie?"

"Momma and Garcie always warned me about the caves, how they could fill up on a sudden with water, but they didn't understand the tides. Them caves don't scare me none." She flushed, realizing she'd given herself away. "Well, I did do a little exploring, if truth has to be told." She brightened. "Maybe he did find him a place. I'm going to go out and look for him. I'm going to the top of the dunes." And she was off like a yellow jacket, her slicker flying.

"Don't go near those caves!" Ruth called after her. "Do you hear me?"

"Let's hope for the best," said Tom.

"We've got to rig up something to close that hole," Ruth said. "I understand you're a good carpenter, Tom."

"Pretty good," said Tom. "Want me to do the repairs?"

"Yes—well—I've been thinking about adding a room. Maybe this would be a good time for it. Right where that hole is."

"You want to add a room?"

"With Garcie gone, the Reverend Cogburn is going to need someone to take care of Jessie when he goes out on the road. I'm planning to take over that job. She'll be spending a lot of her time here with me and she'll need a room. Can't have her sleeping in a sleeping bag all the time. And maybe enough space for an aquarium—room for a little marine collection."

"That's pretty ambitious," Tom said.

"If you think that's ambitious," Ruth said, "you have no idea." She laughed. "I've been helping her to read a great big book on biology by H.G. Wells. It's called *The Science of Life*. It's not really my subject, but I'm learning a lot from it."

"Helping her to read? Are you teaching her to look up words in the dictionary?"

"She already has that habit," Ruth said. "She's a remarkable child. She's been educating herself since she was quite young."

"When she's down at the store," Tom said, "Buttercup and I try to break her of that country talk. I wonder why she clings to it?"

"She clings to it because it's a security blanket. She knows better, but she feels safe with it."

"I think it's wonderful that you're showing such an interest in her."

"It's more than passing, Tom. I'd like to adopt her."

"She's a lucky girl," Tom said. "It's good to know that someone cares about her."

"Her birthday's in November," Ruth said. "Could you have the room ready by then? It could be her birthday present. She'll be thirteen."

"Thirteen!" Tom looked over the dunes in the direction Jessie had gone. "She's growing up, isn't she?"

"She's almost a young woman."

"Yes," said Tom. He seemed to shrug a weight from his shoulders. "I'd be happy to do the job. But right now I've got to get back to Buttercup and see if the Sheriff has showed up. I should take a couple of buckets of water from your cistern down to her. Then I should set to work clearing her cistern out. But I'll get back up here as soon as possible and do this job for you. I think it's a wonderful gift. I'll do it for nothing. You just pay for the material. I'll get everything from the mainland as soon as possible."

"Do you think the Reverend will agree?" asked Ruth. "I mean, about me taking care of Jessie?"

"Why wouldn't he? No pun intended, but it'll be a godsend for him."

"That's what I've been thinking," said Ruth.

Chapter
Sixteen

In a few days, the great galaxy of windborne water called Hazel arrived in Canada; but those on Fortune Island were only aware that it had left them, some of them, not only injury, but choices, not choices, but decisions. Most of the damage had been caused by the sea surge, by the tsunami caused by the northern spin of the big skirt of the eye when it was southeast of them. To their good fortune, and to the misfortune of others, the eye had gone inland and up the continent.

In time, connections were reestablished, most symbolically by the return of the mail boat, which, on one of its visits brought the Reverend Jason P. Cogburn back to the island and on another, took Gullah Garcie Garson away with it, and, two weeks later, brought her back for burial. There was still no trace of Sheriff Walkup. As she and Tom and Jessie cleaned up the store, washing everything down with bleach to kill mildew, Buttercup pined in uncertainty and sometimes certainly mourned, bursting into tears and sobbing so that Jessie went to her and held her, the child comforting the woman. Then one day a volunteer contractor came from the mainland with his crew on a barge holding a large crane with *Dixie Constructors* written on it. The crane ground its way, tilting and sliding, across the mud-flats, which had become dry and cracked, and pulled and lifted the shrimp boat high out of its wedge in the escarpment, swung it on chains in a great circle and started to grind its way down to the Flukes, when something that looked like a yellow seabag detached itself from the keel of the shrimp boat and fell to the flats with a fluttering *FLUMP*. And so the mystery of where the Sheriff had gone was solved. The crew of a coast guard cutter took the Sheriff and Buttercup back to the mainland. She would bury the Sheriff in Morehead City, his hometown. Trial by ordeal had exacted two deaths of the denizens of Fortune Island.

The amateur archeologists of Fortune Island discovered the tombs of the dead—respectively, the black graveyard and the white. They would only need the black. They cleared it before Garcie's remains returned to the island.

Two black men, strangers, perhaps relatives of Garcie's, appeared. They threw themselves into the cleanup along with the natives, those few remaining. They began to dig a grave for Garcie. Tom Judas spoke to them. They got out of the half-dug grave and he finished the job alone. People wondered about it, fleetingly, but were too busy to hold the wonder, that wonder or any, at the time. It seemed as if Tom climbed out of the grave moments before Garcie was lowered into it. Jessie threw a handful of dirt on the coffin, and the two black men finished the job. Tom stood aside, sweating in the cold November air, and watched Jessie as she watched the two men work.

The Reverend Cogburn hired the two black men to repair his screens and windows, fix some roof damage. He frowned at the fact of Garcie's death, but said little. He twisted the top off a bottle of Wild Turkey while the black men hammered. Thanksgiving, the general evil had scarcely touched him—thanksgiving, he could feel the heat of the bourbon reaching his skin, his capillaries—thanksgiving, his house still stood—thanksgiving!

> When the wind blows down the house we thank the Lord
> that we were out that day; or, when the sea
> turns our mast under its swashing opaque belly,
> and we are thrown clear, we swim and pray
> thanksgiving, thanksgiving, selfishly forgetting
> that, like so many bits of bait, our mates
> twirl downward in the darkness,
> being bitten and consumed.

The black men were hammering on his roof and he sat at his table, glowing, playing solitaire. But then, in an abrupt change of mood, he said, "How can a man concentrate with them niggers banging their coconuts together like that?" But then he saw a way of making the game work and fuddy-duddied with the cards under his hand, trying not to let Jessie see that he was cheating. "Now!" he exclaimed. "Now it works!"

It was then that Jessie realized that Cogburn was growing old. It was a shock of recognition—that beard, always short, tight to his face, spiky, growing in different directions, had become soft and pale. It fell in one direction now, as if it had lost its strength. It saddened her to see it—mine enemy grows older—and she felt a rare moment of tenderness for him. How strange that was!

"Weren't you even a tad worried about me?" she asked him.

He picked up his glasses and scanned the storm news headlines of the newspaper. "I knew you'd be all right."

"How could you know that?"

"I was worried about you. I was worried about the house. I was worried about everything. That's my job. I'm a worrier."

"What about Garcie?"

"I was worried about her, too. Was anybody worried about me? I was stuck on the mainland." He looked up over his glasses. "What did you expect me to do? Wilmington got hit hard, but don't bother me with that. I've got problems of my own." He pulled off his glasses and flung them on the newspaper. "You're beginning to remind me of your mother, little Magdalena. What do you want?"

"Do you want me to fix you something to eat?"

"No. Get me my gun out of the pocket of my coat there on the clothes tree, and get me the cleaning equipment."

Jessie gathered the cleaning equipment and brought him his pistol, holding it with a thumb and forefinger. She dropped it on the table.

"Easy!" He began to clean the pistol. "Those nigger workmen won't ask me for so much if they see this cannon on the table." He poured himself another Wild Turkey.

"What problems have you got?"

"I've got to figure out what to do with you, don't I? You're still too young to just be left alone. People would think I was doing wrong by you. Got to find somebody to replace Garcie, somebody to take care of you when I'm away. I been thinking about that Buttercup—or, do you think that gallivanting girl friend of yours... what's 'er name?"

"Ruth. Doctor Ruth Perle!"

"Doctor?"

"Doctor of Philosophy. I bet you didn't even know there was such a thing!"

"Whatever give you the idea that I don't know about such things? Where you ever been, little girl? I been up and down in the world and back and forth in it. There's also a Doctor of Theology. Did you know that? And a Doctor of Psychology." He took a drink, puffed his cigar. "And a Doctor of Laws! But anybody ain't a medical doctor is just plain showing off using that title, which is another thing you don't know. You got you a whole stack of ignorances. Your ignorances stack up taller than you do. But here you are, and here's the house—no big damage done, not counting Garcie, of course—and I have important things to do on the mainland. I have to turn you over to somebody. I've got a parental responsibility."

"*I've got a parental responsibility*!" Jessie mimicked. "I'd say the only reason you came back was so that you could sit around here and get drunk for a couple of days where nobody who looks up to you out there can see you."

"Go ahead, mimic me! And I'll ignore the rest of that. But these things have to be done. Think she'd be interested in taking care of you?" He ran his tongue along his lip.

"She might." Jessie intuited that she should be cautious, tried to show no emotion, knowing that if she showed Cogburn how pleased she was he might not do it, he was that ornery, but it was, by gosh, faceflushingly, heartpoundingly wonderful that he might turn her over to Ruth's care. Or was he just teasing her?

The cylinder of the pistol hung open and he was running a cloth down the barrel. He paused to take a drink, then said, "Some kind of Yankee, ain't she? Ain't she a Jew?"

"She's rich and she's famous. She was the guest of honor at Beaufort. The mayor was there and made a speech about her."

"And you were there, I suppose?"

"She took me with her. What's wrong with that?"

"And what's she so rich and famous for?"

"She writes books."

"Uppity little skirt! Well, I've got no choice. I've got to go over there and talk nice to her about you."

"I'm coming."

"You stay right here. Keep an eye on them niggers. If they get done before I get back, make them wait outside. Rich and famous, eh? I like the sound of that."

He reloaded the pistol and slammed the cylinder shut.

"I'll try charm," he said.

When he left, Jessie vented like an old steam locomotive. Phew! She lit a cigarette, held it out and looked at it, the way Ruth did, and, "cancer stick," she said. Some people called them that. She vibrated with hope and fear, hope that things would go well and fear that they wouldn't. Who

knew with the Reverend Jason P. Cogburn? He was half drunk already.
But maybe he was in just the right mood to get along with Ruth. "Maybe
it'll be okay," she said, with a tongue tangled in smoke. She tried to read
a page of *The Science of Life*, but found it hard to concentrate.

The workmen were still hammering on the roof when he returned a
few hours later.

"She's agreeable," he said. "Get over there and see her—and be on
your best behavior, little Magdalena, you hear me?"

"You got along with her?"

"I got along with her Jew money."

Outside, Jessie waved to the men on the roof and broke into a dead
run across the dunes, Garcie's heavy gold ring—Love and Luck—on a
long gold chain, swinging, punching her chest, her heart counterpunching
through her thin, heaving ribs. She could swear she saw the sun break
through the clouds. She was in a sweat when she got to Ruth's.

"What happened? What did he say? Please, Ruth, stop lighting that
cigarette and tell me what he said!"

"Calm down, sweetie, everything's fine."

"Well, what happened?"

"He's the one with the problem, honey."

"And I'm the problem."

"To him you are. To me, you're the prize. He's got to find somebody
who'll stand in loco parentis for him so he can get off this island when he
has to. So, as you might expect, he behaved himself. He even offered me
what might be considered by some a nice little stipend; but, of course, I
refused it. I've got more money than I'll ever need. You're no problem
to me, sweetie. I love you. I told him I couldn't accept his offer but that
I'd make him a counter offer. So the upshot of it is this—you pretty much
belong to me now, just as I said. Remember? Didn't I tell you that? Now
what do you think of this? What if I were to adopt you? Cogburn is
willing, given the right incentive."

"Oh, glory, glory! Would you do that? What do you mean,
incentive?"

"A sum of money. A tidy sum. The adoption won't be based on that,
but he won't do it unless his palm is crossed with silver. There are lawyers
in Wilmington we can use. They may be able to take your statement and
present it to a judge. It may be possible that you not be there at all. These
things can be done."

"Oh, thank you, Ruth, thank you, thank you!" Jessie threw herself into Ruth's arms. Ruth held her for a moment patting her back with her free arm, the arm holding the cigarette held away, then with both hands she held Jessie at arm's length. "And I've got a surprise for you. I pretty much thought things would go like this, so I hired Tom to build a room on this house—your own room! But you've got to keep it nice and clean and orderly. It's my job now to teach you self-discipline. In fact, it's my job now to teach you everything."

"I already know how to smoke."

"You little devil! I thought I'd been missing cigarettes. We'll put a stop to that, first thing."

But Ruth was laughing.

Jessie was crying. "It's a whole new life," she said.

Winter 1954

Hurricane Hazel was beginning to seem like a bad dream that the island had awakened from to find that life had achieved an approximation of what it had been.

Tom had been doing a lot of repair work on Fortune Island, cleaning up, construction—or, rather, reconstruction—and was being constantly called to work by the few people left on the island. Mixing and pouring concrete, Tom glistened with sweat. He tore off his soaking wet tee-shirt, but he was grateful for the heat, grateful for the fickle weather of the Outer Banks. Winter on these islands could force you to wear heavy garments for the cold or to strip away your clothing for the heat.

Ruth got up from her work and looked out the window at him often, his long black hair dank and flopping about as he heaved over tubs of cement, or was it concrete, she didn't know, had never known which was which. But she did know that it was very hot work that he was doing. His bronzed back was burnished with sweat. She called out to him:

"Hey! Why don't you come in and have something cold to drink. I can fix you a sandwich. Or just to cool off. Come on in. Take a break!"

He stood up and looked at her, wiped his brow on his forearm. He was about twenty feet away. She saw the body of Michelangelo's David. But that face, simultaneously rugged and sensitive, whose face was it, that seemed so familiar?

She was surprised. His desire was for hot black coffee. He sat across from her and sipped it. "I had two eggs this morning," he said. "I usually only eat one. I feel stuffed. I don't eat that much." He lit a cigarette.

"You're really a singer, aren't you?" Ruth asked. "When you got off the mail boat you had a guitar with you."

"The hurricane got it," he said.

"Why do you stay here—on this island—what's here for you?"

"I write songs in my spare time. I like the isolation, the quiet."

"I write books on folklore and poetry. I like it here for the same reason."

"I know," he said. "Would you mind if I were to ask you something personal?"

"That depends," she said. "But go ahead."

"Jessie tells me that you're going to adopt her. Is that true? And, if it's true," he added, getting down to cases, "how are you going to do it? I mean, I thought that it wasn't possible for a young unmarried woman to adopt."

"I've been married. Had a daughter of my own. Both my husband and my daughter are dead." He started to speak, but she waved away his words. "So I've had some experience, you see. But on the technical side, the legal side, I have lawyers who can fix it, make it happen. First I'll get guardianship, then adoption. My situation is a little different from the average."

"You mean you've got the money."

"Why, yes, but—"

"Excuse me," Tom said. "I didn't mean to be so blunt. I've been rather isolated from civilization for a long time. Lost my manners."

"You've been a sailor, haven't you?"

"I've been at sea."

"How do you feel about me adopting Jessie?"

"What would I feel about it? Really, it's none of my business. I was just curious—about how it would work." He finished his coffee. "But, personally, I think it's a great idea. The best thing that could happen to the kid."

"I'm glad you approve."

He shrugged. "Absolutely."

Ruth laid a dog-eared magazine down on the table. "Do you know about this case on the cover? 'The Case of the Veteran's Gang,' or whatever."

Tom was caught off guard. "I'm familiar with it," he managed to improvise. His blue eyes were icy.

"There's an interesting picture in it—a picture of a boy with white hair. It's so strange to see such a youthful face and that shock of white hair surrounding it. Isn't that odd?"

"Odd, yes... "

"Why don't you take it along with you when you go and read it?"

"Don't you want it?"

"Heavens no! I don't really care for that kind of story."

"I don't either."

"Well, if you don't want it, just throw it away. But if you ever want to talk about it, I'd be willing to listen."

Tom said, "I'd like another cup of coffee, if you don't mind. And can I borrow a cigarette? I'm out." He crumpled a pack and threw it in a wastepaper basket where it vanished in reams of rejected writing.

Ruth refilled his cup with coffee, handed him a cigarette, and lit it for him. She sat down across from him and smiled, displaying a mouthful of even, gleaming teeth, and perhaps for the first time he saw that she was a beautiful woman.

He smiled back, but it was a sad, surrendering smile that touched her nonetheless. She felt sure that he was unconscious of his own charismatic powers, that he was unaware of himself, and his unselfconsciousness, amounting to a kind of innocence, intrigued her. She could see that he wanted her but would never make the first move. She said, "You know Jessie won't be back until this afternoon."

His eyes had warmed. "You're a beautiful woman, Ruth."

Ruth shrugged, got up, and stood, waiting. "You're not so bad yourself, Tom."

Tom stood up. But he was uncertain, conflicted. Ruth saw his hesitancy and took his hands in hers, wanting his arms around her, wanting her hands on his back. "There's time enough, Tom," she said, stepping closer.

"Time enough to get acquainted, do you think?"

"Oh, plenty of time, Tom." She moved in between his arms and flattened her hands on his back. "Delicious," she whispered.

He hadn't felt a woman's touch on his body for nearly fifteen years. It was so exquisite a sensation that, for the moment, he needed nothing more. But then the moment passed and he was in another place. He and Ruth were alone in the world. She was the focus of his being. He could see nothing but her and hear nothing but her voice and feel nothing but her body—his body and her body—the one body of them both, a being unto itself, which had found her bed in the no-place that surrounded it, had become one voluptuary that seemed to be speaking in tongues, humming in magnetic attraction.

When it was over, Ruth laughed. "Wow!" she exclaimed. "I feel like I've got bubbles coming out of my ears."

"Me too," said Tom. But immediately his head cleared, and he wanted to know what this would mean for Jessie.

"Jessie'll be all right," Ruth said, lighting them both a cigarette. Then she said, "Why don't you want to be her father?"

Tom jumped out of bed and pulled on his clothes. "She hates her father. Besides, I'm bad luck," he said.

"No she doesn't. She was just terribly upset. And that's nonsense, Tom. People aren't bad luck, they have bad luck."

"I've had most of my life to think about it," he said. "All I have to do is get near somebody and everything goes to hell."

"I remember you pulling us all out of the water, saving our lives, and that was good luck you brought us."

"Luck's a chance," he said, "but trouble's sure. I'll come back in the cool of the evening to work on the room." And he was gone. Ruth lay where she was, satiated, inseminated—she'd taken no precaution, had not wanted to. It was crazy, but she didn't care. She loved him. She turned over and went to sleep.

⌘ ⌘ ⌘

Cherie Marie,

Ruth is teaching me French. Parlez-vous Français? How's the weather in New York? Have you had any snow yet? I've never seen much of that stuff in my life. Ruth tells me that in New York and Boston it stacks up on the streets and covers everything and is really beautiful at first but then it gets dirty. Too bad! Down here today it's kinda cool and the skies are gloomy, but I'm not. I was afraid to ask her what a diaphragm was, because I suspected that it was something biological, so I asked Buttercup, and she explained it to me. So now I sort of understand why you burned yours. I know you were very angry at that agent of yours who got you so many dancing jobs in New York and all and then went off to Hollywood with somebody else, so naturally you burned your diaphragm, but to be honest, I don't really see what good that would do because you'll have to get a new one, won't you? I mean, you'll have to get a new agent, so I suppose you'll need a new diaphragm. Or am I getting things all wrong?

A month ago, Tom that I told you about, and who is really a piece of attractive, and a very nice guy, too, poured the concrete slab for

*my room. Well now he is framing the room and making a lot of noise
with his hammer and you can't hear yourself think over at Ruth's, so
I came over to old Cogburn's house to write this. He is, as usual, on
the mainland. He still leaves the place open so I can get in. It's kinda
creepy, thinking he might walk in the door, but it's quiet.*

*The last time I saw him was when Ruth took me to Wilmington
a couple of weeks ago to talk to a judge at the courthouse. I was
surprised to see him there. There must have been twenty lawyers, all
of them working for Ruth, some from Boston (I could tell because of
their accent—they sounded like Ruth) and some from Wilmington, or
at least from North Carolina. Ruth bought me a new dress to wear
before the judge, who asked me a lot of questions, like how did I feel
about Cogburn and how did I feel about Ruth and how did I feel
about everything and then they stuck me out in the hall with Cogburn
sitting across from me for a long time not saying a word and finally
he went in.*

*I've never seen him like that. He had a shave and a haircut
and he looked a little scared of all of those lawyers who paid very
little attention to him. It was strange. He always seemed to be
the most important person wherever he was, but not this time. He
seemed a bit shrunken up. But it was like he was hoping everything
would work and he could get rid of me, like he was afraid something
might go wrong and he'd be stuck with me, and I could feel it. Ruth
was different. She was the queen of the courthouse. Even the judge
seemed to be under her spell. It was exciting to see what a really
important person she is. You never get that when you're alone with
her, she's so regular. Once, Cogburn called me Cinderella. I don't
know what Ruth did to him, but whatever it was, it made him a lot
nicer. In fact, I think it was the nicest he'd ever been to me.*

*I hope you get a new agent soon and write and tell me all about
it. And now that I know what it is, I'm sure you'll be getting a new
diaphragm. But Marie, there just ain't no sense in burning them.
Temper, temper! That's what Ruth always says to me.*

*Oh Marie, you just couldn't in a million years imagine how
wonderful I feel every time I think of the fact that I am really and truly
going to be Ruth's daughter soon. I love her so much I just have to
run out of words. It's all in my heart that pounds like Tom's hammer.
I know you must love your parents, too. Maggie is super and Capt'n
Jack is the bravest man I ever saw. But I know you don't like them*

trying to tell you what to do. Me, I'd do anything Ruth asked me to
do, just to be with her. I would just die if I ever lost her love.
Love, love, love, kiss, kiss, kiss,
from your Little Sis

⌘ ⌘ ⌘

The joy Jessie's belated thirteenth birthday present in the form of her new
room at Ruth's cottage brought her was as much a gift to Tom as the room
was to Jessie. Ruth had all the accoutrements necessary to the room of
a young girl brought over from the mainland, including a canopy bed, a
beautiful undersized overstuffed rocking chair, and a large aquarium—the
sea life to be supplied by Jessie. Everything that should be was fluffy and
pink. It was as if Ruth had picked things out for her own daughter, who had
died so young, for her own daughter who had magically reached the age
of thirteen. She cut the ribbon at the door to the room and Jessie entered
into a childhood she had never known, and perhaps had grown beyond.
When Jessie turned about to thank her benefactors, they stood arm-in-
arm, smiling in anticipation of her joy. There was joy, indeed, in Jessie's
eyes, but also discernable doubt, inconclusiveness. Ruth and Tom were
let down a little, but tried not to show it. They sang her "Happy Birthday."
They cut the cake that Ruth had brought back from Wilmington. But there
was a green cast to Jessie's blue eyes, and they wondered why the happy
day had not quite come off as they hoped it would. "Next birthday, we'll
take you in to Wilmington for a real party at a hotel," Ruth said, trying to
compensate for something she could not account for, something that struck
her as strange. What's wrong? she wondered. What more can I do?

Tom wondered what had happened, too. He thought perhaps that
Jessie was overwhelmed. When she had gone into her new room that
night, he said, "Maybe it was too much for her."

"Everything was fine until she looked back at us," Ruth said, some
subtle voice whispering beneath the surface of her mind about some new
concern, some trouble to come that she couldn't quite put her finger on.

Tom thought he might know what was going on but was as yet too
constrained to speak openly of it. But he knew that he must tell Ruth
about it—not today, not on Jessie's birthday, but soon. He had not heeded
the flirtatious adolescent eye-batting when it had occurred, but, after the
major incident, he remembered it, and thought that it had boded ill. The
major incident had occurred about two weeks before. He and Jessie had
been walking the beach. It was another warm November day. Jessie was

wearing a tee-shirt. Suddenly she ran into the surf, neck deep, and came back to him and stood there, heaving her chest, her arms goose-pimply and purple. He realized that she was being seductive as she danced before him on the sand. He didn't want to believe it but it couldn't be denied. Her breasts swelled and nippled the soaked tee-shirt, and she knew it, he could see. It was deeply embarrassing to him, but he didn't want to make too much of it. He took off his shirt and draped it around her shoulders. She looked hurt, disappointed, resentful, even angry, and stalked away as if he had done or said something very unpleasant to her. Here it was, he told himself, the bad luck coming, the trouble coming. It had worried him ever since.

Tom's most powerful fear, of destroying Jessie's chances once again, made him wish to withdraw, to leave the island before his burgeoning love for Ruth sucked him into a crazy triangle that could lead to God-knew-what damage to Jessie, perhaps even the loss of her biggest chance for happiness. He brought bad luck to those he held dearest, had always done so. The hopes and dreams of a child must outweigh the passions of a man—his feelings for Ruth—or he's no man at all.

Chapter
Seventeen

November 2000

R uth reached out from her chair beside Jessie's bed, pushed a button, and Jessie slowly rose to face her.

"Not too high," Jessie said. "It squashes my insides. Makes it hard to breathe."

"How's that?"

"Fine," Jessie said, with a sigh. "I don't know what squashes. There's nothing in there anymore."

"Just guts," Ruth said. But Jessie only weighed seventy-five pounds, according to the nurse. Of course, that was just an estimate. Ruth hadn't let the nurse disturb Jessie for a weighing-in. There would be no more treatments, no more medicines, only pain-killers, Ruth had decided. Jessie agreed. She was going to have a drink, if she wanted one. She was going to have whatever she wanted, Ruth had decided, and nothing she didn't want. They both knew this was the end. The metastasizing crab had found its way to Jessie's brain. Jessie would die at home in her bed in Chapel Hill. No more hospitals, no more medicos, no more discomforts, even agonies, of treatment—just Ruth, Juanita, and the nurse, until things took a turn.

"I was remembering the lighthouse," Jessie said, "the one on Ocracoke, the way it twinkled like a star. I'd lie on the sand at night and watch it and think of it as my own, as if others couldn't see it."

"Yes," Ruth said. "Yes." At that moment, she'd have given anything for a cigarette.

"We have defeated the foe," Jessie said. She would have laughed, but laughing hurt her chest. "Not this time," she said. "It's funny, the things people say, isn't it?"

"That was when you saw the Liberty ships when you were a little girl, before I found you."

"A moth-balled fleet, somebody called them. I can still see the cypresses behind them. That was Wilmington, from across the Cape Fear River. It seems like the only thing I remember from back then. No, I remember my mother, with her long red hair and her one bad eye. Poor sad woman. I might have shared her fate, if it weren't for you. Fortune Island... I never hated a place more nor loved any place as much. But it was the loneliness that I hated and loved."

"I always loved the isolation of it," Ruth said, "but I got lonely, too."

"In memory, it was its desolation that was both beautiful and ugly."

"Yes," Ruth said.

"Ruth," Jessie said, "move the oxygen away and give me one of your cigarettes. I know you want to smoke. You can smoke if I'm smoking. Get us both a drink and give me a cigarette. Don't worry, I'll just puff on it. It's just a hand habit."

"I wish I had never let you smoke," Ruth said.

"If it had anything to do with this," Jessie said, "it's secondary. I had a genetic weakness. So far, at least, it seems that you don't. It could have been anything that triggered it, even emotions. A man's wife dies and three months later he drops dead, or gets sick and dies. Or a lifetime of stress, holding something in, or keeping it from yourself, that weakens your immune system, and suddenly you're a target for God-knows-what, except that there isn't any God."

Ruth rolled the oxygen cylinder into the hall, called for Juanita to bring them drinks, whiskey and sodas, and lit a cigarette for herself and Jessie.

"Do you know anything about neuroscience, Ruth?"

"Existential biology?"

"Something like that," Jessie said.

"You were turned away from belief before I got to you," Ruth said. "The older I get the more of a poet I become. I'm not religious, but, as Dylan Thomas said, the wind is."

"The answer is blowing in the wind?"

"That's the other Dylan."

"Oh—I confuse them."

Juanita brought in a tray with their drinks. She frowned disapproval.

"It doesn't make a bit of difference... Juanita," Jessie said, "what I do."

"Si, senorita."

". . .Not a bit," Jessie said, as Juanita pulled the door to behind her.

Ruth said, "I have a letter here I want to read to you. It's a very old letter. It's about the kind of man your father really was. I always told you children that your father died in an automobile accident. After a while it just seemed best to let it stand that way. I didn't want you to know that he died in prison."

"Prison?"

"Yes, he died in prison. It was a great disgrace. I didn't want you children to be burdened by it. But now I think you should know how it happened; because, believe it or not, though he died in prison he was a great hero, as you can tell from this letter. Listen—"

Jessie tried to sit up in bed.

Chaplain Baker had written:

> Here, behind the Wall, things happen suddenly and senselessly. I was umpiring a baseball game. A prisoner disagreed with my call and came after me with a bat. Tom stepped between us and received a glancing blow. He was treated and thought to be all right. He died a week later, as I have described. We are considering charges against the person who struck him, a petty thief who claims to be the notorious Alligator Man. He has been proven not to be, but such is vainglory. I am so sorry. Tom probably saved me from a serious beating, if not death. He was an old and dear friend and a truly wonderful man of great, almost morbid, sensitivity. His was a noble, if melancholy, soul. I was always surprised by his sudden traces of dark humor. A person of talent and depth. I am proud to call him my friend. You will receive further information by and by.
>
> Yours in God,
> Chaplain James T. Baker
>
> P.S. I do not believe him to be any more guilty of this crime than the crime he was previously incarcerated here for. Bad luck rode like a blackbird on his shoulder.

⌘ ⌘ ⌘

That afternoon Jessie lapsed into a comatose dementia, her mind coming and going like the light from her beloved lighthouse on Ocracoke, and Ruth had her removed to the hospital. Once, she looked up and saw David and Hildy standing by her bedside. "Where's little Jessie?" she asked them. "Where's my... namesake?"

"We couldn't bring her," David said. "She's only just due to be born."

"Yes... on my birthday..." Jessie said. "But she came... early. I'll never see her... now." Then she went on a wild ride. *Ruth was driving, young and beautiful and strong. Oh, how she admired her! The big Rover was sliding on sand, and there was a rainbow out at sea. But she didn't know where they were going in such a rush. There was something that she had lost behind them and there was danger ahead but she did not fear the danger because she was with Ruth. Because she was with Ruth the danger was an adventure. Because she was with Ruth she looked forward to it. Now, somehow, she could see herself and she was surprised to discover that she was just a little girl. And how fresh was Ruth's cheek! Ruth kept pushing on the gas pedal and calling to her above the noise of the gear-shifted, grinding machine, and the wheels-sprayed sand and the swashing surf, the distinct but muffled susurrus of the sea, "We'll be there before dark! We'll be there before dark!"*

"Where?" Jessie cried, and the doctor jumped, surprised.

"Oh—" he said.

Outside, he said, "Protocol calls for life support, unless . . ."

"No life support," Ruth said. "I'm her mother."

Ruth, David, and Hildy waited. They tried to eat supper at the Duke University Hospital cafeteria. They went outside so that Ruth could smoke. They walked as the autumn leaves fell around them and crunched underfoot in desiccated chips. "It's her birthday," Ruth said, in a thick voice.

Jessie ran into the house to tell Cogburn that he was not her father. Tom Judas has just showed her a picture of himself and Susannah. Susannah was holding Jessie on her knee. Tom Judas had said, "Here's my proof that I am your father." They were the happiest words she had ever heard. "You're not my father," she told Cogburn. But when he looked up at her from his game of solitaire, he had the face of an alligator. Then he stood up on his tail, so that he was at least ten feet tall, and came toward her waving his little fat arms and his clawed hands. "I'm going to eat you," he growled. Then Tom Judas, a rhinestone cowboy, rode right in through the kitchen on a great white stallion. He was swinging a lariat with one hand and waving a big white Stetson with the other. In a flash, he had the alligator man roped and tied. He dragged him out of the kitchen through

*the door and onto the dunes outside. When he returned he left his mount
outside. "I dragged him into the sea where he drowned and sank," he
said. "You'll never have to fear him again." And then he was on the
great white stallion again and lifted her into the saddle behind him and
they rode away on the water, the great silver horseshoes pounding and
splashing.*

Late in the evening the doctor came into the waiting room and told
them that she was gone.

"Do you want to see her?" he asked. "A last look?"

"No," Ruth said. "I'll see her around the corner."

But whose imagination sees her looking out? Was it a collective
dream of the living that penetrated the mind that had been pronounced
impenetrable—"No brain activity"—to watch the post-mortem movie of
Jessie's dream, that saw her seeing...

*No more, ever, than fourteen years of age, sometimes much younger,
sometimes holding Susannah's hand, looking up at her, sometimes as tall
as Susannah, her height being a matter of volition, like her age, which
she would never allow to be more than fourteen, and it was her fourteenth
birthday and an especially exciting birthday it was, because it was the day
that she found her father, the day he said that she was his... and it was not
only her birthday, he told her, but it was the day on which he and Ruth were
getting married and she was to be the bridesmaid as well as the birthday
girl. Suddenly there was a church and everyone walked up the aisle to the
rhythm of the Wedding March, she walking between them, between Tom
and Ruth, holding their hands, mother, father, and daughter...*

Chapter
Eighteen

Spring 1955

Pamlico Sound was as smooth as a stretched sail, giving no suggestion of its third, dark, dimension, depth. It would have been the doldrums to an eighteenth century freebooter, but to Capt'n Jack, an old, twentieth century salt aboard a chugging, motorized mail boat, it was a day to breathe deeply of the optimistic spring air, to take in with tranquility from the deck the positive, north-migrating birds in a cloudless robin's egg blue sky. He knocked the tobacco from his pipe on the rail and scanned the horizon for Fortune Island.

Tying the skiff to the dock, Tom said, "You could have knocked me over when I saw you on deck."

"I would have called ahead, but there's not even a goddamn telephone line running out here. I don't know how you can stand it."

"You can get used to anything, Jack. Twelve years in prison proved that to me."

"I was just heading south and thought, what the hell, I'll just stop off on that God-forsaken island of Tom's and see the old troubadour. Thought maybe I could talk you into going down to N'Orleans with me. The band's waiting in Wilmington." Capt'n Jack looked around. "Looks like you rode out Hazel. A real bitch of a hurricane, wasn't she? Widdershins, like a witch, as the mountain folk might put it."

"The folks here spent the winter putting the place back together. But I'm afraid it'll never be the same. We've lost more people—left, I mean, gone to greener pastures. Two died. Did you know Sheriff Walkup?"

They were climbing the soft slope from the dock to Tom's shack. Capt'n Jack was breathing heavily, his barrel of a chest-belly heaving, but his voice rang clear, like shots in the air.

"Sheriff of Carteret County until about twenty years ago, I'd say. Retired. Let's see, didn't he get involved with some kid? Minor scandal, you might say." He guffawed, waited, saw that Tom got his pun, and said, "He was in his fifties and the girl was oh, maybe a teenager. He must be... he's dead?" He looked at Tom. Tom nodded. "He must have been in his seventies. Sorry to hear about him dying. Every man's death diminishes me. So do not come to ask for whom the bell tolls, it tolls for thee, said old John Donne. Yeah, he had a reputation for honesty before the scandal. He was well liked, as I remember. Was he still married to the..."

"Breathing a little hard, there, Jack."

"Weight! Blood pressure! Getting old isn't for sissies. How's your head? Do you still get those headaches?"

"I still get them."

"Ought to have that looked into. You should have been over them a long time ago."

"I work for her."

"Who?"

"The Sheriff's wife. Her name's Buttercup. Well, to tell you the truth, I don't know what her right name is—maybe Missus Walkup will do. But everybody calls her Buttercup."

"Pretty thing, as I remember. Folks was more narrow minded in those days. Old man, young girl, you know. So now she's his widow? Well, they stuck it out together, didn't they? Just goes to prove vox populi vox dei not so dei."

"I thought you believed in the voice of the people."

"The voice of the people yes, but beware when the voice of God starts speaking through them. Then it's the Spanish Inquisition all over again."

They paused before a sun-gleaming, newly-whitewashed building. "This is the general store," Tom said. "It was flooded up to the second floor. My new shack is around behind it. The old one was destroyed. Come on, I'll show you."

"I can see how busy you've been," said Capt'n Jack, as they came upon Tom's new digs. "You call this a shack? It looks seaworthy." Capt'n Jack took a bottle of rum from under his jacket. "I ought to break this over its hull."

"Wait till the bottle's empty, Jack."

"You're damn right I will!"

They went inside.

"Did it hit you all up in Manteo?" asked Tom. He found a couple of glasses and gave one to Jack.

"The hurricane? No," Jack said, "didn't touch us. Went inland. Beat up on Raleigh. Heard Ottawa got its pretty little derriere spanked."

"As far up as that?" Tom poured them each a large glass of rum. "I haven't paid much attention to the news. Out here it doesn't seem to matter. Besides, we've been so busy pulling this place together, who's got time to think about where the damn ripsaw went after it left us? The worst of it here was a sea surge of at least ten feet. The good part was that it didn't last long—just whooshed in and whooshed out. But I've still got my hands full here. I'm helping Buttercup and I'm doing a lot of construction. I built an addition on Ruth Perle's cottage. You know her, don't you?"

"Oh, I meant to ask—how is she?"

"That's right, she's an old friend of yours, isn't she?"

"She's quite a woman. She knows more about the Banks than most of the natives. She's written two or three books on the subject. She's pretty well-known, you know. And how's your daughter?"

"The woman who took care of her, and raised me as well, was one of the victims of Hazel. She was like a second mother to me."

"Well, I'm sorry to hear that, Tom. Did she recognize you? You've changed a lot, even since I first met you."

"She did recognize me, but I don't know how. I took her a gift one night and gave her a kiss. She was nearly blind and I don't know if she knew who I was or not, then. But later, when she was dying, she seemed to recognize me. It was kind of strange. But my girl, Jessie... Ruth has sort of taken her over. She made some arrangement with the Reverend Cogburn—you know, the stepfather—who's almost never here, to take care of her."

"Ruth brought her up on a visit," said Capt'n Jack, stuffing his pipe. "I knew that red-headed stringbean was yours, of course, but I kept my mouth shut, the way I thought you'd want me to. Still playing Secret Agent X-9, are you?"

"Ruth knows Jessie is my kid, but we just don't talk about it. I guess she's waiting to see what I'll do, the way I've been waiting to see what was going to become of Jessie. That part couldn't have turned out better. Ruth wants to adopt her. Can that be done? I mean, can a single woman adopt a child?"

"Ruth can do just about any thing she wants to do."

"Oh? Why is that?"

"I don't know if I should say...you'll have to keep this to yourself, but I know you and I know you will...a woman with somewhere between thirty and fifty million dollars can do just about anything. She's probably got an army of lawyers working for her."

"My God! I had no idea. You mean to tell me she's got that kind of money?"

"The kind that can make anything happen. But you'd never know it, would you? She's as regular as warm milk."

"But why does she live like this?"

"Because she likes it. She's a writer. She's a Rough Rider. That's what I like about her. We've both been in some tough places. Well, Ruth has been in places just as tough as we've ever seen. You know she carries a gun most of the time." Capt'n Jack chuckled. "She's a humdinger! She lives her life her own way and she's made a success of it on her own. Her money didn't buy her fame, her books did. You're not sweet on her, are you? Because if you are, and she returns the favor, you're one lucky devil."

"I'm in love with her, Jack."

"Well, that's the kind of miracle you were looking for, isn't it? Now you can end all this pretense and come on with me. Your daughter is safe in Ruth's hands."

"Then you think she can adopt her?"

"She can if she wants to, believe me. And why shouldn't you two get together?"

"Trouble is, Jack, the thing has taken a kind of a strange turn over the past few months. Jessie is growing up. She's at that age, if you know what I mean?"

"I know what you mean, the difficult age. The age of rebellion. My Marie has gone up to New York to live. Finished high school—she was the prom queen—and took off practically still wearing her crown. Hardly writes. She's staying with some people we know up there, at least I hope she's staying with them. I don't really know what she's up to."

"Ruth is home schooling Jessie, preparing her to go to a school where they can get her ready to go on to college. Ruth wants her to go to her school, Smith in Massachusetts, and it takes a lot of preparation to get in. Of course Ruth has got a lot of influence there, I'm already aware of that, so, if she can get Jessie ready, it should work out all right. But—this is a little embarrassing—Jessie has developed a crush on me. Sometimes it's a little too obvious for comfort."

"Oh, what a tangled web we weave when first we practice to deceive! Why haven't you told her the truth by now?"

"Everything's going so well for her, probably for the first time in her life, I didn't want to destabilize the situation. I didn't want to throw an emotional monkey wrench into the fire, but now I've been thinking I'm going to have to tell her, although I'd just as soon let Ruth take her off into a better life—and especially now, since you tell me how rich Ruth is—and just leave it at that. Then I could go off and join you and get back to music."

"But you say you're in love with Ruth; then why would you want to go off and leave her?"

"I don't know—the fact that she's so rich! I had no idea. She might think I'm after her money."

"Well, you can think of more damn problems, can't you? You're never going to get it right, you know. It just doesn't work that way in life. You love her. If she loves you, the money doesn't matter. The right time to tell the truth is always now. Tell everybody everything before some real harm is done beyond just embarrassment. Your daughter! Girl like that, who hasn't had anything, you give her something, and the first thing she's likely to be is scared to death of losing it. Take it from me, I've raised ten children, seven of them girls, get everything out in the open and let her know where things stand. And whatever you do, don't let her feel that she's been a fool. I never liked your plan, Tom, the secretiveness of it. I thought you should come here and tell her who you were. Tell everybody!"

"I didn't want to cause trouble, and it has worked out the way I planned it. I mean, I stayed out of her life and luck walked in."

"And love walked in and screwed everything up." Capt'n Jack slapped his knee. "So you didn't want to cause trouble and you may have, anyway, it would seem. Get it all out in the open, Tom—above board, that's the way to live. I was going to suggest that we go and see Ruth, have a little party together, but I think I'll save it for my return trip. I'll sleep here tonight and catch the mail boat in the morning. This general store got rum? Get us another bottle and I'll tell you about Smiley—how last time he fell off the stage doing a jig on his peg leg—and I'll sing us a lullaby into the land of the luscious lascivious and lewd." He sang:

"And now we're anchored in the bay
With the Kanakas all around
With chants and soft aloha-oos

> They greet us homeward bound
> And now ashore we'll have good fun
> We'll paint them beaches red
> Awakening in the arms of an island maid
> With a big fat aching head."

Capt'n Jack did not awaken in the arms of an island maid, but he did have a big fat aching head. Tom was frying eggs. No, no, no, no, he did not want anything to eat. A little rum in his coffee might help. And it did, or it seemed to, because Capt'n Jack rubbed his head with both hands and believed it to have shrunken to its normal proportions, though his skull still contained a large ball-bearing that refused to stop rolling around inside it.

Tom, too, looked peaked, though he stuffed down two eggs and three cups of black coffee. "I've got a hard day's work ahead of me," he explained.

"Gonna be a hot day," said Capt'n Jack. "I don't envy you. I'm getting too old for this kind of partying. Well, down to N'Orleans for me, and I'll see you and Ruth at the end of the summer, after the harvest fairs, on the way back."

They met Jessie in front of the general store. She carried an algebra book in one hand and a cigarette in the other. She dropped the cigarette in the mud, surreptitiously stepped on it, and stood, looking at them. No gift to Tom but a sullen look. "Hello, Tom." She gifted Capt'n Jack with a girlish grin. "Hello, Capt'n Jack!" With each greeting a wisp of smoke curled from her lips. "I'm just hurrying to Buttercup for my algebra lesson. I love algebra, don't you?" She was looking up at Capt'n Jack. "It's really good for the brain."

"Well, Miss Jessie," said Capt'n Jack, "it's good to see you again. You're growing like a weed."

"That's my job. Ruth says my job is to grow up straight and tall and to learn everything there is to know."

"Well, from the looks of things," said Capt'n Jack, "you're living up to your obligations. How did you like *The Science of Life*, that H.G. Wells book I gave you?"

"Oh, that was a wonderful book! I read the Bible right through and it just don't have any science in it and I read *The Science of Life* and it don't have much poetry in it. That's the way things are. You just can't get to the bottom of things." She looked wonderstruck at her own discovery.

It seemed deeper than she realized when she was saying it. Then she was back with them. "Ruth and I read *The Science of Life* together, and she says we know more about biology and the natural sciences now than most people who teach the subject—that's what she says. Ruth got us a drawing pad and we copied out all the drawings of the stages of life of the little animals and animalcules. You know, how they metamorphosed from stage to stage? Some have as many as five stages, but I guess you know that. What was interesting is to think that people go through stages, too. I'm going through one right now, myself."

"They certainly do," said Capt'n Jack. "I'm at the last stage. Now look at Tom here, puffing away on that nasty cigarette—he might have been a foot taller if he hadn't smoked. Am I right, Tom?"

"Absolutely," said Tom. "I was naturally intended to be seven foot two."

"I get it," said Jessie.

"No," said Tom, "you don't yet, but you will get it when I tell Ruth about that cigarette under your foot."

"I'm not a child, Tom," she said with adolescent dignity. Then she thought better of it and said excitedly, "Oh please, Tom, don't tell her! I promise, that's the last time. I just like one in the morning when I stroll over here. But I won't do it anymore. Don't tell Ruth, please!"

"Okay," said Tom, "but you owe me, young lady."

"How's Marie, Capt'n Jack?" asked Jessie.

"With the swells in New York."

"Are you coming up to see Ruth?"

"Not this trip, honey."

"And how's Maggie?"

"Fine. Maggie's fine."

"Tell her hello from Jessie."

"Will do, sunshine!"

"Well—bye," said Jessie, waving her hand.

"Bye," said Capt'n Jack.

But Jessie was already up the steps of the general store and halfway in the door. Tom looked at Capt'n Jack. Capt'n Jack shook his head, and that damned ball-bearing rolled around inside it. Tom threw him a wink, and they walked down to the dock. It was almost time for the mail boat. They climbed into the skiff.

"You got yourself a bright little girl there," said Capt'n Jack. "Oh, did I tell you that I'm going to pick up Smiley toward the end of the summer, after the fairs? Yeah, the old peg leg pirate's finally getting out." Over the years, Capt'n Jack had come to understand Tom's affection for Chuck Smiley. At first, they seemed like unlikely buddies, but they shared one quality in abundance—loyalty. Capt'n Jack, too, had been a merchant marine, had gone to sea when he was only sixteen, and knew how these friendships formed. He'd known many a Stan Laurel and Oliver Hardy partnership. He thought he understood how a feckless rogue like Chuck Smiley had lightened the burden of Tom's principled seriousness. If Tom meant business, Smiley meant monkey-business. Yes, he could see them kicking around together, one supplying the ballast and the other the balloon, perfectly balanced to keep each other from growing either dull and solipsistic or simply floating off into a dreamer's cloud. "I'm going to take him to Manteo and get him readjusted to civilian life."

"What's he going to do?"

"I don't know. Maybe I can find a place for him in the band."

"Don't let him get you into trouble," said Tom.

"Well, at least I've got a while left to live in safety before he can get me into any trouble. Anything you want me to tell him?"

"You can tell him I miss him, the crazy son-of-a-bitch. The improvident one! Yeah, say that I miss him."

Summer 1955

Becoming more and more of a ghost to the world outside, Smiley was finally able to walk through the Wall. But this irreverent revenant had a spring in his step—literally. With the help of the prison doctor, he sported a wonderful new leg that could turn at the ankle, and now he turned on his heel, as on a dime, back and forth, back and forth, smoking cigarettes and stamping them out, waiting for Capt'n Jack to pick him up.

The immense Central Prison, with its parapets, buttresses and towers loomed over him, resembling a European castle. A modern Raleigh, a la 1955, had arrived at the castle's gate with buildings like siege machines. Down the street something that looked like a huge ball-throwing catapult was making an ear-piercing sound as it lifted what looked like building materials into the sky. He was downtown, in a business district, and this new world looked very strange, indeed. The cars looked like science fiction creations. He fancied that they could lift straight up like autogyros. Light ricocheted from every direction, all of it hot and glarey, as people brushed, and cars rushed, by. Charles "Chuck" Smiley was a stranger in a strange land.

A school bus stopped and unloaded noisy children who were there to tour the prison and see the gas chamber. But Capt'n Jack's bus never came. Smiley waited two hours in the loud bright light of the June day. Capt'n Jack had promised to be there. It was unlike Capt'n Jack not to keep his word, not to be prompt. There must have been an accident, something untoward must have happened. But why hadn't Capt'n Jack phoned to tell the warden, to let him know? There was something ominous, now, in the falling brightness, something worrisome and nervous-making.

At one point, for a moment, Smiley considered going back into the prison, transporting himself through the Wall once again, to find out if the warden knew anything, but immediately dismissed the idea. There was no way that the world was going to get old Smiley back inside that Wall, no way at all. No, he'd rather wander the streets pointlessly than go back inside.

An evil thought shook him, rattled his bones, even vibrating down into his mechanical foot—Capt'n Jack was dead. He would have to be dead to leave him waiting like this, to not find a way to notify him that he would not be here. He would have to be dead. But this was Capt'n Jack he was thinking about. Capt'n Jack couldn't die. What a crazy idea! This waiting in the sun was making him morbid. Flat tire, more likely, not near a phone, something like that—it had to be. But what to do?

Raleigh was not a port city; he did not know it well. He had been to Raleigh once or twice, years before, and he tried to remember what he might know about the place. State capitol. Uppity artsy-fartsy. But also downbeat in places. Wasn't there a Masonic dance hall back in the Forties, and hadn't he gone dancing there? Or was that earlier? Or was that exclusively black?

He looked about at the pageant of the busy streets, realizing only now that he had left the prison behind, that he had just walked away, distracted by his thoughts, and wandered into utterly strange territory. He felt a little frightened, remembering that he had a check for five thousand dollars in his ancient wallet, a very large sum of money.

Capt'n Jack was going to get it cashed for him. Now he had no idea how to cash it. Maybe he could find the insurance company that had issued the check. That was an idea. He had twenty-five dollars in his pocket, awarded by the State, and another hundred dollar bill, his savings, taped to his back—thanks to the good offices of Chaplain Baker—just in case.

What he needed was a cold beer, so he asked several people on the street where he could get one and finally got an answer. "Beer—retail?" He had always found the North Carolina liquor laws maddening—county by county, town by town, wet, dry, and everything in between. "The Beer Barrel on West Martin. Just keep going and turn left at the next intersection." Despite many fittings, his leg had begun to hurt. Maybe it was the heat. He limped on, took a left, and was gratified to see a sign—Cold Beer. It was a middling blue collar bar on a manufacturing back street, sardined with workmen taking a noon break for sandwiches and beer, where air had been displaced by smoke. He fitted himself into a place at the bar and ordered, "A cold one!" The beer was so cold it hurt his forehead the way an ice cream cone did when he was a kid. It felt wonderful to be out of the sun, in a shady nook, and the beer, he promised himself never to forget, was the coldest, most delicious beer he had ever had in his life or was ever likely to have again.

He ordered another. He felt easier now. That touch of panic he had had back there had dissipated. When he wiped the sweat from his brow now it did not reappear.

"The Naughty Lady of Shady Lane" was emanating from somewhere. He couldn't see the juke box for the crowd. Cute song! A man leaned into him and said, "Would you like to meet her?" He looked at the man, who nodded his head in the direction of the music.

"Oh, yeah, I guess I would," he said.

"Just get out?" inquired the man.

"Does it show?"

"All over your body," said the man. "I'm Bookbinder." He was a big heavy smooth-faced fellow. "Not *Mister* Bookbinder, not nothing else, just plain Bookbinder."

"Hello," said Smiley, "I'm Smiley. Chuck Smiley. Yeah, I got out and somebody was supposed to—"

"Somebody was supposed to meet you and they didn't show up, eh? Happens all the time. People forget about their friends behind the Wall. No one cares. I should know. I was a cop and got sent away and nobody knew me when I got out. Maybe I can be of some help to you. What do you need?"

Smiley chug-a-lugged his beer and ordered a third. The beers were hitting him hard but he felt helpless to control himself. He found himself saying, "I have a big check in my pocket and I need to cash it. If I could find a bank—"

"No need for a bank. A friend of mine runs a business out in Forest Hills. He might be able to cash it for you. What's it for?"

"Five grand." Smiley was working on another beer. Had he ordered it? Where had it come from?

The big smooth man whistled. "That's a lot of do-re-mi, my friend, but it won't be a problem for the guy I'm talking about. What kind of check is it?"

"It's an insurance check. I was a Merchant Marine. You gotta be dead or seriously wounded to get it."

"And you got it. I noticed you limping when you came in. Is that the wound?"

"Artificial leg."

"They never did give you Merchant Marines the credit you deserved," the big man said. "I always said that, and I was in the army. Yeah, them U-boats used to give you old boys a shellacking. Gutsy guys, I always said, Merchant Marines. What were you in for?"

"What were you in for?"

"Corruption, they said. Bullshit's more like it. I was a good cop. I like to help people, that's why I joined the police force."

"Conspiracy to commit armed robbery here."

"No shit! And I bet you wasn't even guilty, was you?"

"I didn't do anything," Smiley said, at that moment believing he was telling the truth. This guy had it right—they had been wronged, both of them, him and the cop! His old cohorts, too. "My best buddy," Smiley said, "was completely innocent." Smiley was absolutely sure of this.

Bookbinder put a big paw on Smiley's back. "Did you ever see that movie—*The Best Years of Our Lives*? Vets got treated like dogs, and it was worse for the Merchant Marines, because they weren't even treated like vets."

"You're telling me, buddy!" exclaimed Smiley. He knew he was getting kind of blurry. How did he get out to the car? But there he was.

Bookbinder passed Smiley a brown bag with a bottle in it. They were going to Forest Hills, wherever that was. "Have a drink," Bookbinder said. Smiley took a drink. The bourbon tasted like dynamite juice. "Lord," said Smiley, "I haven't had a drink like that in years."

"I know how it feels," Bookbinder said. "This here place I'm taking you, this here is in a nice neighborhood, nice homes and all, but there's a big old house on a dead end of it and that's my friend's house of business— understand?" Bookbinder looked at Smiley, saw that he didn't, and said,

"Well, you'll see for yourself." And Smiley did.

It was a big old Victorian house and it didn't take long for Smiley, even in his dimmed state, to realize that the place was a swanky whorehouse, upstairs, it was, downstairs was a still. The joint was full to overflowing and everything was flowing, including Smiley. Bookbinder said, "The naughty lady of Shady Lane—I asked you if you wouldn't like to meet her and didn't I go and find her for you? Meet Lana. Lana, this here is Chuck Smiley."

Lana was a pulchritudinous, French-twisted blonde in a low-cut gold lamé gown. The many flowers of her perfume swept up his nostrils and filled his head. He reached out and touched her tanned arm. She giggled, said, "I'll sit with you while Booky takes care of your business, then we'll go upstairs and have a good time together. Party time, eh?" She winked burlesque eyelashes. Bookbinder said:

"Let's get the business over with so we can have some fun. Here, you can use my pen. Just endorse the check, and I'll go get it cashed for you and be back in a minute."

Smiley wondered how the check got on the table in front of him, among the glasses and the wet rings of the glasses. "Now, wait," he said, wondering if he wasn't being stupid. But it was hard to focus. His thoughts were flying loose before he could organize them.

"Of course you're not," said Bookbinder.

"Not what?"

"Being stupid. You said you wondered if you were being stupid."

"Did I say that? I thought I thought it."

"You said it, and it sounded like an insult to me," said Bookbinder, looking aggrieved. "Shit, man, I just wanted to be of some help to you. I told you I was a cop. What's the matter with you?"

"We'll wait right here," said Lana, patting Smiley's sleeve. "Go ahead, Chucky-boy. Sign the damn thing so we can start having some fun."

Bookbinder pushed a pen into his hand. Lana reached over and tousled his hair. "You're gonna be some great guy tonight," she said.

"Did I tell you," Bookbinder said to Lana, "that our friend here only has one leg?"

"Oh wow!" exclaimed Lana. "That'll be something different. I never done it with a guy with one leg. I can't wait. Hurry up and sign that damn thing!"

"You're among friends," said Bookbinder. "I, for one, understand your situation. Yeah, there go! That's it. Sign it. OKAY!" he roared.

"I'll be right back with your cash and then we'll have some real fun, eh, Lana?"

"We'll be waiting," said Lana.

Once, Smiley's eyes opened and he saw a sky full of the stars. But he had to close his eyes and sleep. The second time he opened his eyes it was as if the sun had punched him in each eye with its golden gloves. Then he felt an excruciating pain in his head. He had been to ports around the world and knew what a knock-out drop felt like when you woke to its aftermath. This headache wasn't the product of beer, bourbon, or even white lightning; it was the product of old Mister Mickey Finn, the greatest knock-out artist of them all. Even with his head pounding like a sledge hammer on a ten-inch spike, he could figure out that Lana had slipped it to him.

He was lying in tall grass alongside a highway with fields and little patches of woods stretching in all directions, no city in sight. Well, damned if he hadn't done it again. Improvidence had proven once again to be his strong point. He stood up. He didn't have to look for the check, he knew it was gone. Bookbinder and Lana hadn't bothered with the small change. He still had about ten dollars in ones in his pocket. He reached up and felt behind his neck, down his back, for the hundred dollar bill taped back there, knowing too, that it would be there, because no one would have removed his coat or shirt, since no one had any intention of showing him a good time. Yes, the hundred was still there, the only bandage he had to cover his wounded self-esteem. "What in God's name is wrong with me?" he asked the highway traffic. "You know what you need, Smiley," he told himself, "you need the guidance of a good woman. You're not fit to walk down a street by yourself, you dumb shit!"

No use going back, even if he knew where back was. But as bad as the situation was, one thing had changed for the better. This morning—for it seemed to be morning—this morning he had a direction. He was going to make a straight line, or as straight a line as he could make, a bee-line, to find his friend the erstwhile William Makepeace Thackeray McQueen, a/k/a/ Tom Judas. Yes siree, old Smiley is heading for Fortune Island, he told himself. After all, Tom does owe me money. He stuck his thumb out for a lift, going east, to the sea, to the great Atlantic Ocean, where that danged island of Tom's was, and maybe he would have some luck there, at long and dear last.

✖ ✖ ✖

Dear Sissy,

I got a terrible telegram. Dad is dead. What we know is that he was playing New Orleans, doing everything too much, and he had heart failure. He survived one a few years back. Mom wants me to come down for the funeral but I'm not going to. There's nine other kids to be there, and I don't think he could tell one of us from the other, at least not the seven girls. Besides, I've really got something going with a very rich Greek, and I don't intend to interrupt the magic for one single second. I've got this guy where I want him and I'm going to keep him there. You're a prophet, Sissy, I got myself a new diaphragm and it brought me luck.

Don't think I'm too hard. Capt'n Jack didn't give a damn about funerals. He cared more about his musicians than he did us. As for Maggie, he left her plenty of money. Only her. It's up to her to see if us kids get any. I say let the rest of them have it. I've got my Greek.

> *Love,*
> *Marie*

P.S. Mom says she'll write to Ruth. She'll probably have to write letters to the whole damn American Communist Party. My Greek is a full-fledged capitalist shipping mogul. Ahoy poloi!

Autumn 1955

In her journal entry of the first day of autumn, Ruth wrote that she and Jessie had just got back from a visit of several days to UNC at Chapel Hill, where she had taken Jessie, her feral girl, her Kaspar Hauser, for testing.

Friends and colleagues of mine—after I explained the circumstances of Jessie's life—were extremely impressed with her innate abilities as well as with our efforts to bring her educational level up to par—in fact, we had exceeded par. On standard academic tests, Jessie is now not only at the high school graduate level but has the equivalent of a one year college education. Her Stanford-Binet scores were very high—higher, in fact, than mine; but the psychological testing shows she's very emotionally immature, doubtless as a result of years of isolation. The latter manifests itself in so many ways. One is that she does not want to leave my side to go away to a good prep school that can prepare her for college.

Another troublesome way that this immaturity manifests itself is with regard to Tom. She has a schoolgirl crush on him that is making all of us uncomfortable. Of course she has no idea that he is her father—he should have told her long ago. I've tried to convince him that he should tell her. I told him that if he didn't tell her I would. But he warned me off by telling me that if I told her, he and I were through. In most ways, Tom seems to be a stable and rational man; but when it comes to Jessie, he suffers from some kind of terrible fixation, an idée fixe, almost a phobia, something built in the years of imprisonment he suffered. But I can't help thinking that it is some strange structure in his very makeup, some birthmark of guilt, that he was born with, but that might not have manifested itself if the circumstances of his life had been different.

I have never felt about another man, even my first husband, the way I feel about Tom. I am utterly, passionately, god-forsakenly in love with the man. It amazes me that Jessie has been blind to the fact that Tom and I are lovers, although we have tried to conceal it from her. Still, you would think that she would notice. I say I am going off to New York or Boston for a few days on business, and he says he is going over to Wilmington to do something or other, and we meet there and spend glorious weekends making love. Buttercup—along with her boyfriend, Chuck Smiley, an old friend of Tom's, who lived with Tom in his shack for a time but now lives with her at the general store—keeps Jessie on these occasions, but, according to Buttercup, the thought that Tom and I might be meeting away from Fortune Island apparently never enters Jessie's innocent mind.

Her unworldliness is as profound as are her sponge-like academic skills and innate intelligence. She's such a strange creature, and I love her as dearly as I have loved anything in life. She has a great future to look forward to, but she can be so trying—I imagine an infant who also happens to be a genius. And the infant is clinging and frightened of being removed from its mother and the genius is resentful of the parent who adores it.

Tom told me some time ago about an incident that happened a while back. Jessie found him on the beach and immediately disrobed to her tee-shirt, fortunately long enough to make a short dress, then plunged into the cold water and came back out to show him the result. He promptly covered her with his shirt, and, it seems, gave her a lecture on modesty, to which she did not respond favorably, but stalked off in high dudgeon, like a woman scorned. It was very embarrassing for him. That was when I told him that he had to tell her that he was her father and that was when he warned me off. I told him to consider the fact that he was practically the only man on the island, and not to judge her too harshly, that she was growing up, abuzz with hormones, and that it was only a girlish crush. But something has to be done about it. With much gentle persistence I did rend a concession from Tom. He promised to tell her on her birthday. I hope he means it. But I shouldn't doubt him because he's a man who keeps his word. I thought that was a good idea—telling her on her birthday. It's only about a month away. We're going to tell her about us and our plans to be married. We thought it would be a joyful announcement, that she'd finally have a complete family of the sort she has always dreamed of. But now I'm not so sure what her reaction will be, and I'm nervous about it. Perhaps it's too much to tell her all at once. But she must be told. Tom and I are the two people who love her most in the whole world. Either one of us would do anything for her. Still, I worry about her reaction.

In response to all this talk of school, she seems to think that it's some kind of plot to get rid of her. Nothing could be further from the truth.

And later that day Jessie answered one of Marie's romantically, or sexually, boastful letters with one of her own.

...and so the visit to Chapel Hill has proved me to be a very smart girl indeed! But the big news is this: I have found the man of my dreams! You're always telling me about the men that you meet—and I wonder how you hold on to that Greek of yours with all these other men around and your sex life being what it is and all—and so I'm glad to be able to tell you that your little Sissy has met someone, too. He isn't rich like some of yours—I have to admit that—but I bet he's as good-looking as any of them, a real piece of attractive, if you know what I mean. I know you're always telling me I'm only a kid but I'm going to be fourteen in about a month and between me and you I feel like what you always say, every inch a woman. Wow! And just like your men, he's giving me a hard time. You know how it is. They're so weird, men! His name is Tom and I practically got naked for him on the beach one time and he hands me a shirt and gives me some modesty crap and boy was I pissed! There I am with my little bazzooms and nipples sticking right through a wet tee-shirt and he won't even look.

He hands me his shirt looking away from me like there's something wrong with me. I felt like slapping him good. You know, "What's the matter with you? Don't you get it?" You're always telling me to act coy, like I'm not interested. Well, do men act coy, too? Because this one sure did. But this is the bad part: I think he kinda likes Ruth. What a pissy situation, a real triangle! Wow! Well, I'm deep in it now, just like the woman in that romance novel you sent me. You know, she didn't know which way to turn? Maybe Ruth is plotting against me. She wants me to go away to school. Could it be that she wants to get me out of the way so she can have him all to herself? But you know what the French say—On ne peut pas vivre seul, which you of course know means, you cannot live alone. It's a real drama. But, honestly Marie cherie, I'm scared to death that I'm going to lose all of the happiness that I just found over this folie. No, really, I'm scared. Please send me some of your good advice. I need to say good-bye to tristesse. Help! Sissy.

Chapter
Nineteen

Jessie felt inside her shirt for Garcie's necklaced ring and fingered it, rubbed the gold of it warm, to make a leap in time, be in a better place, be older and unafraid, and the magic worked, and it was a cool November day, the day before her birthday, and she was on a street in Wilmington, entering Efird's Department Store, the best store in town, according to Ruth, wearing jeans and a jacket, with Ruth and Tom, to shop for one of her birthday presents, her first grownup wardrobe. In minutes, she stood surrounded by dressing room mirrors. Oh, it was the first time she had seen herself, multiple selves, from every angle. She wasn't disappointed, as she expected to be, but thrilled, and very nearly hypnotized, by her own appearance. She wasn't looking at a child, or a girl, but a nubile young woman, everything as it should be, biologically speaking. In profile, her small breasts pointed up, and there was a swooping curve at her lower back. She saw that she had a small pink birthmark halfway up her back, shifted to get a better angle, and saw that it was shaped like a little flower, a rosebud, not blemish-like at all, but pretty enough to make you want to kiss it, a lovely little possession of which she had been unaware. Her long legs were strong and well developed from wading the dunes and the water surrounding them. A branching river of red hair, so like her memory of her mother's, rode the falls of her shoulder blades. And when she felt the satin touch of the lace-trimmed bra on her breasts her nipples hardened. Narcissism was not her face reflected in the river of the mirrors but the river that ran through her veins as she put on new lace panties, gartered stockings, and slipped into her first pair of high-heeled black pumps, ankle-twisters that lifted her reflections high and higher to the tops of the mirrors, and she was determined to master them. A long-sleeved, gray woolen dress with purple piping and a flared skirt became a curtain to be lifted over her head to display the true and secret scene of her body. She turned around and around to see a vision of herself superimposed on Botticelli's "Birth of Venus," until the spell was broken by a call from outside the magic-filled dressing room.

"Are you all right in there? Do you need any help?"

"Can't you leave me alone?" Jessie said under her breath. "Always after me!" But she called back to Ruth: "I want to try the suit. I'll be right out."

She tried a Hunter green winter suit. After a few tugs and pats here and there, she studied herself, front, left and right profiles, behind. Yes, she thought the suit made her look even older, like a career girl. She looked like somebody old enough to do anything. Yes! She found her lipstick, puckered, and with several uuum-uuums, freshened her lips. She made faces at herself—funny, alluring, coy—then, impulsively, planted a kiss on the mirror—the heart of a girl's puckered lips. She wrote FOR TOM under it with her lipstick. She stepped out of the dressing room and was delighted to see that the result of her efforts was dramatic, caused what she believed to be a flash of jealousy in Ruth's eyes and Tom's breath to be taken away, but it was Ruth's breath that was taken away while Tom was pleased and approving, like the father he was.

"Oh, darling," Ruth cried, "you're dazzling! I thought that green would work with your coloring."

"We've got a debutante," Tom said.

Ignoring Ruth, Jessie sashayed up to Tom. "But what do you really think, Tom?"

Tom was uncertain what to say. He tried, "I can't believe I'm looking at the same girl."

"Is that good?" Jessie persisted. "How good is that?"

Tom was baffled. "As good as can be, I guess."

"But say it!" Jessie insisted. "Don't you think I'm beautiful?"

"Oh—yes—of course," Tom ventured, visibly confused. "I always thought you were beautiful."

Jessie's face reddened. "No—damn, damn, damn it! You know what I mean. Say what I want you to say!"

"Well, Jess, I'm just not sure what you want me to say."

"She wants you to say she looks like a woman," Ruth suggested.

"Not a kid!" Jessie shot.

"Well," said Tom, "you look like a woman, not a kid. You look like a mighty young woman, though."

"Damn to hell and tarnation!"

"Jessie," said Ruth, "stop that cursing and get back in there and change." She took Jessie by the wrist, pulled her back into the mirrored dressing room, and saw the lipstick kiss and inscription. "Jessie, what is the meaning of this? What will they think?" Ruth spit on her handkerchief and wiped away the kiss and its dedication, saying, "Jessie, this fixation with Tom is embarrassing us all. Mostly, it's embarrassing Tom. Your hormones are attacking your brain."

Jessie was taken back by the harsh tone in Ruth's voice, but she ventured to say, "Oh, no more than yours!"

Ruth placed herself in front of Jessie and backed her into a corner. The small room was spinning with imagery, movies on every side. "I'm shocked at your behavior," Ruth said. "I'd like to slap that lipstick off your mouth. But we're here to have a good time, to celebrate your birthday. Have you forgotten? Tomorrow's your birthday! Why can't you behave?"

Jessie fairly screamed, "Because I'm going crazy! This whole thing about going off to school—you're just trying to get rid of me, both of you!" Tears shot from her eyes. "You want Tom all to yourself!"

The saleslady opened the door a crack, looked in, said, "Ladies, ladies! This is Efird's, not Woolworth's or Perle's."

Ruth said, "Just a moment," and pulled the door closed. In a lowered voice, she said, "Jessie, Tom thinks of you as a daughter, not as a rival to me. And he has a wonderful surprise for you tomorrow. The most wonderful you can imagine. And your behavior today will make you ashamed when you hear it." Ruth caught herself up, regained control. "It's that damned island!" she cried. She could hear the frustration in her own voice. "You're not seeing enough of boys your own age."

"There aren't any boys on Fortune Island," Jessie shot back. "There are hardly any people there anymore. The only new person to come along since I can remember is that one-legged crazy friend of Tom's who's romancing Buttercup. But I've never, ever seen a boy my age on that damned island!"

"All the more reason for going to school," Ruth said, her voice steady now. "You can meet people your own age, girls and boys. You won't have to be so lonely anymore. I understand, believe me. Now fix your face." Ruth dabbed at her with her handkerchief. "You're a young lady. Act like one!"

They had the afternoon to kill, so Ruth suggested a movie. She got a paper and checked what was playing at the two first-run movie houses in town. *Sabrina* was playing at one and *On the Waterfront* at the other. Ruth voted for *Sabrina*, a kind of Cinderella story, staring Audrey Hepburn. Tom was indifferent. "They both sound good," he said. But when Jessie heard that Marlon Brando was the star of *On the Waterfront*, that decided it for her. She had only seen one movie in her lifetime—*Streetcar Named Desire*. She wanted to see that strange piece of attractive again, he of the Grecian muscles, torn tee-shirt, and inarticulate tongue. She had masturbated to the photographs of Greek statues in one of Ruth's art books. She was adamant. "I can't understand a word he says," she said, "but it doesn't matter. He gives me goose-bumps."

So they found the theatre and lost themselves for a time in the alien exotic world of the Hoboken docks. After the movie they went back to the Cape Fear Hotel and had dinner in the dining room. Jessie slouched, picked at her food, and said little. Did she like the movie? "He was good," she said. Ruth asked her what she liked about him. "He wanted to tell the truth," she said.

"Sit up," Ruth said. "Let everyone see your pretty suit."

Jessie continued to slouch, as if trying to hide.

Tom said, "Come on, honey, give us a smile."

Jessie gave him a strained smile, dropped it, and went back to sulking.

Ruth gave Tom a wink. He saw that the people at the next table, two men and three women, were sympathetic, knowing, understanding. He thought that they must have teenagers of their own. He gave them a nod and they smiled in what he took to be commiseration.

He was sure that Ruth, who was sharing a room with Jessie, would have a talk with her tonight, get her back on the birthday beam. Fourteen years old at midnight! He could hardly believe it. He had an impulse to tell her that he was her father, tell her now. He wanted so much to tell her that he was her father that he couldn't eat, picked at his food, dropped a fork-pierced piece of steak to his plate; but the plan was to wait for her birthday, and wait he would. He knew that it would be a birthday that she would never forget, a gift that she would always remember. He didn't want to spoil that, though he knew it would lighten her mood. But the time was not right, was it? She was not right. He was not right. Once given, once told, it would alter everything.

But he was a patient man. He had had to learn patience. Perhaps he had been too patient. When he had changed his name to Judas, Chaplain Baker had told him that there were two Judases, Judas Iscariot, the guilty one, and a Saint Judas, the innocent one, who had been killed in a riot. Chaplain Baker had asked him if he knew for certain which Judas he was. Chaplain Baker had said, "I think you are the latter one, though I know you think you are the former. I think you are the latter one because"—and he smiled—"you have the patience of a saint."

In their room that evening, Ruth and Jessie prepared for bed.

"Why are you acting like this?" Ruth asked.

"Like what?"

"Bitchy!" Ruth said. "This whole trip is just for you. You didn't eat a morsel of food. You just sulked through the whole meal, which Tom, who doesn't have that much money, put out a pretty penny for." Ruth put a dressing gown on over her pajamas. Jessie was brushing her teeth. "Won't you try to brighten up and be cheerful? Tomorrow's the big day—your fourteenth birthday. Think of it! And Tom has something very important to tell you, something very important to you, but he can't tell you when you're acting like this."

"That you two are getting married or something?"

"He has to tell you. I can't. But that's not it. It's something else."

"More secrets between you? Buzz, buzz, buzz!"

"If you'll behave reasonably, he'll be able to tell you tomorrow. Which is what he wants to do, tell you on your birthday. Don't you realize that we both love you? You're the dearest thing in the world to us, both of us. Can't you see that? Whatever we do, we're trying to do it for your own good."

Jessie came out of the bathroom with tears in her eyes. "Oh, Ruth, I'm so afraid I'll lose you both! I don't want to go away to school. I'm afraid you'll forget me."

Ruth, in bed, held her arms out to Jessie. "Come here, baby. Get in bed with me. I'll hold you tight. You're still just a baby, you know. My baby! My troubled baby."

Jessie got into bed and snuggled up to Ruth. Ruth reached over and turned out the light. Almost immediately Jessie fell asleep in Ruth's arms, in Plato's shadowed cave, in the REM world of dreams, one of which, a dream of goodbye, woke her in the night to discover that Ruth was gone.

She sat alone in the bed in the dark, dazed by reality. At first she thought Ruth had gone to the bathroom, but there was no light under the bathroom door. She found the bedside lamp and lit it. "Ruth? Ruth! Ruth, where are you?" How long had she been asleep? Where was Ruth?

She got up and put on her bathrobe over her pajamas. She looked around, then padded out into the thickly carpeted hall, whispering, "Ruth? Ruth?"

Only one room showed a faint light at the transom—Tom's. She raised her hand to knock, but something stopped her, the soft rumble of Tom's voice in an almost animal exclamation of some sort. It frightened her, but she wanted, needed to know, what was going on behind the door, and so bent to the keyhole, but could see nothing, another sinister adult mystery made of silent darkness.

She went back down the hall to get one of the straight-back chairs that bookended a table there and brought it back to the door and stood up on it on tiptoes and tried to see over the door, down through the open transom. And she saw Ruth and Tom naked on the bed, Ruth straddling him and rocking and heaving up and down. She felt faint, and half fell from the chair. She gathered her twitching body up enough to run back to her room, into the bathroom, and vomited into the toilet, dry heaves. All of her horrible fears were true. To be awake was to be betrayed.

She looked at the clock. It was well after midnight. It was her birthday, not theirs. Ruth had deserted her for Tom, Tom belonged to Ruth, not to her.

Ten minutes later, Jessie hobbled away from the hotel in her new high heels, her Hunter green suit, her make-up stained and running, trenched by her tears. It was a cold and misty November night and her hair was wind-blown in seconds and damp with the mist, the fog and spindrift off the nearby docks, the almost rain. The street was empty, dark, except for damp pools of light under the street lamps, the shops closed, locked up, undecipherable. Half a block from the hotel an old car pulled up beside her. There were two young sailors in it. The car rolled slowly along beside her as she walked with determination to nowhere in particular, just away from her betrayers.

"Where you going, lady?" She glanced at the car, saw that it was the sailor who was driving who had called out to her, because of his craned neck, and answered:

"Where are you two going?"

"Just cruising. Want to cruise?" The sailor who was driving stopped the car as she hesitated. It was somewhere to go, something to do. It was out of the wind and the cold, out of the almost rain. What did she care, anyway, what did anyone care? She stepped up to the car. The sailor on the passenger side got out and opened the back door of the sedan. A sweep of his hand invited her to step in.

One last hesitant moment, then she got in. The sailor closed the door for her and got back in the front seat. "Back at base, they call me Devil and him Angel," said the driver. "You see what a gentleman he is."

"Knock it off," said the gentleman sailor.

"What do we call you?" asked the driver.

Confused, surprised at her own boldness, fearful, Jessie said, "It's my birthday! I'm eighteen."

The driver said, "Okay, we'll call you Birthday Girl. Here, Birthday Girl, take a shot of this." He handed her back a brown bag with a bottle of whiskey in it. "It's a happy birthday drink. Go ahead, take a drink—down the hatch!"

The gentleman sailor said, "She don't look old enough to drink. You don't look old enough to drink, Birthday Girl."

"She looks plenty old to me," said the driver. "She looks like a college girl to me."

"Because you're drunk!" Angel turned around in his seat and said, "Don't drink so much of that! Devlin's drunk." He turned back to Devlin. "Look, Devil, let me drive."

Devlin hit the gas, burning rubber and screeching on into the night. "Engels, you asshole," he said, "this is my car and I do the driving. How do you like that booze, college girl?"

"It's like fire."

"Oh, that stuff ain't nothing. I'm going to drive us out to a place I know where they've got a still and white lightning and you can dance there, too. Like to dance, Birthday Girl? College girl?"

Angel turned around to face Jessie again. "Listen, how old are you? Really?"

"I told you I was eighteen and no matter what you say, I look it. I look twenty. Maybe thirty."

Devil laughed. "Ooops! Don't go too far there, Birthday Girl, or you'll be too old for us. We ain't neither one of us twunny."

Angel said to Jessie, "I got an eighteen year old sister and she looks a lot older than you."

Devil said, "What're you talking about, Angel? Shit, she's taller than me. Taller than you, too. And she sounds like college."

Angel said, "But look at her face."

"She looks pretty good to me," said Devil. "Go ahead, college girl, have another swig of that good hooch."

Jessie could see him watching her in the rear view mirror, a dark haired young man with glassy blue eyes. He wore his white sailor cap in a rakish forward tilt. Angel wore his on the back of his blond head. Both wore pea jackets with collars down.

Angel turned to Devlin. "Let her out! In fact, let us both out right now! We'll walk back to the hotel."

"Hey, you don't have to steal her from me. There's plenty of quiff where I'm going. You can have her. But you're missing out on some big fun, Angel. Besides, it's beginning to rain out there. Windshield wiper, thunk thunk! You really want to walk out in that rain? Okay." Devil skidded to a stop. "Go ahead, don't mean nothing to me. But hand me back that bottle, college girl."

Angel got out and opened the back door. "C'mon, Birthday Girl, I'm taking you back where we found you."

Jessie hesitated. They were some way out of the center of town. The two or three drinks she had taken had hit her hard, but maybe the air would do her good. Devil was drunk, maybe dangerous, at least it was dangerous to drive with him. Walking with Angel seemed like the safer choice, even if she would get wet. He seemed like a nice boy.

Jessie got out and took Angel's arm. They watched as Devil roared off, honking his horn. She said:

"How far are we from town?"

"Not far."

"Is your friend really bad?"

"Oh, you mean that Devil stuff? His name is Devlin, so they started calling him Devil. He tries to be a tough guy because he's from Boston."

"I have a friend who has an accent like his. She's from Boston, too. Isn't it funny how they say wahtter for water?"

"What's your real name, Birthday Girl?"

"Jessie, that's my name—Jessie McQueen."

"I'm Ray Bob Engels. I'm eighteen, but you're not, are you?"

"Almost," said Jessie. "Engels, and that's why they call you Angel?"

"That's the Navy. We all get these crazy nicknames." He shook his head. "Devlin's going to get himself in trouble with his drinking, though. He's a nice guy when he's sober, but that's something we should all be careful of, that drinking. I've known it to ruin people, members of my own family. Got a cousin and three uncles go to AA."

"What's that?"

"Alcoholics Anonymous. I don't drink none at all. Don't smoke neither, though I come from tobacco country. I try to live a straight, clean, God-fearing life. The body is a temple of God's. What's got you so ripped up tonight, Miss Jessie? You look like you been to a party—did you have a fight with somebody? Devil and I, we saw you come storming out of the Cape Fear Hotel. Shucks, I couldn't afford to check in there for even one night. Half a night! You in that beautiful outfit you got on— what happened?" The while they talked the rain came straight down and bounced off the asphalt, drop by drop, splash by splash, like little angels with watery wings. After a little way, Angel planted his hat on Jessie's head, then gave her his pea jacket to wear. "Spray don't bother me none. When I'm at sea, I stand up forward and enjoy the wake. But you didn't tell me what happened."

"Something made me hate the two people I love best in the world, that's what happened. Would you do me a favor?"

"Sure, Miss Jessie, what?"

"Would you kiss me?"

"What? Just like that?"

Jessie stopped and threw her arms around his neck. "Like this." Her lips banged into his mouth, hurting him.

"Hey! Easy!"

"What's the matter?" she asked.

"Now that's what I mean about the alcohol. We're going to get ourselves into all kinds of trouble like this."

"I'm a virgin. Don't you want me?"

"Oh my, Miss, yes, course I do; but you don't really want to do anything out here like this. It's because you've been drinking. I done told Devlin you were jailbait. And let me tell you something. There's nothing wrong with being a virgin. Why, every fellow wants his bride to be a virgin, and he should be a virgin, too, so that they know no other forever always until death do them part."

"You're a virgin too?"

"I'm keeping myself for the future Mrs. Engels, miss. I've got me sisters and I hope they're keeping their selves, too. Expect they are. Well, maybe one ain't, but I'm not sure."

"You're a religious boy, aren't you?"

"I'm a Baptist, miss, and I hope a good one."

"I'm a scientist."

"A Christian Scientist?"

"Naw, my great-great-paw-paw was a monkey's uncle. I'm a biological scientist."

"You're joshing me, miss—ain't you? Don't you believe in heaven?"

"I believe in stardust. Oh, there's a glow over left!"

"That'd be downtown. I'll have you to your hotel in no time."

Under the marquee of Cape Fear Hotel, Jessie turned to Angel. There was a new aggressive look on her face. "I have to warn you, Angel, if I'm left alone, I may kill myself. I may just go up to my room and jump out of the window, and you wait down here and see if I don't. I'll be smashed at your feet in five minutes. I mean it! I have nothing to live for anymore!"

"Now what do you want to go and say such things for? You're making me afraid."

"All I want you to do is come up to my room and keep me company until I feel better. Wouldn't that be the Christian thing to do?"

"I can't get into that hotel, Miss Jessie. There's a clerk for sure, watches everybody who comes and goes. I'd sure like to help you, Miss Jessie, but I just can't do that."

"I could go in first, and you could come in and rent a room and then come to my room and sit with me."

"A room in a place like that would cost me my whole pay, and I don't have that much of it left, anyway."

"I have money. Here, take this."

"No, miss, I can't take your money."

"Not even to save my life? Suppose you read in the papers tomorrow that a young girl—that a young woman has jumped from a window of the Cape Fear Hotel; then you'd be sorry that you didn't take the money and save her, wouldn't you?"

"I'd be mighty sorry, miss. I would, indeed!"

"Then you'll come? And I'll give you back your pea coat and cap when you leave. Parting is such sweet sorrow!" She wobbled up the steps of the Cape Fear Hotel.

Angel felt that he had no choice but to do as she asked. He had to get his coat and cap back, and he felt pity for this strange girl, and fear for her, that she might do something—well, he just didn't know what she might do. If one of his sisters ever became so desperate-seeming, so lonely and desperate, he hoped that somebody like himself would try to be of help. He waited a few minutes and went into the hotel and checked in. She had given him more than enough money. He felt guilty spending it. He felt embarrassed before the night clerk, who seemed to look at him with curiosity, suspicion even. Angel thought the clerk must be wondering why a young sailor with no cap and no coat on a cool rainy night was spending so much money on a hotel room in a swanky hotel like the Cape Fear, but the clerk said nothing and did his business with his nose in the air and with cold, if curious eyes. A bellboy was summoned to direct him to his room but Angel said he could find it himself. He took the elevator directly to Jessie's floor. Everything about what he was doing felt wrong, creepy and sneaky, and just plain not right. Now he knocked on the door just to get inside—to hide.

Jessie opened the door and pulled him inside, locking the door and shoving a chair under the knob, moving with such speed that Angel had no time to protest. All he could say was, "Oh, my Lord, miss! What are you doing?"

Because Jessie was naked. "I had to get dry," she claimed.

"Oh Lord, miss! I've got to get out of here." He looked around the lamp-lit room, saw the rumpled bed. "Why, I swear, miss, you can't be much over fifteen. I can see that now that you've got all that grown-up rig off. You're what they call jailbait, you are! I ain't never... I would never do..."

"Please, Angel! Please, please, please! Just sit down for a few minutes. Just stay here with me. Please! Give me a chance!"

Outside in the hall, Ruth tried the door. "Jessie, I can hear you in there. Why is this door jammed? Who's that in there with you?"

Angel answered Ruth: "I'll get it open, ma'am. I'll get it!" He jerked the chair out from under the door knob and fumbled with the lock. "I ain't done nothing, ma'am," he called through the door. "Honest to God, as God is my witness!"

Jessie retreated into the room and lit one of Ruth's cigarettes from the night table. She stood by the bed, holding the cigarette out, the way Ruth did, in one hand, and with her other hand on her hip, in what she believed was a posture of bold sophistication, trying to look as unabashed as Vivian Leigh, the Blanche Dubois of *Streetcar Named Desire*, might have looked in a similar situation. She watched Angel fumbling with the lock, his hands shaking, and cried, "You religious jerk!"

"No need to get mean, miss," Angel said. Finally, he got the door unlocked.

"Open this door, damn it!" Tom roared.

"Yes sir! But you see, the harder you push, the harder it is for me to open the door."

"Who in hell are you?" cried Tom.

"Nobody, sir—Seaman First Class Engels, sir."

The door flew open and Tom stepped in. "What's going on in here?" He saw Jessie naked and backed out into the hall. Ruth stepped in. She cried, "Oh, my God!" Jessie's cigarette-holding hand wavered; otherwise, she stood, insouciant as a statue. "Get your clothes on, young lady!" Ruth didn't seem to know where to place her voice. Her order came out of her mouth with an uncharacteristic thickness, as if she were gargling and speaking at the same time.

Tom shouted from the hall, "That girl is under age! If you've laid a hand on her—"

"God in heaven may strike me dead, sir, if I ever—"

"Or I'll strike you dead!" cried Tom. His voice, too, was off-pitch.

"Tom, this obviously isn't the boy's fault," Ruth said, with more self-possession. She pushed Angel into the hall. "Now take this boy down to your room and talk to him."

Tom said, "What do you mean, it's not his fault?"

"Think about it," Ruth said.

"Come on, boy," said Tom, trying to think, taking Angel by the arm. "Maybe you can explain it to me." Jessie broke her pose, swooped up Angel's pea coat and cap, ran to the door, and threw them into the hall. "You really ain't no piece of attractive, Angel!" she yelled after him. "And don't come back, hear! I never want to see you again!"

"Shut that door!" Ruth commanded. "And get your pajamas on. What in hell has gotten into you? Did he lay a hand on you? Or maybe I should ask if you laid a hand on him."

"He didn't have a chance, the sissy-boy," Jessie cried, "but I wanted him to."

"You what?"

"Like you and Tom."

"Tom and I? I just went down the hall to borrow some cigarettes—"

"Aw, cut the rebop, Ruth! That's what Stanley Kowalski says. I saw you through the transom. Beasts in the field!"

Ruth flushed with embarrassment, with anger. "Don't you use that kind of language with me, young lady!" She took a deep breath, shook her head, and said, "Oh, honey, no!"

"You're going to send me away to school so you can have Tom all to yourself." Jessie began to sob.

Ruth saw Jessie's robe on the bed and handed it to her. "Here, put something on. You don't understand."

"I hate you!" Jessie shouted. "I hate Tom! I don't know which one of you I hate the most. I hate you both!" Jessie dropped her cigarette on the rug, picked up a large table lamp, ripped the cord from the wall, and threw it across the room. The ceramic lamp hit a glass covered picture and both shattered. Jessie ran into the bathroom and locked herself in with a click. The phone rang. Ruth let it ring while she lit a cigarette. Her hands were shaking. She picked up Jessie's cigarette from the rug. The carpet was burned. She stepped on the spot and turned her foot. The phone was still ringing. She dropped Jessie's cigarette in an ash tray. She picked up the phone on the fifth or sixth ring. "Yes? Yes, yes, I know. I'm sorry. Look, can you get me a doctor up here? A young girl. She's having hysterics. I know. I know it's late. Well, get him up!" she ordered in a harsh voice. "He'll be adequately compensated, and so will you. Yes. Hurry, please! Yes, thank you. Now put me through to Tom Judas's room. I'm not sure... 308, 309. Just put me through, dammit! Yes. Thank you. Hello, Tom? I've got a doctor coming up here to give Jessie a sedative. I want you to keep that boy there with you until I call and tell you everything's all right. I'm going to have her examined. Yes. Just hang on. Nice kid, eh? Thank God for that! I'll call you." There was a knock on the door. Ruth cradled the phone, went to the door, opened it. A sleepy looking man wearing a burlap-baggy brown suit and gum shoes said:

"I'm the house detective. Is everything all right in here? We've had complaints." He stepped in without invitation.

"Not exactly."

The detective saw the broken lamp and picture. "Oh, my! We'll have to put that on your bill." He looked around. "What's that, a cigarette burn? Might have to buy a whole new carpet." He eyed the shut bathroom door.

"Of course," said Ruth. "And here's something for you." She handed the house detective a bill.

"Five-spot. Thank you, ma'am. Anything I can do?"

A grey-haired man in a plaid bathrobe appeared at the door. He was carrying a medical bag.

"Please come in," Ruth said to the doctor. She saw that he had pajamas on under his bathrobe—he was wearing slippers. "I'm so sorry to disturb you at this hour, but—"

"Where's the patient?"

"She's locked herself in the bathroom."

The doctor went to the bathroom door and knocked. "You'll have to come out of there." He turned to Ruth. "A young lady, is it?"

Ruth nodded.

The detective said, "I can get the door open in a jiffy."

The doctor said, "Better not to frighten her. Why don't you go downstairs and tend to business? I can handle it from here."

"But I've got a way with locks," the detective said.

"That won't be necessary," the doctor said. "She'll come out, *won't you, my dear?* Let me suggest that everyone leave the room."

"I want you to give her a thorough examination," Ruth said. "I want to be certain that she hasn't been molested. Do you understand?"

"I understand," the doctor said. "All right, now. Let me be alone with her. What's her name?"

"Jessie."

The doctor turned to the bathroom door. "Come on out of there, Jessie. Nothing to be afraid of. How old are you, Jessie? You know, I've got granddaughters of my own. They think I'm just swell. Come on out and let's talk."

Ruth was reassured. She followed the house detective into the hall and closed the door behind her. The detective said:

"If she's been molested in this hotel—"

"There will be no lawsuits," Ruth said. "Don't worry about that. I don't think she was actually molested, anyway. I just want to confirm that she wasn't."

"I checked the books," said the detective. "You have the room for two more days, but if you should leave early—well, I get off at six"—he checked his watch—"which is only an hour from now . . ."

Ruth went through her purse and handed him several more bills. "Thank you for your trouble and I guarantee that there won't be any more trouble here. How's that?"

"Thank you very much, madam, indeed, and I hope that the rest of your stay will be more pleasant." He gumshoed off and vanished into the elevator.

Ruth waited in the hall, trying to put a plan together and at the same time wondering what she had done wrong, what to do next and why everything had gone so badly. The picture in the room and the lamp could not be put together again, but could she put the birthday back together— was there some way of doing that? Maybe she had no gift for motherhood. She saw what was before her eyes, but did she understand it?

Ruth was not a person to have doubts, but she doubted herself now.

Jessie was not an ordinary girl. She had had few of the average child's experiences, but she was very intelligent, socially ignorant while at the same time intellectually gifted—and perhaps too much of a challenge for Ruth to have taken on. No, Ruth didn't believe that. She could get a handle on this problem. She could work it out. Jessie was her daughter now and she loved her and that was all there was to it.

The examination took twenty unbearable minutes. The doctor finally stepped into the hall.

"She's fine," he said. "But she'll probably sleep most of the day and she'll have a headache when she wakes up. There was no sign of molestation. The girl's a virgin. Sweet girl, really, just got herself a temper to go with that red hair." The doctor's gentle words were a relief.

"She is a sweet girl," Ruth said, wistfully.

"Oh, yes, ma'am," the doctor said. "She told me that she had seen that movie—what's it called?—with that, eh, Brando fellow? Said she thought he was—what was it? Funniest expression—"

"A piece of attractive?"

"That's it!" The doctor laughed. "Say the darndest things, don't they?"

"She does." Relief rose to risibility. Ruth laughed. "She comes up with some of the darndest, darndest things you ever heard. How much do I owe you?"

"Oh—"

"Will this be adequate?"

"More than adequate. Thank you very much, madam. It was a pleasure meeting you and your daughter. I'm sure she'll be fine now. Goodnight!"

"Goodnight, doctor." Ruth went into the room and looked at Jessie. She was wearing her bathrobe and sleeping peacefully. Ruth went to the phone and asked to be put through to Tom's room.

"Yes?" said Tom.

"She's fine. The boy didn't touch her. Let him go about his business and come in here and we'll make plans." Ruth collapsed into a chair and shook her head slowly, sadly, at the sight of Jessie sleeping. "You've almost got what you always wanted and you don't know how to handle it. In dreams begin responsibilities, sweetheart. That's an old Irish saying, and a great one. But you had no way of knowing that. That side of life was always shut off from you. How hard it must be for you!" Ruth looked up to see Tom looking at Jessie. He stood by Ruth's chair and she took his hand. He looked at Ruth, now. "Were you talking to her?" he asked.

"Just mumbling to myself. I was just thinking how hard it must be for her. It must be hard for you, too, Tom. You're so filled with guilt, you're afraid to tell her. It shows that you have more conscience than most of us, but with you I'm afraid it's turned into an obsession. You've dreamed your responsibilities into guilt. Thus conscience makes cowards of us all," she paraphrased Shakespeare.

"I just followed my light. But you're right. I should have told her sooner. Capt'n Jack told me to tell her. You told me to tell her. Even crazy Smiley told me to tell her. But what have I ever brought anyone but trouble?"

"My dear, you've brought me love and happiness. You brought Jessie into the world and I snatched her up like the great gift that she is, and then you came along yourself and I snatched you up, too. You bring happiness—no, joy!—but trouble comes, too, with everything. We can't escape it. When it comes to trouble, you're no more special than anyone else, and I wish you'd get that through your thick head." She squeezed his hand. "Ah, yes! Well, I think we've got to get her back to Fortune Island. She ought to be in a familiar place. I'm truly concerned about a nervous breakdown. Maybe it's my fault. There, you see, everything isn't your fault. I've been pushing her so hard with her studies, maybe too hard. That's what's confusing about her. She's so bright, and you begin to think you're dealing with an adult, but life hasn't really prepared her to be one, not even to be a fourteen-year-old."

"What should we do?"

"Wait here with her until it's late enough for me to find a boat to take us back to the island. I'll try to find someone who's willing to take us over later in the day, perhaps even this evening, so she can sleep it out."

"I can find a boat."

"No, I want to do it. I want to get out. All you have to do is stay here. You can order up some breakfast later. Just be here if she wakes up. The doctor said she'd have a headache. Give her some aspirins. Keep her calm, for God's sake! Don't say anything that will get her excited again."

"Like the truth?"

"Now isn't the time for the truth. Now is the time for patience, which you're good at."

Ruth kissed Tom and lay down next to Jessie on the bed. Tom settled into the easy chair, warmed by Ruth.

At nine o'clock the sun streamed in through the window blinds, striping the bed. It must have stopped raining. Tom heard Ruth in the bathroom. He reversed the blinds, shutting out the sun. Jessie sat up in bed, looked at him without recognition, and flopped back into a deep sleep. Tom went back to the chair and dozed off. He had a dream of Smiley, running somehow on one leg, a horseman chasing him down. The pounding of the horse's hooves became the drumbeat of rain. For some strange reason, it made him laugh in his sleep. A guard was holding him back, tugging on his arm. Then he realized that Ruth was the guard and that she was trying to wake him.

"It's six o'clock, Tom. I had to chase all over Wilmington in the rain to get someone to take us back to Fortune Island. Have you eaten anything? I stopped and ate lunch, but that was the only stop I made on a regular detective hunt for a fisherman named Oglethorpe. He's willing to take us. It's a long story, but he's waiting now on his boat down at the docks. He talked the price up saying it was going to be a rough trip in the rain, but I think he's something of a con artist because I found him by asking if anybody knew of anyone who was going over to Fortune Island and was told that he was going over for the fishing tomorrow. Let's wake Jessie up, gather our things, and go home."

"What's in the box?"

"It's a birthday cake. I thought, maybe, when we get home—well, we could salvage something out of this birthday."

But Jessie would not speak to Tom or Ruth, whether out of embarrassment or anger they could not tell, on the long journey home across Pamlico Sound, and when they reached Ruth's cottage, she went straight to her room without a word. Ruth had to give up on her hope of salvaging the day, and she and Tom, exhausted, wet, disappointed, having talked the subject of Jessie's mental state to death, retired to Ruth's bedroom in silent frustration. Ruth, who had had the least sleep of the sadhearted three, began to snore as soon as she hit the sheets. Tom lay listening to the stormy skies and finally fell off. Jessie, in her room, lay with her eyes wide open, sorting through chaos. Eventually she leaped up out of bed and made her way to a kerosene lamp and lit it. She pulled off her nightgown, went to her suitcase, the contents of which had not yet been put away, found underwear, and put it on. She found her new Hunter green suit and put it on, found her new high heeled shoes and put them on, and sat down next to the lamp with her mirror before her and made up, as if going out on the town. She ran a brush through her still damp hair, then repacked some articles in her suitcase, made her way into the main room, took up pen and paper and wrote, "I'm going home. It's my house." She left the note on the typewriter, stared at the cake for a moment, stuck her finger in the cake and obliterated the legend, "Happy Birthday Jessie." She licked the icing from her finger, then knocked the cake to the floor.

She donned her raincoat and rain hat and stepped out into the dark and damp of the dunes, carrying her suitcase and pocketbook, and began the quarter-mile hike to Cogburn's house, her high heels plunging in the damp sands of the dunes, making the tracks of the hunted, the rain washing her makeup askew.

Chapter
Twenty

Chemical fireworks, ignited by a large consumption of bourbon, discernments firing, misfiring, sputtering discrimination—playing solitaire on a stormy night, cheating because why not?—the malfunctioning electric mind at three o'clock in the morning, St. John of the Cross's dark night of the soul, blundering and correcting blunder with blunder—"Issues from the hand of God the simple soul." The Reverend Jason P. Cogburn studied, for a moment, the wrinkled sleeve of his soiled white shirt, upheld by an arm grown flaccid and bony, the gnarled hand of which poised a dark bottle over a glass. Beyond the bottle, the door swung open and a strange young woman stood looking at him.

He had heard of alcoholic hallucinations in the white lightning stills of the North Carolina and Tennessee mountains, of men who were frightened by what they saw, or thought they saw. "Is it Susannah come back from the sea?" He lowered the bottle to the table, gripped its neck, the knuckles of his hand pale as bone. "Is it a souvenir of the sea, with its green garment and long, wet, red hair? Magdalena, is that you? Have you come back from the deep?"

"A souvenir of the sea? What's the matter with you, old man?"

Jessie dragged her suitcase in from the porch, leaving it inside the door, and came over to him at the table and sat down across from him. But he continued to stare at the shut door.

"Why do you stand there like that?" he asked.

She put her hand on top of his that was on the bottle and shook it. "I'm over here, look at me!"

He blinked and swiveled his head to look at her there, at the table, the bones of his neck snapping twice—click, click—so that Jessie could hear them.

"Pour me a drink, Magdalena. My hands shake so much."

"You don't scare me," said Jessie. "You're just a crazy old coot!"

Now he looked at her over his glasses, his jowls whiskery, grizzled. "Why do you look like that?" he asked, his puzzled eyes scanning her.

"Like what?"

"You look like a... you look like... you're all wet."

"It's pouring pigs and goats. Can't you hear it? What's the matter with you? Have you had a stroke?"

"It's Jessie, isn't it? All done up like a woman! How did you get so old?"

"How did you get so old?"

"What's this? And suitcase in hand!" He took a slug of bourbon, most of which ran down the creases of his mouth. "What happened? Have a fall-out with the Jewess? Well, by God, don't you look like your mother! Don't you look like the perfect Magdalena?"

Jessie got up and took off her raincoat and hat and hung them along with her pocketbook on the clothes tree inside the door, knuckle-dusting the shooting iron inside the pocket of his long black dustcoat. She spun around to face him, taking up several poses. "I'm all grown up, do you see? I'm twenty-five or thirty years old, and that must make you over a hundred. Look! Look at me!" She found a pack of cigarettes in a pocket and lit one—approaching him, she blew smoke in his face.

"You look cold," he said, fanning the smoke. "Do you want a drink?"

Jessie went to the cabinet, got a glass, and brought it to the table. Cogburn poured her a drink, his hand shaking, spilling bourbon on the table. "Your mother wouldn't drink with me," he said. "Only sometimes... that last time..."

"You wouldn't let her."

"What do you know? She had T.B. She'd get drunk over one little drink. I wanted to sit and talk. By God, she's come back in you! Magdalena's back," he yelled at the ceiling, "the high-heeled painted whore from Wilmington, with whiskey-wet lips and a lipstick-stained cigarette!"

"I'm Jessie McQueen, and this is my house! This is my mother's house and my father's house and his mother's and father's house before him. My grandparents built this house. Where did you come from, you crazy old son-of-a-bitch? Why are you always here and not here? Why do you always sit and drink like this? Why are you always playing solitaire?

Who in the hell are you and where do you come from? Out from under
what rock do you come?" She drank down a half a glass of bourbon.

His neurons were firing blanks—blankety, blankety, blankety, but he
couldn't curse. He shrank down in his chair, waved his hand across the
table, breaking up the solitaire he had been playing. He looked at the
cards. They were meaningless. "I drink because I hate life," he said,
finally. "But I go on the road to make a living and I come back here
to forget how I make it. You don't know this, but I come from snake
handlers and people who speak in tongues. I hated my mother and my
father as much as you hate me."

"But you're not my father!"

"No, I'm not your father. He's a criminal in the Central Prison in
Raleigh. Or maybe he's out and gone by now, or maybe he's dead. What
do you care? What did he ever do for you? Who are you, little girl?
You're nobody, that's who you are! Maybe now you're a Jew, because I
sold you to the Jewess."

"What do you mean, sold me?"

"I signed you away for five thousand dollars to a bunch of her
shyster lawyers. If you belong to anybody, you belong to her. You're her
indentured servant. You can be bought and sold, like the slaves of Egypt,
like the slaves of the old south. Have another drink, slave girl! Pour one
for me. You wearing high-heeled shoes? My God, you're bigger than
your mother!"

"Ruth paid you five thousand dollars for me?"

Cogburn lifted himself out of his chair and wobbled into his bedroom,
which had once been the pantry. He was back before Jessie could
understand what it meant to her that Ruth had bought her the way you'd
buy an animal at auction—or, once upon a time, a slave. Cogburn was
back and dumping money on the table, what seemed hundreds of bills,
green floating and mixing with the scattered pink-backed cards, the face-
up Jacks, Queens, and deuces, a discarded small-time high-stakes poker
game soaking up the tabletop bourbon. "I partake of what life has to
offer," he said—"that is, venom. But a God-bit man like me is immune.
No, maybe that ain't the right word. I just don't give a single shit." He
paused, thinking. "My maw and my paw built up in me an immunity to
most of life, and, listen—gobble-gobble, gurgle-gurgle, gooble-gooble—
that's the truth of it all! That's what it all means! Amounts to!"

He lunged at Jessie and dragged her to the floor. "Gobble-gobble,"
he cried. "I've got a snake for you! A copperhead is what I've got! You

think I can't do it, Magdalena, but I can! Now that you're young and beautiful again, I'll be damned if I can't!"

"You ain't strong enough for me, old man," cried Jessie, struggling out from under him.

She jumped back from his flailing hands, but not in time to stop one from seizing her ankle. She pulled loose. He was between her and the door, rolling on the floor, a fallen scarecrow, reaching for her. Then, with demonic will, he rose, his arms outstretched like a goalie's, and danced from side to side, blocking the door.

She turned and ran up the stairs to the second floor. She heard him clump up the stairs after her. She took off her painful shoes and threw them, one after the other, down the stairs at him. She was in the dark, but at the end of the hall was a window, lit from outside by lightning. She found the attic door and struggled with it, then dropped to her knees and let her fingers search for the key among the floorboard cracks. "Copperhead coming!" Cogburn called, still struggling to mount the stairs. The house vibrated with thunder. She retreated up the attic stairs, but he was still just behind her, adrenalin-charged. She groped her way toward the trunk containing her treasure trove of books and hid behind it in the dark, tin-roofed, rain-roaring attic. Deafness tasted the air with its forked, flicking tongue.

Then Cogburn's hands found her, clawed at her, tearing her clothing away, her suit jacket, her blouse. He bit cruelly into her shoulder. She could not hear herself screaming. He punched her on the jaw, and she fell back, passive, unknowing. Growling, grunting, he forced her legs apart, got between them, pulling her panties aside, and thrust his copperhead at her until it bent in half, collapsed. She was impenetrable, a virgin's membrane protected her, and the crazed potency of his youth was gone. He was delivered up to a strange new sensation, new to him now but not new, old as his earliest childhood. Whatever this sensation, this ghostly stranger, was, it pulled him away from her, eventually stood him up, swayingly, on his feet, hissing for air, and finally led him away from her, muttering to himself that he had made a mistake, a big mistake, that he was sorry, sorry. sorry. He groped in the dark for a way to a place of light, a place where the rain on the roof could be made to stop sounding like a freight train grinding through a lonely town at night, a place where the wind would stop shrieking like one of Garcie's banshees. Only now did he realize that he had been deafened with madness, but his ears had opened again, and he could hear, even through the uproar of the storm,

Jessie screaming in the attic. But she was closer than he thought. When he reached the second floor landing, he felt the thud of Jessie's shoulder in the small of his back and was propelled down the stairs. He could hear his body thudding against step and wall as he tumbled, and clearly heard his ankle crack at the bottom. Pain shot up to his knee, down to his toes. "You little bitch," he whispered, but he felt no anger, felt that he was adjusting to some kind of defeat, felt acceptance, even passivity. He rolled about on the kitchen floor, at the foot of the stairs, gripping his leg at the ankle with both hands. He could feel a shard of naked bone. "You broke my leg!" he called.

"You raped me!" she said flatly, descending the stairs. No longer fearing his hands, she stepped over him, picked up her shoes, went to the kitchen table, sat down, and put them on. She watched him writhing on the floor, and he saw in her eyes a craziness, not just what could be expected in the situation, not just anger, not outrage, but that an alien spirit had possessed her, and he looked away, frightened.

"I didn't," he said, softly, carefully. "I couldn't!"

"I know when I've been raped!"

"No you don't! I couldn't get inside you."

"I felt you there."

"You don't know what you're talking about." He sweetened his tone. "C'mon, Jess, help me get to the couch. My God, I'm in pain."

"Good! I only wish I had killed you. You really are the alligator man, aren't you?"

"The alligator man! That's newspaper rubbish. There's no such thing as the alligator man." Cogburn tried to drag himself to the couch. He cried out in pain. "For God's sake, Jessie, I've seen you with animals. You wouldn't let a horned toad suffer. You'd shoot a horse with a broken leg, wouldn't you?"

But he was surprised when this new Jessie with the strange look in her eyes and the meaningless smile on her face got up and helped to drag him, kicking his way with his good foot, to the couch. He asked her to get him a drink. She brought him one. Then she sat down at the table and examined her shoulder. "You've bitten a chunk out of my shoulder."

"Now you're snake-bit, too," he said. "Won't hurt you any. I've lived with it all my life."

"What you said," she said, "about shooting a horse with a broken leg? That gave me an idea." She got up and went to the clothes tree, pulled Cogburn's pistol from his coat pocket, came back to the table, and sat in his place, facing him across the room.

"What are you going to do with that thing, Magdalena? You're not planning on shooting the old man, are you?"

"Jessie's not going to do anything," she said, "Jessie's not here. But Magdalena is going to put you out of your misery. You said it yourself, that I hate to see animals suffer."

Cogburn laughed nervously, snorted with pain. "Damn ankle," he said.

"Who is Jessie," Jessie said, "what is she, that all our swains commend her?" Plain as day, she saw Susannah drifting downward in the ocean, her long red hair like wavering flames. She felt the faint smile on her face as she pulled the trigger, once, and then again. Then she saw two spots of blood on Cogburn's shirt, and the amazed look on his face, then how the amazement faded. She felt that the slight, puckered smile on his face matched her own, almost as if they were kissing good-bye. "Jessie doesn't live here anymore," she said. "But I do."

✳ ✳ ✳

Tom's hands shook as he lit a kerosene hurricane lamp, turning the wick up only high enough so that he could find his way about, not so high as to wake Ruth, who, it seemed, had not felt the body blow of the electric explosion in the sky as he had, perhaps because she had had less sleep than any of them.

He wondered if Jessie had been wakened and went into her room. He saw a heap of bedclothes in the middle of the bed and called in a whispery voice, "Jessie?" He didn't want to wake her if she had slept through the blast, as Ruth had been able to do, but the bed didn't look right.

He turned up the wick of the lamp to the point where it spread a fair light. He pulled the bedclothes aside. Empty. The storm must have wakened her after all. She could have gone to the outhouse. Or maybe she was in the main room and he hadn't seen her in the dim light cast by the lamp at that point. He went into the main room, holding the lamp up to see the chairs, and stepped in something soft and sticky. He held the lamp down and looked at his foot, saw that he had stepped in the birthday cake, toppled to the floor, broken. He held the lamp up and turned, looking this way and that; then he saw the note in the typewriter, a note written in longhand, finger-marked with icing. "I am going home." Home could only mean one place—Cogburn's house. He woke Ruth.

Ruth went to check Jessie's room. She was back in an instant. "Her suitcase is gone," she said. "She's either taken her best clothes, or she's wearing them. She's not in her right mind. She might harm herself. I'm her guardian. I have a duty to see to her welfare—a legal obligation."

"Listen to yourself," Tom said. "You sound hysterical."

"I love her."

"I know you do. That's part of my love for you," Tom said.

"And mine for you," she said, dressing.

Tom pulled on his boots. "How can she still think of that place as home?"

"Don't you see? She's trying to go back."

"Back to what? She had nothing."

"And nothing to cope with—except Cogburn, and he wasn't there most of the time."

"She probably thinks she'll have the house to herself." Then it occurred to Tom—"What if he's there now? He's a drunk, crazy old coot, and she hates his guts."

"I don't suppose he'd do her any harm."

"What makes you think that? Didn't you tell me you found her hiding from him? Isn't that how you met? And what about her? You said it yourself—she must be out of her mind. If she finds him there, he might be the one who's in trouble."

"Now who sounds hysterical?" Ruth said. "But let's get over there."

Jessie pulled the trigger the first time as Ruth and Tom approached the house.

"That sounded like a shot," Ruth said.

"It's the storm," Tom said.

A second bullet pierced Cogburn's chest.

"Two shots," Ruth said. "I know the sound of a pistol when I hear it."

They broke into a run. Ruth did not knock at the door but bounded through it, calling, "Jessie! Jessie!"

Jessie sat at the table, holding the gun, looking at Cogburn, who was slumped on the couch across the room, blood on his chest. "He bit me," she said, in a faraway voice. "He bit me and he raped me."

They could see now that her clothes were torn and her shoulder was bleeding.

"Check him out," Tom said. Ruth went over to Cogburn and felt for pulsation in the arteries of his neck. "He's—"

"Don't say it," Tom stopped her, holding his hand up, going to Jessie.

"Give me the gun, Jessie," he said, gently, his hand pushing the gun down. Jessie looked up at him as he took the gun from her, and he saw in her pale blue eyes the missingness of her being.

"Jessie doesn't live here anymore," she said.

Tom lifted back bloody flaps of clothing to examine the wound on Jessie's shoulder. Teeth marks and broken, bleeding skin.

"Look at her," Tom said. "I don't think she knows what happened."

"Yes I do," Jessie said, in an almost unrecognizable, infantile voice. "I pushed him down the stairs and broke his leg."

"Is it true?" Tom asked Ruth.

Ruth examined Cogburn's legs. In a moment, she said, "He's got a compound fracture. The femur's sticking right out through the skin."

"Then he couldn't have walked on it?"

"Impossible," said Ruth. "The pain would have been agonizing."

"Then how did he get to the couch?" Tom wondered aloud.

"I helped him," Jessie said. "I put him over there so I could sit and look at him and shoot him."

Tom said to Ruth, "He was no threat to her when she shot him."

"He just sat there," Jessie said, in that same strange little voice, as if she were telling a children's story. "We talked. He said he didn't rape me and I said he did—so I shot him, bang, bang, and he'll be a better person now. I know he will."

"Of course he will," Tom said. "You didn't hurt him any. In fact, what you said is just a story, a good story, but not the real story. You really had nothing to do with this. The real story is that I came over here to play cards with him. Ruth, look at the mess on the table. Money all over the place. We were playing poker, you see. Drinking too much bourbon. There was a fight over the cards. He pulled a gun. I wrestled it away from him—that's when his leg was broken, in the struggle—and shot him. That's the real story. That's what really happened." He looked at Ruth, waiting. Her big dark eyes were unbelieving. "Tom!" she exclaimed. "You can't!"

"Come over here," he said, "and put your hands on Jessie's ears. I don't want her to hear."

Shaking her head, not knowing what Tom had in mind, Ruth hesitantly did as she was told. She cupped Jessie's ears.

"What is it?" she asked.

"Have you got a handkerchief?"

"In my pocketbook, on the table."

Tom pulled a handkerchief from Ruth's pocketbook and wiped down Cogburn's revolver. Then he took the gun over to Cogburn's body and pressed the dead man's prints back on it. He came back to the table, turned around, and fired a shot into the wall next to Cogburn's head. Ruth jumped at the sound.

"I'm trying to put it together," Tom said. "What's important is that her prints won't be on the gun. Nobody's going to question the confession of an ex-con like me, and, if I confess, I don't get a jury. The judge gives me six, seven years maybe, for manslaughter. It's a good bet, and I get out sooner than that, probably, and I join you and we start a new life. How does that sound?"

"I don't know what to think," Ruth said.

"You don't want this to touch her, do you? I know I don't."

"No."

"It doesn't look good, you know. It looks like premeditated murder."

"But the rape?"

"Rape won't justify what she did. How she did it. It wasn't an immediate response. It wasn't self-defense. He couldn't even get near her on that leg."

"But she's only a child!"

"All right, they treat her like a child. It might mean a lock-up in a juvenile facility until she's of age—maybe six or seven years. And even if they don't send her away, she'd be exposed to public notice, stigmatized. You don't want it known that she was raped, do you? I want her to have a clean record, don't you? A good life, don't you?"

"But I can get lawyers down here to defend her."

"Your money can't solve this one. Lawyers'll bring investigations. If I confess, there won't be any investigation, and she'll be in the clear."

"They can defend you—self-defense?"

"What case for self-defense is there when he's got two slugs in him and one in the wall next to his head, and him with a broken leg? Look at the size of me and look at that old man sitting there. No, it won't wash. No, somebody's got to pay for this, and I'm determined to be the human sacrifice." He waited for Ruth to think. "Well, then, let's get her out of this," Tom urged. "Are you with me?"

"With you and Jessie? Always!"

"You're willing to wait, aren't you?"

"You know I am. As long as I have to."

"Find Oglethorpe. Then you and Jessie get off this island—up to

Boston. He'll take you if you give him enough money. Give him enough money and he'll take you anywhere. Take some of this on the table, if you need cash. Nobody will ever know the difference. You've got your pocketbook. Don't take anything else except Jessie's suitcase and bag. I'll wait until eight or nine o'clock in the morning and go down to the general store and tell them what happened. My version of what happened, I mean. The police will come and find me good and drunk and I'll confess. They'll be happy not to have any problems solving a murder. I've spent almost half my life in prison. You'll see, it'll go like that!" He snapped his fingers. "It won't be the end of her. It won't be the end of that bright future you promised her."

Ruth put her hands on Tom's shoulders and looked into his eyes. "You're the best man I've ever known, Tom. I love you."

He bent down and kissed Ruth very hard for a long moment, then pushed her away. "Now take her and go. Get out of here! Get her bags. Don't leave anything. Take this." He handed Ruth a lipsticked cigarette. "Take it and go. Now just get off this island. Go, go, go!"

Chapter
Twenty-One

December 2000

In Georgetown, Hildegarde, at her computer, had just found the web site for the Cape Lookout National Seashore. She clicked on Fortune Island, scrolled, stopped, and picked up at:

...as Fortune Island declined, the post office remained one of the village's few links with the outside world. By about 1955, a postage stamp was the town's only purchasable item, but it was toward the end of that year that the post office closed its doors for the last time. Though the few remaining islanders had made a valiant effort to come back after the devastation of Hurricane Hazel in 1954, economically the island was defunct. Summer kitchens and dairy houses provide glimpses of an earlier time without generators or electricity. The kerosene stoves of the past could leave homes sweltering in the summer. Thus cooking was restricted to separate kitchen buildings.

Hildegarde wondered why Jessie had written so little about Fortune Island in *Souvenirs of the Sea.* It was so interesting.

Unfortunately, the McQueen/Cogburn House, once the biggest house on the island, was lightning-struck and set ablaze in 1962, and burned to the ground. Erected on its site is a memorial stone commemorating the birth of the scientist and writer, Jessie Judas, a member of the McQueen family. Click for photograph.

Hildy clicked.

Jessie M. Judas

Marine Biologist and Author
Born on this Site

1941

Hildegarde supposed that Ruth would want to disperse Jessie's ashes near this monument. She imagined them all standing by that large stone with the bronze plaque, and Jessie's dust scattering off in the wind. She clicked back to the text:

> *If you come in season be prepared for the notorious mosquitoes and for unpredictable weather. If you come out of season, you will be on your own, and come at your own risk. Fortune Island is a protected historic and archeological site. Please do not disturb artifacts, burials, or any portion of any historic ruin or site. Help the National Park Service protect and maintain this rich cultural site for future visitors by reporting any violation you observe to your nearest National Park Service office.*

Of course, it was a sad occasion, this imminent visit to Fortune Island to scatter Jessie's ashes, but Hildegarde could not help but feel the excitement of going there, especially in winter when it was truly isolated and deserted, of seeing for herself the place of Jessie's birth and of her childhood, the humble birthplace of a famous woman.

Hildegarde reached over her computer to a bookshelf, brought *Souvenirs of the Sea* down to her lap, and slid a beautifully manicured nail between its pages. It was a random selection. Anything Jessie wrote suited her. She read a passage subtitled "The Sex of Water."

> *Water is naked but for its diaphanous gown, which can best be detected when the water falls over an escarpment. Then the gown shimmers like silk in the sun or at night with the glow of the moon. She who is underneath the gown is Water, who is always a dancer, and is then a hula dancer, or a belly dancer, but can be at*

other times a ballerina, an adagio dancer, or whatever, but always
a dancer, at least always ready to dance. The Water in your glass,
if it is not a glass made opaque by color, seems to be sleeping (in a
black glass it seems dead). But Water does not sleep for very long.
It catnaps, but is as ready to swing into action as is a cat who has
detected the slightest creeping of a mouse. Water appears to be
feminine, but a great, broad-shouldered wave, one of those that
come from the sea and flow over land, destroying whole cities,
Water in that form would give us the sense of powerful masculinity,
like a football player. Everyone knows that Water is graceful—a
fountain spray, for instance—but it can also seem clumsy, as in
a stagnant flood of several weeks duration, when dead animals
float on it, and its lovely perfume dissipates and is replaced by
a sulphurous stench, the odor of the dead. This is when Water
seems to be connected to the warriors of the wasteland, and
distinctly masculine, the destruction men make, which is so unlike
the fecundity of the sparkling, egg-rich stream full of fish, which
seems feminine. So Water is both Yin and Yang, Lingam and Yoni,
or appears in such aspects, apparently at will. Of course how it
is contained tells the story, in a tall clear glass or falling between
two jutting rocks. Water, then, tends to conform to its surroundings
and is coy in its pretenses. So, if we think of Water at all, it is as
an hermaphrodite, as he-she or she-he Water, a sideshow trickster,
like that star one can point to, that glittering dew drop in the night
sky, which has been gone for a billion or more years.

She had loved that passage when she first read it in German. How
could she have known then that she would be part of the author's life and
death, that her own child would be Jessie's namesake?

❄ ❄ ❄

Hildegarde thought Ruth looked haggard when she got to Georgetown.
"It's such a drive for a woman of your age. Why do you do it?"

"I guess I'm trying to prove I'm not a woman of my age. Hildy, you
remind me of Buttercup. She went on and on about how I shouldn't make
the drive, how I should take a plane instead; and, my dear daughter-in-law,
I'm going to tell you the same thing I told her, and then I don't want to
hear any more about it. I like to drive. I'm determined to drive. I'm not
going to be made old. Now that's it. And no, I'm not hungry. I stopped
to eat. What I want is a drink, then a hot bath, and I'll hit the sack. But

first, let me see that granddaughter of mine."

Hildy took her into the nursery to look at little Jessie. Ruth hadn't seen it coming, and gripped the crib with fascination and delight. A rusty crown had begun to form on the baby's head. "A Jewish-Irish-Cherokee-English-German-American redhead. What a wonder!"

Ruth left the box with Jessie's urn and ashes in it on the dining room table. When she had gone to bed, Hildegarde lifted the box and looked at it. "All that is left," she said. "I wish she'd been buried. We could visit her grave."

"It was in her will," David said, "that her ashes be scattered on Fortune Island."

"I know, but if she was so unhappy there, why do you suppose she wanted to go back?"

"I suppose her life was an odyssey," David said, "and odysseys end where they begin. She left us the house in Chapel Hill, you know, to sell or whatever. I don't know what she had in mind. Maybe some crazy idea of little Jessie growing up there."

"We should keep it open for the public, like Carl Sandburg's house."

"That's a thought," he said, giving Hildy a kiss on the cheek.

"I mean it," she said. "Jessie ought to be remembered."

⁂

The next day they drove to Chapel Hill in two cars. The plan was to spend the night there and then go on to the coast and to Fortune Island the next day.

Ruth was refreshed. If it had not been for the size and color of the big red Hummer, David would have lost her. For her part, Ruth kept track of David's BMW in her rear-view mirror and tried not to lose him. Unlike herself, he had always been a slow and cautious driver. She thought of him getting out of the taxi in front of the Institut des Sciences in Paris. She had in her mind such a vivid picture of him—and he looked so like Tom—his eyes searching the crowd for her, his grin when he found her on the steps of the Institut. She knew then that Jessie was seriously ill, but was not about to spoil Jessie's big moment by telling anyone just how ill she was. January. A year goes by and people go with it in their hecatombs. Jessie was just one among many who had been taken this year. But it was hard to believe that it was not quite a year ago that David smiled up the steps of the Institut at her, that not quite a year ago Jessie had one of her greatest triumphs, and now she sat there next to her, nothing but dust, bones in an urn in a box. Where was that bright spirit that rode beside her over forty-five years ago on her first great adventure? Gone! Jessie was dead, David was married, and there was a new Jessie riding in the car behind her, all in the speed of less than a year. Life and death are both Hummering ahead of you, David. Keep up! All of you back there—keep up!

E.M. Schorb

E.M. Schorb's novels include *Paradise Square*, winner of the International eBook Award Foundation's Grand Prize at the Frankfurt Book Fair in 2000, and *A Portable Chaos*, winner of the Writers Notes Magazine Book Award for Fiction, 2004.

His poetry has been widely published and his latest volume, *Time and Fevers*, was a recipient of the Writer's Digest 16th Annual International Self-Published Book Award, as well as an Eric Hoffer Award for Books. An earlier collection, *Murderer's Day*, was awarded the Verna Emery Poetry Prize and published by Purdue University Press.

WWW.EMSCHORB.COM

Printed in the United States
140051LV00001B/117/P